KHAN

Heath Gunn

ISBN: 978-1-9162957-2-8 (E-Book Kindle)
ISBN: 978-1-9162957-3-5 (Paperback)

A CIP catalogue record for this book is
available from the British Library
Any references to historical events,
real people, or real places are used fictitiously.
Names, characters, and places are products of the author's imagination.
Front cover image by Stuart Bache, Books Covered.

First printing edition 2020.
Page Turner Publications 20-22 Wenlock Road London, N1 7GU
www.heathgunn.com

DEDICATION

For Rhianne, whose endless support, encouragement and patience - listening to me rattle-on about characters and plot lines, makes my stories possible.

1

The sleek black Range Rover slowed in the humming evening traffic and the tailgate eased open. A tightly wrapped cloth bundle was pushed from the rear of the 4×4 and slammed unceremoniously onto the black tarmac. As it hit the road it rolled into the path of a dirty white van. The driver of the van saw the bundle drop and braked hard, but the gap was too short and the van skidded over the cloth bundle, snagging it and dragging it along the road. The Range Rover tailgate closed, the suspension dipped and it accelerated away, disappearing into the mass of cars.

Ice-cold pins of rain spiked DI Lomas Baxter's face as he walked from his car, his shadow dancing on the shiny road under the glow of the street lights. He dug his hands deeper into the pockets of his peacoat, pulling it tightly around his body. A team of uniformed officers was keeping back a growing crowd of on-lookers as Lomas headed towards the scruffy white van. DC Drew Taylor had got there before him and was talking to the driver of the van. Lomas nodded a greeting to Taylor. She raised a hand briefly then turned her attention back to the interviewee.

'So, Sherlock, what've we got?'

The forensic pathologist turned to face Lomas, maintaining his crouched position. 'Asian male, approximately thirty-five to forty years old, visible head trauma and some other injuries. I'll know more when I get him back.'

'Was he dead when he was thrown out of the car?'

'Yes. Initial checks indicate that he died six to ten hours ago.'

'OK, thanks. Can I have a look?'

'Be my guest. I'm leaving the sacking around him until we get him back, but I've opened it up as far as his shoulders. It looks like he's taken quite a battering, but again...'

'Yeah, I know, you'll know more when you get him back.'

Lomas crouched down by the wrapped body to have a closer look. He recognised the dead man as local businessman and sus-pected drug dealer, Inzamam Khan.

'How did you end up on the road, Mr Khan?' He stood up and turned away from the corpse, taking in the scene around him. 'Thanks, Sherlock. Keep me in the loop, will you please?'

He moved in the direction of his car. The air smelled fresh, renewed by the recent rain, untarnished by the death that marred the street.

Drew made her way over towards Baxter as the icy rain began to ease.

'I've finished talking to the driver of the van. Malcolm Thomas, a forty-seven- year-old driver for a small office-supplies company. He was driving home after his last drop of the day. He says the traffic was medium to heavy. A black Range Rover slowed in front of him. He eased off a little but was probably still a bit close, then the tailgate opened and the wrapped body was dropped out of the back of the vehicle before it took off through the traffic. He's shaken up – says he tried to brake, but couldn't stop in time and heard the body hit the underside of his van. He keeps apologising for being too close to the Range Rover, saying if he'd left more space he wouldn't have hit the body.'

'OK, nice work. Did he get a look at anyone in the back of the Range Rover? Or the registration number?'

'No, he said the back flipped open and the body dropped out pretty much straight away. He panicked and slammed on the brakes, his attention was on the bundle in the road, not the car.'

'That's a shame. When you get back, pull all the local CCTV feeds, please. I want to see what they captured.'

'He did say that he thought it might have been a Range Rover Overfinch, with privacy glass, but it might have just been a look-a-like body kit. He's a bit of a petrol- head. He also added that the way it shot off into the traffic, it was a quick one.'

'OK – there won't be many of those around. Get him to sit down with someone back at the station and work through the events slowly. He might remember more than he knows.'

'Will do. Is there anything else you want me to do here? I thought I'd coordinate some of the uniformed officers to interview the other drivers, see if anyone saw anything else.'

'Sounds like a good idea. Keep me up to date, please. I'm going to head back and give the DCI an update.' Lomas watched Drew turn and head back towards the crowd of people standing under a makeshift rain shelter the scenes of crime team had put up.

Lomas stood for a while and looked around at the scene. He had a panoramic view of the road and pavements, which were lined with shops displaying their wares in glossy, rain-sprinkled windows. The shop fronts were interspersed with stoic grey buildings, one of which was a bank. At each end of the building hung a small black camera.

'Drew!' Lomas called after the young red-headed officer. She spun around to face him.

'Boss?'

'The bank – could you make sure you include their CCTV footage?' He pointed at the bank and the cameras.

'Will do.'

2

DCI Marie Carlton stood with her arms folded, looking out of the window at the rain hammering down. Lomas knocked on the door. Carlton turned away from the window, her steely blue eyes catching the light as she turned to face him.

'Hi Lomas, what have we got this time?'

'Asian male, mid to late thirties, no official identification yet, but I had a look and I'm pretty sure it's Inzamam Khan. He was dropped from the back of a moving Range Rover, in traffic. Possibly not linked to the nightclub killings but I'm not ruling anything out yet, given his acquaintances. Sherlock's initial exam shows some injuries consistent with violence. I'll have more detail later when he's finished checking him over.'

'Witnesses?' she asked.

'Uniform are interviewing everyone who was at the scene. Luckily most of them stopped when Khan was dropped onto the road. A poor bugger in a van immediately behind him didn't stop in time and ran over the body.'

'Ouch.' She winced, imagining the van rolling over the dead man. She and Lomas had worked on many cases together over their years of service and, although Marie liked to be kept informed of progress on all the cases under her charge, she knew Lomas would cover every aspect of the investigation. He was a solid, dependable and vastly knowledgeable detective who had brought some of the south coast's deadliest criminals to justice.

3

Seven days earlier

Inzamam Khan slammed his iPhone onto the white tablecloth and shouted at the top of his voice. 'Fucking sons of infidels! They have less sense than they were born with. Do I have to do everything myself? Is there no one around here with an ounce of initiative?'

'What is it, boss?' A smart-looking, bearded, Indian man scurried forward. In the background a pair of scruffy white men in their early twenties leaned against the doorway that led to the kitchen of Inzamam's restaurant. Khan looked over at the loitering pair with disdain. They were a necessary evil, a means to an end. He tolerated their presence, humoured their feeble attempts at wit and paid them handsomely for their endeavours. They, on the other hand, thought that they were in with 'the man'. He knew that this was how they referred to him when they were at a safe distance from him, but when they were in his presence they hung back until he called for them. He knew they were afraid of him and what they had seen him do to others who had displeased him.

Seeing the two youths reminded Khan of a recent incident. Another youth had challenged Khan over the size of his cut. Inzamam had not reacted to the young man's verbal taunts, nor to the tirade of predictable racial abuse that had accompanied his attempt at increasing his payment.

'Come on, you fuckin' thick Paki, I'm due more than that. I'd get more than that in tips waiting in this fuckin' shit-hole of a restaurant!' he had yelled across the kitchen.

Inzamam had stopped checking the takings. He'd turned and walked calmly across to the three youths without uttering a word or changing his expression. As he had got within arm's length of the gobby one, his hand had shot out and grabbed the youth by his throat. The loiterers had eased backwards, leaving their accomplice alone in Khan's clutches. Gobby tried to struggle, but Inzamam grabbed a fistful of his hair. As he did so, he simultaneously released the lad's throat and slammed his face down onto the stainless-steel worktop. He did this three times, then a large silver pot had fallen off the end of the worktop, clattering to the floor. With the third strike the youth's body had gone limp. Inzamam had released his grip on the youth's hair, letting him drop to the floor. His legs spasmed as he hit the ground. Khan had then turned his attention to the other two, who both turned to run.

'Stay there, gentlemen,' he had said quietly. The pair had frozen to the spot as the restaurateur walked around them slowly until he was standing before them, staring intently at them. They'd glanced over their shoulders at their acquaintance, who was sprawled motionless on the floor. With fear filling their eyes, they turned back to face Khan.

'Are either of you unhappy with your level of remuneration?' They'd looked at each other briefly and silently shook their heads.

'Good,' he continued. 'Then this conversation will not need to be repeated, will it?' Again both shook their heads, neither uttering a sound.

'You know where the door is. You may leave.' They glanced round at their associate.

'Oh, don't worry about him. I'll take care of him.'

Not needing to be told twice, the pair ran from the restaurant. No repeat performance had ever been required.

Inzamam snapped out of his recollection. 'Get me a coffee, Raj, and none of that cheap filtered crap we serve up to the monkeys who come in here.' He shot a glance at the Asian youngster.

Raj was well over six feet tall, with a thin beard and an athletic build. He was a regular visitor at the kitchen and a regular recipient of the verbal abuse Inzamam chose to dole out. He was Khan's right-hand man. As well as being gifted with great technical knowledge, he spent his days working at the centre of Khan's business, as well as covering for Inzamam when his wife, Husna, called. At these times Inzamam was invariably shut away in his office with one of the many young waitresses he employed. He usually hired women based on their looks, age and vulnerability, which – as he did with most people in his life – he then exploited. As ever, Raj did what he was told, without complaint or argument.

Khan watched Raj as he made his way silently to the rear of the kitchen and set about brewing a fresh pot of expensive, rich-fragranced coffee in the meticulous way he always did. Khan smiled and moved his attention to the two youths who, upon noticing his shift in attention, shifted their weight off the door-frame and stood up straight.

'So, what are you two doing here? Hopefully it's good news. I've heard enough shit for one day.'

'We … we've run out, Boss,' the skinnier of the pair stuttered, blinking furiously.

'Run out? Really? What, of everything?'

'Everythin' except the green, boss. We had a really busy night in town.'

'Yeah, the coke went really quick,' his partner interrupted.

He was a mop-topped chav, dressed in a knock-off Adidas tracksuit and high-top Nike basketball boots. He had a round, chipmunk-like face with cratered skin from acne in his early teenage years. They were a useful, if not overly bright, pair. Inzamam had supplied them each with a free mobile phone so he could get hold of them day or night – a privilege he made frequent use of. He also knew they were using the phones to call premium-rate sex lines – at his expense. Inzamam viewed their perverted needs as a further example of infidel weakness, he considered the phone bills a small price to pay compared to the income the pair generated. Khan knew the two low-level thugs served their purpose, to him they epitomised the picture of an inferior race that Inzamam Khan had been cultivating since his youth; one he had used to fuel his business empire.

As a boy Inzamam had spent much of his time in the company of his father, Malik, who he idolised and despised in equal measure. Malik Khan had been a middle-ranking commander who had helped set up and run an al-Qaeda training camp near Kandahar in Afghanistan. The elder Khan had oversight of training impressionable young recruits in the use of small arms, explosives and orientation, among other subjects. The syllabus was delivered within the framework of the Taliban's interpretation of sections of the Qur'an. The trainer's plans were underpinned by their belief that they were messengers of God's will and if they were successful, it was due to their actions being ordained at the highest level.

Whether the enemy was the Russians as it was in the 1980s, or later, the allied forces of the USA, UK and others, the locals who fought for the Taliban retained their belief that the infidels were weak, ruled by their greed and debauchery, and promiscuous in nature. From an early age Inzamam had questioned the logic of fighting these forces with bullets and bombs, convinced that the preaching of his father and his brethren was misguided, shortsighted and unambitious. While he agreed with the cause, he found it difficult to believe that they would ever truly overthrow these superpowers without first infiltrating their land and destroying them from the inside. It was then, as a teenager, that he had begun to formulate his plan: his contribution to the jihad.

Young Inzamam's epiphany came one day while he shared a meal of spiced goat and potatoes with some of the young trainees. They were descended from farming families. As the conversation unfolded, Inzamam learned that their fathers had changed their crops almost without exception to the opium poppy. As an inquisitive child Inzamam had asked questions, keen to know more. The farmers' sons bragged about how their families had forged great business arrangements with district officials, warlords and drug traffickers who targeted greedy, weak Westerners with their high-quality opiates. Inzamam had a lightbulb moment that day, and since then he had developed a carefully crafted plan, the central part of which was to supply the finest Afghanistan product to people in the West. His main focus quickly became convincing his father to move the family to England: to his parents, he sold a heavily researched concept of a better life for his brothers and sisters. The pivotal part of his plan had been shared in a conversation one evening when he got the chance to speak to his father privately.

'Father, our move would enhance the progress of the holy war against the weak British fools. We could use our connections in Afghanistan and Pakistan to flood England with opiates: a flood that I could orchestrate by using the infidel's own sons, to sell our products to the weak-minded, addicted non-believers. I have done lots of research Father and we should open a chain of high-quality restaurants, serving native Afghan dishes to the paying British public. This would give us a respectable business that would be our face to the outside world.'

Khan

His father has been impressed and this was the only aspect of his plan that he had altered once they reached English shores and discovered the nation's hunger for spicy curries, generalised by the British as 'Indian' food. The Khan's restaurants served generic Indian food, fronted by the father-and-son duo of Malik and Inzamam. They quickly became pillars of their local community, commended for their charitable giving and community spirit, while their restaurants became a well-managed front for what speedily became the largest drug trafficking and dealing business in the south of England.

***

Inzamam called on his sidekick once more to restock the grubby-looking pair. 'Raj, get these two sales machines some more nose candy, would you?'

The pair nodded at each other proudly, not understanding the back-handed nature of the compliment.

'How about the smack? How's that been going?'

'I done most of mine,' the bony one retorted quickly. Silently Khan shifted his stare to Chipmunk, who blushed and shifted his weight uneasily from one foot to the other.

'I've not moved much, boss. Sorry, boss. I've tried, but the peeps, they just want the coke, innit.' He wiped his nose on the shiny sleeve of his tracksuit top and sniffed in a lungful of curry-scented air. Inzamam Khan moved slowly to Chipmunk's side. Chipmunk leaned away from him, towards his associate. Khan placed an arm around Chipmunk's shoulders, gripping a fistful of tracksuit in his strong hand and feeling the youth tremble. He smiled a broad, menacing smile, his perfect straight white teeth glinting at Chipmunk.

'Don't worry. Raj will get you more coke and you can sell double the amount of nose candy to the clubbers, while your skinny friend here can wind some more smack into the junkies, can't you, Darryl?'

Bony gulped. Khan knew he'd thought his speedy shifting of junk would keep Inzamam's attention on Chipmunk, rather than make their sales a joint effort.

'Yes, boss, course I can.'

'Good – a joint sales force. You boys are going to have more cash than you know what to do with soon, if you keep sales up at this rate.' Of course, Inzamam knew that they couldn't keep up their newly found momentum, because they were both too keen on sampling the product themselves, but this was an accepted consequence of using junkies as pushers. The payoff was worth the cost, and Inzamam was making plenty off the back of them.

Raj loaded a blue rucksack with enough of both drugs to keep the two going for a couple of days. As he passed it over to Bony, he took a crumpled Tesco bag full of cash out of Chipmunk's hand. Khan watched as Chipmunk made a token effort to resist letting go of the bag. Khan was pleased to see that Raj didn't even acknowledge it as he pulled the carrier from the chav's hand.

Inzamam observed as, with well-practised ease, Raj emptied the contents of the plastic bag onto a large silver tray and began to count it. He had an excellent brain for numbers, weights and amounts especially, and Khan knew that not only did Raj know the exact weight of the cocaine and heroin he had just handed out, but he also remembered perfectly the previous supply and what that should equate to in monetary terms. He didn't take long to count the £2,500, then he nodded at Inzamam and passed him £500.

Khan took the cash and divided it into two equal shares. 'Well done, boys, there's a two hundred and fifty quid bonus each.' Reaching into his own pocket, he pulled out two crisp £50 notes. 'And here's a little something extra as a thank you for turning it around so quickly and coming straight back in with the green.'

The two grinned at each other, then said in unison, 'Cheers, boss, you da man!'

Khan smiled and turned away, returning to the table where he had slammed his phone down. The youths scurried out of the door, whispering to each other.

'How much did you give them, Raj?' 'Fifty of each. Is that OK?'

'OK? That is fucking genius, Raj. So what would that be at current prices?' Before Khan could work out the value of the drugs, Raj answered. 'Seven-grand.'

'That's sixty-three hundred quid profit, young Raj. Good work. You might even get a bit of a bonus if they turn that around quickly.' Khan threw a small bundle of folded notes onto the table. 'There's your cut. Enjoy.'

Raj walked slowly over and picked up £250. His cut was the same as the dealers'.

Although Khan had promised him a pay rise if he carried on cutting the gear so the junkies kept buying, Khan didn't want to give it to him too soon. He knew Raj was loyal and would carry on working towards the pay increase.

A few weeks earlier, three or four of the pushers had run into the back of the restaurant, panicking because six junkies had died of overdoses during the night after they had bought Inzamam's gear. Instead of their employer joining them in panic, he celebrated and put his prices up, shouting that the junkies would pay more because they knew they were getting the best high. Although the pushers thought he was mad, within two days they had all sold out of their usual four-day supply and had come back for more.

The evening in Khan's continued on as if nothing had happened in the rear of the restaurant. Inzamam was the perfect host: charming, smiley, accommodating, ensuring that the diners were all well catered for and happily parted with their money. Some were such regulars at the buzzing Southampton restaurant that they talked to Khan as if he were a member of their own family: laughing, joking and chatting.

Inzamam stood with his hand on the back of a chair after cracking a one-liner that made the table erupt in laughter. He surveyed his restaurant with a smile of satisfaction. He was truly master of all.

The pungent scent of spices filled the air, small candles made shadows dance playfully above elegantly dressed tables, glasses chinked and his customers ate and drank the night away, none of them in a rush to leave. Inzamam didn't run a 'turn them around quickly' place; he liked people to feel relaxed, and he was happy for them to stay and soak up the congenial atmosphere.

He moved to open the door for a professional-looking young couple who were leaving. He nodded at the man, who was in his early twenties, clad in a smart blue suit.

'Goodnight to you both,' Inzamam said, looking the young man's partner up and down. His gaze hovered first over her thighs, where her black pencil skirt clung, revealing an hourglass figure. He stole a glance inside her blouse as the opening door created a draught that ruffled her top. He was sure she saw him look, but she smiled politely and followed her companion quickly, reaching for his hand as they left.

'Ah, young love,' Inzamam muttered as he closed the door behind them. As he turned back towards the restaurant he caught a glimpse of Raj, peeking around the doorframe from the kitchen. Inzamam stalked over to his sidekick.

'What is it, Raj?'

'It's Gonzo – he's in a flap about some of the … er … customers,' Raj stuttered, looking around to check that no one was in earshot.

Gonzo was one of the pushers – Khan nodded and ushered Raj through to the rear of the restaurant. They worked their way through three locked doors, each one of which had a different combination lock. Raj and Inzamam were the only people who knew how to get through from Khan's to the centre of the drug operation; pushers came in through an overgrown, unmarked alleyway at the back of the property. They made their way hurriedly through the last door and into the familiar room. Before them stood a visibly shaken Gonzo, wearing an oversized Adidas hoodie that hung down to the middle of his thighs, at about the same level as his low-slung, grubby jeans. Pasty white skin and an acne-riddled complexion framed the nose that had earned him his nickname, and on his right cheek was a fresh red mark, already starting to darken. Gonzo had clearly been hit by someone – or something.

'What is it, Gonzo?' asked Inzamam.

The youth chewed nervously on his bottom lip. 'It's the Albanians, they jumped me and took my gear and my cash, and when I tried to stop them, one of them pulled a BFG and slapped me with it.' Tears filled his eyes.

'Fucking Albanians!' Khan shrieked. Raj jumped and Gonzo stood frozen, like a rabbit caught in the glare of a car's headlights.

Inzamam walked over to Gonzo and cupped his head in his left hand. 'You did the right thing coming straight back and telling me. Now, who are these lairy motherfuckers?'

'I've seen one of 'em about. But there was three of 'em. I tried to stop 'em, honest I did.' Tears again filled the young pusher's eyes.

'It's fine – we'll sort it, don't you worry about that. Raj, I want to know who these fuckers are, and I want to know by tomorrow morning. I don't give a shit if we have to knock on the door of every junkie in this neighbourhood. No one does this to me, and no one pulls a Big Fucking Gun on one of my boys.'

'Yes Boss, no problem,' Raj replied.

'Now, Gonzo, think carefully. Did they say anything?'

Gonzo gulped and shifted his weight from one foot to another. 'Well?'

'They did say one thing,' Gonzo stuttered. 'Well, come on then, what was it?'

'I d-d-don't really want—'

'Oh, just fucking spit it out,' demanded Khan.

'They said "tell that pussy Khan we're going to wipe him out".' As he finished the sentence, Gonzo flinched and took a step back.

At first Inzamam didn't react. He could feel Gonzo and Raj watching him. His face held exactly the same expression for a few seconds, then he erupted in laughter.

Raj and Gonzo looked at each other, puzzled.

Inzamam Khan laughed louder and harder until tears rolled down his cheeks. He wiped them with the back of his hand and regained his composure. 'Was that it? Was that the best those Eastern European fuckwits could come up with? Raj, get Gonzo some ice for his face, then get to work finding out who these fuckers are so we can give them a little geography lesson.'

4

Six days earlier

Raj Gadhi worked through the night speaking to everyone he could get hold of, using the descriptions that Gonzo had given him of the three assailants. It only took an hour to track down the name of the bald man with the tattooed neck who had hit Gonzo with the handgun. Kreshnik Tanush was well known for using this method of delivering messages to those he wished to intimidate, so finding out his name was easy. Identifying the two men he was with was harder, as it appeared that Tanush's crew was extensive and mostly made up of illegal immigrants, if rumours were to be believed.

Raj was relentless. Driven by the desire to please his employer and not wanting to anger him by failing to complete his task. The young man had witnessed the wrath of Inzamam Khan many times and it wasn't something Raj wished to experience.

'Paddy, it's Raj. Yeah, I'm good, thanks. Listen, did you hear about what happened to Gonzo? OK, good. I need to find out who did it. I'm pretty sure he got bitch-slapped by Kreshnik Tanush, but I need to know who was with him.

You saw Kreshnik yesterday? OK, who was he with, do you know? Oh, you don't know them. Can you tell me what they looked like?'

'Yeah,' Paddy replied. 'One was tall and skinny, in a long green parka jacket with the hood zipped round his face, and the other was short, fat and bald – and get this, he had gold-rimmed shades on. Looked like a proper dick, swaggering about like he was da man, innit.'

'OK, that's pretty much how Gonzo said they looked, so at least we've got that straight. Laters.' Raj cut the call and dialled Inzamam's number.

'Raj, give me some good news.'

Raj relayed Tanush's name and the matching descriptions he'd had from Gonzo. 'You fucking genius, that's great. I'll be at the restaurant in an hour to pick you up. Have a go at finding out where this Albanian fucker hangs out.' Inzamam hung up.

Raj set about hunting down Kreshnik Tanush and his crew. He figured the best way to do that would be to head to where Gonzo had been attacked and buy some gear.

Raj grabbed an open-face crash helmet from the desk behind him and rushed out of the back door, down the alleyway to his scooter, the olive-green Vespa he rode everywhere. He loved it. It rasped into life. With a quick twist of the throttle Raj headed off across town towards Gonzo's patch. All of Inzamam's boys had very clearly defined areas they were allowed to trade from; Khan insisted on it.

'There's no sense in competing with yourself. Anyone who sells for me gets their own patch, and no one is to wander outside it. If anyone tries, they get cut off,' he had told Raj in his first week. After a month, Raj was the one marking up the map and showing the pushers where they were permitted to sell. He went to far greater lengths than Inzamam had ever done, making sure that the areas all had equal opportunity to maximise income for his employer. He researched the demographics of the local popu-lation, ensuring that there was either a densely populated housing estate nearby or a wealthy private school, college or university halls. All of these were guaranteed to generate income. In the two years since Raj had been coordinating the pushers, Inzamam's turnover had gone through the roof. Profits had soared again since Raj had been let in on the cutting.

Before he started working for Khan full time, Raj had been doing a Biomedical Science degree and had been on track to ace his course and walk into a job with one of the local teaching hos-pitals. He'd been introduced to Khan by a mutual friend after they'd eaten in Khan's restaurant and stayed on drinking into the night. Khan had been fascinated by what Raj was doing and asked him if he'd like to earn some money on the side. Within six months Raj had earned more, working part-time for Khan than he would have done in a year, or more as a Biomedical Scientist and he'd gradually made the shift across to working with Khan full-time.

Raj met Gonzo outside a Tesco Express which took up the ground floor of a concrete high-rise.

'Gonzo.'

'Raj.'

'So, have you seen him?'

'Yeah, he was around the back of the flats about twenty minutes ago. I hid so he didn't see me – I didn't want any more grief.'

'No, course you didn't, mate. No worries. Do me a favour, sneak round and see if he's still knocking about, will you?'

'Will I fuck!'

'OK, let me put it to you another way. Get your fucking arse around there and see if he's still there, or I'm gonna cut your supply in half.'

'You fuckin' wouldn't.'

'Try me. Now get a fucking move on. I've got to get back to the boss.' Raj had learned a thing or two watching Inzamam intimidate the 'weak white infidels', as Khan referred to his pushers when no one but Raj was around. Raj was quietly pleased with himself for pushing Gonzo into doing his bidding; it felt good to be dishing it out for a change.

***

As quietly as he could Gonzo sidled around the side of the tower block, his stomach churning like an old cement mixer. He could smell the acrid stench of piss as he crept past a metal wheelie bin, keeping as close to the wall as he could in an attempt to remain undetected. As he drew closer to the corner of the building, he could hear heavy Eastern European accents and the smell of cigar smoke.

'Kreshnik, I go for piss, then we move the rest. Yes?'

Gonzo stopped dead in his tracks as he heard the voice of the short, fat, bald man.

He took a couple of hasty steps backwards and his heel caught an empty beer bottle standing next to the wheelie bin. It wobbled for a second, then toppled over. It chinked as it hit the ground, then rolled under the bin. Gonzo froze, fear filling him. As he turned to run, a hand slammed down onto his bony shoulder.

'You! What the fuck?' The fat man's voice was clear and close – so close. Gonzo wriggled out from under the hand but the short man was quick. He kicked the skinny pusher's ankles out from under him, sending him crashing to the ground in front of the bin.

'Did you not listen to our warning, small man?' taunted the Albanian.

'I dunno what you mean,' stuttered Gonzo. The heavy-set man slammed a foot onto Gonzo's shin as Gonzo desperately tried to pull himself away from the angry Eastern European.

***

Khan

Rosen Kepi had spent the majority of his life in the Albanian underworld. He'd been brought to the UK by his bosses, who had promised him a better life and an endless supply of free money, courtesy of the British government. Kepi had fallen for it, had packed up his life into two holdalls, then hitched, scammed and stowed away to get to the UK. Upon arriving in the promised land, he realised that not only did he have no way back to Albania, but he also had little choice but to do whatever his employers told him to do, regardless of how it sat with him. This only served to make him more angry – an anger that manifested itself in some of the most horrific beatings he had ever given out, earning him a fearsome reputation and ensuring that he was passed all the jobs that required his unique skills. Broken bones were not an unusual result of one of Kepi's beatings, although most of the injuries he inflicted were carried out in a red mist of fury – not with the person he was beating, but with himself for allowing him to end up in that situation.

'There is no point in you trying to escape, little man,' Kepi calmly informed Gonzo.

He gave a menacing, toothy grin and, without breaking eye contact with Gonzo, he ground the heel of his boot into the youngster's shin, sending a shooting pain up Gonzo's leg. Gonzo screamed – then he saw Kreshnik Tanush come around the corner.

'You again? You do not learn.'

***

Gonzo watched as the two grinned at each other, then Kreshnik said, 'Deal with him, and properly this time.'

Gonzo saw Kepi close his eyes for a moment. He was still pinning Gonzo to the ground by his leg. Then Kepi grabbed Gonzo's hoodie and hoisted him off the ground, up and off his feet, in one easy motion. He dangled for a moment, then felt himself being dropped. As Kepi let go, he smashed Gonzo in the jaw with his right fist, sending him hurtling against the bin. Gonzo groaned, and air rushed from his lungs. Kepi grabbed the back of Gonzo's head and bounced his face off the top edge of the bin.

Gonzo slid to the ground. He felt a shoe slam into the side of his face. Then felt the cold concrete and then the short Albanian faded to black.

***

Hidden in a dark corner, Raj had silently watched every part of the brutality and had texted Inzamam their location. He dare not venture out to help his colleague for fear of suffering the same fate: a decision he reassured himself was the right one, the more pain he saw inflicted on Gonzo.

To his left, out of the corner of his eye he saw the familiar shape of Khan's Range Rover. Moments later the headlights went off and it rolled silently to a stop. Raj watched Inzamam step out of the big, black 4×4 and carefully push the driver's door closed, hardly making a sound. The tailgate opened automatically as Khan walked to the rear of the car. Raj saw him retrieve a shotgun, which he held in latex-gloved hands. He walked towards

Raj, holding his finger to his lips. Raj nodded and pointed towards Gonzo and the Albanians. Silently, Raj followed Inzamam, who walked with cat-like stealth holding the shotgun out of sight just behind his right leg. The pair stepped from the cover of the bins and confronted Gonzo's attackers.

'If it isn't our Albanian cousins,' Khan mocked, standing slightly turned away so as not to reveal the firearm.

'What the fuck do you want, Paki?' spat Kreshnik. Raj's glance flicked between the two, from just behind Khan.

'Isn't it obvious? Your head, you dumb piece of shit!' And with that brief retort, Inzamam Khan lifted the shotgun and blasted Kepi in the face. Before his corpse hit the ground, Khan had shifted target. Without a word, he fired into Tanush's left shoulder. The force of the shot spun the Albanian's whole body around and he collapsed to the ground, gripping his shoulder with his right hand. He didn't scream, didn't cry out in pain, just gritted his teeth and scrambled to his feet. Raj watched as the Albanian stood and looked Inzamam straight in the eye, blood oozing through his fingers.

'Well come on you weak fuck, finish the job. Or have you not got the balls? Have you any idea—.' The sentence was cut short as Khan unloaded the shotgun directly into Kreshnik Tanush's chest, silencing the large Albanian. Tanush's lifeless body slammed onto the hard concrete.

Raj watched in shock as Inzamam threw the untraceable shotgun onto the ground between the two dead drug dealers. Without saying a word to Raj, he carefully scooped up Gonzo into his arms and carried the young pusher to the rear of the Range Rover.

He laid him carefully on a plastic sheet that covered the floor of the boot, pulled the load cover across to conceal him, and pressed the button to close the boot.

'Come on, Raj, jump in.'

'I've got my bike here,' Raj stuttered.

'OK, grab your bike and meet me back at the office.'

'Will do.'

A million thoughts raced through Raj's mind. *What was Khan going to do with Gonzo? Why was he on a plastic sheet? Why had he left the shotgun? He fucking shot the Albanians!*

Raj pulled on his crash helmet. As he did, he heard the distant sound of sirens.

Time to go.

5

Inzamam pulled up outside the rear entrance to the restaurant fifteen minutes later. Gonzo had remained silent and motionless in the rear of the Range Rover the entire journey.

'I hope you're not fucking dead,' Khan muttered. He checked his phone and saw that a text message had come in. He pressed the screen and opened the text, it was from his wife.

Husna and Inzamam had been married for eighteen years. They had avoided the more traditional route of arranged marriage by gathering their families together, successfully convincing them of their suitability for each other and how perfectly matched their families were. Once their parents and grandparents were in agreement, they had married within weeks. Inzamam's business empire had grown during their time together, affording them a lifestyle that they and their two children, Kamila and Muna, had all become accustomed to. The girls had come along in the second and fourth years of their marriage and Inzamam had immediately felt a conflicting mixture of emotions: a feeling of being blessed with the arrival of two beautiful daughters, and an overwhelming sense of responsibility for their protection and well-being. Two feelings that had intensified as the girls had reached their teenage years.

The text read:

Hi, hope your night has been a good one, do you know when you'll be home? Xxx

He heard a soft moan from the back of the car and glanced automatically over his shoulder, although he couldn't see the young pusher in the boot. Quickly, Inzamam replied to the message then pocketed his phone, feeling a sense of relief at the noise from behind him.

All good tonight – busy! Hope you and the girls had a good night. Shouldn't be too late xxx

He jumped out of the car and moved swiftly round to the back. As the tailgate started to rise, Inzamam could see that a groggy Gonzo was starting to come around.

'Take it easy,' soothed Inzamam, reaching in to help the young man out of the rear of the car. The silence that surrounded him was broken by the familiar sound of Raj's scooter approaching. Khan turned and waved Raj over to join him. Raj parked the bike by the Range Rover and hung his helmet on the handlebars.

'Is he – is he alive?' Raj blurted out.

'Yeah, he's coming round.'

'Thank fuck for that. I thought with the beating he'd had, he was a goner for sure.' Khan and Raj turned their attention to the young pusher as he let out another groan.

Each easing a hand under each of Gonzo's arms, they helped him out of the car and onto his feet. Gonzo wobbled unsteadily, swaying against their grip, forcing them to hold him upright. The metallic smell of blood and wet clothes clung to the battered man, whose face was a maze of cuts, with smears of sticky, clotting crimson.

Struggling to stay conscious, he leaned heavily on Khan and Raj as they supported him to the office.

'Let's get you inside and cleaned up,' said Inzamam, noting a puzzled look on Raj's face as he spoke. 'What? He took a beating for us tonight and he didn't run or turn grass. He deserves some care,' Inzamam said, feeling the need to justify his unusually soft tone.

Gonzo's left leg buckled as they moved him inside. Raj took a firmer hold of Gonzo's arm to steady him, and Khan pushed the door open with his foot.

Once inside, Inzamam swept everything off the cutting bench onto the floor. With one wide scything movement of his arm, tools, powder and scales scattered across the room. Raj looked shocked.

'Stop fucking looking at me like that. It'll all clean up. Like I said, he needs help.'

Inzamam fussed around Gonzo like a conscientious nurse, tending to his wounds with sterilising liquid and dressings. He perched on the corner of Raj's cutting stool. Every time Gonzo winced, Inzamam apologised and reassured him that he was going to be fine. He carefully rolled up the leg of Gonzo's trousers, where Kepi had pinned him to the floor with his boot. There was clear evidence of bruising starting to appear, and dried blood from where the Albanian's heavy foot had broken the skin. Khan wiped it clean and wrapped a light bandage around it.

'OK, that's you, I think. Raj will grab you some food and there's a bed through there, in the back room.' He motioned to a door. 'Get yourself through there and get some rest. We'll chat once you're up and about. I'll get you some painkillers. If there's anything you need, you just shout and Raj will sort you out. Got it?'

'Yes, boss, thank you.' The young pusher looked as shocked as Raj had been at Khan's kindness.

Khan turned to Raj. 'Go through to the kitchen and find Gonzo something to eat – heat something up if you need to. And get something for yourself. Stay with him, please. I'll be back early in the morning.'

'OK, will do.'

And with that, Inzamam Khan left the two youths together.

***

Raj made his way through to the kitchen of the restaurant. The air was still filled with the pungent aromas of the night's trade. As he expected, everything had been washed up and put away and the kitchen was spotless. Mohamed, the head chef, was a meticulous man and insisted on his kitchen and his staff being pristine. Raj headed over to a large fridge in the corner of the prep area. When he opened it and looked inside he realised how hungry he was. The night's events had taken over and time had flown by. A quick mental check told him that it was nearly twelve hours since he'd last eaten, and that had only been a KFC box meal. The fridge contained a range of sealed, labelled dishes, including some wonderful-smelling saag aloo, a pepper-and-vegetable biryani and, Raj's personal favourite, a chicken tikka madras.

He popped some rice into a heavy pan to boil, and reheated the biryani for Gonzo and the madras for himself. Once he'd prepared the meals, he washed up and stored everything he had used, not wanting to upset the chef. He loaded a tray with their food and carried it through to the rear of the restaurant.

Raj helped Gonzo out of the bed where he'd been resting to a table in the corner of the room. The two sat in silence at first, both tucking into their food. Then Gonzo broke the quiet.

'Thanks for the food, man.'

'No problem.'

'Did you see what happened?' Gonzo asked. 'What do you mean?'

'I remember gettin' a bit of a beatin', and bein' thrown against a fuckin' wheelie bin, but the next thing I know I was waking up in the boot of Khan's Range Rover. What the fuck happened in between?'

Raj wished he hadn't asked, because the fact that Gonzo hadn't seen what Inzamam had done was a bonus. He knew that Gonzo would find out exactly what had happened within an hour of being back out on the street. Raj decided to take the cautious route, so as not to dig a hole for himself by lying, but also so he didn't piss off Khan.

'You got a proper kicking. I thought they were gonna kill you, but the boss turned up just in time to stop them finishing you off. He picked you up and put you in the back of the car, and drove you back here.' Raj hoped his summary might be slick enough for his inquisitive dining partner to accept and move on. He was wrong.

'What do you mean, stop them finishing me off?'

'Well, like I said, I thought they were gonna kill you. The bald one had you pinned to the ground by your leg, and they're always tooled up.'

'So what happened to the fuckin' Albanian wankers?'

'What do you mean?' Raj attempted to dodge again.

'I mean, what the fuck happened, Raj? Stop fuckin' stalling. Did Khan deal with them?'

Khan

'Fuck, yeah.'

'So what did he do? Come on, Raj, fuckin' spill. Oh my God. He fuckin' killed them, didn't he? He fuckin' killed them and you don't wanna grass, so you're not saying anythin'. Fuck! I'm right, aren't I?' Gonzo sat back in his chair, eyes wide, jaw hanging open. Raj didn't answer. His silence was all the response Gonzo needed. It hung in the room like a heavy dark cloud, oppressive and menacing.

'Fuck, that means you know, you saw – you're a fuckin' witness, Raj.'

Raj hadn't thought about it that way before. He'd only thought about what might happen if – or when – Khan realised that Gonzo knew. He hadn't considered what it meant for him, or how his employer would view his loyalty. With a quick, nervous calculation, he arrived at the conclusion that he knew enough about the rest of Inzamam's operation to guarantee his safety. After all, Khan had to have someone on the inside. It might as well be Raj, and he made a fortune for Khan every month. He nodded silently to himself. Without another word he stood and collected the empty plates, slid them onto the tray and turned to return them to the kitchen. Then Gonzo broke the silence again.

'So what the fuck do we do now, bruv? Come on, you always have a plan. What the fuck are we gonna do?'

Raj spun to face Gonzo. '*We* are going to do fuck all! Do you hear me? Because I, for one, don't want to piss Khan off, and anything we do is likely to do just that. So what *we* are going to do, Gonzo – or, more specifically, *you* – is keep your fucking mouth shut, pretend like nothing happened, and that you never went to see the Albanians. That way, you stand half a chance of staying alive long enough to see this as a lucky escape. After that, you're going to do whatever the fuck Khan asks you to do, because at the minute, I have no fucking clue what he's going to do next. Got it?' As he shouted, Raj had walked, tray in hand, until he was standing over Gonzo, who still sat at the table. The tray of empty plates was almost pressing on Gonzo's throat.

'Alright, no need to lose your shit. I just fuckin' asked, is all. Anyway, I'm no grass!'

'Well, don't fucking ask, and you'd better not be, or you'll be joining the Albanians, that much I do know.' Raj calmed slightly and turned to walk away from Gonzo, intending on taking the tray back to the kitchen, when a thought stopped him in his tracks. He spun around, slid the tray back onto the table and turned to face Gonzo.

'Give me your phone.'

'What?'

'Give me your fucking phone, Gonzo.'

'Why the fuck am I gonna to give you my phone? Are you fuckin' mental?'

'Listen to me, you dumb shit, I'm trying to keep you fucking safe.'

'How the fuck does takin' my phone keep me safe?'

'Because if the police suspect you, or any of your spotty junkie mates, of being involved and your phone has pinged off the local tower, or they take your phone and use the tracking built into it to see where you've been, you're fucked!'

Raj stood looking at Gonzo, holding his hand out expectantly, while the young pusher stared at Raj, agog.

'How the fuck do you know this shit?' he said, shaking his head.

'I just do. Now give me your phone.'

Gonzo complied and handed Raj a battered iPhone with a web of cracks covering the screen. Raj took the phone over to his bench, which Inzamam had swept clear earlier. He placed the handset on the bench and took his own phone from his pocket. Unlike Gonzo's phone, it was spotless and in a shiny black cover. He looked in the drawer for a SIM key and proceeded to remove the SIM card from Gonzo's phone, then he took a pair of electrician's side-cutters and chopped the SIM into six pieces, dropping them into a clear plastic bag. Raj then picked up his own phone and sent Khan a WhatsApp message letting him know that he would have a new number by morning.

Then he removed his own SIM card and followed the same procedure, while Gonzo looked on over his shoulder. Once he had sealed the bag, he walked over to a large grey cabinet. He took out a claw hammer, walked back to the bench and dropped the hammer through the screen of both phones. He glanced over at Gonzo, who did not look impressed, but did stay quiet.

Then Raj took two new handsets out of the same cabinet, slotted in two new SIM cards, and handed one to Gonzo. 'Right, you're all set up. Call this number.' He scribbled a mobile phone number on a scrap of paper. Gonzo did as he was instructed. A couple of seconds later, a quiet ringing came from Raj's bench. He scooped up the phone and pressed decline then gave Gonzo his new number, simultaneously saving it to the phone. He repeated the exercise with his own phone, then messaged Khan again with the new number.

'That's fuckin' awesome. Cheers, Raj, you're a G.'

Raj smiled at the note of appreciation in Gonzo's voice.

'No worries. Now go and get your head down – you've had a hell of a night.'

'You're not fuckin' kidding. Cheers, Raj – you're alright.'

Raj picked the tray up again and made his way through to the restaurant to wash up.

6

Five days earlier

Inzamam Khan arrived at his large house in Chilworth a little after 2 a.m., taking care to minimise the noise he made opening the door and entering his home. As he walked into the darkened hallway without turning on the lights, he closed his eyes and took a deep breath in through his nose, drawing in the reassuringly familiar smells of home. He stood motionless for a moment or two, attempting to wash the events of the night from his mind. It didn't work. Although he felt relieved to be home, he replayed the actions he had taken: he clearly saw the Albanian flying backwards as the round he'd discharged from the shotgun blasted into the man's chest. He flicked his shoes off and silently padded through to the kitchen. Quietly he closed the door behind him and checked the kettle to see if there was water in it. Topping it up slightly, he put it on to boil and took a cup down from the cupboard. He brewed a cup of strong black tea then made his way through to the lounge, where he sank into a large cream armchair, cup in hand.

As he sipped his tea, Inzamam Khan allowed himself a smile at the thought of some of the Albanians being out of the picture. They were by far the biggest threat to his continued domination of the local drug scene, with Kreshnik Tanush one of the most prominent among them. Khan decided that Gonzo getting himself a beating would have a couple of positive outcomes. The removal of Tanush and his henchman was the first, and by far the most significant. The spin-off benefit was that Gonzo would have an unquestioning loyalty to Khan that money couldn't buy, but fear could certainly guarantee. This, Inzamam decided, would be a quality he would exploit to the maximum over the coming days and weeks. He also recognised the loyalty Raj had demonstrated, yet again, and made a mental note to reward his young trainee.

He finished his tea, washed and put away the cup, then headed up to bed, still in darkness. On his way to bed, Inzamam looked in on each of his girls. Both teenagers were sleeping peacefully. Then, after placing his clothes in the linen basket, he climbed into bed next to Husna, who instinctively rolled towards him.

***

The next day, Husna left Inzamam to sleep in later than usual. He failed to stir when she got up to make sure the girls were ready for school. This was a common occurrence in the Khan household, given the hours he kept at the restaurant. By the time Inzamam surfaced, not only had she dropped their two girls to school, but she had also completed half of her to-do list for the day. This included updating her online jewellery shop, which sold an array of custom-made pieces, created for wealthy individuals who liked to wear something no one else would be wearing.

Husna had set up her business five years earlier, going to the bank with a fully constructed business plan to secure initial funding. At first Inzamam teased his wife about selling 'costume jewellery', as he had called it, but the meteoric success of Husna's venture soon silenced him. Like her husband, Husna ran a tight, well-ordered enterprise, which turned over a handsome profit and allowed her to buy, among other things, a beautiful white Mercedes SLK, which she had always wanted. Since it was a two-seater the girls had to take turns in going out in it with her. She kept all the jewellery in a huge safe in the office at their home. The back half of the garage had been converted into a photography studio Husna used to photograph the jewellery.

As Inzamam walked into the kitchen, Husna held a cup out to him. He smiled and kissed her on the cheek, gratefully taking the cup from her and cradling it in both hands. He took a seat at their kitchen table. As he took a first slug of the rich, black coffee he rolled his head round in a circle, and his neck cracked.

'Late one last night?' Husna asked playfully.

'Yeah, a little bit. It was a good night, though – the restaurant was buzzing and Mohamed did an amazing job. That couple who just opened up the new clothes shop were in, Joe and Sally. They were saying they've been getting a bit of stick from the girls who work in the high street stores.'

'Really? What for, opening up a nicely kitted out clothes boutique that doesn't stock the same tat as the high street?' .

'I know. They're not fazed by it, and they even think that some of the more switched-on girls will be applying for the job they've just advertised.'

'Oh, I hope they do well. It would be great to have something a bit different to choose from.'

'Like you need more clothes,' Inzamam teased.

'You want me to look nice, Mr Khan, you will have to pay,' she joked in response, with a playful flick of her long, black hair. It had been years since Inzamam had bought any clothes for his wife, apart from presents. Out of the corner of her eye she caught him look her up and down, smile, and drain his coffee.

'Have you got a busy day?' he asked, walking over to refill his cup.

'Not massively. I've done the shop, and the girls are both out after school. I just have to take Mum to the opticians and I'm good. How about you?'

'The usual. I need to sort an issue out with a couple of the boys and do a bit of buying.'

Inzamam knew that Husna was well aware not all of his business ventures were totally above board, but she didn't ask any questions as she didn't want to know the details. The only thing she'd insisted on, years earlier, was that Inzamam kept anything that wasn't legal away from the house and away from her and their daughters. He had readily agreed to this and he had gone to great efforts to honour his promise.

Husna knew that 'the boys' were nothing to do with the restaurant, but she didn't want to know any more.

She grabbed her keys from a hook on the wall, walked across to Inzamam, gave him a long kiss on the lips, her hand placed gently on his cheek, then turned and headed for the door.

'See you later, have a good one. Love you.'

'Of course you do! Who wouldn't?' he called back.

She closed the door behind her, and Khan finished his second coffee.

7

Raj's phone lit up and began to ring simultaneously. Inzamam's name flashed on the screen, with his surname in capital letters.

'Morning, boss!' Raj answered.

'Morning, Raj, how's Gonzo?'

'He seems OK this morning. He ate dinner last night and crashed out.' Raj began wondering whether to tell Inzamam that Gonzo had figured out what had happened to the Albanians.

'Raj!' Inzamam shouted. Raj had drifted so far into thoughts that he had zoned out of his actual conversation with Khan.

'Yes – sorry. Didn't sleep very well,' he covered quickly.

'OK, no worries. I asked if Gonzo said anything about the Albanians?' Khan repeated.

'He asked how he got back to the office and I told him you came and picked him up.' Raj paused, hoping that was enough information.

'OK, good. Now, I need to know what's been said around town. Put some feelers out and see what you can pick up. Oh, and I need a new handset. I need to ditch this one – can you sort me one out?'

'Yeah, we've got a couple in the cupboard.' Raj was relieved that Inzamam hadn't pushed the conversation further regarding Gonzo. He hung up quickly, before Khan had time to ask him any more.

Raj had been watching Gonzo pacing the room at the rear of the restaurant like a caged animal on and off since he had woken. He could see him getting increasingly anxious and Raj was becoming increasingly irritated by the skinny pusher, so had enlisted Gonzo's help in cleaning up the mess that Inzamam had made clearing the cutting bench to tend to Gonzo's wounds. Once everything was back as it should be, Raj began working on cutting the latest batch of product. With exacting precision he weighed out the ingredients that would see the pure cocaine increase to three times its original weight. However, he was used to working in solitude, and his unwelcome guest's pacing was beginning to grate.

'Will you sit the fuck down?' Raj shouted at Gonzo.

'No, I can't. What's Khan gonna do when he gets back? What the fuck is he gonna say? You know him best. Am I fucked?'

'You are if you don't sit down – you're doing my fucking head in.' His rant had no impact and Raj watched as Gonzo continued pacing nervously. Acknowledging that Gonzo wasn't going to calm down, Raj stopped what he was doing.

'Look, Khan's a businessman and you're a valuable asset. If you weren't, he wouldn't have come and rescued you from the Albanians, brought you back here and looked after you the way he has, would he? He'd have left you to be killed by that bald freak, and stayed well out of the way. The fact that he waded in means he places value on you being part of his crew, and the thing he values most of all is loyalty. So it's simple: all you've got to do is show him that first, you're grateful he saved your life, second, you absolutely understand the risk he took to do it. And third, you will do whatever he needs you to do to repay the debt you now owe him.'

'You think?'

'Yes, I think. Now will you grab a beer and relax until he gets back and we find out what he wants us to do next?'

Gonzo stood motionless for a moment in the centre of the room, looking as though he was contemplating what Raj had said. He rubbed his hands over the top of his head, took a deep breath and said, 'Yeah, you're right. He's a businessman and this is sort of the business we're in, init.'

Raj nodded sagely at the young pusher, while at the same time he was staggered that Gonzo thought he was 'in business' with

Khan. But if that's what Gonzo wanted to tell himself, then it worked for Raj.

'Want one?' Gonzo asked as he unscrewed the cap from a bottle of Budweiser.

'No, I'm good, thanks, but could you put the kettle on while you're up?'

The room in which Raj worked was exceptionally tidy. One wall had a heavy door in the centre of it. The door had an oversized handle and led into a walk-in fridge, similar to the one in the restaurant kitchen. It was lined from floor to ceiling with well-ordered storage units. Raj knew exactly what chemicals were where in the fridge, without referring to the labels. It had a just-cleaned smell to it, and bright lighting that bounced off the steel flooring, adding to the clinical feel. Raj always placed a small wooden wedge inside the door whenever he ventured in, paranoid that someone would shut him inside and he would die of hypothermia.

His favourite cutting ingredients were benzocaine and phenacetin, both of which were stored in large quantities, bought by Khan's buyers in person and in bulk from European pharmaceutical suppliers. Raj liked these two cutting elements as they didn't reduce the numbing effect of the cocaine in the same way glucose did, which he had used when he first started mixing for Khan. The additional benefit of phenacetin was that it gave his blend a shimmer which mimicked that of high-grade, pure cocaine. Khan liked this: he had told Raj it gave their product a classy look.

The last delivery of the cutting agents consisted of five hundred kilos of each.

Raj had diligently separated it into smaller five-kilo bags which he sealed in airtight containers before dating, labelling and storing them in the chiller cabinets, ready to use. He could easily cut thirty kilos of street-ready product in a day if he needed to – more than enough to keep the local team of pushers supplied. His process, post-cutting, included checking the purity of the product using a forensic testing kit, then pressing the drugs into wrapped blocks. He then placed Khan's trademark scorpion stamp on the top of each block. Although this added no value to the product in cutting terms, it added street value. The pushers and bigger dealers that Khan supplied were impressed by the visual impact of the stamped blocks, and Inzamam reflected this in the prices he charged when he sold outside his own patch.

Raj would even use the blocks for pushers, like Gonzo, who he ran for Khan. They would ask for scorpion by name – something Raj got a buzz out of, as he had come up with the logo.

The hydraulic press was on its own stainless-steel bench along the opposite wall to the fridge, with the testing area on a similar, stand-alone unit. Both were immaculately clean and ready for use.

For smaller batches, Raj used a tub – a small stainless-steel bath with a bowl-like base. This meant he didn't lose any powder into any cracks or seams. Into this he would pour the coke, then mix in the adulterants in just the right measures to ensure the product gave a good hit, but also stretched it to deliver a reasonable amount to pack and sell on. He prided himself on the rigour of his process: he sieved the coke multiple times, through sieves of varying grades, until he was happy with it. He then tested the purity, and only when he was satisfied with the mix would he weigh it and press it into one-kilogram and five-kilogram blocks, for local use and selling on respectively.

The feedback from pushers was always positive: they told him it was the best gear they'd ever had, or sold, and their customers couldn't get enough. Each of them – the smarter ones, at least – were building a solid, repeat customer base that gave Raj a good idea of how much he needed to send them out with when they came for more. He gauged how much they needed for existing supply and for targeted growth, depending on their patch. He showed each of the pushers on Google Maps exactly where their patch started and stopped.

Initially Raj had needed to report back to Khan that the Albanians had delivered quite a blow to his operation, but before long their sub-standard product had meant that people came back for scorpion. This had pleased Khan, and he had gone out and bought Raj his scooter.

The heroin they supplied was a different matter. That arrived pre-packed and ready to stack in a dry storage cupboard, in a storeroom through a blue door to the left of the hydraulic press.

The only aspect of Khan's business that Raj had not been invited to be part of, so far, was the front end: purchase and trafficking. Everything Raj came into contact with arrived at the rear of the restaurant. He didn't know where it came from or who Khan's suppliers were. It would just arrive, often in a bakery van or similar, and nearly always packed in plain cardboard boxes.

His suspicion was that the coke was Columbian and the heroin was from Afghanistan, but he had never had the balls to ask Inzamam directly. It was a funny thing Raj had noted about working for Khan: sometimes he could be generous and kind, sharing stories and intimate details with him, like some really graphic details about his nights with the restaurant waitresses. Other times he would react furiously to the slightest of provocation and could be fiercely protective of his privacy. Rarely could Raj gauge which it would be; he just took each day as it came.

Raj felt eyes burning into the back of his head. He spun around on his stool to see Gonzo staring blankly at him, holding a cup of tea.

'You OK?'

The spotty pusher snapped out of his daze and looked at Raj. 'Yeah, yeah, I'm fine. Just thinkin' about last night and how close I came to being shot, stabbed or beaten to fuckin' death.'

'It was pretty close, but try not to get too freaked out by it. You're fine now, a bit bruised and battered, but generally you're OK. Aren't you?'

'Yeah, I guess. I hurt everywhere, like I've run a marathon – that, or been run over by a fuckin' train, but I guess that's normal.'

'If you weren't hurting after the kicking you took, you'd be superhuman.'

'Well, I am, aren't I? I'm like the skinny Superman!'

The pair laughed out loud. It felt like the first time Raj had laughed in a long time.

'Thanks for the tea.'

'No worries. How long does the cuttin' take you?' Gonzo asked, wiping his nose on the back of his hand.

'Depends on how many kilos and what for.'

'How much do you get through?'

Suddenly Raj felt uneasy at the direction Gonzo's questioning was taking and closed the conversation down.

'Don't you worry about that, you've got enough on your plate, don't you think?'

'S'pose so,' Gonzo said, shrugging and turning away from Raj. He walked over to the small leather sofa, which faced a medium-sized flat-screen TV. Raj watched him drop into the sofa. The leather squeaked in protest as he dug in to make himself comfy. He flicked the TV on and started surfing the channels, settling on a rerun of an old *Rocky* movie.

Raj turned back towards his cutting bench, smiled to himself and shook his head at the choice Gonzo had made. He wasn't one for action movies, preferring instead to pick up a good book. As he turned his attention back to his work, his phone buzzed in his pocket. Suddenly he felt even more uncomfortable. The name on the message banner, next to the WhatsApp icon, was Sarah.

Raj shot an uncomfortable glance across the room towards Gonzo, but he was fully absorbed in the movie – so much so that he bobbed his head to one side, mimicking Balboa, who was avoiding a punch on the screen.

Raj held his phone up in front of his face. He could feel perspiration starting to form in his palm as he opened the message.

Hey you, got time for a quick call? xxx

Raj tapped rapidly at the screen then hit send.

Hey yourself. Things a bit tense here, how about later? xxx

The response came back almost immediately, accompanied by a crying emoji.

I guess if you can't find time for me, I understand xxx

When he read the message, Raj's stomach knotted instantly. He really liked Sarah and didn't want to piss her off, but he was relatively inexperienced when it came to women and he didn't know whether he should leave it or message back. He thought about it for a second, he even considered what he thought Inzamam would do, but decided quickly that he didn't want to treat any woman the way Khan did. Raj ran a hand through his thick black hair, and elected to respond.

Sorry, yes of course, I can always make time for you. Give me five minutes to get out and then call xxx

Yay! OK, five xxx.

'I'm just popping out. I won't be long.'

He got no response from Gonzo, who was still focused on the movie.

Quickly Raj packed away his cutting gear, locking away anything that Gonzo could abuse out of sight. Once it all was cleared, he grabbed his phone and jacket from the back of a chair and left through the back alley.

8

Inzamam searched his phone for the name Chantel, then smiled as he typed a text.

I've got a couple of hours to kill, baby, what you up to? Xx

He didn't have to wait long for a reply.

Hey you, I'm not up 2 anything. I'm all yours. Where n when? Xxxx

I'll pick you up outside the park, half an hour xx

Ok baby I'll b there. cant wait 2 c u xxxx

Inzamam smiled, slid his phone into his pocket, bounded upstairs, sprayed himself with his favourite Tom Ford, Private Blend aftershave, headed back down and grabbed the Range Rover keys on his way out of the door. The big 4×4 made him feel good as he cruised out of the quiet street he lived on. The plush black leather seats and air conditioning, set at just the right temperature, made it a nice place to be, and the high seating position made Khan feel like the king of the road.

As he eased the steering wheel slowly around to the right, the park came into view and he could see the young waitress waiting for him, as arranged. She was a pretty, petite blonde, dressed in tight black jeans, heeled boots and a low- cut red top. At just turned twenty, she wasn't quite the youngest employee Inzamam had done this with, but she wasn't far off. He had been screwing her for a couple of months, after getting her drunk one night after the restaurant had closed. The first time had been on a table in the restaurant, after that he had taken her to some classy out-of-town bars and restaurants. He'd even managed to take her away for a couple of nights to a boutique hotel by the sea in Devon. He'd told Husna that he needed to go and meet a new fish supplier for

Khan's. She had smiled as she kissed him goodbye on the morning he'd gone, telling him she was going to miss him while he was away.

Fifteen minutes later, Inzamam had picked Chantel up from outside the park, wearing a little, floaty dress, an overnight bag in her hand.

A broad smile lit up the young waitress's face as the Range Rover drew closer. Like he had with all the others, Inzamam had made a point of making Chantel Minson feel special from the first week: like a prize flower, picked from a bunch.

She jumped into the car and leaned across to give Inzamam a playful kiss on the cheek.

'Hey, baby, it feels like forever since we had some time together.'

'I know – it's been driving me insane trying to get out and see you.' Inzamam had become accustomed to spinning a convincing-sounding yarn.

'So where are you taking me?' asked Chantel.

'I haven't got long, so I thought we might head out of town to that country pub we like.'

'Aw, that's a shame. I was kinda hoping we had all night.' The waitress twirled her hair around her finger and blew Inzamam a kiss.

'Sorry, baby, you know I'd love to, but I can only get away for a couple of hours, then I've got to head out of town.'

'I could come with you.'

'No, you can't.' Khan shut her down quickly. Realising how harsh he had sounded, he softened it by following up quickly with, 'You know I would take you if I could, baby, but the people I'm meeting would bore you to tears. They're all business.'

Chantel pouted and nodded.

Over lunch Inzamam was a complete gent, listening intently to Chantel recount stories about her friends' love lives, during which she dropped in that all her friends would kill to have a man who treated them like he treated her. This made Khan smile. He felt like a deadly spider who could drag any woman he wanted into his web, and he would only release them if and when he wanted to set them free.

Inzamam enjoyed the game, he took pleasure in the sex, but it was more than that; he reveled in the adoration, the way the young woman he played around with came running at the drop of a hat. He loved the challenge of gently lulling them into a false sense of security, making them feel like they were the only girl in the world, even though they all knew about Husna. Then, when he'd had enough, or when they got too clingy, he would engineer a series of interactions via text and face to face that would make them go off him. Then they, without fail, told him they didn't think the relationship was going anywhere and they wanted something more. On a couple of occasions they'd even apologised to Khan as they said goodbye. This made Inzamam feel all-powerful and uncatchable. His basic plan, which had served him well to date, was that if they dumped him instead of him dumping them, they were far less likely to drop him in it with his wife.

One girl, a seventeen-year-old waitress called Julie, had threatened to tell Husna once. The fiery verbal assault she had received from Khan scared her so much that she not only ran away from him in the middle of the night, but also never came back to work in the restaurant again.

He dropped Chantel back at the same spot he had collected her from, gave her a long, gropey kiss goodbye, and sped off once she had closed the car door.

Inzamam joined the motorway and headed for a West London mosque he frequented, a place of massive inspiration for him. He prayed as often as his busy life would permit, but was by no means devout and the mosque he was going to wasn't necessarily for his spiritual enlightenment. The cleric who occasionally preached there had been known to the Khan family for years. Inzamam had known him since his early childhood in Pakistan. The cleric had arrived in the UK about three years after the Khan family and had quickly gained popularity among those with extremist views. He had started to believe that there had been a shift in home-grown radicalisation. Inzamam had been captivated by the passion in his teachings, even as a child, and he fervently believed the cleric was defending his own interpretation of Islam. The cleric had made such an impression on Khan that he had helped set up visits to like-minded mosques to spread the word.

Some of the preacher's speeches had been met with anger and violence, and on occasion Inzamam had to use his own contacts to get the cleric out of an area quickly and safely, for which the holy man had been very grateful. One such violent reaction had resulted in fighting on the street outside the mosque. This had quickly got out of hand and had ended in cars being set on fire and people being arrested. It had also been filmed on mobile phones by passers-by, and shared on Facebook and YouTube. The posts had been viewed hundreds of thousands of times and fuelled the cleric's reputation, almost instantly broadening his reach and influence. Following this incident, he had featured on the evening news and Inzamam had narrowly avoided ending up on camera.

The rhetoric the cleric used to incite those who flocked to listen to him was highly provocative and delivered with such venomous enthusiasm that Inzamam couldn't help being drawn in. The cleric had recognised Khan as the son of Malik when he first saw him at an early UK speech, which had surprised Inzamam, given that he had not seen the holy man since he was a child. They got on well from that point on and Tahoor Mohammad Passi, or Passi, as he had asked Inzamam to call him, had spent hours talking to Khan about his plans and business activities.

Inzamam parked on a crowded street, a short walk away from the mosque, and made his way to the men's entrance. Stopping just before the door and removing his shoes, he silenced his phone. He placed his shoes on a rack and stepped, right foot first, through the door. The usual greeter nodded towards Inzamam.

'*Assalamu alaikum,*' he said. *Peace be upon you.*

Khan responded with the traditional reply. '*Wa alaikum.*' *Peace be upon you too.*

No sooner had Inzamam stepped foot inside the mosque than his friend appeared, as if from nowhere. He grasped Inzamam's right hand in between both of his slim hands and greeted him with a warm smile.

'Inzamam, I am so glad you could make it – we have much work to do, my brother. There is much to be planned, and many followers who need to reset their path and follow the true meaning.'

'Great to see you, Passi, my brother. Are you speaking here today?'

'Here? No – there are many souls here, but few that have the foresight to really grasp the true meaning. There are many here who hold with blasphemous views and in the final reckoning, they will be laid bare for all to see. There is an uprising in the young; they are becoming intolerant of our impotent elder statesmen and their will to keep the peace at all costs. We are seeing our dynamic young being attracted to what is rightfully theirs. However, we must plan carefully so that we do not end up in irons – or worse. We can use the power of social media to enlist those who want to act for the true righteous cause. We will strike out at the very heart the infidels and their soft, weak and pampered culture, but we will also strike those Muslims who are un-Islamic. A wave is coming: they will either join us, or be drowned by its power.'

The cleric ended his speech by patting Inzamam heavily on the shoulder and turning towards the mosque. The two men walked in together and prayed in unison, with a number of others who had congregated for *Salat al-'asr*, the late afternoon prayer.

Inzamam stood in contemplation, considering his *rakah* and the meaning he attached to the prayers he offered. Raising his hands up beside his ears, he said clearly, '*Allahabad Akbar*'. *Allah is the greatest*. He folded his arms across his stomach and recited the opening prayer, the *Istiftah Dua*. Inzamam continued through the rituals of prayer, led by the imam, until he had completed his offering to Allah.

He took a moment to absorb the beauty of the mosque before standing to leave, Passi beside him. The two men paused, saying in unison, '*Allshumma inner as-aluka min fadhika*'. *O Allah, I ask of Your bounty*. Then they reclaimed their shoes and stepped from the mosque, left foot first.

'So, brother,' Passi began, 'are you returning to your restaurant?'

'I am. I have lots to do and we're fully booked this evening. I also have other business to attend to that requires my urgent attention.'

Passi's curiosity was piqued. 'Other business? Nothing too challenging, I hope?'

Inzamam had confided in Passi and had expressed his frustration at the unwelcome competition the Albanians had presented when they had started dealing in Southampton. Passi had counselled Inzamam to adopt a patient approach to his new trading neighbours, saying that, in the fullness of time, Allah would present him with a solution.

'Yes, very challenging – my trading neighbours overstepped and had to be dealt with. It will require a certain amount of cleaning to minimise repercussions.'

'I see. That is unfortunate, but perhaps not untimely. Maybe it was the right time to make a statement and help your neighbours to better understand where the line is, that they will not be permitted to breech. Were there casualties?'

'Yes, two, but there's little chance of a connection to me, or my business.'

'That may be a positive outcome, Inzamam. I'm sure the local rumour mill will define its own version of events. Have you considered how you might feed the lines of communication with the right kind of messaging?'

'I thought I'd allow a steady trickle of information to leak out through my frontline teams.'

'Hmm, they are a good resource, and one I remember you saying you had used to good effect previously. Yes, I think your approach is a sound one, brother.'

The two men embraced briefly. Passi placed a hand on Khan's shoulder. '*Fi amanullah,*' he said, bowing his head. *May Allah protect you.*

Khan responded in kind and walked to his car.

9

Valmir Shala, an intimidatingly tall, broad Albanian, was unaccustomed to not getting his own way. He sat in a booth behind a round table at the back of his Portsmouth nightclub. He was seething. Erion Hasani, one of his top men, had just told him that Kreshnik Tanush and Rosen Kepi had been found dead in a Southampton alleyway, shot at close range. Shala slammed his huge fist against the shiny-black surface of the table and glared at Erion.

'Erion, this does not please me.'

'Yes, Mr Shala, I understand, but I thought you would want me to let you know straight away.'

'This was the right thing. Now tell me, who do we hold responsible for costing me one of my most profitable distributors and fixers?'

'I am asking our sources, Mr Shala. My guess is Khan. He's by far the biggest supplier in the area and Kreshnik was intending to take some of his territory.'

'Ah yes, the scorpion king,' Valmir said with a smile. 'How do we narrow down to Mr Khan?'

'I will work on this now, Mr Shala. As soon as it is confirmed, I will let you know.'

'Very well, do what you need to do. But do not take long – the longer we leave this without taking action, the more people will think we are weak.'

'I understand. I will deal with it swiftly and decisively.'

'No – before you take any action, speak to me. I do not want any unauthorised action risking our business.'

'Yes, Mr Shala.' Erion turned to leave.

'Where are you going? Come, sit for a while. I want to know of our business to the east. What news of Brighton?'

Hasani did as requested and took a seat beside the smartly suited Albanian. Shala swept a glass of raki towards him and downed his in one swig.

10

'So what do we know about our two dead Albanians, Drew?' DI Baxter asked.

'We know they're both part of the Albanian drug mafia. Kreshnik Tanush and Rosen Kepi are both thought to be employees of Valmir Shala. Both are linked to cross county-lines distribution and supply, along with being suspected of various attacks on members of rival drug gangs.'

'OK, so we're looking at drug related killings. No surprise there. What about the gun found in the alley?'

'Ballistic analysis confirm it was the murder weapon, but it's untraceable and there were no prints on it.'

'Of course not, that would be too easy. OK, thanks Drew. Anything else?'

'No, I think that's it for now. Although I was wondering who you think it might have been?'

'Drug related killing, in a Southampton alleyway. My money's on Inzamam Khan, but I very much doubt he'll have got his hands dirty and I'm sure he'll have a sixty person alibi.'

'Do you want to pay him a visit?'

'Let's go to Portsmouth first and talk to Shala and get a sense of how pissed he is at two of his men being killed. Then if it feels like the right direction to go, we'll pay Mr Khan a visit.'

11

Khan left London and instead of going towards Southampton he headed straight for the M1, aiming for the north of England. The Khan family had settled briefly in Rotherham, in South Yorkshire, when Malik had first brought them to the UK.

As Inzamam drove the familiar route towards the Yorkshire town, he remembered the small two-bedroom house they had lived in. There he had made lifelong friends who had bought into Khan's vision of how a devastating jihad could be waged against the white Christian masses in the UK.

He listened to an audiobook version of Thomas Harris's *Hannibal* as he pointed his sleek Range Rover up the motorway. Khan loved the way Harris described how Dr Lecter hid in plain sight and erased those who tried to capture him.

Just north of Coventry the phone interrupted the audiobook. Caller ID showed it was one of his northern friends calling: Vihaan Patel, who had grown up on the same street as Inzamam. As children, they had been inseparable.

'*As-Salam-u-Alaikum,*' said Inzamam.

'*Wa alaikum assalam wa rahmatuallah*. It's been a long time, my brother, and I hear you are coming up. Sadiya was talking to Husna earlier.' Replied Vihaan.

'I am indeed – I'm already on the M1. It's been too long, what have I missed?'

'We have been continuing with your mission. The flow of substances and people is

good and your plans are coming closer to fruition.'

'That all sounds very good – perhaps we can pray and then have some food when I get to you? It's been a busy day and I could do with a sensible conversation about how we can bring the plan forward, as quickly as possible. Things have been moving too slowly recently and I'm keen to see them move on.'

'I have some new girls arriving this afternoon. If you like, we could view them together over some food?'

'Yes, let's do that. Shall I come straight to you?'

'Yes. When will you arrive?'

'In about an hour.'

'Excellent, see you soon.'

The call ended. Inzamam switched the audiobook off, selecting a radio channel with an ageing rock star presenting his favourite eighties hits. He glanced to his right at a young man in a red Ford Focus, with an exhaust that was way too loud, overtaking him in the outside lane. With a slight smile, Khan floored the Range Rover. The big V8 engine roared and he slipped past the Focus, leaving the boy racer in his wake.

Fifty-five minutes later, Inzamam left the M1 at Junction 33 and peeled off towards Rotherham town centre. As he passed through Canklow, he remembered when the side of the road into town had been a row of car sales garages, selling cheap runabouts for his dad's generation. He smiled as he recalled an old gold-coloured Bluebird his dad had bought. He patted the steering wheel and gunned the car down the dual carriageway, over the roundabout, between the football ground and scrap metal yard before hanging a left towards Vihaan's house. Inzamam blipped the key to lock his car as he knocked on the black front door of Vihaan's two-bedroom terraced home. Kids skateboarded down the road, screaming as they reached the bottom of the hill.

'Inzamam!'

Vihaan – a portly Indian with thinning jet-black hair, goatee and round, pitted face – greeted Inzamam with a hug. He stood to one side and motioned for Inzamam to go inside. Inzamam stepped straight into the lounge, which was decorated in dark green and gold. The TV in the corner was playing a twenty-four-hour news station, with a journalist dressed in khaki doing a piece to camera from a war zone.

'Please come through – let's have some tea before we get down to business,' said Vihaan.

'This is a flying visit, V. I need to get back. There have been some recent events that need my attention,' replied Khan.

'Hopefully nothing that is detrimental to the good work you have been doing?'

'It has the potential to be problematic, but nothing I can't handle.'

'Of course, I don't know anyone better at handling difficult situations than my old friend Inzamam Khan.'

'Less of the old, if you don't mind.' They laughed and sat down at the small kitchen table as Vihaan's wife Sadiya silently brought them tea.

'Now, down to the business of the day,' Vihaan began, ushering his wife out of the room. Her head bowed, she left the room, closing the door behind her. Inzamam nodded his approval.

'She's a good woman, but this is not for her ears. We have managed to bring together a collection of fine young specimens for a gathering this week. All who are attending have paid up front, as usual, and I don't think they are going to be disappointed. We have developed a good reputation for providing good-quality, discreet entertainment in pleasant surroundings.'

'Good – that keeps people coming back for more. Now, where are you holding them?'

'Just down the road. We have a friend who has a large, comfortable home with many rooms, all well equipped for keeping our investments safe, as well as for entertaining.'

'That all sounds excellent. And we are going over to them?'

'I thought that, since you are here for a brief visit, you would like to see how things are running here in your absence.'

'You've always had a good head for business, V. I have always been confident having you running things up here.'

'Thank you, that's good to hear. You are too kind. Let's go. I'll show you how things are done in the north.'

As Inzamam and Vihaan stood up to leave, Vihaan's wife came back into the room and silently cleared their cups. Khan paused and watched her, admiring how her light, flowing sari clung to her hips as she moved. He made brief eye contact with Sadiya as she turned to leave the room, smiled, nodded then followed Vihaan out of the house.

Their journey took less than ten minutes and took them out of the town centre to a large house on the outskirts. The imposing building came fully into view as Vihaan turned his white BMW into the driveway. Inzamam looked around at the stone house, set back from the road, surrounded by well-kept lawns and mature trees. They stopped in front of a double garage and Vihaan led Inzamam to a side gate that had wisteria growing in an arch over it.

'An impressive house.'

'We were lucky to find the house – and Arjun, who has been a great supporter of our work.'

'Where did you find Arjun?'

'He was introduced by a mutual friend, and is as dedicated as you will find.'

Inzamam paused. Trusting people outside his small circle of friends had always been a struggle for him, but he credited his suspicion as being one of the things that had kept him safe and out of the reach of the law for so long. He did, however, trust Vihaan so nodded and followed him inside.

The house was as grand on the inside as it was outside, with large paintings on the walls and ornate chandeliers hanging from the high ceilings. Within a few seconds of them walking through the side door, a smiling, bald man in his early sixties, wearing a pink striped shirt, came to greet them.

'Vihaan, so good to see you,' he said loudly, reaching for Vihaan's hand with both of his. As he shook Vihaan's hand, he turned his attention to Inzamam. 'And you must be Inzamam. It is a pleasure to finally meet you. I have heard much about you, and I must say I am in awe of what you have managed to achieve in such a short space of time. You are truly driven, and very welcome to my humble home.'

Khan smiled politely and shook Arjun's hand. 'Thank you for being such a supportive member of our community. It isn't often that such generosity can be found. You have a lovely home.'

'It's a pleasure to be involved in something which brings such pleasure to others and is for a greater good. Now, please, you must come in and have something to drink.' Arjun Bakshi led the two men through into a beautiful, modern kitchen, where they sat and drank tea while they made small talk. The house and its grounds, which were extensive, were silent. Inzamam felt unusually at ease sitting at the kitchen table, talking to the affable Bakshi. After a while Inzamam began to feel that the conversation could go on all day and into the night, so he tried to hurry things along.

'So Arjun, what do you and Vihaan have planned for this evening?'

'Ah yes, of course – enough idle chat, on to business. Come, let me show you what we have in store.'

They stood and followed Arjun out onto a patio that spread the width of the house. Around the far side of the house was an annexe. It was hidden from sight by the house and a dense line of mature trees that formed a copse between the annexe and the end of Arjun's land. Inzamam looked around and nodded his approval. Arjun held the door open for Inzamam and Vihaan, and they stepped into a dimly lit, lavish bar area with small, round tables, plush booths and a fully stocked bar.

'It's nice, isn't it?' said Vihaan excitedly.

'Yes, it looks lovely. Tell me, Arjun, how long have you lived here?'

'I've been here for about eight years now. I refurbished the annexe a couple of years ago. I'm glad it's being put to such good use.'

'And your family?'

'I don't have family to speak of – a son in London, who I haven't spoken to for ten years, and an ex-wife in Birmingham, who is enjoying her free house.'

Inzamam nodded again, liking the sound of the solitude and privacy that Bakshi's life gave him as it greatly reduced the risks surrounding their activities.

'One more question, if I may?'

'Of course, anything.'

'How do your guests know where to come?'

'Ah, a shrewd question. We collect them in a private taxi from an agreed place, ensuring the highest level of discretion. The windows are blacked out and they do not know where they are when they arrive. They enter via a side entrance that is surrounded by trees, with a path leading only one way. Their phones are taken from them as they get into the taxi, and turned off to avoid any unwanted attention.'

'It sounds very well planned.'

'Yes, it is,' Bakshi assured Inzamam. 'Now, can I interest either of you gentlemen in a drink?'

Inzamam was aware that V. was looking at him, waiting for him to speak first. He smiled at Vihaan's deference and watched as Arjun walked behind the long wooden bar.

'I'm driving back later today, so just a beer for me. Nothing strong enough to weaken the conscience.'

Arjun smiled at the religious reference and opened a bottle of Chang beer. 'And for you, Vihaan?'

'I'll have a JD and coke, please,' Vihaan said hesitantly.

'Excellent choice! I'll join you. Now let's get on with things, shall we? Mr Khan has a long journey ahead of him, and I'm sure you're keen to see what we've brought you here for.'

He watched as Arjun pressed a buzzer at the end of the bar, but heard no sound. Within a minute a tall, attractive, young-woman, with long blonde hair tottered through on heels that were slightly too high for her. She was dressed in a figure-hugging black dress. Khan noticed that she instantly recognised Vihaan, as she smiled timidly when he raised his glass to her.

'Tracey, these fine gentlemen would like to see what we have in store for our guests tonight. Could you be a gem and bring the girls out, exactly as they will be presented later?'

'Of course, Mr Bakshi, I'd be delighted,' she said, obviously trying to suppress her northern accent. She turned to leave the bar, holding Inzamam's gaze for a few moments as she did.

'An eye for the ladies, Mr Khan?' Arjun said with a wry smile.

'Life's pleasures are to be enjoyed in whatever form they take, wouldn't you agree?' replied Inzamam.

'Oh, I would indeed, and this is one of the reasons I am so pleased to be involved in your enterprise – to aid others in that enjoyment.'

'That, and the fact that it pays very well, I'm sure,' Khan responded with a laugh.

'There are many ways to be paid, and all have their benefits.'

Tracey opened the door and Inzamam watched as she beckoned an awkward- looking procession of white girls, who looked to be in their early to mid-teens, into the bar. Some wore dresses, some just wore underwear and some wore tight jeans and bra tops. All but two were looking down at the floor as they lined up along the rear wall of the bar. Khan could feel Vihaan watching him for a reaction, but he didn't give him the satisfaction. He stayed completely poker-faced as he watched Tracey walk along the line, encouraging the girls to stand up straight and ever so quietly getting them to smile and lift their heads. Each one did as they had been instructed, but none of them made eye contact with the three men.

'So, what do you think?' asked Vihaan, clearly unable to wait any longer for a reaction from Khan.

'I think I need to understand some of the finer points of what you're doing to make sure I'm OK with the level of risk versus reward,' Inzamam said, quietly enough so that the girls couldn't hear him. Arjun and Vihaan looked at each other, clearly shocked by Inzamam's response, but Inzamam held their stare, making it clear he wanted answers.

'Come, let us go somewhere more private and talk in more detail,' Arjun said to Khan.

'OK, where?'

Arjun pointed to the door the girls had come through. All three men walked through, into a long corridor and once the door had closed behind them, Inzamam let fly.

'What the fuck are you playing at? A line-up of underage girls who all know your names – are you fucking stupid? Your private cab routine – how long do you think it will be before the local police are following you in unmarked cars, or a rich, pissed wanker shoots his mouth off and uses your name? I'm guessing you praise-hungry motherfuckers let the visitors know your names, as you've let the little white slags know who you are!'

'I'm sorry, Inzamam, I didn't think—' Vihaan stuttered.

'Come now, let us discuss this calmly. Come and have a drink,' Arjun interrupted.

Khan turned and smashed his fist into the older man's face, once, twice, three times. Heavy blows rained down on Arjun's nose and mouth. He tried in vain to cover his face and, as he did,

Khan

Khan grabbed him by the scruff of the neck, pulling him close, so close that Inzamam could feel Bakshi's hot breath on his face.

'Now listen to me, you stupid, arrogant wankers. This isn't a fucking game, and I'm not going to get caught because you want to play Mr Big. Do I make myself fucking clear?'

'Yes,' replied Arjun, spluttering through his bloody lips. Khan looked at Vihaan.

'Well?' shouted Inzamam.

'Yes, I understand. We'll do better, you have our word.'

Inzamam released his grip on Arjun Bakshi and, with an open hand, slapped Vihaan hard.

'Don't be so fucking careless, you dumb twat. I expect better from you. And you—' he said looking at Bakshi. 'Go and get yourself cleaned up, then get back out there to the bar and make sure tonight goes without a hitch. Tomorrow you will have a completely different operating model – understand?'

'Yes, I understand, totally. Thank you for pointing out the error of our ways. We won't let you down.'

'Fucking right you won't – because if you do, it will be the last thing you ever do. Now, hurry up and get cleaned up. I want to enjoy something from this fucked-up trip before I head back.'

A few minutes later Inzamam was joined in the bar by Vihaan and a battered Arjun.

Inzamam immediately took control of proceedings.

'So, Tracey, how long have your friends been staying with us?'

The young woman smiled and answered confidently. 'They've been here for a couple of days, and most will be staying with us for a little while. As most of our girls don't have regular homes,

77

they like to stay here. Mr Bakshi treats them well and their rooms are like their very own hotel rooms.'

Khan was well aware that the girls were mainly from the social services system, or daughters of illegal immigrants. He'd spoken to Vihaan at length about how they could make money from the exploitation of young girls. What he didn't know before this trip was how Vihaan ran the logistical side of things.

Inzamam nodded his approval at Tracey. He noticed that, as Tracey had been talking to him and walking along the line of girls, Vihaan had been unable to take his eyes off her.

'So, Arjun, how does this work?' Inzamam asked.

'If you would like to enjoy some of the finer pleasures of the flesh before you leave, please choose any of the girls. Tracey will show you to one of our beautiful rooms,' replied Arjun, obviously being careful not to use Inzamam's name.

'Any of them?'

'More than one, if you wish – they would all be pleased to make you happy,' Vihaan said with a toothy grin.

'No, no, one will be enough,' Inzamam said, standing and walking along the line-up of young girls. He glanced over his shoulder and winked at V as he took Tracey's hand.

'I choose you,' he said to Tracey, smiling. Tracey blushed and looked from Arjun to Vihaan, as if asking for permission.

'Tracey, please go with our guest,' said Arjun, looking like he was attempting a smile through his swollen lips. She nodded and smiled broadly at Inzamam.

'In that case, follow me, please. You won't be disappointed with your choice…' She paused, as if waiting for him to give her his name.

Inzamam nodded. 'Good.'

12

Four days earlier

Raj bustled through the door, shaking rain from his bike jacket while juggling his crash helmet and rucksack. Gonzo wandered out of the toilet, rubbing his eyes with the back of his hands, naked apart from a pair of boxers, which had Iron Man's face on the front.

'Nice pants,' Raj said with a laugh.

Gonzo looked down and grinned. 'Iron Man is the man, Raj – could've done with his help with the Albanians. Well, before Inza-man came along.' The skinny youth beamed at Raj, his ribs visible under his tattooed skin, much of which was bruised a dark purple.

'What's happenin' today then, Raj? A bit of cuttin'?'

'How are you feeling? You sound better,' said Raj, changing the subject.

'Yeah, not bad, thanks. I'm sore as fuck, but I'm breathin'.'

'So, you should probably start by tidying up the sofa and the table in there. If the boss comes in and sees the little pit you created for yourself yesterday, he'll go mental.'

Gonzo glanced over his shoulder at the empty crisp bags on the table and the bedding hanging over the arm of the sofa. He nodded at Raj, who watched as Gonzo walked over to tidy his makeshift bed. Raj said nothing, but was relieved that he'd managed to successfully change the subject. He didn't want Gonzo getting too pally, and he definitely didn't want to tell him about the daily tasks he carried out to keep Inzamam's drug empire functioning and growing. Once Raj was satisfied that Gonzo had cleaned up and was absorbed in morning TV, he started his routine. First he went into the drug store and did a stock take. Next he cleaned his cutting bench and all the equipment, which was neatly arranged. As he was replacing the scales, his phone rang, Inzamam's name popped onto the screen.

'Morning,' he greeted Khan.

'Good morning. How's Gonzo this morning?'

'He seems fine – he's really bruised, but cheerful enough. He's sat watching TV at the minute.'

'Good. I'll need a little chat with him when I get back, which should be in about three-quarters of an hour. Can you have

Lawrence meet me in the office as soon as I get back? There are a few things we're going to need cleaning up.'

'Trouble up north?'

'Nothing we can't handle.'

The phone went dead and Raj was left wondering what Inzamam was referring to.

He decided not to waste too much time trying to figure it out, as he knew that Khan would only share what he wanted to. Instead he flicked through the contacts on his phone until he found Larry.

Larry – Khan was the only person to call him Lawrence – had grown up in the local area and was a similar age to Inzamam. He was well known in the criminal community as being the person who could source anything and get pretty much anything done, including getting rid of people. He had contacts that reached halfway around the world and was great fun to get drunk with because he had so many stories about things he'd done.

'Hi Larry, it's Raj. How you doing?'

'Raj! I'm great, thanks, buddy, how's you?' 'I'm good, thanks. Are you local?'

'I am, as it happens. Got in from LA yesterday. Why? What's up?'

'Inzamam asked me to give a call and see if you can meet him here in about three- quarters of an hour.'

'Yes, mate, of course I can. What's he fucked up this time?'

'Who knows? He's on his way in now. I haven't seen him yet.'

'OK, no worries, mate. I'll see you in thirty, get the kettle on.'

'Will do. Cheers, Larry.'

Half an hour later, true to his word, Larry bowled through the door. His charisma instantly filled the room. He was a tall, tanned, good-looking guy with cropped salt and pepper hair and matching stubble. Larry had been mentoring Raj for the last year, when he'd told Raj that he saw some real potential in him that Khan would struggle to see and probably wouldn't invest the time to develop. Raj had been grateful for the support and had learned lots from Larry. A bright-white smile beamed from his bronzed face and his arms went out to hug Raj.

'Raj! Great to see you. It's been a while.'

Raj hugged him back, then turned to make tea. 'Good to see you too, man. What you been up to?'

Before Larry had time to answer, the door swung open again and in walked Khan.

'Thanks for coming over at short notice. Raj, make that two teas, will you? Lawrence, come through to the office, let's have a chat.'

Larry rolled his eyes at Raj then followed Inzamam into his office. The door swung shut behind them.

Raj made the teas and carried them through to the two men. He placed the cups on the desk then turned to leave.

'Raj, stay – you could do with hearing this. You need to know how to clean up shit like this. As the business grows, I can't always be the one sorting out the crap. Isn't that right, Lawrence?'

'Yeah, Raj, you can't always have Inzamam cleaning up after you. Grab a seat.'

Larry smiled at Raj, who didn't react but did as instructed, pulling up a seat and grabbing himself a bottle of water from Khan's office fridge.

'So, what can I help you with, Inzy?'

Larry was the only person Raj had ever heard call him Inzy.

'We need to sort out some crap up north. There's a business I've got up there that's being run by a guy I've known for years. He's brought someone in to help him without running it by me, and—'

'Let me guess. You don't approve?'

'He's a complete fuckwit to be honest. He's endangering the business – and me along with it. So I need him out of the way. But there's a complication.'

'Oh? You've never let that bother you before.'

'I know, which is why I'm talking to you. He owns an asset that's useful to the business and I want to keep control of the asset.'

'OK, sounds simple. Trade him his life for the asset, then make sure he's far enough away before we get rid of him for good. It's going to cost, Inzy. We can fly him to Brazil – I have someone there who can remove him permanently. Is that the kind of thing you had in mind?'

'I knew you'd know how to clean it up. Didn't I tell you, Raj? Lawrence will know how.'

'You did.' Raj nodded. He'd been looking from one to other throughout the exchange, staggered by how easily they talked about killing someone.

'Just one question.' Asked Raj.

'What is it?' Replied Khan.

'If this asset has reasonable value, which I'm guessing it does, do you need Will?'

'That's good thinking. Yes, can you get Will on the phone later today?'

'I would imagine so.'

'Who's Will?' asked Larry.

'He's my lawyer. Don't worry – he's on the inside.'

'OK, that's fine then. How quickly do you want this done Inzy?'

'Yesterday?' Khan said with a smile.

'OK. It'll take a day to convince him to sign over the asset and then get him out of the country. Can you get Will to draft an asset transfer contract quickly?'

'I don't see why not. So, how much is this going to cost me?'

'Twenty-five plus expenses.'

'I can live with that. And confirmation of completion?'

'Secure message, as usual?'

'Fine, let's do it. Any other bits we've missed, Raj?'

'No, I don't think so.'

'Good! Game on, then. So, to specifics. The target is Arjun Bakshi, the asset is his house on the outskirts of Rotherham. Do you remember V.?'

'Yes, your mate from Rotherham?'

'That's him. He's going to need frightening, but nothing that will cause permeant damage. Just enough to make him think and stop him doing something stupid again.'

'Got it. Anything else?' Larry said as he stood to leave.

'No, I think that's it. Thanks.' Raj and Inzamam shook hands with Larry and he left the office.

'See you, Gonzo!' Raj heard Larry shout as he walked towards the back door. Raj was fully aware that Gonzo's eyes had been on stalks since Larry walked in. Raj glanced in Gonzo's direction and saw the pusher's head sink beneath the top of the sofa.

'What's been going on, boss?' Raj asked tentatively, unsure whether Khan would share anything with him.

'That fucking idiot V. has brought in this muppet, Bakshi. He's got a huge house, a bigger mouth and an even bigger ego, and he's fucking dangerous.'

'How so?' Raj pressed, interested, and sensing that Inzamam was in a sharing mood.

'The girls we've got up there all stay in an annexe in Bakshi's grounds, which in itself isn't a problem. It's quiet and secluded. But his house is right next to it and they bring the punters up to the house in blacked-out minibuses, which will draw attention. Then, to top it off, they all know their fucking names – girls, punters, the lot. Fucking idiots! I can't believe V. would be so fucking stupid, but he hasn't got your brain. I'd get you to go and run things up there, but you're too valuable down here.'

Raj sat listening to Khan, quietly pleased that he was thought of as valuable, but sensing that he wasn't going to get anything more out him about his northern exploits.

'Right, let's get Gonzo in here and sort him out before I need to add him to the cleaning list.'

'Gonzo, in here!' Raj shouted to the youth, who was still watching TV. Gonzo jumped up from the sofa and scurried through to the office.

'Morning, boss.'

'You alright, Gonzo?' Khan asked him.

'Yeah, not bad, thanks. I'm a bit sore, but I'll be alright. Raj has sorted me right-out with some sick painkillers.'

'Good. I'm glad you're feeling better. We need to have a little chat about what happened with the Albanians. Tanush and Kepi were both nasty pieces of work and they'll be missed by the Albanians and others. When people are … removed in the way they were, other people start asking questions, and it won't be long until the questions get to you, as it was your patch. So, what are you going to say?' Inzamam asked.

Raj stood silently watching Khan starting to pile pressure on Gonzo, who was shifting his weight uncomfortably from one foot to another, clearly unsure what to say.

'I-I don't know. What do you want me to say?'

'Well, let's start with what you know. Or, rather, what you think you know.'

'Boss?' Gonzo stammered.

'Let me make this simple.' Khan broke into softer tones than Raj was expecting him to use. He walked over and put an arm over Gonzo's shoulder. 'You were in the street, Rosen Kepi was giving you a kicking, you woke up here. Now, what do you think happened? Simple question.'

'Er … I … er … dunno … you came and got me and fucked-up the Albanians?'

'OK, let's say for argument's sake that's what happened. How do you feel about that?'

As Inzamam kept asking questions, Raj began to understand what he was doing, and why the softer tone.

'Dunno what you mean?' Gonzo asked.

'I mean what I say. It must have been scary in the alleyway, by the bins. So how did you feel when you woke up here?'

Raj smiled. Inzamam was dripping in enough information to confirm to Gonzo that he had been there, and had saved him from being beaten to death.

'I guess relieved, and … grateful?' Gonzo phrased his answer as a question, checking it was the right one.

'That's an interesting word, grateful. Why so?'

'I don't think I'd have got out of there in one piece on my own, and if it hadn't been for you, I'd have been dead, I reckon.'

'That would explain feeling grateful, I suppose,' interjected Raj.

'But, Raj, young Gonzo is one of our own, and we look after our own, don't we?'

'We do indeed,' said Raj, understanding immediately where Khan was heading.

'Isn't that right, Gonzo?' repeated Inzamam.

'Er, yeah, boss, course we do.'

'Of course we do. So let's get back to the topic in hand. At some point people are going to ask you what you know about the Albanians, and it would be really useful if we all knew how that was going to play out.'

'I'm gonna to tell them I don't know nothin', 'cos I don't.'

'Depending on who's asking That might work. But you may be asked in different ways,' said Inzamam, tapping Gonzo on the shoulder.

'I don't know what you mean.'

'Well, let's say it's the local pushers and crack whores. If it's them, I'm guessing your answer will fly because, let's face it, you're the man as far as they're concerned. But if it's the Albanians or the police, they're going to be a bit harder to convince, especially as you're a fucking terrible liar.'

Khan's soft, sympathetic tones had vanished, replaced by sarcasm and a building anger. Khan's face contorted as he spat the words at Gonzo.

'Take this fucking seriously, you stupid drug-pedalling motherfucker!' Khan screamed in Gonzo's ear. Raj winced, and Gonzo started to tremble.

'Sorry, boss. I mean, I am takin' it seriously, just tell me what you want me to say and I'll say it. I'll not tell no one nothin'. Not even if they say they're gonna kill me,' Gonzo said, his voice cracking.

'I'm glad you're taking it that seriously, Gonzo, because if the police or the Albanians get hold of you, they'll either lock you up until you talk or they'll beat the shit out of you until you talk. Either way, they'll make your spill your guts, you whiney little fucker. And I'm not going to get picked up, or shot, because you couldn't keep your fucking mouth shut. So let me tell you how it's going to be.'

Inzamam was as animated as Raj had ever seen him.

'No matter who gets to you, or what they ask you, you repeat that you know nothing. You keep repeating that you know nothing if they lock you in a cell, or if they fucking waterboard you. You keep repeating you know nothing if the Albanians break every fucking bone in your body, if they gouge your eyes out or feed you to their pet fucking pigs. Because you owe me, Gonzo, and if I think for one minute that you're going to grass me up, I'll string your family up outside the crappy block of flats you call home, while you watch them die. Then I'll blow-torch your face and tear you apart, limb by limb, making sure you stay awake through the whole fucking thing. Do we understand each other?'

'Yeah, I understand. I won't grass you up, boss. I wouldn't do that – you saved my life.' Tears streamed down Gonzo's face and he shook as he spoke.

'And don't you fucking forget it, you scrawny little twat! Now help Raj with today's deliveries. You're going nowhere.'

Raj was shocked for a second but kept a straight face, so as not to give away his surprise to Khan. He knew that Khan would want to keep Gonzo under close surveillance, but helping him? That was a shock. That meant Gonzo wasn't going anywhere; he would be staying in the office permanently, under lock and key. To confirm his suspicions, Raj asked Khan if he should make up a proper bed for Gonzo instead of him using the sofa.

'Great idea. You see, Gonzo, this is what "taking it seriously" sounds like. Raj knows when things need doing, and why. You could do a lot worse than listen to Mr Gadhi – and you never know, it might even keep you alive longer.' Khan gave a menacing grin. 'Now go and sit in front of the TV while I talk to Raj, then you can help him set you a bed up. And keep the place tidy. It's not a fucking crack den.'

'Yes, boss, thank you.'

Raj followed Inzamam into the office and closed the door.

'What we have there, Raj, is a petrified pusher,' said Inzamam, trying not to laugh.

'You could say that. I thought he was going to piss his pants.'

Inzamam laughed. 'He did look a bit scared, didn't he? Good. I meant what I said: if he fucking grasses me up, I'll fucking kill him and his no-good junkie family.' As Khan spoke, his eyes darkened.

'Understood. Don't worry, I'll keep him here. He won't be going anywhere.'

'Good lad, Raj, I know I can rely on you. Keep him busy – he has to earn his keep.

Otherwise I might as well get Lawrence to clean him up when he's done with the northerner. But I think he's more use to us breathing. What do you think?'

'What do I think?'

'Yes, what do you think? You've always got an opinion. Even if you don't voice it, I know you have a view.'

For the second time that day, Raj was shocked. Khan was asking for his opinion and seemed to mean it.

'I think enough people will have been killed by the end of this week. If too many die, people will start pointing the finger. The Albanians could have been anyone, the northerner is far enough away not to be connected to us, but if Gonzo or his family end up dead, the police will start to join the dots, and we could do without the additional attention. Business is good, all the patches are turning over plenty, and the export side is flying. Why would you jeopardise that over a skinny little pusher that we can keep locked up?'

'You see, I knew you had an opinion, and one worth listening to. I agree – keep the little twat alive and working. I'm off out.'

'No worries. Anything I need to do while you're out?'

'Only what we've just discussed. That'll be enough for one morning.'

13

After speaking to Larry, Inzamam Khan headed home for an hour – just long enough to get a bite to eat and have a quick catch-up with Husna. He walked through the front door, announcing his arrival with a cheerful 'Hi'. Getting no response, he went through into Husna's home office, where she was updating her jewellery website.

'Hey, how was your trip up to see V.?' she enquired.

'Good, thanks,' said Inzamam, kissing the top of her head. 'He's up to no good as usual.'

'What about Sadiya? How's she doing? I was chatting to her on Messenger and she said that she hadn't been well.'

'She seemed fine, but she never talks to me much. V. never mentioned that she wasn't well. It was only a flying visit, so not too much time to catch up.'

'We should go up and see them for a weekend soon.'

'Why not? Sounds like it could be fun.' He turned to leave the office, not in the mood to extend the conversation about Vihaan.

'Put the kettle on, would you?' she shouted after him.

'Consider it done, my queen. Your wish is my command.'

'Too right, and don't you forget it, Khan!'

Husna laughed and returned to tapping on her keyboard. He half-filled the copper kettle and flicked the switch to boil, grabbed one of Husna's cups from a cupboard and stood flicking through messages on his phone. One stood out. It was from Ray Johnson, a wealthy, influential businessman and someone with whom Khan had built a useful relationship. Conveniently for Khan, Ray was also a home-grown sympathiser and muslim convert with a taste for the more extreme views of Inzamam. Five years earlier, Johnson had funded a new supply route for Inzamam to expand his drug distribution lines into neighbouring counties, after they were introduced by a mutual friend. Since then they'd made each other a lot of money.

Good afternoon, my young entrepreneurial friend. If you are around today, I am up from London. It would be good to catch up over a coffee. Ray

Inzamam smiled at Ray's sign-off. He was about the same age as Khan's father and, despite his business acumen, he still used Messenger as if he was writing a letter. It had taken him a year to stop using 'Dear Inzamam' at the beginning of every message.

Inzamam replied as the kettle clicked off.

Hi Ray, that sounds good to me. Where and what time? I've got a pretty free afternoon.

He made Husna's tea, took it through to her, kissed her on the top of her head again, and went upstairs to change.

Ray messaged back straight away.

Hello Inzamam,
I can be free in the next hour. How about Ocean Village?
Ray

Perfect, see you in an hour.

Inzamam changed from chinos and polo shirt into a pale grey Ted Baker suit and pink shirt. Glancing at his reflection in the mirror, he smiled. He liked his wardrobe and thought nothing of spending two or three thousand pounds on a shopping spree –

something Husna and his girls enjoyed too. He headed back downstairs and popped his head around the office door.

'I'm off out. Do you want anything picking up on my way back?'

'No thanks, are you going to back in time to drop the girls off, they're going over to a friend's house later?' replied Husna, turning around to face him. 'You look good. Going anywhere nice?'

'Just going to meet Ray for an hour or so and yes I should be able to drop the girls off.'

'Ah, I see. Have fun and don't worry about the girls, I'll ask Carla to pick them up and take them to hers.'

Khan knew Husna liked Ray. They'd been to his home on the outskirts of Windsor for some lovely garden parties, but he also knew she was smart enough to know that he made money in similar ways to her husband, which meant she wouldn't want to know specifics.

'See you later. Say hi to Ray.' Husna stood to kiss him before he left. He held her face in his hands as he gave her a long, lingering kiss. As he let her go, he drew in a deep breath, letting the smell of her perfume fill his nostrils.

'See you later, love you,' he said.

'You'd better, Khan.'

He rolled the Range Rover slowly down the gravel driveway and turned right towards the main road that led down to The Avenue, a long, tree-lined road that led towards the centre of Southampton. He drove down to the waterfront and the high-rise development surrounding the marina in Ocean Village. Inzamam remembered when there were just a few bars and a couple of restaurants around the marina; now it was a sprawling mass of glass towers, overlooking expensive yachts and powerboats.

He parked and walked over to a magnificent structure on the far side of the marina: the hotel, spa and bar fashioned in the shape of a cruise ship was one of Inzamam's favourite places. The architecture was beautiful, and the staff made sure they looked after everyone well. It was the kind of place that attracted those who wanted to be seen somewhere cool, as well as those who wanted to eat and drink somewhere out of the ordinary. Khan took the lift up to the sixth floor and was greeted by a well-dressed, good-looking man in his mid-twenties.

'Good afternoon. Are you joining us for lunch?'

'A table for two, please,' replied Khan.

'Certainly. This way, sir.' As the young man led Inzamam to a table overlooking the marina, Khan glanced around the restaurant and bar to see if there was anyone there he knew. There wasn't. He took a drinks menu from a waiter, who introduced himself as Thomas, and without really looking ordered a bottle of Australian Malbec from the top end of the list. As the waiter was returning with the wine, Inzamam saw Ray come through the door into the reception area. The same young man greeted him then escorted Ray to the table. Inzamam stood to greet his friend with a warm handshake and a big smile.

'Ray, it's great to see you. I've ordered a bottle of red.'

'Ah, my dear Inzamam, how well you know me.'

They sat as the waiter offered to pour a tester, which Ray waved away.

'Just throw it in the glass, young man. I very much doubt it will be going back.'

Inzamam waited as their glasses were filled and the bottle was left in the centre of the table. Ray sat across from him. He wore a double-breasted cream suit and similar pink shirt to Khan's. His tanned complexion, thick blond hair and white teeth made him look like a much younger man.

'So, tell me, how's business?' Ray asked Inzamam.

'Things are going well. We're working across three counties and have a distribution chain that reaches along the south coast.'

'That does sound good. What's this I hear about you experiencing Albanian interference?'

'They're a minor inconvenience, an occupational hazard that's to be expected. They're greedy and clumsy, with an overinflated sense of their own importance.'

Khan was unsurprised that Ray knew about the Albanians; his connections spread far and wide. He held his glass out towards his friend. 'Cheers.' Glasses chinked and Ray nodded and took a big mouthful of wine.

They ordered food and settled into an easy conversation about family, laughing frequently and loudly.

Ray brought them back to business. 'With distribution spreading so well, your holy war must be gaining traction, Inzamam.'

'It is proceeding to plan, *inshallah*. We are making excellent progress: the infidels are weak, their offspring are easily coerced into playing their part in the supply chain, and they are easy to keep in line. It never ceases to amaze me how enthusiastic they can be, when given the smallest reward for their efforts.'

'How so?' Ray smiled and refilled their glasses.

'Something as simple as an extra fifty, or a gram for personal use, on the house, and they're over the moon. They really are fucking stupid.'

'That's why they make the best employees.'

'They do – and the state of them. I don't think I've met one yet who knows how to dress themselves, and they all have faces only a mother could love.' The pair laughed loudly and drained the wine bottle. Inzamam waved the waiter over, ordered a second bottle then excused himself.

On the way to the toilet, he messaged Raj.

Won't be coming in tonight, can you let the restaurant know? What's happening with Gonzo?

A reply came back quickly from Raj.

Will do. I've had him working all day. He's cleaned the floors and done a crap job of the windows :-)

Sounds about right. Did you get hold of Will?

Yes, he's drawing the asset transfer paperwork up and will send it over to me later today. What do you want me to do when it gets here?

Send a PDF over to L pls.

OK, will do.

Khan pocketed his phone and re-joined Ray. 'So Ray, I'm sure you didn't just want to know about my fuck-ugly distributors, or the Albanian rumour. What's on your mind?'

'Insightful as ever, dear Inzamam. Although you are incorrect about one part; it is Albanian connected.'

'Oh?'

'They're starting to take an interest in moving into Brighton. They've left a couple of the local pushers in skips, almost beaten to death, but not quite. The beatings were intended to send a message.'

'To who?'

'I have a local distributor. He's not of your calibre, or vision. But he is dependable and … well, let's just say I'd rather he didn't come to any significant harm.'

Khan knew exactly what Ray meant. He had known for years about his friend's secret preference for young men. His wife, Inzamam assumed, didn't have the same knowledge – if she did, she had hidden it very well on the occasions Khan had met her.

'What would you like me to do, Ray?'

'I think we could mutually benefit from your involvement, Inzamam. In as much as Roman could learn from you and perhaps become someone you could utilise. And Brighton could become the next territory that you expand into – a bit of a win-win. What do you think?'

'I think you have a problem with the Albanians, you heard about my recent run-in with them, and you figured I could clean it up for you. Tell me more about the situation. Who and where?'

'I'm glad we're on the same wavelength, Inzamam. My strong belief is that Valmir Shala has deployed one of his best to take control of supply in Brighton. Erion Hasani has been seen by some of Roman's team, and a couple of them have been approached directly.'

'Approached how?'

'With a proposal for switching suppliers and increasing their earning potential, would probably be the best way to describe it. Now, I don't know what these Albanian wankers think they're playing at, Inzamam, but this is just not cricket. Years gone by, if someone wanted a cut of your business, they would at least have the courtesy to arrange to meet with you and discuss terms first, not just pitch up to the street urchins and deploy such crass poaching methods. It's just not on. You understand me, don't you?'

Inzamam smiled at Ray's yearning for the code of the past: honour among thieves. He knew that Ray was not as righteous as his disdain for the Albanians' actions made him look. Ray was no fool and had, in his younger days, done exactly what Hasani was doing to him now. Maybe Ray was just getting too old for the game.

'Of course I understand you, Ray. To be clear, you want me take over Roman's operation and mentor him, while taking care of the Albanian problem?'

'Exactly, my dear Inzamam. I couldn't have put it better myself.'

'And the product we would be moving? My scorpion blend?' Khan let the question hang, fully aware that, since Ray needed his help, he would have to give up a share of the cut.

'But of course. That's precisely what I had in mind. With a percentage for me, in recognition of my making the territory and ground troops available for transfer to you.'

'Of course – I wouldn't have it any other way. We've always made sure that our dividend has been shared fairly, and I see no reason why that can't continue.'

Inzamam watched the tension in Ray's face ease. 'Shall we order some food?' asked Inzamam.

'Yes, that would be superb,' Ray replied, clearly pleased to have resolved the business part of their meeting. Inzamam motioned once more to the young waiter and watched Ray eyeball the man as he walked towards them, a flirtatious smile creeping across Ray's lips.

When their starters came, Khan decided to find out more about Ray's Brighton venture.

'Tell me about Roman and his team.'

'A handover would be useful, I suppose. Roman is a darling boy – well educated, very bright and understands the scene in Brighton. Who's buying, what their latest fix is, and how to move it in volume.'

'He sounds promising.'

'Oh, he is – he reminds me of you at times. Very astute and focused on delivering a good product for top dollar. His disciples are like those that you have in other territories. Mainly young white men from deprived areas, or well-off, silver-spoon types, out to rebel against their parents, selling to their university peers and fellow clubbers.'

'So far, so good. What about saturation?'

'Market saturation is high in the central areas, with good margins, less so in the outer city parts. Some real room for growth and profit generation on the outskirts.'

'I'm going to need to a cash injection for production to move scorpion into there. That will need investment and I'm not sure I should carry all the risk, Ray.'

'Of course. I'm always happy to invest if there's a good rate of return – you know that, Inzamam.'

'Good. I'll give you some baseline figures later this week. On the face of it, I think we could have another successful venture. So, onto the other part of the equation: how deeply are our Albanian interlopers invested in the city?'

'They've made inroads in the clubs and bars district in the city centre, but by no means a strong foothold.'

'And this Erion Hasani – what do you know about him?'

'He's a nasty piece of work by all accounts, cast from a similar mould as your Mr Tanush.'

Khan nodded, but said nothing. 'How many foot soldiers?'

'Less than twenty, I would say – some of Roman's initial team, a handful at best, but no one who would have any significant loyalty, I wouldn't imagine.'

'OK, that makes life a bit easier. What about the police?'

'They pick up the odd street vendor but we've had no interest at a higher level, and no one has knocked on any doors that could lead to us. Like other forces, they're making positive noises about tackling gun and knife crime along with drug-related crime and county lines.'

'Good, that's all really useful. This lamb is lovely, by the way.' Khan smiled and scooped up a cube of curried lamb.

14

Larry's phone vibrated in his pocket, it was a message from Raj.

Will is drafting the asset transfer agreement. Should be with you later today. IK is aware.

That should be a fun piece of news to share with AB.

Ha ha, yes, I guess being told you're going to hand over your house and doing it are two different things.

I'm sure he'll be very cooperative.

Larry had stopped at services not far from Silverstone race circuit for a bite to eat. The news from Raj of the agreement being drafted meant that all the pieces of his plan had now been lined up. His contact in Brazil was ready and waiting. Larry had priced up flights earlier and found one leaving from Heathrow, flying direct to São Paulo, that still had seats. Larry had stopped in a high-street travel agent and paid £1,140 in cash for the ticket, telling the agent Sue an excited story about flying out to surprise his best friend for his birthday. She hadn't batted an eyelid when he'd given her Arjun Bakshi's name and frantically patted his pockets, telling her that in the rush he'd forgotten his passport. 'You'd better not forget it when you get to the airport,' she'd joked with him, handing him his ticket.

'Oh don't worry, that will be planned out very well,' he had replied.

Larry picked up a chicken Caesar wrap and a bottle of water, paid and strolled back out to his car. He fired up the Audi S5, listened to the powerful V6 engine burble as he ate his wrap, then continued his drive north. An hour and a half later, he was turning off the M1 and gunning the sleek German coupé towards Rotherham. He'd taken a brief call from Inzamam on his way up assuring him that everything was in place and he was sure things would go smoothly.

Larry was intrigued to see what Arjun Bakshi would be like. In his line of work he often found that, when confronted with non-negotiable realities, people reacted in very different ways. Some would plead, others would try to play hardball and negotiate in return, while some would be reduced to simple animal fight-or-flight reactions.

He decided to go first to see Vihaan Patel, whom he had met a couple of times with Inzamam. As he watched the grey expanse of Tinsley Viaduct disappear in his rear- view mirror, he muted the car stereo and considered how he would greet, and subsequently handle, Vihaan.

Cruising slowly down the rundown street towards Vihaan's house, Larry spotted a space behind an old Toyota Rav-Four, which gave him an unobstructed view of the Patel's front door and side passageway. He sat and watched for about half an hour, during which time no one came in or out of the house. With the exception of the kids playing at the bottom of the hill, the road was quiet. He got out of the car and walked across the road. Without looking around, he went into the brick passageway that ran alongside Vihaan's home. He came to a tall gate with a rusty latch. Larry pressed slowly on the latch and eased the gate open. Despite its age, the gate opened quietly. To his left, he could see the back door of the Patel's house and their kitchen window. Not seeing anyone moving around inside, Larry moved stealthily to the back door. He checked the handle, as he suspected, it was locked. He picked the lock within a few seconds, eased open the door and stepped over the threshold into the kitchen. Still no sign of anyone. Good, he thought, that makes life easier.

He checked around the house. Once he was sure that no one was home, he slid the bolt across to lock the back door and headed to the lounge where he sat in an armchair that faced the front door. Larry sat in silence for over an hour, listening to the sounds of kids playing outside and a clock ticking on the wall.

Eventually his patience was rewarded and there was the rattle of a key in the front- door. Larry didn't move. He sat quite still, eyes focused on the upper half of the door.

As it swung open into the lounge, a woman bustled in, shopping bags hanging from her hands. She raised her head and when she saw Larry, she froze. A man Larry recognised as Vihaan walked into her, obviously not expecting his wife to stop dead.

'Sadi, what are you…' His words trailed off when he saw Larry.

'Hello Vihaan, and Mrs Patel, I assume? Come on in and close the door, please.' Larry motioned for them to step inside. Sadiya looked over her shoulder at Vihaan, who nodded for her to do as instructed. Larry nodded and smiled at the pair. 'My sincere apologies, Mrs Patel, for intruding in your home, but I really need your husband's help with something.'

Sadiya didn't reply, but walked through to the kitchen. Larry watched her leave the room and close the door behind her.

'Vihaan, do me a favour. Open the kitchen door and ask your wife to make some tea. I'm parched.'

Vihaan did as requested, then sat on a sofa opposite Larry, who sat and waited, all the while just looking at Vihaan, saying nothing and giving nothing away. Sadiya brought the tea through and placed a cup in front of each man.

'Thank you for the tea, Mrs Patel. Now, I know this is your home, but would you mind going upstairs while I speak to your husband? It's a rather delicate matter and I'm not sure he'd be comfortable discussing it in front of you. Oh and could I have your phone please?'

Sadiya looked at Vihaan.

'Give him your phone and go upstairs, Sadiya. I'll come up when we've finished.'

Without saying a word, Mrs Patel handed him her phone and left the room via the stairs in the corner. Once he was sure she had gone into one of the bedrooms, he turned his attention back to Vihaan.

'You've been a silly boy, Vihaan, a very silly boy indeed. Inzamam has asked me to come up here and clear things up – you know, take care of his business interests. He was less than impressed with your little set-up and as you know, better than I do, he likes things to be done properly. So let me tell you what's going to happen. You're going to give me your phone. Then once we've sorted out our lines of communication, you're going to take me to see Mr Bakshi.'

'But, but—' Vihaan tried to interrupt.

Larry held up a hand to silence him. 'No, no, now is the time for you to listen, not to speak. Your time for speaking was when Inzamam was here, but from what I've heard you were too busy showing off your underage knocking shop. Just in case you're in any doubt about how serious this is, I am under strict instructions to ensure that this situation is resolved, permanently, before I leave.' Larry didn't break eye contact with Vihaan the whole time he was speaking. Vihaan wriggled uncomfortably under Larry's stare and when Larry finished speaking Vihaan did not try to jump in and speak again.

'Come on, give me your phone, we've not got all day.'

'What are you going to do to us?'

'To who?'

'Me and my wife – what are you going to do to me and my wife? She hasn't done anything, she doesn't know anything.'

'Your wife's of no concern to me. That is, as long as she doesn't try to tell anyone about my visit.'

'She won't! She doesn't even know who you are.'

'But you do, don't you, Vihaan?'

'You're Lawrence. You clear things up for Inzamam.'

Larry smiled. 'Yes I am, and yes I do. So now we've established that you know what I do, pass me the phone. Do not make me ask again – that would be a mistake on your part.'

Vihaan did as he was told and handed Larry his iPhone. Larry took a SIM card pin from his pocket and popped the SIM cards out of both phones. Once he'd got the cards, he put them in his pocket, along with the pin.

'Come on, we'll take my car.' He pointed over the road towards his Audi. They got into the S5. Larry looped around the hairpin at the bottom of the street and headed towards the centre of town.

Nervously Vihaan guided Larry towards Arjun Bakshi's house on the outskirts of town. Even though Larry knew where it was, he let Vihaan navigate. He stopped by the side of the road about half a mile past Bakshi's and checked to see if the agreement had hit his inbox yet. It had. He smiled and downloaded the PDF, ready to print off.

'Right then, let's go and pay Mr Bakshi a visit, shall we?'

'What are you going to do?'

'All will be revealed in good time. This one, was it?' he asked as he turned into Arjun's driveway.

'Er, yes, this is it.'

'When he comes to the door, I want you to introduce me as a friend of Inzamam's who was in the area, and Inzamam told me I had to come and see the way you had the place set up. Do you understand me?'

'Yes, I understand.' Vihaan ran his hand nervously through his thinning black hair.

'Good. No heroics, no secret hand signals, just breathe and relax, OK?'

'OK.'

The pair walked to the door of Arjun Bakshi's impressive home and Vihaan rang the bell. They didn't have to wait long before Arjun answered the door.

'Vihaan, how lovely to see you. I didn't know you were coming today, or did you mention it and I forgot?'

'Hello Arjun – no, it was a spur of the moment thing. This is a friend of Inzamam's. He's been on business in Leeds and Inzamam told him he had to visit while he was here and see how we have the place running.'

'Well, any friend of Inzamam's … Arjun Bakshi, and you are?' Arjun extended a hand to Larry.

'Larry. Lovely to meet you.' Larry shook Arjun's hand and stepped inside as Arjun moved back to welcome them in.

'You have a lovely home, Mr Bakshi.' Larry studied Arjun's face, including the swelling of his lips and small cuts to his face. He looked curious and a little worried, clearly not sure about his unannounced guests.

'Call me Arjun, please. Thank you, I like it very much. I was just about to have some tea – would you care to join me?'

'Sounds fantastic, I'd love to,' said Larry with a wide smile. The three men walked along the spacious hallway and into Arjun's kitchen. Vihaan and Larry took a seat along one side of an island. Bakshi busied himself making tea.

'How would you like your tea, Larry?' Bakshi asked in a congenial tone. 'Black is fine, thank you.'

'A man after my own heart.'

'Have you lived here long?'

'Oh, a few years now. I loved it the moment I saw it and don't think I'll ever move.'

Vihaan glanced uncomfortably at Larry as Arjun spoke fondly of his home. He didn't acknowledge Vihaan, and remained smiley and engaging.

'I don't blame you. It really is lovely.'

'Here you go, gents. So, Larry, what do you do?'

Larry sensed that Arjun's question carried much more weight than the words alone suggested. 'I work in asset management. Really boring stuff – land and property acquisitions for wealthy people with money to hide.'

They laughed together politely and sipped their tea. Larry was pleased with how things were going and could see how uneasy Arjun felt. This suited Larry. He could see why Vihaan had brought Bakshi into the fold: he was a charming host, engaging and clearly wealthy.

'You must show me around. This is a flying visit and Inzamam told me so much about the place when we spoke earlier on the phone. I was about to head off up to the Lakes but Inzamam insisted I look Vihaan up and come to see what you've both been up to. He says it's quite the enterprise.'

Larry saw unease creep across the older man's face, but he remained polite.

'Inzamam is too kind. Of course you must see. Come, let us go and take in the sights.'

Arjun put down his tea and led them out of the kitchen towards the annexe. As they walked into the detached building Larry saw the woman Khan had told him about. He could see why she had stuck in Khan's mind: she was tall, leggy and wearing a spray-on black dress and heels that highlighted her toned calves and lower thighs.

'Tracey, my dear, this is Larry. He's a friend, here for a flying visit. Do you have any of the girls in a state of readiness?'

'Hello.' She smiled sweetly at Larry. 'Yes, of course, I think we have two or three who could come out to entertain.'

'Splendid, would you mind bringing them out, my dear?'

Tracey left the room. Larry waited until she had gone, then turned to Vihaan. 'So, Vihaan, tell me, how do you and Arjun attract girls to come and stay?'

'Er, they're happy to come and stay. Many of them have diffi-cult pasts and are immigrants or involved in the social services system,' Vihaan began.

'We offer them a lifestyle and comforts they would otherwise never experience,' Arjun interrupted.

'Ah, I see. So you prey on the weak and take advantage of the poor?' Larry stared into Arjun's eyes, just long enough to make him wriggle uncomfortably in his seat.

'Er…' Vihaan began to answer.

Larry held up a hand. 'Shh now, Vihaan, the grown-ups are talking.'

Larry heard Vihaan draw in breath to reply, but he must have thought better of it.

'That was a rhetorical question. We both know what you're doing. Building a little harem out of underage, underprivileged girls. Quite the businessman, aren't we? Again, a rhetorical ques-tion.' Larry held up one hand to silence Bakshi. 'Do you have a printer I could use?'

Larry saw the bewilderment on Arjun's face. 'Er, yes, yes, of course, there's one in the room to our left,' he said pointing to a door.

'Excellent.' Larry took his phone from his pocket and opened the PDF Raj had sent him. He located an air printer and turned his phone towards Arjun.

'This one?'

'Yes, that's it.'

'Good, thank you.' Larry pressed print and asked Vihaan to go and get the document from the printer, and a pen. He did this without question. As he returned with the document and handed it to Larry, the door opened and Tracey walked in, followed by three young girls dressed in skimpy outfits and all looking uncomfortable. They lined up with their arms folded in front of them, until Tracey walked in front of them and spoke very softly. As she passed each one they unfolded their arms, stood straighter, pushed out their boobs and pouted. One of the girls tousled her long red hair and looked Larry in the eye, clearly trying her best to be seductive. Larry looked blankly at the girls then returned his attention to Arjun, who had pressed himself into the corner of his chair, as far as he could get from Larry.

Larry looked briefly back to Tracey and smiled.

'Tracey, I'm not interested. Thank you for bringing the girls out, but I'm sure they'd be much happier in more clothes and doing something more age-appropriate. Could you all please leave the three of us to talk? Thanks again.'

Tracey looked at Arjun, who waved them away, then she ushered the girls quickly out of the room and closed the door behind them.

Larry stood and walked in front of Arjun Bakshi, who was shaking. 'What do you want?' he asked, a nervous tremble in his voice.

'What an excellent question, and one that deserves an honest answer. I want a couple of very simple things, Mr Bakshi – sorry, Arjun. First I want your signature on this paperwork. Then I want you to pack a bag – an overnight bag will do. Then I want you to accompany me to the airport, where I will help you board a flight to Brazil, with this ticket.' He waved the airline ticket in the air.

'Do this, and everything will be very straightforward. Don't … and, well, let's just say you'll find out what I really do for a living. You see, you've both been very careless. Your business model is flawed and leaves you open to exposure, which in turn leaves Mr Khan open to exposure – and that cannot happen. You've played fast and loose with the rules of anonymity, and become carried away with feelings of power. On top of this, the girls, as you call them, are children. Now, I don't care how you horrible little men make your money, but keeping kids who should be in the care of the local authority, prisoners and sex slaves in exchange for some crappy cheap clothes and a bed? That is deplorable.'

Despite Larry's ambivalence when it came to killing, or disposing of the variety of criminals he was often paid to deal with; the exploitation of children made his skin crawl. He firmly drew the line at any involvement in anything that included kids. He'd been in the care system as a youngster and understood how scared and impressionable the children who found themselves there could be.

Larry loomed over the two men. Vihaan and Arjun looked at each other then back at Larry, speechless, fear etched across their faces. Eventually, Arjun spoke.

'What's on the paperwork?'

'It's an asset transfer. Your house and all its grounds will become the property of Inzamam Khan, with immediate effect.'

'My house? No, I won't do it. He has no right to ask that of me.'

Larry slipped a small knife from his jacket sleeve. Without saying a word, he drove it through the top of Arjun's left hand and into the chair arm where his hand rested.

Arjun screamed and his body spasmed in pain. Larry left the knife sticking out of the older man's hand.

'Now, let's try that again.' Larry glanced at Vihaan, who looked like a rabbit caught in headlights. Arjun reached to pull the knife out with his right hand.

'No, no, no, that stays in for the moment,' Larry cautioned him. 'Where were we? Oh yes, you were signing over your house to Inzamam.'

'But you're going to kill me once I've done that. My only insurance is this house,' Arjun said, trying to remain calm, sweat popping out on his forehead.

'I understand your train of thought, but here's the thing. I can either subject you to excruciating levels of pain and you'll eventually sign your house over. Or, you could do as I ask and the rest will play out exactly as I described. You will wake up in Brazil, near a beach, alive. Inzamam doesn't want you dead any more than he wants Vihaan here to suffer for being stupid and making poor decisions for Mr Khan's business.' Larry shot a glance at Vihaan, who paled at the sound of his name.

'I won't, I can't. What will I do? I don't know anything about Brazil,' Arjun objected.

Larry reached down and twisted the knife in Arjun's hand. Arjun writhed around in his chair, screaming.

'I'm not sure that's the best strategy. What do you think, Vihaan?' said Larry in a mocking tone.

'Just do it, Arjun, he'll kill you where you sit if you don't,' Vihaan said.

Tears were streaming down the bald man's face as he pressed his right hand on the top of the knife, trying hopelessly to relieve the pain.

'I get that it's a difficult decision, but it's better that you live to appreciate old age in a nice sunny climate than die here, alone, cold and in pain.'

Larry's tone had changed again. This time he sounded sympathetic, as if he was trying to console Arjun. Bakshi's shoulders bounced as he sobbed and Larry waited patiently, knowing that Arjun couldn't endure much more. He gave the knife another small twist and then walked over to the bar to fix himself a drink. 'Drink, either of you?'

Neither man replied.

'OK, just me then.' He poured himself a large gin and tonic and carried it over to where Arjun and Vihaan were sitting. Arjun was still sobbing silently. Larry looked at Vihaan, who hadn't taken his eyes off the knife. Larry turned a chair around and sat on it facing backwards, resting his arms on the back, cradling his gin.

'I'm going to ask you once more, then I'm going to take that knife out of your hand, run it down your right forearm, peel back the skin and fillet the muscle from the bone, all of which you will be conscious for. Or you could sign the form.'

Arjun Bakshi looked at Larry with pleading eyes. Larry returned the look with an unemotional stare. He'd played this game many times and was impressed by how long Arjun had held out. Larry put his drink down and reached over towards the knife. He moved Arjun's right hand, with no resistance, grabbed the handle and quickly withdrew it. Bakshi screamed once more. Larry rotated the knife between his fingers, noting that Vihaan and Bakshi were watching him intently. Then, with his left hand, he grabbed Arjun's right wrist, pinning it to the chair arm. Arjun struggled and tried to pull away, with no success. Larry drove his elbow into the side of Arjun's nose, breaking it on impact.

Once more he pinned the older man's right hand to the chair arm and pressed the blade of the knife against his upper forearm. He broke the skin easily and made a two-inch incision in his arm before Arjun caved.

'OK, OK, please stop, I'll sign the transfer.'

Larry released the pressure and withdrew the blade from Bakshi's arm. 'That wasn't so hard, was it? Vihaan, grab that table, would you?'

Vihaan hurried to a small round table and brought it over, placing it in front of Arjun. Larry put the document on the table, laying a shiny, silver pen beside it, and said - 'Read it, then sign on the dotted lines. Do you understand?'

'Yes.'

'Good. Let's get this over with.'

With a shaky hand, Arjun Bakshi took the pen. Blood oozed from the wound in his hand.

'No, no, stop, you're going to get blood all over the paperwork. Vihaan, go and get me a bandage or something, will you?'

Vihaan scurried away. Arjun looked at Larry with fearful eyes.

The way the vulnerable girls who lived in Arjun's home were being treated and abused for the entertainment of Bakshi and his friends made Larry's skin crawl. Because of this Larry enjoyed the suffering he was inflicting on Arjun.

'Let me tell you what's going to happen next, just in case you've forgotten. You're going to sign the paperwork, then you're going to pack a weekend bag of essentials. Once you've done that, you will say goodbye to Vihaan and then you and I will take a drive to the airport.'

'What happens then?' Arjun asked, his voice trembling.

'I'll let you know when we get there, but broadly the plan remains the same as it was. You will be getting on a plane to Brazil and you will not return.'

Arjun nodded, clearly too afraid to ask any more.

The noise of a door opening shifted Larry's attention. Vihaan Patel came rushing back into the room carrying a rolled-up bandage, some cotton wool and some tape.

Larry took them from him and held out his hand, palm up, to Arjun. The older man gingerly put his injured hand in Larry's and the cleaner went to work, dressing the wound. He wrapped the bandage expertly around Arjun's hand after packing the wound. Arjun winced as Larry applied the dressing, jerking his hand back occasionally. Larry fixed him with a stern look and taped the bandage in place.

'Would you like to try again, Mr Bakshi?' Once more Arjun picked up the pen and slid the document towards himself. Without reading it, he signed in the three places that had been highlighted. Larry nodded and smiled as this part of his plan fell into place.

Right, asset transfer done. Next, to get this piece of shit onto a plane and over to Brazil. But first, Vihaan, he thought.

'Good, now sit still and rest for a little while. We'll get you packed soon.'

Larry moved his attention to Vihaan, whose eyes darted nervously from one to the other.

'So, Vihaan, my little northern friend. You have been very careless. Inzamam trusted you with his operation here in Yorkshire and you've royally fucked it up, to the extent that I've had to come and clean things up. As you can imagine, Inzamam is none too impressed. Not only do things need sorting out, like Mr Bakshi here, this house and its contents – I'm sure you know what I mean – but you clearly can't be trusted, can you?'

'Of course I can,' Vihaan protested.

'It would appear that the evidence is to the contrary, wouldn't it?' Larry shrugged at Vihaan, whose bottom lip began to tremble.

'Please don't hurt me, Larry,' Vihaan began.

Larry held a finger to his lips. 'Hush now, Vihaan. What will be, will be, you know that. Besides, as you've seen, I've got a job to do and I take a certain amount of pride in my work.' He motioned towards Bakshi, who sat silently shaking, watching the exchange.

'But you know that I'd never do anything to jeopardise Inzamam—' Vihaan began again. Larry slapped Vihaan hard across the face. The smaller man's head snapped round to the left. As Vihaan's hand instinctively came up to his cheek, the ball of Larry's foot struck him hard in the centre of his chest. The perfectly delivered kick sent Vihaan tumbling backwards over a small table. Larry watched as Vihaan scrambled to his feet, fear etched into his rounded features.

Larry flipped the table out of his way and grabbed a handful of Vihaan's shirt.

Dragging the terrified man in front of him, Larry held him for a second, feeling Vihaan shaking in his grasp, then ploughed an elbow into his cheekbone. Vihaan screamed and dropped to his knees. Larry kicked him in the side of his head, sending him sprawling across the floor, unconscious. Larry turned to face Arjun Bakshi, who had sat silently watching, exactly where Larry had left him, bleeding from his own beating.

'Arjun, time to get you packed for your trip.'

'What, now? B-b-but what about Vihaan?'

'I think you have enough on your own plate without worrying about Mr Patel, don't you?'

Arjun didn't answer. Larry studied Arjun Bakshi's face: he wore a new look of determination, almost as if he held the upper hand.

'You can't get away with this. I'll be missed. People know me,' Arjun said with conviction. Very calmly, Larry kept eye contact with Bakshi.

'Arjun, while I appreciate you having the balls to stand, injured as you are, and try your best to offer a level of defiance, let me be clear. You have precisely ten minutes to pack a weekend bag of belongings that will go through an airport scanner without issue. Or you'll be travelling to Brazil as you stand. For the sake of absolute clarity: if you fail to complete this simple task, or refuse to comply, you will die right here.' Larry waited for a moment for his message to sink in, then added - 'Do I make myself clear?'

Larry maintained eye contact until Arjun looked away, his lip trembling once more.

The cleaner cast a glance over Arjun's injuries – bandaged hand, bloodied nose – waiting for a reply.

'Well? I haven't got all night, and if I have to clean up your corpse it's going to take a while. So which is it to be? Pack a bag, or die here in your beloved knocking shop?'

Arjun Bakshi remained silent for another two minutes – time that felt like a lifetime to Larry. But he'd been doing this long enough to know where someone's tipping point was, and had seen the last-minute display of defiance many times before. His victims, fuelled by desperation and pride, often tried to resist him either physically or verbally, as Arjun had. In the end Larry always brought things to a head pretty quickly, after their last-ditch attempt. Bakshi would be no different.

'Say I do as you ask. What exactly happens next?'

'Compliance is your best option. That means we take your bag to the airport and you board a flight to Brazil, never to return to the UK. It's that simple.'

'What about Vihaan? What happens to him?'

Larry looked around at Vihaan Patel, who was still out cold on the floor, and figured he had nothing to lose by telling Arjun the truth.

'He'll be fine. My instructions were to scare him, not kill him. I'll drop him off home and tell him to call Inzamam tomorrow. Inzamam will tell him what he wants him to do next.'

Arjun's shoulders dropped. He seemed relived at the thought of Vihaan being OK, and appeared to be genuinely concerned for his well-being. Larry wasn't accustomed to this with the kinds of people he generally dealt with. He admired Arjun for it, but he could smell the fear on him and knew he was close to doing as he was told.

Larry took a moment to look around the well-designed room, imagining how important the guests who came here to abuse the girls felt. Safe in their exclusive surroundings, their wealth and social standing offering them the protection required to commit such acts. It made him sick to his stomach. Right then and there Larry gave himself an additional job, one that would require no payment and he would share with no one.

'So you will definitely not hurt him more, or worse?'

'Mr Bakshi, you have my word,' said Larry, sensing this would close the conversation. 'No further harm will come to Vihaan.'

Arjun nodded at Larry. 'Very well. I'll pack a bag and go with you.'

15

Raj stopped what he was doing and grabbed his mobile phone. He glanced at the screen and saw Sarah's name pop up. He checked the other room to see what Gonzo was doing. Seeing that he was sleeping, Raj opened the WhatsApp message. By the time he'd moved, another message had popped up and replaced Sarah's name. It was from Larry. There were no words, just a picture of a signed document. Next came a text message.

All done, Bakshi gone. Show IK the picture then delete and clear.

Got it, will do, Raj replied. A flutter of excitement shot through him as he looked again at the signed document and wondered what Larry had done to get the signature.

He flicked across his recent call history to Khan's name. A picture of the scorpion stamp from their product came up on his screen as he called the number. Raj had taken the photo himself and assigned it to Inzamam's number, for a joke. When Khan saw the image of the scorpion being used as his avatar, he laughed so hard that he nearly fell off his stool.

'What is it, Raj?' Khan answered abruptly.

'Sorry it's late. Lawrence just forwarded me a picture – the signed document. I wanted to check whether you wanted me to forward it to you.'

'Yeah, send it now.'

'Will do.' Raj hung up and forwarded the picture, followed by a screenshot of Larry's message. Within seconds, his phone rang.

'Boss?'

'Good work, Raj. Now double-delete those images and send Lawrence his money, would you?'

'No problem. Anything else?'

'What's Gonzo been up to?'

'He's been helping me. I've had him lifting and carrying all day, but I've kept him away from anything that might compromise us.'

'OK. Sorry to saddle you with the useless little shit, but I need him where we can keep tabs on him, and I don't trust anyone else to keep him on a short leash.'

Raj smiled at the compliment.

'Are you sure you've got enough for him to do?'

'Yes, plenty. I'll get him cleaning when he wakes up. He sat and watched another crappy movie with a beer tonight. I think he feels like he's won the lottery.'

'Well, he's going to have to earn those fucking beers. Keep him close.'

'No problem. See you tomorrow?'

'I'll be there in the morning. Get some sleep, and thanks again.'

Raj hung up and allowed himself a moment of solitary satisfaction. He checked on Gonzo, who was sound asleep, a half-empty beer leaning against his thin ribs. Raj shook his head then returned to the message from Sarah. He arranged to meet her at 10 a.m. the following day, stuffed his phone into his pocket and set about clearing up the office and cutting bench. When he went out, he liked to leave the place tidy. He really wanted to meet Sarah. Once he'd tidied everything away and cleaned all the equipment, he headed into the back room and made himself comfortable on his sofa bed. Raj slept over about three nights a week; it made things easier when it came to getting big shipments either in or out. He worked ridiculous hours but Khan looked after him, regularly throwing him a bit of extra cash. In fact, in the last month alone Inzamam had given Raj £1,500 in backhanders – the kind of cash Raj would never earn if he had a normal job like his friends. Inzamam had also kitted out the back room especially for Raj, with blackout blinds and comforts to help Raj get some rest in the middle of the day, if their schedule allowed it.

Raj got into bed in complete darkness, eased himself into a relaxed state and fell gently to sleep.

16

Erion Hasani thumbed the steering wheel control of his BMW. Valmir Shala's booming tones filled his car.

'Erion, my friend, tell me, what news of our shooting?'

'Mr Shala, good evening. I have narrowed down the area that Tanush and Kepi were working at the time they were killed. They had been infiltrating the territory of Mr Khan, as I suspected. They had recruited a handful of his lower-level street workers – no one with any influence or insight into his operation.' Hasani paused and Shala jumped in.

'Good work. Tell me how do you intend to proceed?'

'As it is likely that Khan is going to find out I am on his territory, I thought a direct approach would be best, to let him know that I know what he's done and do not appreciate this level of aggression between businessmen.'

'An excellent idea. I do like to face a problem head-on. However, choose the place and time of your meeting well. If Mr Khan is as ruthless as he appears, he may not take kindly to you being so frank. I do not want to risk adding you to the list of people I need to replace.'

'Understood, Mr Shala, and thank you.'

'No need to thank me. Just make your point and update me after your meeting. One more thing, tread carefully Erion, the police have been to see me about Tanush and Kepi. A Detective Inspector Baxter and he does not seem the kind of man who will leave this alone.'

'Of course.' Hasani ended the call and stepped out of his car onto the unlit back road. He dropped his phone into his jacket pocket and pulled his coat around him against the cold night air.

Hasani walked along the side of a boarded-up building and punched a code into a dirty metal keypad. An old steel door clicked open. Hasani pulled it towards him. He walked into a brick corridor with an uneven concrete floor. A dim light cast by caged wall-lights lit the way ahead. At the end of the corridor was another door, above which was a small CCTV camera. Hasani looked straight into the camera and flicked his hand in a motion clearly intended to instruct someone to open the door. The door clicked and he pulled it open.

Unlike the grim-looking corridor the last door had revealed, this one gave way to a packed nightclub with concrete walls and high-backed booths, lit by the spinning glow of blue and purple wash lighting. A heavy bass line thumped into Hasani's ears and as he rounded a corner, going further into the club, he saw a throng of sweaty bodies on the dance floor. Most of them were purchasers of Mr Shala's drugs. A thick-set bouncer nodded to Hasani. He nodded back and turned left, up a set of private stairs, through another door.

Erion Hasani was the kingpin at Jete Nate nightclub – English translation, 'nightlife'. It was a buzzing club just off Bedford Place, popular with young people up for a full-on night out. Hasani had helped Valmir Shala, to buy the club, which had been there for years. They had pumped money into it, giving it an urban- industrial feel and attracting the best DJs and stage dancers to come and perform there. The investment had paid off. Shala had been so happy with Hasani for pointing him in the direction of such a goldmine that he had taken the previously unheard of step of giving Hasani shares in the club. With his stake secured, Hasani had been determined to make the club a success, and it was.

As he walked into his plush office above the club, a pretty young woman brought him a drink and took his coat with a smile and a flutter of her eyelashes. Hasani smiled, took the Russian vodka and perched on the end of his desk, looking at a bank of monitors that covered almost every inch of the club. It was a busy night as usual and he sat in silence for a while admiring his handiwork, sipping his vodka and watching the punters on the dance floor, in the booths, and at the bar. He noted his security team and their positions around the club. As he did, he reached along the desk and pushed a button set into a chrome keypad. This triggered a pager worn by his head of security, Dardan Rama. Hasani watched as Rama touched his ear, looked up at the closest camera and nodded. Hasani waited for a couple of minutes, then Rama appeared in his office doorway. He was a big, muscular man with a thick neck, a shaved head and a tattoo snaking out from his collar up the side of his skull.

'Good evening, Mr Hasani.'

'Dardan, how are things tonight? Is business good?'

'Very good. The door is up again, the bar has been non-stop and at least two deep since about midnight. The bar team are working through people quickly.'

'And our products?'

'Pills are selling well, as you would expect. Cocaine is up week on week. The young ones seem to like the quick hit.'

'Good, good. Any trouble?'

'Nothing out of the ordinary – a couple of boys arguing over girls, and a handful that needed removing.'

'Put into cabs and sent home?'

'Always, as you instructed.'

'Good, if we're known locally as the club that looks after our guests, they will keep coming.' Hasani smiled at Rama and raised his glass. 'Enjoy the rest of your night.'

'Thank you, Mr Hasani, you too.' Rama turned and left the office.

Hasani stood up and moved across the room to stand in front of the monitors. Once he'd satisfied himself that all was running as smoothly as Dardan had told him, he took a seat on a large leather sofa that ran along the wall opposite his desk. Taking his phone from his jacket pocket, he unlocked it and flicked through his contacts. Finding the one he was looking for, he hit call. The phone rang three times before being answered.

'Gonzo, my friend, this is Erion Hasani. How are you?'

'I'm … er … OK, thanks.'

'You don't sound very sure. Is there something wrong?'

'Um … no, I guess not, except how did you get my number?'

'I heard about your unfortunate encounter with Kreshnik and Rosen, and wanted to call personally to see how you are. I do hope they didn't hurt you. You must believe that I had no idea they were going to attack you the way they did. Their actions were unauthorised and were a shameful act of cowardice.' Said Hasani, ignoring Gonzo's question about obtaining the number.

'OK.'

'Why don't you come to the club? I would be very unhappy if their rogue actions affected our friendship.' He said in his clipped Albanian tones.

There was a pause. 'I, er, can't at the moment, Mr Hasani.'

'Nonsense! I will not take no for an answer. Let me know where my driver can pick you up.'

'I'm, well, I'm at Khan's, Mr Hasani, and I'm not sure I can get out.'

'You are a resourceful young man, I have every confidence in you being able to excuse yourself from Mr Khan's hospitality. My driver will be at the end of the road in one hour.'

'OK, thanks.'

'No need to thank me – that's what friends are for.' He ended the call and smiled, then called his driver. He directed him to collect Gonzo then hung up without waiting for confirmation of his instructions.

***

Gonzo had taken the call from Erion Hasani quietly while Raj had been cleaning. Then he had stayed in bed, pretending to be asleep, a half-empty beer bottle leaning against him, until he had heard Raj go through to his room and close the door. He'd stayed silent for another forty minutes, listening for Raj coming back out, constantly checking his watch, keen not to miss his pick-up time by any longer than was necessary to make a clean exit. Exactly an hour and ten minutes after he had spoken to Hasani, Gonzo was in the back of a Mercedes, being driven to Jete Nate.

When they pulled up outside the club, the driver opened the door for Gonzo and a muscular, bald guy with a tattoo that snaked up the side of his head greeted him. 'You are a guest of Mr Hasani, yes? – please come with me.' The big man motioned for Gonzo to follow him through the main entrance, bypassing the queue of people eager to get in. Gonzo felt like a celebrity. He nodded and smiled at two girls at the front of the queue, instantly feeling more confident and attractive due to the special treatment he was getting. The girls giggled and waved.

Once inside the club, Gonzo was escorted to a private booth on a raised platform overlooking the dance floor. Hasani was seated in the centre of the booth. He raised a glass to greet Gonzo.

'My friend, come, sit down, let me get you something to drink.' He had to shout to be heard above the thumping music.

Gonzo watched, feeling awkward, as Hasani motioned to a woman standing behind the booth. She turned and left, only to return moments later with a tray of shots, which she passed to Gonzo, Hasani and three young women who sat on either side of Hasani.

Gonzo took a shot and sat down at the end of the booth. As soon as he did, a gorgeous blonde in a short skirt and sparkly top slid along next to him and gave him a huge smile. Gonzo felt immediately self-conscious and wriggled uncomfortably in his seat.

'Come, drink!' Hasani shouted, raising his shot glass. Gonzo watched as everyone around the table did as Hasani had instructed, then realised afterwards that he had done the same. They threw back their drinks in unison and ceremoniously tapped their glasses on the table. The woman behind the booth immediately passed around another round of shots and Hasani repeated his rallying cry. Once more they all drank together. Gonzo started to feel the warming effects of the shots and began to crave more. He smiled back at the blonde, starting to feel more confident. She leaned in and asked his name.

'Mike, my name's Mike.' He surprised himself by using his actual name, rather than the nickname he had been known by for years. 'What's yours?'

'That's nice. I'm Emina.' She gave him another big smile that made Gonzo tingle a little bit. He was glad he'd decided to change before coming out. He'd dug out a pair of skin-tight black jeans and a Ben Sherman short-sleeved shirt from the bag of clothes Raj had taken him to pick up. He'd have been mortified if he'd met Emina wearing his old trackie bottoms and hoodie.

He glanced up and saw Hasani tap Emina on the shoulder. She turned to face Hasani, who leaned in and said something in her ear. She nodded and turned back towards Gonzo. 'Mike, would you like to switch places with me so that Mr Hasani can speak to you?'

Gonzo looked at Hasani, who nodded, as if approving the move.

'That's fine,' He stood up to let the young woman out. As she stood to switch places, he picked up the smell of her perfume. She smelled good, and she was so close. He fought off the urge to touch her and instead slid into the booth next to Hasani. As soon as Gonzo sat down, Emina slid back in next to him, really close. She smiled and reached past him to pick up another drink. He returned her smile then turned to face Hasani.

'Mr Hasani, thanks for sending your driver to pick me up. This place is great.'

'Nonsense! As I said to you earlier, that's what friends do, and we are friends,

yes?'

'Yeah, I guess so.'

'How do you like the lovely Emina? She's very beautiful.'

'Er, yeah she is.'

Hasani leaned in as if to whisper to Gonzo. 'I think she likes you too, my friend. She never sits so close to anyone I've introduced her to before.' He laughed and patted Gonzo on the shoulder. 'You have a way with the ladies, I think.' He winked and gave a hearty laugh. Gonzo smiled and glanced around at Emina, who was watching the dancers and swaying her head in time with the music.

'Tell me, why do they call you Gonzo?' said Hasani.

'It's because I have a big nose that makes me sound like a muppet,' Gonzo said in a self-deprecating tone.

'Your nose is much smaller than those of my Albanian brothers. Well- proportioned for your head, I think. As you age you will grow into it, trust me.' Hasani pointed at his own nose and winked once more. 'So what is your given name?'

'Mike,' he said for the second time that evening.

'Mike – yes, I prefer that. I will call you Mike from now on.' Gonzo smiled and felt himself straighten up, immediately feeling more valued.

Hasani patted him on the leg and snapped his fingers, raising his hand for more drinks. 'Now why don't you tell me about what my fellow countrymen did to you, and let me again express my apologies for their unauthorised action.'

Gonzo hesitated, then decided that Hasani knew everything anyway. Gonzo told him how he had come to meet Kreshnik Tanush and Rosen Kepi. The Albanian didn't break eye contact as Gonzo spoke. *He's really listening,* thought Gonzo. Maybe he didn't know. When he got to the part where Kepi rendered him unconscious, Hasani leaned in closer.

'And next?'

'I don't know. I woke up miles away from the alley.'

Hasani's face remained interested and non-judgemental. Gonzo wasn't able to gauge what he was thinking.

'Come now, there's no need to hold back. I am not looking for any kind of vengeance against those who helped you. Kreshnik and Rosen were acting completely outside the instructions they were given – and in this business, if you do that, you pay the price.'

Gonzo was starting to feel intimidated, but determined not to show it. 'I guess so, but I honestly don't know. Between Kepi knocking me out and waking up, it's a blank.'

'You obviously have friends who look after you, or a well-armed guardian angel,' replied Hasani, once more laughing out loud. Gonzo laughed with him and felt Emina's hand rest on his thigh, sending tingles through his body.

'Enjoy yourself, Mike. We talk later,' said Hasani, nodding towards Emina. Without needing further prompting, Gonzo, who was quickly getting used to being called Mike and the respect it seemed to bring, turned away from Hasani and faced Emina. She immediately leaned towards him.

'Would you like to come and dance?'

Gonzo blushed invisibly, wishing he could actually dance. 'Yeah, if you like.'

Emina grabbed his hand and pulled him towards the dance floor. He couldn't take his eyes off her body as she walked. He had one hand in hers and the other on her tiny waist, feeling her hips move as she walked through the crowd to an empty spot on the dance floor. Once there, Gonzo realised gratefully that he didn't actually need to do much dancing. Emina took control and moved around him as he swayed and bounced awkwardly, but she seemed to like how he moved. He was having the night of his life.

She blew him a kiss as she dropped down in front of him, her hands sliding down his chest. She moved so well, coming up slowly, hips swaying, smiling a big, inviting smile. Gonzo was more than a little aroused as Emina danced with him, but he kept bobbing and moving as best he could with the music. Then, as if she were reading his thoughts, she threw her arms around his neck and kissed him. Gonzo felt as if he was going to explode. Her hands were moving over him as if she had eight of them. He moved his own from her waist up her back and into her thick blonde hair.

'Come, Mike, there is somewhere we can go.' She grabbed his hand and dragged him off the dance floor towards a side door, where a bouncer stood. She waved at him as they approached and he stood to one side, holding the door open for them. They burst through a door into an office with thick carpet and a long sofa against one wall. Emina turned him and almost threw him on the sofa. Sitting astride him, she tugged at the buttons of his shirt, kissing him frantically. Gonzo didn't need any persuasion; she was the most beautiful woman he had ever seen and he was pretty sure she wanted him, right then and there. He slid his hands up her thighs, lifting the bottom of her dress as he did. He felt the thin lace sides of her underwear and ripped it away. Emina didn't stop him.

He felt her pulling at his belt then the zip on his jeans and before he knew it, he was inside her. Her dress only covering a small strip of her stomach, her breasts cupped in his hands, Emina rode him hard. *My God!* he thought. *Is this really happening? She is fucking amazing and she's fucking me.*

Finally, they collapsed into a sweaty heap on the sofa, facing each other.

'You are amazing. That was amazing. I have never done this with someone so soon after meeting them.' She said.

'Me neither – you are fuckin' beautiful.'

'You're so sweet, but I bet you say that to all the girls.'

'Yeah, you're right, I do,' he replied then burst into a raucous laugh, the kind of laugh he hadn't done for years. *She is fucking amazing*, he thought as he stared into her deep blue eyes.

'Whose office is this, Emina?' he asked, suddenly aware of his surroundings.

'I don't know.' She shrugged.

'We'd better get dressed and get out of here before we get caught, don't you think? I wouldn't want you to get into trouble with Mr Hasani.'

'You really are so sweet. Come, let's get dressed and get a drink.'

They straightened their clothes and visited the en suite toilet then, giggling like teenagers, they made their way back to the booth and Erion Hasani.

When they got to the booth, Hasani looked them up and down, smiled and waved his hand over a tray of shots. Gonzo eased into the booth first, holding tight to Emina's hand. She slid in next to him, virtually glued to his side. This made him feel ten feet tall.

Hasani waved Gonzo towards him. 'You are enjoying your-self, yes?'

'Yes, thank you, I'm having a great night,' Gonzo replied, grinning like a Cheshire cat.

'That is good. I like when my friends can enjoy themselves. Now to business, yes?'

'Yeah, sure,' said Gonzo, trying to keep the elation out of his voice.

'You and I could do some mutually beneficial business. You are well-connected and influential in your area. I am new to this region and wish to have an impact. Tell me, how could I have immediate impact that gives recurring income?'

Gonzo thought for a second. *Should I sell Khan out? Hasani treats me way better, but Khan did save my life from those low-life Albanian scum.*

'What did you have in mind?' he said, deciding to play it cool and keep on Khan's good side without upsetting Hasani.

'I was hoping we could work out a distribution network – on a scale that has not been seen in these parts before. It could make you a very rich man.'

'You mean, with me?' Gonzo asked in surprise.

'Of course, a partnership of sorts. Don't decide now. Business decisions should be considered, and I'm sure you are a man who likes to reflect on business opportunities.'

'Er, yeah, definitely. I'll have a think and let you know,' he replied, trying to sound business-like. Gonzo felt Emina's hand on his leg once more. Hasani smiled and turned back towards the two young women on the other side of him.

It was four-thirty a.m. when Hasani's driver dropped off Gonzo and Emina, swinging by Emina's home first. She gave Gonzo the longest kiss as she got out of the car, checking three times that he'd got her phone number and he was going to call her, once more assuring him that she didn't normally sleep with people so quickly. Gonzo was buzzing. He asked the driver to wait until he'd watched Emina walk into her flat and close the door.

At Khan's, despite feeling pretty drunk, he crept to the sofa, careful not to disturb the sleeping Raj and hoping that he hadn't got up while Gonzo had been at the club. He changed back into the clothes he'd worn earlier, puffed up the sofa cushion under his head and smiled as he thought about his night with Emina.

17

Three days earlier

'Lawrence, Inzamam. How goes it?'

'Morning Inzy. All good with me, thanks. You?'

'My day is off to a great start, thanks to the work you did yesterday. Very efficient, as ever.'

'We aim to please. So what can I do for you today? I know you didn't call to praise me on my expediency.'

'I'm truly offended. I did, of course, but you're right; that's not the only reason I called. Are you local? And if so, is there somewhere we can meet? I have something I need to discuss with you, of a delicate nature.'

'It always is. I'm in Portsmouth this morning, if that's helpful. We could meet in Gunwharf?'

'Perfect. What time works for you?'

'Eleven-thirty?'

'Sounds good. There's a Nero's at the top of the escalators.'

'I know it.'

'Great, see you there.' Inzamam ended the call and floored the accelerator. The 4×4 shot along the winding country road that ran past Marwell Zoo. He sped along the scenic network of country lanes he often took when he needed time to make calls or think. On either side of the road were fields, broken by the occasional outcrop of cottages, houses and smallholdings. It was a sunny morning. Inzamam turned off the air conditioning and opened his window halfway, feeling the mix of cool air and the sun's heat on his arm. He caught a waft of freshly cut grass as he passed a house where the owner was using a ride-on mower to trim his lawn. The radio was playing Jack Johnson, the car engine lending a pleasing, thrumming backdrop. On top of all this, Lawrence had dealt with Arjun Bakshi and Khan was now the owner of another large house in Yorkshire. It was a good morning.

Khan decided against going into the restaurant. Instead he joined the motorway and headed for Gunwharf, with the intention of having some rare time to himself before meeting Lawrence. He stabbed a different button on his steering wheel and said, 'Call Raj.'

The phone rang twice before Raj answered it. 'Morning, boss.'

'Morning, Raj. All OK there?'

'Yeah, all good. I've just had a delivery that I need to put away.'

'And Gonzo?'

'Yeah, he's good. He seems a bit happier than usual.'

'What do you mean?'

'He's walking round singing, which is doing my fucking head in if I'm honest. I don't remember telling him he could be happy.'

Khan laughed. 'Maybe he's just enjoying being around you and your glowing personality.'

'Ha, yeah. Maybe.'

'Anyway, I didn't call to chat about yours and Gonzo's blooming bromance. I'm going to be in later – I've got some bits to take care of. You'll have another delivery this afternoon. I brought a shipment forward and I'm going to need a decent-size batch of scorpion packed and stacked by tonight. Can you handle that, if Gonzo helps?'

'Yes, if you're alright with that. Him helping, I mean.'

'That's fine he's not going anywhere. You might as well make use of him. Just don't let him sample anything. With a nose that big, we'll be broke in a week.' He laughed again.

'No problem. See you later.'

'Later.'

He hung up and headed towards Portsmouth and Gunwharf Quays shopping centre. As he drove past the sculptured sails that towered over the motorway on the way into the city, he was pre-occupied by a heavy, nagging thought, regardless of how hard he tried to block it out. He drove into the underground car park that sat beneath Gunwharf.

As he left the car park, the Spinnaker Tower loomed over the harbour to his right. He leaned against a barrier, gazing at a naval warship that was making its way slowly into the dockyard. The grey ship dwarfed the boats that were moored along the small jetty. Khan checked his watch. He still had twenty minutes until he was due to meet Lawrence. He turned away from the water and headed into the shopping centre, smiling at two women pushing buggies as he stepped into the Ralph Lauren store. After killing a few minutes looking at shirts, he made his way to the coffee shop to meet Lawrence, who as always arrived promptly.

'Good of you to meet me at short notice.'

'No problem. It sounded like something that can't wait. Which usually means it can't.'

They ordered coffees and took them to a quiet table at the back of the coffee shop.

'So, where to start?' mused Khan.

'The beginning is generally thought to be the best place.'

'Hmm, maybe not quite that far back. When you were in the office, you saw that Gonzo was in?'

'Yes, I saw him on the sofa. What's the dumb little shit been up to?'

'In truth, nothing that I would have discouraged him from. He's been getting tapped up recently by a rival supplier.'

'Albanians?'

'You guessed it.'

'So what have they said to him?'

'It's not so much what they said, more what they did.'

'Did? Past tense?'

'Yes, this is definitely past tense.'

Lawrence leaned in closer. 'What the fuck have you done, In-zamam? These Albanians don't play games. They're fucking hard-core.' There was an unusual note of intensity in his voice.

'What am I, a fucking Scout leader?' Khan snapped back.

'No, not at all, but you know what I mean. They're full-on, take-no-prisoners types. Whereas you try to keep a lower profile … usually.'

'I've well and truly blown that – literally. The other night, Raj saw them giving Gonzo a kicking. He called me in a panic, said he thought they were going to kill him. So I jumped in the car and went to sort it.'

'And?'

'When I got there, they were kicking the shit out of him, had him pinned to the floor, about to blow him away, I'm sure of it.'

'And? What did you do? No, actually you don't need to tell me. I heard about the two men who were found in the alley.'

Inzamam said nothing.

'Fuck. Now I know why it's a sensitive matter. A bit of an un-derstatement, don't you think? Killing two Albanian drug dealers is a bit more than *sensitive*.'

'Never mind that – we need to deal with it, and quickly. There's another business opportunity coming my way that will mean upsetting the Albanians even more.'

'Upsetting them more! How the fuck could you upset them more?'

'By taking over one of their territories and relieving them of their crew.'

'Nothing much, then.' Larry shook his head and took a swig of his coffee, then

continued. 'So, how much do you know about the two you blew away?'

'Not much. Their names were Kreshnik Tanush and Rosen Kepi—'

'Kepi?' Larry interrupted.

'Yes, why?'

'He's fucking mental – well, was. He's the guy the Albanians sent to deal with people who did things … well, who did things like you've done. Sorry, carry on.'

'Both work for Valmir Shala, via Hasani. They have links with the Albanian underground network – clubs, drugs, prostitutes, the whole nine yards.'

This time Khan paused to sip his double espresso.

'Well, I'll say one thing for you. You don't do things by halves. This other territory, is it local?'

'Brighton.'

'Again, no half measures. It couldn't be Fareham or Gosport, somewhere easier to crack.' Larry finished his drink and stood up, picking up his jacket from the back of his chair.

'Going somewhere?' asked Khan.

'Yep, this is going to be a longer chat than I thought, and coffee's not going to cut it. Let's go round the corner for some food and a beer.'

Inzamam nodded and followed Larry out of the coffee-shop. They made their way to a nearby bar and restaurant which was virtually empty. Inzamam led the way to a quiet corner where they wouldn't be overheard if the other tables filled up. They ordered a couple of beers and some starters and carried on their chat.

'So, tell me what you have in mind. In fact, no – back up a bit and tell me first what you did with the weapon you used, and your car.'

'OK. I ditched the gun in the alleyway, it was an untraceable. My car needs to be valeted, but there isn't much blood in it. Gonzo was out cold when I put him in there. He'd done most of his bleeding on the ground of the alleyway, and I always have a plastic boot liner in it.'

Khan looked to Larry for a response. Larry paused before he responded, rubbing his hand across his chin, looking deep in thought. 'Right, we need to get your car cleaned, thoroughly. That's easy, I can do that today, if you like.'

'That would be really helpful, Lawrence, thanks.'

'OK, that's that sorted. Now, what do you have in mind for our friendly neighbourhood Albanians?' he asked with a wry smile.

'Whatever we do with them needs to be big enough to have an impact and send a message, but not so big that it draws any unwanted attention outside of their circle, if you get my meaning?'

'I think I'm following. Go on.'

'We need to deal with the local Albanian threat, in terms of underlining the fact that Southampton and the surrounding areas are my territory. The ripple effect needs to be strong enough to reach our friend Mr Shala in Portsmouth and make him reconsider his growth plans for Brighton.'

'So again, nothing too much, then?' Larry asked with another smile.

'No, not at all, just a gentle tickle.'

They laughed and chugged their drinks. Once they'd finished their meal and the waitress – who Khan couldn't resist smiling at every time she came to the table – had cleared their plates, they moved on to planning.

'Is Hasani still running Shala's club up at the top of town?' asked Larry.

'Yes, he bases his operation from there. Why, what are you thinking?'

'He's Shala's right-hand man, right?'

'Yes,' Inzamam said, taking a mouthful of beer.

'Good, I thought so. We send a message to Shala, via Hasani, which serves two purposes. First, sending it via his right-hand man means it will make Shala listen. Second, it demonstrates that no one in his empire is out of reach. And I think I know just how we'll do it.'

18

Vihaan Patel called Inzamam, as instructed, the morning after Larry had visited Yorkshire and removed Arjun Bakshi from his home.

'V. what the fuck do you want?' Khan said.

'Lawrence told me to call you this morning,' he replied, his voice muffled. His face was swollen and his top lip and the side of his face were still numb from the blow Larry had inflicted on him the previous day. He'd also found it difficult to call Inzamam, as his vision was blurred.

'You sound awful. What did he do to you?'

'I think he's broken my jaw or cheekbone, along with other stuff.'

'Shit, that must hurt' Khan sounded shocked.

Vihaan ignored what sounded like mock sincerity and continued. 'He said you'd tell me what you want me to do next.'

'Fucking right. The way you two were running things was a shambles. The place looks great, but allowing people to know who you are and not having any kind of insurance is ludicrous.'

'How do you mean?' Vihaan asked, confused.

'OK, let me spell it out for you. The girls – fine, you get them where and how you can. You look as though you've got some good ones, who will do as they're told and not cause any trouble. Tracey is very nice too.'

Vihaan winced at the sound of her name. He was sure Khan had chosen her because of the obvious connection the young woman had with Vihaan.

'But you've got to protect yourself so that the punters have something to lose. Let me give you an example. When you collect them in your blacked-out pimp bus, you ask for their passport, which you hold until you drop them back. You copy it and at the end of the night, after they've had their fun, you tell them you have a copy and that they need to keep to themselves all the details of where they've been, who they've met and what they've done, otherwise they may find themselves implicated in child abuse allegations. That's your starting point. You've then got them literally by the balls. You not only own them but you have guaranteed repeat customers who will be completely discreet. Do you see where I'm going with this, V.?'

'Yeah, I think so. You're talking about having a hold over the people we provide a service to, to protect ourselves.' Vihaan's answer was painful for him to articulate, and his anger at his old friend was growing.

'Exactly! Once you've got them by the balls, you can put the prices up, depending on what they want to do with the girls, but no rough stuff, you don't want to run the risk of injuries. They can't object because the power balance is in our favour. Then you have to make sure you look after the girls. They need regular new clothes and decent make-up. Now, let's talk about the house, then you'd better go and get checked out.'

'What about the house?'

'It needs a bit of redesigning. No one is going to live in it, so we might as well turn it into our northern centre of operations. It will need planning out properly, but if we do it right, I think we can make some proper money out of it. How many bedrooms does it have?'

'I don't know – six, maybe seven.'

'And downstairs, how many rooms?'

'At a guess, about the same. You've seen it, you know how it's laid out.'

'I can't really picture anything but the kitchen and the annexe. What I'm going to do is get an architect I know to come and have a look. You can show him around.'

'OK, fine,' Vihaan replied in a clipped voice.

'You OK?'

'Not really.' Vihaan got the impression that Inzamam didn't care whether he was OK or not, but he wasn't prepared to risk any additional visits from Lawrence.

'Oh yeah, sorry, it must be pretty painful. I'm not going to keep you much longer. I'll get the architect to call you and arrange, and then you let him in and walk him round.'

'Inzamam, can I ask you something?'

'Of course, what is it?'

'What's happened to Arjun? He wasn't a bad guy, just a bit naive.'

'I wouldn't worry about Arjun if I were you. You've got enough on, getting this back on track.'

'Is he dead?' Vihaan persisted, ignoring Khan's instruction to back down.

'Dead? What do you take me for? Some kind of fucking madman?' Inzamam's pitch and volume rose. Unmoved by this, Vihaan continued.

'It wouldn't be much of a stretch to imagine him not making it as far as the airport, let alone Brazil. And why Brazil?'

'Not much of a stretch? Watch yourself, V. The only reason you haven't joined him in Brazil is because you and I have known each other for years.'

Vihaan could hear the outrage in Khan's voice.

'You're right – we have known each other for years. That didn't stop you and your hired hand scaring the shit out of my wife and breaking my face though, did it?'

Khan took a long deep breath then answered in a calmer tone. 'Look, V., mate, I'm sorry if any of what happened scared Sadi.

And you have to believe me, I didn't know what Lawrence was going to do to you. If I did, I'd have told him to tone it down. When you get checked out, if there's anything you need, let me know, yeah?'

Despite the pain and numbness in his face, Vihaan responded. 'Yeah, OK. You still haven't answered me.'

'He's in Brazil. I just needed him out of the way once the house was sorted.'

'OK, I'll talk to the architect, but don't try to hurt me or mine again, Inzamam, or we're done.'

'No problem, Vihaan. I would never hurt Sadi, and you're like a brother to me. Let me know how you get on at the hospital.'

Vihaan dropped his mobile onto the kitchen table and looked into his wife's tear- filled eyes. Sadiya had been sitting at the table throughout Vihaan's conversation with Inzamam. They had been up all night, since Vihaan had returned from Arjun's in the early hours of the morning. Sadiya had insisted on knowing what was going on, and Vihaan was in too much pain to argue. He had given her the barest of outlines, not going into detail about what he and Arjun did at Arjun's house. He had, however, told her that he was running a part of Inzamam's business from there, and that Inzamam had taken badly to Vihaan involving Bakshi. When Sadiya asked what Larry had been doing there, Vihaan told her that he was the one who had beat him up, that he'd forced Arjun to leave with him.

'Try not to worry too much, it'll be fine,' he tried to reassure her as he put the phone down.

'Don't worry? You're sat there with your face smashed up and I'm supposed to not worry? Are you mad?'

'Can we just go to the hospital, Sadi? My face is really hurting.' She nodded and stood up to get the car keys.

'Just one thing.'

'What is it?'

'Once you've done what you need to with this architect, I want you to get out of business with Inzamam. He's dangerous, Vihaan, and I don't want you to get hurt even worse. Once you've done, I want us to move away and never talk to Inzamam again.' Her eyes were pleading, yet strong. Vihaan wasn't sure what he'd done to deserve her.

'OK, where do you want to go?'

'Somewhere on the coast – but not south, where he is.'

'OK, we will. I promise.'

He knew she meant it and if he was honest with himself, he knew she was right. If he stayed around Inzamam he would end up hurt, or dead, but he also had no idea how to cut ties with Khan and get away.

Sadiya picked up his jacket and passed it to him, ready to go to Accident and Emergency.

19

Raj got to the park early. His stomach was doing excited backflips and he checked his phone constantly, half expecting Sarah to cancel. He sat on his scooter, his crash helmet hanging over the right mirror and his gloves stuffed into the front of his half-open jacket. To his left he could see orderly lines of cars waiting to board a ferry to the Isle of Wight, while in front of him a cruise ship edged past, a huge, floating resort. Raj checked his phone again. It was exactly 10 a.m. He looked around the park but he couldn't see her.

Maybe she's stuck in traffic or held up somewhere. Or maybe it's only just ten and she's going to be here soon. For fuck's sake, calm down, Raj, his internal monologue rambled on. Just as he was about to launch into another round of self-doubt, he saw her drive into the park. He turned and watched her park next to his scooter, her long black hair covering the side of her face, hiding it from his view. Feeling a flush of excitement, he got off his bike.

Raj stood mesmerised as Husna Khan got out of her car, walked around to where he stood and, without a word, placed her hands on the sides of his face and kissed him – a long, lingering kiss that made Raj feel like he was floating. He ran his hands through her thick black hair and held the kiss. When they eventually came up for air, she smiled. His stomach flipped again.

'Hey you, it's good to see you,' she said. 'You too – it feels like it's been ages.'

'It has.'

'It's been three days.' He laughed.

'Exactly – ages.' She smiled again. He shook his head and took her hand as they walked along the waterfront towards the bench they always sat on. They sat facing the water. The cruise ship had made its way out of view.

'So, how long have you got?' he asked, keen to know if this was a rushed half hour or something longer. He hoped it was the latter.

'I've got a couple of hours. I wish it was longer.'

'I'll take a couple of hours – any time is better than none.'

That was great: he could spend some time here, escaping his insane world, watching the boats with Husna.

'Can we not talk about when I have to go? Instead, can we talk about how we're going to be together more?' she said, melting him with another smile and a soft kiss.

'You know there's nothing I want more than to spend more time with you, but things are insane at work – and if Inzamam finds out… Well, let's just say I'm OK with us taking it slow.'

'Oh, you are, are you? What if I'm not, and I want us to be together more?'

'That would be great, but how?'

'I'm working on something. Let's leave it at that for now, OK?'

'I'm intrigued, but OK, yeah, sure.'

'Good, now come here and kiss me.'

She wrapped her arms around his neck and pulled him close, sliding onto his lap. He couldn't believe he was this lucky. He knew how dangerous what they were doing was, but she was gorgeous and when he was with her he didn't care about the consequences.

Husna and Raj had started seeing each other six months earlier, after she had come to the restaurant one night looking for Inzamam, who had been off with one of the young waitresses. Raj had covered for Khan and had spent the whole night, through into the early morning, talking to Husna. He'd never met anyone like her; she was funny, clever and so sexy. Everything about her had made him want to see her again.

When she had asked for his number as she left, he never imagined that she would call him an hour later to arrange meeting up, but that's exactly what she did. From that moment he had been hiding a secret that he knew could end with them both being seri-ously hurt, or worse. He knew how badly Inzamam would react to the news. Nor was he blind to the level of violence Khan was capable of. Even with this knowledge, he couldn't stop seeing Husna. Every time his phone went off and 'Sarah' appeared on the screen, his heart skipped, and whenever he had a chance to see her, he found an excuse to take it. Raj also knew Husna was playing an equally dangerous game; her white Mercedes was not inconspicuous, with its private plates and blacked-out windows. She ran the risk of being spotted every time they met but, it seemed to Raj, the more they saw each other, the less she cared about being caught. Sometimes he thought she almost enjoyed the risk.

They sat and chatted effortlessly, planning a weekend away. Easy conversation, interspersed by long, heavy kisses. But for Raj the time always passed too quickly, and all too soon Husna glanced at her watch. He knew this meant she was getting restless and he was running out of time. He didn't protest. Instead he held her hand and walked her to her car, leaning back against it as he gave her a final kiss.

'See you soon?' he asked keenly.

'Of course, if you can fit me in to your busy schedule, Mr Gadhi?'

'Ha ha, I'll see what I can do. So many women, so little time.' He avoided addressing her as Mrs Khan in response, as just re-cently he'd noticed it made his stomach churn when he thought about her being married to Inzamam. This feeling kept him awake at night sometimes: he didn't share it with Husna.

Khan

He opened the car door when he heard it unlock. She ran her soft hand down his cheek then got into her car. Raj stood and watched as she drove away, waving out of the open window. He watched until her car blended in with the traffic heading over the roundabout towards West Quay and Ikea, then he put on his bike gear and started his scooter. He had work to do.

20

Gonzo woke early but lay still, not opening his eyes, not wanting to let Raj know that he was awake. He heard Raj leave. Only then did he get up and head into the bathroom to get dressed. He knew exactly what he wanted to do with his day, and it didn't involve sitting around Khan's drug den or helping Raj; he wanted to see Emina.

Once he was dressed, he grabbed his phone and opened his text messages. He smiled as he read the texts they'd exchanged after Hasani's driver had dropped them off. He'd been awake texting Emina for at least two hours after he'd got back. Gonzo couldn't get the image of her beautiful face out of his mind, and he knew he had to see her again.

Hey! How did you sleep? Are you around today?

Gonzo sent the first message of the day. He checked his phone every few seconds for about ten minutes, then decided that Emina was probably still asleep. Just as he was boiling the kettle to make a coffee, his phone rang. Excitedly he pulled it out of his pocket. His excitement was short-lived; the name on the screen was Erion Hasani.

'Hello.'

'Mike, my friend, how are you this morning? Did you enjoy yourself last night?'

'I had a great night.'

Hasani chuckled. 'Emina is very pretty, yes? And she obviously likes you.'

Gonzo didn't answer, instead waiting to see what Hasani wanted with him this early. Hasani didn't keep him waiting.

'Are you free today? I would like to continue our conversation. I think you have great potential and would like to discuss how we could explore it.'

'I'm sorry, I'm not sure I follow, Mr – sorry, Erion.'

'Don't be modest. I think we both know that Mr Khan is underutilising your talents and that your earning potential is far greater, yes?'

'Er, yes,' Gonzo said, still not sure he liked where this was going, but willing to play along until he found out.

'So what I'm proposing is we explore your potential, that is all. If you do not like what you hear, we remain friends. What do you have to lose?'

Nothing, apart from my head if Khan finds out, thought Gonzo. 'OK.'

'Excellent! My driver will pick you up in half an hour. If that is OK?'

'Half an hour, at the end of the road?'

'Yes, of course. See you soon.'

Gonzo ended the call and sat trying to figure out what angle Hasani was going to try and play – and whether he should go along with it or tell Khan. He was still feeling torn as a text pinged onto his phone. It was Emina.

Hey Mike, good morning. You're so sweet, I slept well, thank you. I really enjoyed our time together last night. I am around later today xx

Gonzo's stomach flipped. He sent a text back straight away.

Do you want to meet in town this afternoon? How about All Bar One at 4? xx

He pressed send and a reply came back almost instantly.

Yay! See you there xx

The message had blowing-kisses emojis at the end. He grinned like a Cheshire cat at the sight of them.

He quickly changed into his jeans from the night before and a white polo shirt, sprayed himself with CK One aftershave, grabbed his parka and headed out to meet Hasani's driver at the end of the road. The S-class Mercedes was already there, waiting, as Gonzo jogged up to the rear door. As he got in the back, the driver gave him a broad, knowing smile. It was the driver who had dropped Gonzo and Emina off the previous night. As the car moved away, Gonzo ran his hands along the plush leather seats. The windows in the back of the car were blacked out and Gonzo felt like a rock star or a rich businessman. He decided that, when he made his fortune, he would be driven around in a car just like this, with dark tinted windows. Gonzo allowed himself a moment to dream about what his life might be like if he made it. He imagined being in a tailored suit, no tie and expensive shoes, being driven to a meeting to discuss a multi-million- pound shipment. Next to him would be a bodyguard, who would be so feared that no one would dare to make a move on Gonzo. He wouldn't do his own dirty work. The driver stopped outside Jete Nate, as he had the night before; this time though, there was no line of people waiting to get in, no scantily clad girls. Instead one of Hasani's men pulled the door open and let Gonzo in. His daydream continued for the first few steps into the club: he imagined that the club and everything in it was his – his own empire of drugs, drink and money.

Before following the doorman through into the office, he paused to compose himself and exit his daydream.

'Come in, please,' he heard Hasani say cheerfully from inside the office. The doorman stood looking at him, holding the door and waiting patiently. Gonzo stepped through the doorway and smiled at Hasani.

The office was huge and smelled of expensive cigars. Along one wall was a long black sofa, at the end of which stood a four-foot-high stone gorilla, which stared menacingly into the distance. In the centre of the room was the biggest desk Gonzo had ever seen, with a high-backed leather chair behind it. On the wall opposite the desk was a big flat-screen TV. On it a football match played, the sound off. Underneath the TV was a drinks cabinet, on which was a decanter of brown liquid that Gonzo assumed was whisky, on a silver tray with six matching glasses. He took a moment to take in the splendour of the office, including the thick-piled carpet he was standing on. Hasani didn't say anything for a couple of seconds.

'You like my office?'

'Yes, very much.'

'Good – a man who appreciates the result of hard work is valuable. It means you will work hard to achieve similar. Drink?'

'A Coke?'

Hasani burst into a loud, bellowing laugh.

'You're a funny guy. I like you,' he said when he stopped laughing. 'Now, what would you really like to drink? Vodka, whisky, or maybe a beer?'

Gonzo smiled and nodded as if his request for a Coke had been a joke, aware that he was being weighed up and judged the whole time he was with Hasani.

'Beer would be good, thank you.'

'Good, can you get us two beers, please?' Hasani asked the doorman, who had stayed inside the office. 'Come, sit.' He pointed to a low-slung chair on the visitor side of the desk. Gonzo sat down and Hasani sat in an identical chair facing his. This surprised Gonzo, who had expected Hasani to sit behind the desk.

'Now let us talk about what you would like to do. Yes?'

'OK.'

'You are one of Mr Khan's distributors, so you have a network, a knowledge of your area and customers – and, from what I understand, a high number of repeat customers. Am I correct?'

'Yeah, I guess so.'

'But I cannot imagine that you are getting well paid for your efforts. In fact, it is my strong suspicion that you, Mike, are underpaid for your talents.'

Gonzo felt flattered. Khan had never spoken to him like this. He remained silent, waiting for Hasani to get to the point.

'How would you like to make five times what you make now, and be in complete control of your earnings and destiny?'

'Sounds great, but how?'

'A very astute and direct question, which deserves a direct answer.' Hasani finished his bottle of beer and waved to the doorman for another round. 'I would like you to run my operation in Southampton. I have other business interests and I need someone who knowns the territory and has enough contacts to gain traction in a short space of time. My two unfortunate associates, who behaved so poorly towards you, were supposed to be expanding our reach across the city. However, they underestimated you and Mr Khan; that is a mistake I will not make. And, I recognise when someone like Mr Khan requires respect in the way he is dealt with. You know him well – he clearly values you or you would have not been spared. You and I could form an alliance that would shift the balance of power and distribution across the city.'

'So, you're talkin' about me and you takin' on Khan? That's a big ask, and would bring some serious shit if it went sideways. You do understand Khan would have my head on a stick if he knew I was even talkin' to you.'

'And yet, here you are,' Hasani replied.

Gonzo nodded. 'Yeah, here I am.'

'Which indicates to me you are open to the possibility of a different working arrangement, yes?'

'I suppose it does.' Gonzo smiled. The thought of taking on Khan was scary as hell, but there was something about Hasani that made Gonzo think that he might be able to make it work. If he could earn five times what he earned now, he'd have that chauffeur- driven car in no time.

'OK, let's say I'm interested. How would it work?'

'In simple terms, I introduce you to my suppliers and other business associates to discuss volumes and products. You, in return, would keep my identity from your local connections and associates, it is important that you are the face of the venture and your people know you are running things. We would then work out an acceptable profit split and begin our working relationship.'

Gonzo took a minute before responding. He had never been involved in the supply or bulk product end of things and felt instantly out of his depth, but he didn't want Hasani to think he couldn't handle it. He was also starting to feel like he was in too far and couldn't say no without getting in deep shit with Hasani.

'Of course. When you say "products", what range are we talkin' about?'

He'd only been responsible for moving two or three different drugs for Khan, at most.

'I think we'd start with the most popular, based on your local knowledge. But anything is available to us. We have suppliers in many countries and our reach means we negotiate the best prices.'

'Great, so weed, cocaine and heroin then. We should start with those. They move the quickest and we can take the biggest margin from them.' He was trying hard to sound confident, as though this kind of conversation was the norm in his dealings with Khan. The Albanian raised his beer bottle to Gonzo, who chinked his own bottle against it.

'Excellent. To our new partnership, Mike.'

Gonzo smiled and held eye contact with Hasani as he toasted them. He felt a mix of excitement and fear. *What happens if Khan finds out? I'm fucking dead, that's what happens.*

'Now Mike, I'm sure you're a busy man, so why don't we discuss the details in a day or two? Could my driver drop you anywhere? Perhaps to the lovely Emina's?' Hasani grinned as he asked the final question.

'A couple of days sounds good and no, thank you, I think I'll walk.'

'A good idea – always good to get fresh air when big decisions are called for. I can see you and I are going to get on well.'

Gonzo stood and shook Hasani's hand, feeling the Albanian squeezing his hand ever so slightly, making a subliminal point. Gonzo was under no illusions; he was playing with the big boys now.

He left the club and walked through town past the Guildhall, with its impressive stone pillars. The wind was biting and he pulled his parka tightly around him and fastened the zip all the way up, then dug his hands deep into the pockets. He walked quickly, powered by a mix of youth and nervous energy. He pulled his hand out just long enough to check the time on his phone: 2.30 p.m. He had an hour and a half to kill before he met Emina. Just the thought of seeing her again stopped the tightness in his stomach he'd experienced since he had started feeling out of his depth with Hasani. It was replaced by excited butterflies. He couldn't wait to see her and decided, rather than walk back out of town, he would pass the time by having another beer and playing the fruit machines in a pub.

Gonzo passed a ten-pound note over the bar at the Titanic pub and sat down with his pint. He got his phone out of his pocket and checked his messages. He opened Emina's reply, revisiting the feeling of pleasure he got just from seeing something she'd written to him.

Get a grip, Gonzo, he thought as he smiled and switched apps to look through Facebook. Chipmunk had posted a picture of a bag of weed in the middle of a glass coffee table. The photo was accompanied by the text:

POLICE: Is this marijuana?
ME: It's Vegan tobacco, officer.

Gonzo chuckled quietly and shook his head, knowing that the picture would be one that Chipmunk had taken at his house, rather than a stock image. He knew that people like Chipmunk would have to be won round if his partnership with Hasani was to be a success, but the thought of taking on Khan didn't fill him with pleasure. He carried on flicking through random posts of family and friends, easily whiling away an hour, by which time he'd finished his second pint and decided not to have any more before he met Emina.

He waved at the guy behind the bar, an older gent who was polishing pint glasses and putting them away, taking an obvious pride in his work. The barman nodded in reply. Gonzo pulled his coat around him once more as he headed out into the cool air.

It wasn't a long walk up to the string of restaurants and bars that had been built outside the West Quay shopping centre. They overlooked the old city walls and it had become one of Gonzo's favourite Christmas locations: he loved the ice rink that was erected on the build-up to the festive season.

He checked the time on his phone. He was ten minutes early. He considered hovering outside the bar then caught sight of Emina, standing just inside. A flush of excitement came over him and he felt a flutter inside his chest. He yanked the glass door open and Emina shot him the biggest, warmest smile he'd ever been greeted with. She walked straight over to him and, without saying a word, threw her arms around his neck and kissed him. A polite cough tore them from each other's embrace. They turned to face a waiter, who wore an embarrassed smile.

'Good afternoon, do you have a reservation?'

'Er, yes, for four o'clock. Mike,' Gonzo answered.

The waiter checked his list, nodded and turned to walk away. 'This way, please,' he said over his shoulder. Mike and Emina followed, their fingers interlocked, both grinning from ear to ear. She giggled as he pulled her chair out for her, something his gran had always schooled him to do.

'Good manners cost nothing, Michael,' she used to say. He missed her – a lot. She'd died of cancer four years earlier. It ate her away until she was a frail, skeletal version of the fun, boisterous woman she'd been in his early youth. He'd spent every day with her in the three months leading up to her death and afterwards he hadn't spoken to anyone for days. He'd decided earlier that day that his gran would have liked Emina.

They chatted comfortably as they ordered drinks, then starters and mains, laughing out loud at their shared love of garlic prawns.

'So what have you been doing today?' she asked with a smile. He wondered if he should tell her that he'd met Hasani. He figured that she'd hear about it the next time she was at the club if he didn't say anything. Also, there was something about her that made him want to tell her everything.

'I had a meeting with Hasani earlier.'

At the mention of the Albanian's name, her smile slipped. 'You should be careful, Mike. Erion is a dangerous man. He takes pleasure from other people's pain and misfortune. I have seen him do terrible things to people in the rooms at the back of the club.'

He reached across the table and took hold of her hand. 'Don't worry. I know how dangerous he is. I work for someone now who is just as dangerous, but the opportunity Hasani has offered me is somethin' I will never get from Khan.'

'You work for Khan? I have heard Hasani and his men talking about him. They say he is the one who killed two of Erion's men a few days ago.'

Her face filled with worry lines, and Mike started to think it was a mistake to have told her about the meeting.

'Did you have anything to do with that? Because if you did, I would not spend too much time with Erion. He will do horrible things to avenge his men.' She pulled her hand away.

'I was involved, but not in the way you might think. I was the one they were beatin' up when Khan came and took them out. I was unconscious and didn't see him do it, but someone else I work with saw him and basically told me what he did. Khan saved my life.' He lowered his voice to a whisper. 'Those fuckers would've killed me if Khan hadn't come along. I know they'd have left me dead in the alley.'

He had just told her that people she knew had almost killed him, and that the man he worked for had killed them – and she had remained calm and held eye contact with him. He wasn't sure how to read this, but he was pretty sure that this wasn't how a typical first date went.

'You OK?' he asked tentatively.

'Yes, I am worried about you. I like you and don't want you to … to end up dead.' A tear welled in her eye.

'I'll be fine, promise.'

'You shouldn't make promises you can't keep.'

'But I can,' he said, taking her hand again. 'I will be fine. I've got a plan. It's gonna to take me a while to make it play out, but I think I have a solid plan.'

She smiled, but this time it was a hesitant half smile. 'OK, I trust you. Make your plan work and make sure you are OK. Can I ask you one thing?'

'Yeah, anythin'.'

'Am I in your plan?' She blushed, breaking eye contact and glancing away.

'Do you wanna be in my plan?' He tested the water before he gave his reply, wary of giving away how he felt about her. He'd only met her less than twenty-four hours ago; it was crazy.

'Of course, Mike, I thought that would be obvious.'

He felt a sense of relief as Emina answered him and thought quickly about how best to respond, keen not to dampen the mood again. He decided to keep it simple.

'That's sick. I just wasn't sure, you-know, with only knowin' you for, like, a day.' He glanced down at the table. Their hands were still joined; she hadn't pulled away again. He pulled her hand towards him and kissed it. She giggled softly, just as their garlic prawns arrived.

21

Two days earlier

Khan called Raj through to the office. Raj was in the middle of cutting the latest batch of cocaine, just as Inzamam had asked him to. He'd asked Raj to come in early and get started on the gear – he needed a good-size batch for a meeting he had planned in Brighton later that day. As ever, Raj had agreed without question and arrived at the same time as Inzamam.

Larry arrived about an hour later. He and Inzamam sat talking through Larry's idea for dealing with the Albanian contingent for about fifteen minutes. Once Inzamam had a good grasp of what

Larry had come up with, he decided the best way to have Raj's buy-in was to bring him in from the start. For success in Brighton, while simultaneously keeping Southampton growing, Inzamam decided he would need Raj on board.

Raj opened the office door. 'Boss?'

'Raj, come in, grab a seat.'

Raj did as instructed. Khan waited for him to take a seat next to Larry before he continued. 'Now, Raj, you're an essential part of this operation. You know that, don't you?'

'Yeah, I guess so.' Raj sounded hesitant.

'Guess so? Well, let me be clear, you absolutely are. We were just discussing how much you've developed over the last couple of years and how you might be supported to develop further. Weren't we, Lawrence?'

Larry nodded, but much to Inzamam's annoyance he remained silent.

'Sorry, I'm not sure I follow,' said Raj.

'OK, let me explain. We've been presented with a business opportunity; to expand over county lines.' Inzamam paused for effect, but not long enough to let Raj speak. 'We're going to take a run at Brighton and I've got a meeting later today, which is why I asked you to come in and make up a decent batch. I'm going to take our product and flood the streets of Brighton, extending our reach further along the coast. So, what I need from you is to be my eyes and ears in Southampton. Before you say anything, I know you're already my eyes and ears, but if I'm going to really nail Brighton I need you to have hold of the reins properly here.'

Khan paused again, but this time the silence invited Raj to speak first.

'Brighton is a huge market – that would be awesome. And of course I'll hold the reins here – it's pretty much set up and running.'

'It's not quite that simple, Raj. If you're truly going to take over things here in town, you'll need to step up and be the name that people associate with our operation here. That means dealing with the shit that comes up on a daily basis. The Albanians, the pushers who think they can skim off the top, all the scrotes who try to muscle in on our territory: they'll all have to learn to fear you as much as they do me. Now, I know this is not your usual style, so I've spoken to Lawrence here and he's agreed to give you some support while you get established. Your cut will obviously increase – I thought thirty per cent seems fair – but your spend on Lawrence's services will come out of your cut, just like I pay him now when we need his help.'

Khan stopped talking and gave Raj a second to take in the offer. He watched his young protégé's head spinning as he calculated what thirty per cent meant to him in real terms. He knew Raj well enough to know that he would immediately have worked out his new wages in his head; he calculated income and profit for Inzamam and never needed a calculator to do it. Inzamam clapped his hands loudly, snapping Raj from his thoughts.

'So, are you in?'

'Hell-yes, I'm in. Thanks!'

'Good, why don't you shout Gonzo to get us some drinks? That's the other thing you're going to need.'

'What's that?'

'A right-hand man. You're going to need someone you can trust to help you run things – it's too much for one person.'

Khan watched as Raj shouted for Gonzo and asked him to get him, Khan and Larry some beers. He had a good way about him: polite, but with a presence that Khan was sure could command the respect that he would need to be a viable proposition as a junior business partner. Gonzo brought three beers into the office as requested and placed them carefully on the desk in front of the men. He gave Khan an uncomfortable, tight-lipped smile then turned and left, closing the office door behind him.

Inzamam raised his beer and tipped the bottle towards Raj and Larry. 'To new business ventures.'

Raj had a huge grin on his face, like a child in a play park.

'What about Gonzo? How's he been getting on this past few days? Could he be right-hand material?' Inzamam fired the questions at Raj. He watched as Raj went back into calculation mode. Khan liked how measured Raj was, always thinking things through.

'He might do. He owes us – well, you. He's reliable – I mean, I'm pretty sure he's the only pusher who doesn't skim for his own use. And he's been here for the past few days and I haven't had any trouble from him at all. He's respectful and can hold a decent conversation.'

Khan nodded approvingly. 'Well, it's up to you. Whoever you choose, he's going to be your eyes and ears. Tell me, do you think he'd have your back?'

Raj turned and looked out through the office window towards Gonzo. 'Yeah, I think he would. He's let us know about shit going on out there a few times and can clearly take a kicking without running away.'

'What do you think, Lawrence? You're a good judge of character,' Khan said to his cleaner.

'I don't know the kid well enough to have much of an opinion. The only thing I'd say, Raj, is that you need someone who will go in to bat for you, even when it's not right for them. Someone who'll put themselves in harm's way before they put you there. Like you would for Inzamam. The fact that Gonzo feels indebted to you may be enough.'

Inzamam looked across at Raj, who was listening closely to Larry, weighing the advice he was being given.

'Why don't you have a think about it? There's no rush, but you will need someone.'

'OK, will do.'

'Good. Now, how's the batch coming along?'

'Oh, that's nearly done. Brighton won't know what's hit it. This is the best cut of scorpion we've done for a while – the compounds are really good quality and the purity of the base product is amazing.'

'Good. Have it ready by later this afternoon, will you? And I forgot to mention, you're coming to Brighton with us later.'

'Me? Why? I mean, that's fine, but why?'

'Because you've got shit to learn, and what better way to learn than by coming along and getting involved?'

'Sounds great. I'll go and crack on then, shall I?'

'Yeah, good idea.' Inzamam waited until his sidekick was out of the office and the door closed, then turned to Larry. 'That went well, don't you think?'

'Yeah, really well. He'll do a good job for you here, and I'll keep him out of trouble.'

'I appreciate it. I'm sure he'll get there, but he's a bit too nice to be feared just yet.'

'Yeah, he's a nice guy, but I think people could underestimate him at their own risk. He's really sharp and seems to learn bloody quick. He's certainly figured out how to maximise your business model.'

'He has that. He's mustard with the numbers too. I can guarantee you he already knows what his thirty per cent is worth and what he's going to do with it,' said Khan with an air of pride. 'I'm just going to go to the loo, then back to business, Lawrence.'

***

Larry drained his beer then wandered out of the office to get another one. As he was standing by the fridge opening two bottles of Cobra, Raj came over. A look that said *I need to talk to you* was written all over his face.

'You OK?' Larry started.

'Yeah, fine. I wondered if we could have a little chat – you know, about what Inzamam just said.'

'Which bit?'

'The bit where you're going to keep me out of trouble and I'm going to pay you to do it.'

Larry smiled and took a swig of his beer, impressed that Raj was being so up front with what he wanted.

'Oh, and what in particular did you want to chat through?'

'How much it's going to cost me, mainly. I know how much Khan pays you and, well, I don't have that kind of money. So I wondered how it's going to work.'

'Ah, I see. So you want to set up a line of credit with me? Is that what you're driving at?' He waited Raj as he thought about his response.

'Either a line of credit or a cut of the take, depending on how much help I'm going to need.'

Larry was impressed for a second time. This kid really did think things through quickly. He'd only been offered the keys to the kingdom in the last half hour and already he was working out a plan to bring people in with him. Khan had certainly never offered Larry a cut of the take but, on the other hand, Larry did charge him handsomely for his services.

'So how do you think that me having a cut of the take might work?'

'Well, I figure you're not going to be on hand all the time, because you still have work to do for Inzamam, plus your own work, which I know keeps you busy. So unless you're anticipating me needing your help more often than I do, I thought you'd probably average a day per week for me, for which I'd give you five per cent of the take.'

'And how did you arrive at five per cent?'

'Oh, that was easy. One hundred per cent of the business, over seven days, is 14.28 percent per day. Then the one day you do for me divided by 2.5.'

'Why 2.5?'

'You, me and my assistant, which is us 2 at full share and them at half. So your cut would actually be 5.7 percent, but I rounded down for ease.'

Larry could see why Inzamam liked having Raj as part of his business; the kid was sharp, and confident with it, which was not something Larry often experienced among the people he met.

'OK, sounds like a reasonable offer. One that doesn't seem to disadvantage either of us.'

'How do you mean?' Raj asked.

'Well, I'm not getting cash immediately, which is the way I normally do business, but I am getting a fair cut of your takings for the days I work for you. And you don't have to find the cash to hire me when you have a problem. It sounds to me like you've got this all figured out. If I didn't know better, I'd say you've been planning this for a while.'

Larry gave Raj a broad smile, drained his beer, grabbed another from the fridge and headed back to Inzamam's office without another word.

'You've got a smart one there, Inzy.'

'Who, Raj?'

'Yeah. He's just negotiated rates for me working for him with a maturity that far outweighs his years, or experience.'

'He's a bright guy – reminds me of a younger me, only without the temper and the bad habits.' Inzamam laughed and shook his head. 'Now let's get Raj back in here and fill him in on your Albanian plan.'

22

Vihaan Patel woke early. Sunlight streamed through the gaps in the blinds that hung at the window of a bedroom in what used to be Arjun Bakshi's house. A soft groan let him know that Tracey was stirring from the position she'd maintained for most of the night; her head resting on his chest, her arm across his rotund belly. He smoothed a hand through her hair and a pang of guilt knotted his stomach. He'd told Sadiya that he was going to meet up with Inzamam, to clear the air, halfway between Rotherham and Southampton, and he'd have a few drinks and be back the next day. In truth, he'd headed straight to Khan's new house, asked Tracey to make sure the younger girls who lived in the annexe were all taken care of for the night, then spent the evening drinking and talking to Tracey. This routine was invariably followed by him and Tracey having drunken sex then falling asleep together.

Gently, he rolled her onto her pillow, still smoothing her hair, so as not to wake her. His feelings of guilt, although they weighed heavy, didn't stop him from repeating the deceit. He knew what he was planning as soon as he had left home, and how it was going to end, but he couldn't get enough of Tracey; she made him feel important, not a feeling he'd been used to. Although he and Sadiya had a relatively traditional marriage, he had never exploited the freedom that some of his peers had, always feeling like he shouldn't take advantage of Sadi – until he'd got involved with Inzamam's business venture then hooked up with Bakshi. Once he started keeping company with Arjun Bakshi and some of his influential customers, he'd started to crave a taste of the freedom and power they had. Then one day Tracey had arrived at Bakshi's annexe. He had known straight away that he had to have her. It hadn't taken long – she was young, impressionable and keen to please. Arjun had soon spotted their attraction and encouraged Vihaan to pursue her, and Vihaan was pretty sure that Arjun had done some behind-the-scenes encouragement with Tracey too. But he didn't care. The result was exactly what he'd wanted. It also meant that she had been off-limits to customers for months, he and Arjun had made sure of it. When Inzamam had picked her and taken her for the night, Vihaan had raged with jealousy.

He stood looking at her for a moment. His face was still swollen and painful from the beating Larry had given him. Tracey had been really sweet and insisted on bathing it for him the previous night. It hadn't made any difference to his injuries, but at the time he had forgotten about the pain, about Inzamam, even about Bakshi being taken off to Brazil by Larry. She had the ability to do that to him. Vihaan grabbed a guest robe from the wardrobe and closed the bedroom door quietly behind him. He made his way down the stairs to the kitchen that Khan had been so impressed with.

He made tea and stood at the door, looking out onto the lawn that ran the width of the house. Thoughts of his friend Arjun Bakshi came to him.

Did Larry actually take him to the airport and put him on a plane to Brazil, as promised? Or did he kill him and dump his body somewhere? Vihaan had known for years that Inzamam had 'friends' who were capable of doing the kind of things he'd seen Larry do to Arjun, but he wanted to believe that his friend wasn't in the same league. He now knew this wasn't the case, and Khan was capable of similar brutality. This made him nervous about continuing his business relationship with Inzamam, which he knew in truth he had no way out of. He also knew that he had a massive amount of knowledge of Inzamam's activities – and that his knowledge made him vulnerable as well as giving him strength. There was no way Inzamam would forgive Vihaan any more mistakes. If he put a foot wrong Vihaan, and possibly Sadiya, would end up dead. Vihaan knew he had to figure out the best way to play the hand he was holding.

He looked around him. The house that Khan had all but stolen from Arjun was grand and needed keeping on top of. The first thing he had to do was get a new housekeeper – one he could trust. They only needed to take care of the main house; the girls took care of the annexe as part of their deal for living there. Tracey made sure of that, and he was pretty sure he could trust her. Next, he needed to rethink how the customers gained access to the girls, along the same lines as Inzamam had suggested. As he worked his plan up in his head, he stepped outside onto the patio. The chill morning air bit into his skin and he shivered. He didn't turn and go back inside, enjoying the cold on his arms and the concrete against his bare feet. He didn't enjoy the feeling for long, before the pain in his face distracted him. As he sipped his tea, a thought occurred to him. *Inzamam stole the house from Arjun, but he can't live in it. He's miles away and we only need the annexe for the business with the girls. I can do what I want with the rest of the house.*

With this thought he started to hatch another plan – one that would see him clawing back more of the control he craved.

23

Raj had finished cutting the batch of scorpion for Inzamam's trip to Brighton. While Khan was in with Larry, he decided it was a good time to check out where Gonzo's head was at, in terms of career development. He wasn't about to make Gonzo an offer if he didn't want to make something of himself. It didn't matter that Khan had suggested it; it was his money and he intended to protect and maximise it.

Gonzo was slouched in front of the TV as usual, but looked unusually well dressed.

'Where've you been, all dressed up?'

'What do you mean, dressed up?' the skinny pusher replied.

'Oh, come on, it's the first time I've seen you out of trackie bottoms, like, ever.'

'Cheeky bastard,' he said, a wry smile on his face.

'Oh, here it comes. Come on, spill. Where've you been, man?'

'I've seen a girl, innit?'

'A girl – get you. Does she have a name?'

'Course she has a name – it would be a bit fuckin' weird if she didn't. "Oi" would wear a bit thin after a while.' He laughed at his own humour, and Raj chuckled along with him.

'Well, who is she? She must be pretty fucking hot to get you all dressed up in your finest.'

'You wouldn't believe me if I told you.'

Raj sensed a change in tone and thought he'd pushed the dressing-up line a little far. Gonzo turned back towards the TV. Raj hadn't come over to talk to him about some mystery woman, but if the opportunity presented itself…

'Come on, mate, don't go all moody on me. Why wouldn't I believe you?'

'You just wouldn't, that's all.' He edged slightly back towards Raj, re-engaging.

Raj decided to carry on.

'Try me. After the shit we've seen here, not much is going to shock me.'

Gonzo shrugged at him and turned towards him with a serious look on his face.

'Can you keep it to yourself? I've got to tell someone about her or I'm going to fuckin' burst.'

'Ew, don't be bursting round here.' Raj grinned at Gonzo, who chuckled in response. 'Of course I can keep it to myself – who do you think I'm going to tell? The boss?'

'Well, yeah, I guess so.'

'No way! You must think I'm insane. I don't tell him every-thing. I'd get too much grief if I did.'

Gonzo seemed to be reassured by this. He nodded as Raj spoke then he took a deep breath. 'OK, I'm going to trust you. Like you say, we've been through some shit together and I know if you hadn't got involved in the alley, I wouldn't be here. So … her name's Emina and she's Albanian.'

Raj nearly spat out his tea.

'Albanian? Fucking hell, Gonzo, you know how to live dan-gerously, I'll give you that.'

'Just hear me out.'

'Sorry, mate, carry on.'

'So, like I say, she's Albanian. I met her at their club at the top of town.'

Raj opened his mouth to interrupt again, but stopped himself. 'She's not like anyone I've ever met. She's gorgeous and funny and she likes me – I mean, really likes me. I was with her last night and again this afternoon. She calls me Mike, not Gonzo, and it just feels … different.'

Raj watched Gonzo. He'd never seen him look like this: he was animated, meaning every word. He really did like this girl; she had clearly got under his skin. Raj just hoped Gonzo wasn't being played. He'd been given a pretty rough ride recently and could do with a bit of luck.

'That sounds amazing. Just one thing… Mike? Since when were you called anything but Gonzo? I've known you for years and I've never heard anyone, even your mum, call you Mike.'

'I know – proper weird, right? But it sounds good comin' from her and I kinda like it.'

'Does she live in town?'

'Yeah, she's from Lordshill, up near Sainsbury's.'

'So where did you see her today?'

'This afternoon, in All-Bar-One at West Quay.'

'Nice work, Mike.'

'OK, steady, it doesn't sound the same comin' out of your mouth.' Gonzo pushed him playfully and they laughed.

Raj figured this might be a good time to chat to Gonzo about work. 'Can I ask you something, Gonzo?'

'Yeah, sure, what is it?'

'How do you see this playing out?' Raj asked, waving an arm towards the room.

'What, you mean, Khan?'

'I was thinking more about you – where do you see yourself? Surely you don't want to be a street pusher forever?'

Gonzo's smile disappeared and he looked serious again. 'Why do you ask? What's going on?'

'I was just wondering, that's all. I was talking earlier about how I can grow my part in Khan's set-up and I wondered if you'd had similar thoughts.'

Gonzo's brow furrowed and he flushed. Raj thought he looked worried, nervous even.

'What is it, mate? What did I say?'

'What have you heard?'

'Er, nothing, what do you mean?'

'Fuck off, Raj. You fuckin' hear everythin' round here. I'm not a big believer in coincidences. So what have you heard?'

Raj was puzzled, but intrigued. *What the hell is Gonzo getting wound up about?* he thought. *I must have hit a nerve. Something is going on.*

'Gonzo, what could I have heard? Is this something to do with the Albanian girl? Or the Albanians?' He paused. Gonzo's expression had changed as he spoke. 'Oh, now I see. It's not the girl, it's the Albanians. What have you done? Please don't tell me it's something stupid. Khan won't dig you out again – you know that, don't you?'

'I didn't approach them, you've got to believe me. They approached me.'

'Who?'

'Erion Hasani. He called me and asked me to come to the club. Sent his driver to pick me up and everythin'.'

'Fucking hell, Gonzo! Hasani? What did he want?'

The silence was longer this time. Raj could almost see the cogs turning in Gonzo's head, trying to figure out how to phrase his response. 'Well?' he pressed.

'OK, OK, give me a minute… So Hasani called me out of the blue a couple of days ago and asked me to come to the club, said he'd send a driver to pick me up and everythin',' Gonzo took a deep breath. 'When I got to the club, they took me to a private booth where Hasani was surrounded by fit girls and some of his goons. We sat and drank for a bit, then we talked about me gettin'' a kickin' from his blokes, which he says had nothing to do with him. Then he said he wanted to talk to me about a business proposition.' He paused again. 'He asked me if I wanted to help him take over Southampton, 'cos he knows I've got contacts on the streets that him and his blokes don't have. And, I know what the punters are buyin' at the moment, and then he told me he wants me to be his business partner.'

Raj sat listening, hoping that Gonzo had seen the massive risk he was taking just by talking to Hasani, never mind being his business partner.

'When he said "partner", what did he mean? How much of a partner?'

'What do you mean?'

'Did he say how much of the business he'd be expecting you to handle as his partner?'

'Oh, yeah, pretty much everythin'. He said he'd introduce me to his suppliers and then I could handle the rest.'

'The rest? You mean cut, package, distribute and control?'

'Um, I guess so, yeah.'

'You do realise you haven't got the first fucking idea how all of that works, Gonzo, don't you? And I can't see Hasani being the kind of bloke that's going to be happy with you learning on the job, can you?'

Raj began to worry for his associate: he knew that it would need a big operation to take on Khan's set-up. He decided to slow things down a little, give himself time to think about how to handle this. His first thought was that Gonzo could prove useful in more ways than one, especially if he had an inside track to the

Albanian drug gangs – dangerous, but useful. 'OK, so what did you say to him?'

'I told him I'd think about it.'

'Good – at least you didn't commit to him. If you'd done that I'm pretty sure you'd be fucked within a couple of weeks.'

'So what should I do?'

'I don't know yet. Let's think about it carefully and weigh up how it could work to our advantage.'

'How do you mean?'

'Well, he's invited you into his inner circle, so that means he either trusts you – which, let's face it, is unlikely as he doesn't really know you – or he has a plan for how he intends to use you. Knowing how the Albanians work, that won't end well for you. Either way, we need to work out what's the best angle to play.'

'Thanks, Raj, you're a fuckin' hero. I've been freakin' out. I didn't know whether to go along with it or run.'

'So where does the girl fit into this?'

'Emina? She was there – Hasani introduced us and left us to it.' Gonzo's face lit up when he said the girl's name. Raj wondered if Hasani was using Emina to bait the hook for Gonzo, which meant he wanted him to accept his business proposition and have him working for the Albanians.

Fuck! What would Khan do? he thought. *He'd beat the shit out of Gonzo for talking to Hasani, that's what he'd do.*

'OK, so how did the evening play out? And I don't mean the gory details of you screwing Emina either.'

'It's like I said – he sent his driver to pick me up at the end of the road, took me to the club—'

'No, I get that. I mean, how did the business offer play out?'

'Oh, that. The actual offer was yesterday.'

'What do you mean, yesterday?'

'He called me yesterday mornin' and said he wanted to talk to me again about his offer. He sent his car for me and this time he took me through to his office, which is fuckin' lovely.'

Raj flashed him a look that said 'get on with it'. Gonzo coughed and carried on.

'Sorry, but it is. Anyway, we chatted in his office for a while and then he got us a beer and we toasted our new partnership.'

'Whoah, hang on! A minute ago, you said you told him you'd think about it.'

'I did, on the first night. Then when he got me back into his office yesterday, I thought the best thing to do was agree.'

'Oh fuck-it! Gonzo, what have you done? Khan would fucking kill you if he knew you'd got into bed with the Albanians.' Raj thought quickly. He was pleased that Gonzo had been confident enough to share his news with him, but he wished he wasn't in the middle of it. Khan wouldn't take kindly to Raj knowing about it and not telling him but Raj knew, if he told Khan, he'd kill Gonzo for sure, or get Larry to do it. *Fuck, what am I going to do with this lunatic? Everywhere he goes, shit follows him.*

'OK, this is what we're going to do. If Hasani calls you in the next couple of days, you stall him. You do not go and meet him, are you clear?'

'Yeah, yeah, got it. Why?'

'Why? Because I need a couple of days to work out how to keep you from getting fucking shot by either Khan or Hasani, that's why! Unless you don't mind the thought of ending up in a gutter somewhere, with a bullet in your head, or your throat cut...' He watched Gonzo's eyes widen as he spoke. He was deliberately feeding him with fear, as it was the only way he could think of to keep him quiet.

Gonzo asked sheepishly - 'What about Emina?'

'What about her?' Raj snapped.

'Well, can I see her if she calls?'

'I don't know, Gonzo, do you trust her? She does work for Hasani.'

'But I'm only avoiding his calls – it's not like I've disappeared for real, is it?'

'No, I guess not. If you have to, keep it local and away from the Albanian end of

town.'

'OK, thanks, mate. You're not gonna to tell the boss, are you?'

'I don't know what I'm going to do yet. But I don't think telling Inzamam fucking Khan would go well for you, do you?'

'No, I guess not. Thanks again. Sorry for droppin' this shit on you man.'

'It's OK, we'll figure it out. Just don't have any more secret meetings with the fucking Albanians, OK?'

'I swear I won't.'

24

Raj had managed to get Gonzo to sit and watch a movie, so that he could have a bit of time to himself to think. That lasted about five minutes. The internal phone rang and when Raj picked it up, one of the waiters from the restaurant was on the other end.

'Is Inzamam around?' he asked. 'Mrs Khan is in the restaurant and asked me to call through to the office and let him know she's here.'

'OK, I'll let him know.' Raj ended the call and gathered his composure. Husna was in the restaurant! Why? She never came near the place – well, hardly ever.

Khan

He knocked on Khan's office door. Larry and Khan were still chatting, but Larry was standing up and looked as though he was getting ready to leave.

'Sorry to interrupt, boss, but Mrs Khan's in the restaurant. One of the waiters has just called through to let you know.'

'Husna's here. Inzy, there's a nice surprise for you,' Larry said with a smile.

'Time for you to go then, Lawrence. I don't want to introduce you to my wife and have to explain what you do for a living.' Khan laughed and shook Larry's hand, and the two parted company.

'Thanks, Raj, I could do with a few minutes. Would you go through to the restaurant and let Husna know I'll be there soon? Get her a glass of wine and have a chat to her. You could use a break.'

'What, me?'

'Yes, you – don't worry, she won't bite. Honestly, Raj, you're going to have to learn to be comfortable in the company of women, especially if our new business relationship is going to work. Now go on, be charming.'

'Yes, boss.'

Comfortable in the company of women – cheeky bastard. If he knew, he wouldn't be so fucking lairy, thought Raj as he stomped down the narrow corridor towards the restaurant. As he got closer he got the familiar feeling of butterflies in his stomach that he always got before he saw Husna. He ran a hand through his thick black hair, trying to make sure it wasn't a mess, and pushed the door open. There she was, standing in her own restaurant, just yards away from where he worked every day. She looked amazing in tight faux leather trousers and a camel-coloured coat with a subtle checked scarf wrapped around her neck. Her hair and face were immaculate, as always. Raj stood and stared for a moment, just before she caught sight of him and smiled. He walked over to her, reminding himself where he was and that she was here to see her husband, not him. He smiled back, a polite, controlled smile.

'Hi, Mrs Khan, how are you?'

'Raj, lovely to see you.' She stepped a little closer, leaned towards him and gave him a kiss on the cheek. She smelled great. Immediately he felt himself blush, and became even more uncomfortable. Husna looked totally relaxed, with a gentle, playful smile on her lips.

How is she so chilled?

'You too.' He glanced round the restaurant. The waiters were busy setting up tables around them and he could hear a distant rattling from the kitchen, as the door was slightly open. 'What brings you to the restaurant?'

'Oh, I've popped in to see Inzamam. I need to go to London for the day on business and it might be a late one so I thought, rather than phone or message him, I'd pop in on my way past.'

'Great. He's tied up at the moment, but he knows you're here and he'll be through soon. Would you like a drink? A glass of wine, maybe?'

'That's a great idea, but only a small one. I'm driving.' They walked over towards the elegantly appointed bar and Raj went to get them both a drink, as Khan had instructed.

'What would you like?'

'I'll have a glass of that lovely Pinot, please. Are you having one too?'

He watched her mouth as she spoke. He had an overwhelming urge to kiss her, and wondered if she felt the same. Her playful smile was still there; she looked like she was enjoying this.

'It would be rude to let you drink alone,' he said, trying to sound more confident than he really was. The waiters were all at the far end of the restaurant, and Raj and Husna were out of earshot of anyone. As he passed Husna her wine, he leaned across the bar.

'I'm really struggling not to kiss you right now,' he whispered. Her smile broadened and she let out a little giggle.

'Now, now, Raj, you must behave yourself. I'm a respectable married woman and your boss's wife.' She stroked the side of his face as she spoke. Raj looked around to see if anyone had seen her touch him, and was relieved that no one was facing towards them.

'Why do you think I've come in? I never come to the restaurant. I wanted to see you and let you know that I'm trying to sort out a free evening,' she continued in hushed tones. Raj couldn't stop a smile from stretching across his face.

'Really?'

'Yes, really. So are you going to be able to free yourself up?'

'Yes, of course. What did you have in mind?'

'Not sure yet – let's play it by ear. Let me know what time you can get out.'

'OK, great. It won't be late.'

'Good – we can have all evening together.'

Just then, the door swung open and Inzamam walked in, announcing his presence with a loud, 'Ah, my gorgeous wife! What brings you here?'

Raj's face dropped and he felt a crushing feeling in his chest.

'To see you, obviously,' Husna replied without missing a beat. Inzamam walked over and kissed her.

'One day you'll have a woman as gorgeous as this on your arm, Raj.'

The knot in Raj's stomach tightened. *It doesn't stop you shagging everything that moves though, does it, boss?* Unable to stay in the room with them, he looked from Husna to Inzamam then excused himself and returned to the back room.

25

'Ray, how's your day going?' Inzamam asked the investor brightly.

'Inzamam, how lovely to hear from you. My day is going well, thank you. Tell me, how goes your progress with our Brighton project?'

'That's what I'm calling about. We had our first meeting there today, with the chap you recommended, Roman. Things went well. He has a street network which, until now, has been getting patchy supply from our Albanian friends. We took some of our product, which of course they loved, and I agreed to start supplying them from next week – after they've market-tested the sample we left with them. It should be all systems go from there. I've agreed their cut with Roman, who seems happy to have a regular, reliable supply, and I've made it very clear that this is an exclusive arrangement that means they work for me from the first delivery. If they do any distribution on behalf of the Albanians, that would be met with a less than sympathetic response. Again, Roman seemed to be good with that – he's focused on consistency of product and regular deliveries over county lines.'

'That all sounds very promising, Inzamam. I'm assuming our usual arrangement is appropriate for Brighton?'

'Absolutely. I'll keep everything at a safe distance from you and your return will go via your offshore investment route.'

'Very good, Inzamam. I knew you were the right man to invest my money in. The good people of Brighton won't know what's hit them once they sample your superior product. I feel the beginning of another fruitful partnership.'

'Absolutely, Ray. I wouldn't have it any other way. Let's catch up for lunch again soon.'

'That would be lovely. I'm away in Europe on business for the next couple of weeks, but when we sail back in, what say I send the chopper out and pick you up and bring you out to the boat for the day? You and that lovely wife of yours.'

'Sounds fantastic, Ray. See you soon.' Khan ended the call and glanced in his rear- view mirror before changing lanes to join the M27. To his right he could see the green expanse of Portsdown Hill dominating the skyline and overlooking Portsmouth. He gunned the Range Rover along the M27 until he reached the 50 mph area marked out for smart motorway work.

'Fucking roadworks,' he muttered. Glancing in the rear-view mirror, he saw Raj tapping on his mobile. Lawrence sat next to him in the front.

'Sounded like a good call?' said Lawrence.

'Ray's good value. You can rely on him for funding and discretion – not an easy balance to find, as I'm sure you can appreciate in your line of work.'

'Absolutely, rare qualities indeed,' the cleaner replied in a deadpan tone. Khan struggled to work Lawrence out sometimes: he was aloof, but without arrogance. He glanced across at his passenger. Lawrence was looking straight ahead, as he always did, rarely showing any emotion. Khan figured that the ability to remain detached helped him do what he did. He certainly didn't give anything away.

Khan checked the mirror again and asked Raj who he was messaging. He got a rather bland response.

'Just one of the guys.'

Not in the mood for silence, he pushed on. 'So what did you make of Brighton?'

'In what way, boss?'

'Well, how did you think the meeting went? Did you have a view on Roman? Or would you have done anything differently?'

Lawrence turned his head to the right, waiting for Raj to answer.

'I guess it was OK. If I'm honest, I think Roman was a bit too keen and didn't ask enough questions. I'd have thought he would want to know where the supply was coming from, how we were going to get it to him, and what weights it would be packed in, but maybe that's just me. Maybe I just need to know more than most people about our business model.'

'You definitely do. I haven't met many people in this business who want to know as much as you do, but that's a good thing.'

Out of the corner of his eye, Khan saw Lawrence smile. The cleaner was clearly impressed with Raj. It was difficult not to be. He had the business nailed; he understood how to maximise the margins and control the geography. He was a sharp young guy and Inzamam was aware that he needed to keep both him and Lawrence close.

The rest of the drive back to Southampton passed in relative silence. As they neared the city, each of his passengers seemed engrossed in thought.

26

Raj sat quietly in the back of the Range Rover as Inzamam spoke to someone called Ray on the phone. Raj could tell he was someone Khan needed on-side by the way he spoke to him, all bright and upbeat, a very different tone to the one he used when speaking to people he didn't need to impress.

His phone was on silent. As he scrolled through Instagram, a bar flashed onto the screen: 'Message from Sarah'. He shot an uncomfortable glance at Khan in the rear-view mirror, but Khan wasn't looking at him.

Hey you, it was great to see you at the restaurant. Sorry if it felt a bit weird. Are you still going to be able to get away later today? xxx

Raj smiled and replied.

Hey! It was a bit weird :-) but good to see you too. We're out at the moment, but should be back in time to get away xxx

Her response came back instantly, which made him feel good.

That's great – I've sorted the girls out and Inzamam thinks I'm away for the night on business. Why don't you meet me near yours at about 7?

Raj started to type.

Sounds good. We're on the way back from Brighton. I've only got a couple of bits I've got to do when I get back xxx

Khan

OK, 7 it is, I'll message you when I'm on my way. I've booked us a room xxx

He tingled all over at the thought of having Husna to himself for a whole night.

Then Khan interrupted him, asking him who he was texting.

'Just one of the guys,' he said as blandly as he could manage.

'What did you make of Brighton?' Khan continued.

Raj gave him a brief summary of his view of the pusher, Roman, they'd met earlier in Brighton. He decided to keep it brief and made the point, without labouring it, that he was less than impressed with him. Raj figured, even before he'd heard Khan's call with Ray, that Khan had been given the contact by someone he either trusted, or needed, to make the Brighton deal work, and he didn't want to rock the boat too much.

Raj thought Roman was a typical junkie, with very little in the way of business savvy – certainly not someone Khan could build a drug empire off the back of. Raj had asked Roman only one question, and he'd had failed spectacularly, in Raj's opinion, to give a measured answer. Raj had asked how old Roman's average street distributor was. Roman had stumbled and stuttered a bit, then thrown a vague answer: 'Seventeen to nineteen-ish.' That was all Raj needed to know. The average age of Raj's street team was thirteen, with some as young as ten. There was a good reason for this - the police were unlikely to use their resources hunting children on account of the lack of potential for a conviction, which had a negative impact on their arrest and crime detection figures. Raj knew this because he'd done his research. He'd read local crime stats to find out how many arrests resulted in successful convictions for underage drug offences. Roman on the other hand, clearly didn't have a clue. This made Raj feel smug – and even more valuable to Khan. He thought he probably knew the local business better than Khan and although he didn't share Khan's more extremist views; Raj did know that he would pay him well for his dedication and loyalty. This had worked to his advantage to date, placing him on the cusp of taking over Khan's Southampton operation. On top of this, he was going to be spending the night with Husna. It was a good day.

Inzamam had stopped talking to him, instead turning his attention to Larry. Raj took the opportunity to think about how to handle Gonzo. The problem had the potential to blow up in their faces. He couldn't believe that Gonzo had been sucked in by a chauffeur-driven car, a few beers at the Albanians' club, and a bit of bullshit flattery.

He's a fucking idiot, but I don't want to see him dead. How the fuck am I going to get him out of it without things kicking off with Hasani – or Khan? Come on, think, Raj. What would Khan do? He'd fucking kill Gonzo, that's what he'd do. For talking to the Albanians in the first place and for thinking he could actually take the Southampton business and the network of pushers off them. Raj took a swig of lukewarm water from a bottle, then looked out of the window. They were turning left by the huge student accommodation block, City Gateway Halls, which loomed over the junction.

Khan

Telling Khan might be the only way to sort this out. Maybe he'll understand that Gonzo has been a dick, but this might give us a way in to the Albanians' operation. We could use Gonzo's relationship with Hasani to our advantage. What if the Albanians find out? They'll kill him for sure. Fuck.

It seemed that most options led to Gonzo ending up dead. Raj decided he needed help – and he knew just the person to ask. He stayed silent for the rest of the journey, only messaging Husna once to let her know they were back in town and he'd be out in time to meet her.

27

Vihaan Patel was getting out of his car on the driveway of Arjun Bakshi's old house when his Bangla-music ring tone sounded. He dug his phone out of his pocket and shielded the screen from the sun with his hand, expecting to see Inzamam's name. The caller ID said Rio de Janeiro, accompanied by a number he didn't recognise.

'What the fuck?' he mumbled. He considered not answering it for a second, then decided to press green.

'My dear Vihaan, how are you?'

The words were spoken by a voice Vihaan thought he would never hear again.

'Arjun? Is that you?' he asked, not sure if he could believe his own ears.

'It is indeed. Tell me, are you safe?' Arjun Bakshi asked.

'Yes, but never mind me, where are you? I mean, I can see from my phone where you are, but how? What happened?'

He was finding it difficult to process. He'd decided that Arjun had more than likely been flown to his death. The line was silent for a moment, then Arjun replied.

'I am, as you know, in Brazil. Larry was true to his word and didn't kill me, although I had expected him to. He took me to the airport and escorted me to the plane. Even as we were taxiing away from the terminal, he waited at the departure gate, watching the plane take off. I must say, he is very thorough.'

'What happened when you got to Brazil?'

'I was greeted by a couple of Brazilian chaps called Paco and Odo. They recognised me instantly so I had no time to try to escape. They said that Larry had asked them to look after me. I was pretty sure that meant they were going to kill me.'

'What did you do?' Vihaan butted in, keen to know how his friend had come to be phoning him.

'As I was saying, I was sure they were going to kill me. Paco spoke very good English, so I asked him what they had been instructed to do and how they intended to go about it. Sure enough, they confirmed they had been paid to drive me out into the hills, far enough that I couldn't walk back, shoot me and leave me to die.' Arjun sighed, then continued. 'Luckily for me, Brazilians are as greedy as people of every other nationality and I still have access to my money, even here. So I offered them double what

Larry had paid them to tell him they had completed their task and let me live.

They were pleased to have made such a good daily rate for very little work and seemed to have no loyalty to Larry. I even managed to get them to give me their car.'

Vihaan sat in stunned silence, listening to Arjun's tale. He had not anticipated this outcome and wanted to know what Arjun intended to do next. He had no idea how to ask, so he just blurted it out. 'So what are your plans?'

'Do you mean, am I going to return to the UK? No, I think not, Vihaan. If someone wants you dead and believes you to be so, then use it to your advantage. Inzamam and Larry believe me to be out of their hair for good – and I intend to keep it that way.

Brazil is a big place, with many interesting people. I'm sure there are business ventures here waiting to be explored – and exploited. I wanted to let you know that I was alive, as I'm sure you were wondering what had happened to me. Despite your history with Inzamam, I truly believe I can trust you.'

'You can,' Vihaan assured him without hesitation.

'Thank you. Besides, my new position puts me in a rather sanguine frame of mind. The world is my oyster, as long as I don't come across Inzamam or Larry. However, I will seek atonement for their theft of my home.'

Vihaan suddenly felt nervous. 'Atonement? What do you intend to do, Arjun? Please remember my life is still very much in the UK. How will you get revenge without them knowing you're alive?'

'Now, now, Vihaan, relax. I won't do anything that places you or your family in danger, nor will I reveal to Mr Khan – or his accomplice – that I am alive. However, there are many ways to skin a cat – and they must pay.'

'I'm not sure that's a good idea. If they get a whiff of you still being alive, they'll go mad.'

'Don't worry, Vihaan. I'll speak to you again soon. In the meantime, look after my home and our business, and for your own sake and that of your lovely wife, keep the fact that I am still alive to yourself. Not even Sadiya can know. Do you understand me?'

'Yes, of course. I won't say a word. It wouldn't end well for me either.'

'Quite. Anyway, I'll speak to you soon. Take care, Vihaan.'

With that, the line went dead. Vihaan Patel was left looking at his phone in shock, disbelief and fear. Just before he put his phone back into his pocket, a text notification popped up on the screen. It was from the same number Arjun had just called him from. He opened it hurriedly.

Sorry if my call startled you. Appreciate things will be tough for a while. I've put a little something in your account to keep you going. A.

Put something in my account? What the fuck? Vihaan opened his online banking app. He logged in and his account balance appeared on the screen. It was much higher than he had expected. He opened the recent transactions page and saw that Arjun had deposited £5,000 into his account earlier that day. He stood staring at his phone, unable to believe what he was seeing.

Vihaan was even more determined to look after the house now. Knowing that Arjun was alive and well filled him with positivity. He would keep the secret and use the knowledge to his advantage. He decided to carry on playing Inzamam's game, changing the way the wealthy businessmen accessed the girls and making sure that he had some leverage over them, as Khan had suggested.

He also resolved to keep in close contact with Arjun and make sure he knew what his friend intended to do – and how best to protect himself and Sadiya from any potential fallout, should Arjun do something reckless. It felt like a great opportunity to place himself in a strong position. Inzamam couldn't – and wouldn't – come up to Rotherham to run things. Arjun couldn't – and wouldn't – come back to the UK. Vihaan was in the driving seat.

Just as he was starting to enjoy his new-found feeling of control, his phone rang again.

'Hello?'

'Vihaan – Larry. How are you feeling? How's the face?'

'Broken,' he replied, his mood instantly dulled.

'Shame it had to play out the way it did,' the cleaner continued. 'Still, onwards and upwards, eh?'

Vihaan was unimpressed by Larry's bright, bubbly tone. He shuffled uncomfortably and became more aware of the pain in his face.

'What can I do for you, Larry?' he asked, wanting to get the call over with.

'Nothing too complicated. I've been chatting to Inzamam and I would like you to send a list of your, er … let's call them customers … to my mobile by the end of the day.'

Vihaan paused. 'Our customers? What for?'

'Never you mind, Vihaan. Just get me the list by the end of the day. Don't make me come up there to collect it – that would be a mistake.'

Larry's tone was polite, but menacing. Vihaan knew only too well how a refusal, or delay, would play out for him, but he felt the need to challenge Larry's bully-boy tactics.

'That's impossible. I haven't got time to do that today, Larry, and I can't get my hands on everyone's details that quickly. You do know I'm not at your beck and call 24/7.'

He heard Larry draw in a deep breath then let it out in a long sigh. 'Vihaan, a man called Samuel Johnson once said, "men are generally idle, and ready to satisfy themselves, and intimidate the industry of others, by calling that impossible which is only difficult." Now, get it done.' Larry ended the call.

'What the fuck was that?' Vihaan mumbled, holding the side of his face. His injuries were really letting him know that he was overdue pain relief. He made his way through to the kitchen and got a pack of peas from the freezer. He held them to his face and felt an instant relief flood over him. Next he rummaged around in the cupboards and found some Tramadol. He grabbed a glass of water and chugged a couple of pills, then went through the house into a study. Arjun had kept everyone but Vihaan out of this room.

A well-stocked bookshelf covered one wall and large prints of Arjun's favourite pieces of art hung on the walls. The only one Vihaan liked was Van Gogh's head of a skeleton, which had a cigarette hanging from its mouth. He liked what it symbolised about modern society, even though it was well over a hundred years old.

Vihaan took in a deep breath and sat at the large oak desk that monopolised the room. The air was heavy with the smell of books and leather. He rearranged the desk calendar to show the right date, then slumped into the high-backed leather chair. *Right, you need to get that fucking list sorted out,* he thought. Reaching across the front of the desk, he opened a drawer and took out an old-looking key. He spun around in the chair to face the wall and pulled the cord on a recessed roller blind. Instead of a window, the blind rolled up to reveal a safe. There was a circular key cover in the middle of the door. Vihaan flicked the cover up to reveal a keyhole. Using the old-fashioned key, he unlocked the safe, reached inside and took out a silver MacBook. He spun back to face the desk and opened the computer. Vihaan typed in a long password and the home screen appeared. He clicked on the numbers icon and opened a file called Visitor Log. A spreadsheet opened and Vihaan clicked on a tab along the top edge of the screen. It opened to reveal a list of names, dates, charges made and services given. He took out his phone and took a photo of the screen, then scrolled to reveal another page of names, which he also photographed.

'Right, Larry, that'll do you to be going on with. I'll be fucked if you're getting your hands on everything,' he muttered. He attached the pictures to a message to Larry and pressed send.

As he pocketed his phone, the study door swung inwards. Vihaan instinctively closed the laptop. Tracey walked through the door and his face changed instantly to a warm smile.

'I was just on my way to the kitchen and I heard you in here,' she said as she walked across the study.

'I'm just tidying up some of Arjun's filing,' he answered vaguely. She smoothed a soft hand gently down the side of his face.

'How's your face feeling?'

'Painful, but don't worry – it'll be fine. I've had broken bones before. They all heal, given time.' He tried to smile reassuringly, but it hurt too much and he gave up, instead leaning his head against her. She stroked his head, planting a tender kiss on the top of it, then moved away towards the door.

'Do you want anything?'

'Tea would be good if you're putting the kettle on.'

'I'm sure I can manage that.' She pulled the door half closed behind her as she swept out of the room. Vihaan locked the laptop back in the safe then took a key from under the desk calendar, which he used to lock the study door as he left.

His phone buzzed in his pocket. He didn't look at it, assuming it would be

Larry acknowledging receipt of the pictures. Instead he walked through to the kitchen, wrapped his arms around Tracey's waist and kissed the back of her neck. She smelled good and he felt an instant sense of arousal as she pressed back into him.

28

Valmir Shala stepped out of the Mercedes. His size fourteen feet seemed to reach halfway across the pavement. Dardan Rama was one of the few men who were as tall and broad as Shala; both men had to duck to fit under a standard doorframe. Rama held the door open for the Albanian drug lord. Shala noticed that Dardan had a serious, thoughtful look on his face.

'Dardan, what is bothering you?'

'Nothing, Mr Shala. I'm fine.'

'Nonsense. I've known you for many years, and have seen your faraway look before. It's always when you have something on your mind. Now, what is it?'

'It's not my place to question the decisions made by other people who work for you, Mr Shala. Especially as I may not know all the facts of a situation.'

'Ah, I see. You disapprove of something Erion has done? Am I right?' He looked the faithful bodyguard square in the eye, holding eye contact until Dardan nodded. 'Tell me, Dardan, what has Erion done that you do not agree with? It will go no further.' He smiled.

'As I said, I may not be fully aware of all the facts, but he invited an associate of Khan into the club, set him up with one of the girls, then offered him a partnership in the Southampton business.'

'And you disapprove?'

'I know of the individual. He was the one that Kreshnik and Rosen were … dealing with when they were killed. He cannot be trusted and he should not be allowed into the inner workings of your business. That is only my opinion, obviously.' He had maintained eye contact with the intimidating Shala the whole time he had spoken. Shala liked Dardan; he had been a reliable and solid member of his security team for over fifteen years and had dealt with many sensitive issues on Shala's behalf.

'Hmm, I see what you mean – that is a concern. Thank you for sharing your thoughts with me, Dardan. You have done the right thing. You know I must act on what you've told me.'

Rama nodded.

'But I will not let anyone know that it was you who let me know.'

'Thank you, Mr Shala. I wouldn't want Erion to think badly of me. I only mentioned it because—'

'Because I asked you to, and you are a loyal friend.' Shala patted the muscular bodyguard on the shoulder and pulled his suit jacket closed, fastening it around his large frame.

Dardan Rama closed the car door and stepped in front of Shala to open the door to the club. Shala had to turn slightly to fit his shoulders through the single door. His navy-blue single-breasted suit was made to measure, and fit perfectly. He wore spotless black brogues and a crisp white shirt, two buttons open at the collar. He was always clean-shaven and his piercing blue eyes cut through people when he glared at them. He knew that his accent made him seem more intimidating to the young English people who worked for him.

Shala made his way into Jete Nate and did a slow, measured lap of the closed nightclub. He went behind the bar and checked that the bottles in the fridges were all lined up neatly and facing front. Taking a shot glass from under the bar, Shala checked the inside of it with his finger to make sure it was clean and dry. Satisfied that his staff had done their job well, he reached up onto a mirrored shelf behind the bar and took down a three-quarters-full bottle of Beluga Gold Line vodka which, at over £150 per bottle, wasn't ordered much by Southampton clubbers. He poured himself a full measure, downed it in one, and immediately refilled the small glass. He stood for a moment looking across the vast expanse of the nightclub. Lights suspended from the ceiling waited to be ignited and bring the place to life, and glossy tables glinted under the daytime lights. He swirled the clear liquid in the shot glass, contemplating the information Dardan had given him. He had entrusted Hasani with a large part of his empire, making him a partner in the club, and the thought of him making such a decision, at a time when their business was under threat, did not amuse him.

Valmir Shala had become a very wealthy man by having a keen eye for the next big thing, especially where leisure, drink and drugs were concerned. He was a ruthless businessman, making deals and building businesses quickly, and he had gained a reputation as being someone not to be crossed. When crossed, he had expressed his disapproval in the most extreme ways – often at the direct expense of those who wronged him. He knocked back the remaining vodka and walked through the club to the private office area.

Halfway along the wood-panelled corridor, one of Erion's henchmen came out of a door, straight into Shala's path. He staggered backwards against the door, a look of shock on his face. 'Mr Shala?'

'As you were, Paul,' Shala said, nodding at the doorman as he walked past him.

'Er … yes, Mr Shala. Would you like me to…' He stuttered.

'Don't worry. I know my way around my own club,' Shala interrupted him. He stopped outside a pair of closed doors adorned with a silver plaque that read 'Mr Hasani'. He smiled and tugged at his shirt cuffs, revealing an inch of crisp white cotton and gleaming black cufflinks. Shala grabbed the door handle and thrust the door open.

'Doesn't anyone knock?' shouted Hasani, who sat at his desk, facing away from the door.

'I did not feel the need, Erion,' replied Shala.

Hasani spun around to face his boss, clearly shocked to hear his voice.

'Mr Shala, I'm sorry, I didn't know … I mean, I did not expect it to be you. What are you doing here?'

'Am I not allowed to visit my own club?'

'Yes, yes of course. I just normally know when you're coming. Is everything OK?'

'Apologies for the unannounced visit. What is it they say? I was in the neighbourhood so thought I'd drop in.' He smiled a wide toothy grin at Erion, who was visibly rattled by Shala's presence.

'It's always good to see you. Would you like a drink?'

'That would be good. The club looks to be in good order, Erion. It's been a while since I've been here, and it would appear that you and your team are doing a good job.'

'Thank you, things are going well.'

Hasani passed Shala an elaborately carved glass tumbler, a good slug of vodka in it.

'This is a nice office, Erion. Giving the impression of being the owner is a shrewd move – it helps with your standing with our business associates, yes?'

'Er…yes, I suppose it does.' Erion looked uncomfortable as he glanced around the office. Shala took a seat on one of the sofas that ran along the wall of the office. Hasani came out from behind his desk and joined him, glass in hand.

'Tell me, Erion, how is business outside the club? How are your associates doing in their bid to gain ground over Mr Khan?'

'Business is going well. We make progress in our plans to increase our share of the local market, and our connections are starting to increase the number of street-based suppliers.'

'Good, good. And what of Khan?'

'What do you mean?'

'I mean, what are you doing about Mr Khan? He is responsible for the death of two of our most valuable assets. He is the greatest threat to expanding your reach in Southampton and he is now attacking Brighton, which means our business will not prosper there. I seem to remember, the last time we spoke of him, you were going to make a direct approach and meet with Mr Khan.' He eyed Erion as he spoke, looking to see how rattled he was by the visit.

'I decided to try a different approach.'

'Oh?'

'I have brought in one of his closest associates, flattered him and made him an offer he would be foolish to refuse.' Hasani paused, took a swig of his vodka and continued.

'I thought about my original idea of meeting with Khan, and decided that it served no purpose to let him know he had inconvenienced us, or our operation, by killing Kreshnik and Rosen. If anything, I think it would weaken our position. I felt that gaining information from someone who is stupid enough to cooperate, but scared enough to keep quiet about it would be more use.'

Shala nodded and sipped his drink. 'So, tell me about this associate.'

'His name is Mike. He is one of Khan's higher tier, with his own network of street suppliers and contacts across the city. So far, I have met with him and offered him a partnership in Southampton – in conflict with his position with Khan. This means he would have to move his network across to our supply, eventually cutting ties with Khan. Once that happens and his network and contacts are ours, I will remove him from the field of play and we will have made a sizeable dent in Khan's business.'

'Very shrewd. As ever, you do not disappoint. However, if he is at the level you say, what of his loyalty to Khan? You are employing a very high-risk strategy, Erion. If he turns to Khan, you have not only lost the advantage you were hoping to gain, but also any hope of securing the kind of reputation you will need to dominate the area.'

He let his comment hang for a moment, watching Erion think over his alternate viewpoint. 'But you have already started the ball rolling and so you must live with the consequences of your actions. Knowing you as I do, I'm sure you will have everything in hand and will not place our business at risk. Now I must go.' He stood up and emptied his glass. Erion stood up too. Shala gathered him into a hug. As he pulled him close, he said softly, 'I hope for your sake that your plan works, Erion. I would hate to see *you* removed from the field of play.'

He felt Erion's shoulders stiffen, then he released him, turned and left, without looking at Erion or saying anything more.

As he left the club, Rama was on hand to open doors for him. Before Shala climbed back into his car, he stopped and spoke to the bodyguard. 'Thank you for your loyalty, Dardan. You are a good man. I have discussed your concerns with Mr Hasani. Do not worry, you were not mentioned. *You* have nothing to worry about, my friend.' He embraced Dardan and got into his car. 'Take me back to Portsmouth. I have business to attend to,' he said to his driver.

29

Raj was home and ready for his night with Husna with twenty minutes to spare. He threw a change of clothes and some toiletries into an overnight bag and headed out. The temperature had dropped as evening set in. He shivered as he left the warmth of his flat and came out onto the street. Excitement had been building in him since he'd got the text message from Husna. A whole night away with her was something he never dreamed would be possible, let alone something she would instigate. He had a spring in his step as he reached the end of the road and crossed The Avenue at the Cowherds Pub. He moved quickly along Southampton Common, between the towering trees, fuelled by an eagerness to see Husna and wanting to fight off the cold. Cutting across the common, he came out of the top end and headed towards Vermont School. They'd arranged to meet at a quiet spot at the end of the road.

Raj didn't have to wait long before he saw the familiar shape of the Mercedes SLK. As it got nearer, he could see Husna's private plate, HU55NA K. He had teased her before about how conspicuous the plate made her car. She had laughed at him and said she wasn't hiding from anyone, which they both knew wasn't true; hiding from Khan was something they'd both become adept at.

She flashed her lights as she got close to him and he waved, bursting with excitement at seeing her and having her to himself. He got into the car and they kissed before saying anything.

'So, where are you taking me?' he asked.

'That's a surprise. Now, put your seatbelt on and let's get out of here.' She shot him a gorgeous smile and he did as he was told, clicking his seatbelt in place and putting his hand on her leg.

She drove out of town to the motorway, then headed west. Before long they were chatting and laughing, like a couple who had been together for years. Raj flicked through the radio channels and found an eighties pop channel. The sound of Rick Astley immediately filled the car and they took turns singing lines from 'Never Gonna Give You Up'.

'You're too young to remember this, aren't you?' Husna teased.

'You can never be too young for a classic,' Raj replied with a grin. Husna drove the SLK along the M27 until it became the

A31, and as they passed the services she took a left into the New Forest.

'Out in the forest? Where are we going?'

'I've told you it's a surprise, but I guarantee you'll love it.'

Dark was drawing around them, and outside the New Forest started to take on an imposing feel. Heavy clouds blanketed the sky and made the evening even darker, with no stars or moon breaking through. The silhouettes of trees loomed on the dark horizon and they turned right at a lovely-looking pub called the Swan Inn, heading deeper into the forest.

Suddenly a BMW X5 sped out of the pub car park, roared past them, cut sharply in front of the SLK, then shot off into the distance. Husna flashed her headlights repeatedly at the car.

'Bloody idiot! How close does he want to get?'

'The road can't have been wide enough for his big man's wheels,' said Raj, trying to take the edge off. Husna looked at him and smiled.

'Sorry – a bit too road-ragey?'

'Maybe a touch.'

He squeezed her naked thigh. She put her hand on top of his and moved it further up her leg and under her dress. Then she winked at him and floored the Mercedes along the dark, tree-lined road. Raj loved the feeling of speed, mixed with the danger of what they were doing. As Husna sped around a long, sweeping, bend, a car came towards them, full beams glaring at them. Husna flashed her lights, signalling for the driver to dip their lights. Raj was stroking her inner thigh as she drove. He glanced up at the oncoming car.

'Damn, they're bright,' he said, shielding his eyes with his free hand.

'I know – the road's full of idiots tonight.' Husna flashed again. Raj looked over at the dashboard. She was doing just over eighty. The lights got closer, still on full beam and moving fast.

'What the fuck is wrong with this bloke?' said Husna, flashing repeatedly. 'Fuck it!' She turned her full beams on. As the car got closer, Raj realised that it was in the middle of the road. Husna saw it at the same time and moved over, still doing well over eighty. Suddenly the car swerved onto their side of the road.

'Husna!' Raj screamed, but it was too late. She'd jerked the wheel to the left to avoid colliding with the oncoming car. They careered off the road, getting faster and faster. She lost control of the car as it slid on the grass. It leapt off the verge and into the trees. Raj braced himself against the roof of the car and Husna screamed. In what felt like slow motion, the car tipped and flipped forward, end over end, until it smashed into a tree. With a sickening crunch of metal, it stopped dead. Airbags exploded all over the car.

Raj looked to his right. Husna was motionless, her bloody face resting on a deflated airbag. The side of the car was pressing in against his left leg and he felt the warm ooze of blood seeping down his thigh. He couldn't move, held tightly in place by his seatbelt, which had locked on impact. His ears were ringing and his head pounding. He knew he had to get free and check on Husna.

'Husna! Husna! Can you hear me?'

Nothing. She gave no response at all. He pushed the airbags out of the way and struggled to unclip his seatbelt. As he did so, he realised that the car had hit a tree and was lying at an angle. The roof and his side of the car were caved in from the impact.

'Husna! Oh shit! What the fuck?' He began to panic and hot tears filled his eyes.

'Husna, answer me, please!'

Still nothing.

He managed to get his seatbelt undone, flicked the interior light on and then held on to the steering wheel while he reached across to Husna. He turned her head slowly towards him. Her face was covered in cuts, her eyes were closed, and she put up no resistance to him turning her head.

'Think, Raj, think,' he said desperately, fighting off tears. As he moved, he felt a searing pain in his ribs.

'Oh fuck!'

He ran his hand down the side of his left leg. When he held up his hand, he could see blood. He knew he had to get them both out of there. He held his bloody hand in front of Husna's face, and felt the weakest breath against his palm.

Thank God, she's alive, he thought. *Right, I've got to get us the fuck out of here before the police come.*

He knew he couldn't afford to be found with Khan's wife, otherwise he might as well have died in the crash. The he remembered that Khan had told him, when he started running the supplier network, that if any of the boys got injured – by which he meant stabbed or shot – Raj was to call a private ambulance. 'No NHS or A and E visits,' he remembered Inzamam saying. 'Our boys go direct to our own doctors.' Khan had given Raj the number and told him it was a completely confidential service.

Raj fished his phone out of his pocket, and was relieved to see it was still working. His hand hurt like hell, but he opened the phone and scrolled through his contacts until he found NOT NHS. He pressed call. Within seconds, the call was answered.

'Hello, this is Lisa. How can I help you, Mr Gadhi?' asked a woman with a cheerful northern accent.

'Er...' he stuttered, freaked out by his name being used without him giving it. 'Er, I've been in a car accident and I need an ambulance.'

'No problem, sir, just let me ask a couple of questions. Are you alone?'

'Er, no, there's two of us.'

'Is the other person conscious and breathing?'

'No, she's unconscious, but she is breathing.'

'Is there any serious bleeding?'

'Her face is covered in blood.'

'Is the blood spurting, or gushing?'

'No, she's just covered in blood.'

'Can you confirm your number for me in case we get cut off?'

Raj read out his number to Lisa.

'Where are you?'

'I'm not sure – somewhere in the New Forest.'

'Can you see anything from where you are?'

'No, we swerved off the road and hit a tree.'

'Have you passed any landmarks?'

'Yes, we turned right at the Swan Inn, heading into the forest.'

'From which direction?'

'We came from the M27 and headed into the New Forest.'

'Have you got the what3words app on your phone?'

'No, why would I have that?' Raj glanced across at Husna. She still wasn't moving. He bit his lip and his chin began to quiver.

'Don't worry. Can you download it? It will help us pinpoint your location.'

'OK, hold on – let me download it.' Raj located what3words in the app store and
downloaded it.

'OK, I've got it, now what?'

'Open the app and let me know what three words are at the top of the screen for your location.'

Raj watched the blue dot move around the screen and land in the centre of the white box. The words that were displayed at the top of the screen were: slug, brands, arts. Raj relayed these to Lisa and she told him that help was on the way.

'What is the patient's name?'

'Er…' He hesitated, not wanting to disclose Husna's true identity to the call handler.

'I really need to know who they are so we can get them the right help.'

He decided that not telling Lisa could result in Husna dying, so blurted her name out. 'It's Husna Khan – her name is Husna Khan.'

'Can you spell that for me, please?'

He spelled the name out. Still, Husna hadn't moved. He couldn't help wondering fearfully what Inzamam would do when he found out. He would be dead for sure.

'Can you give me Husna's date of birth, please?'

'No, I don't know that,' he said, feeling foolish.

'It doesn't matter. Can you tell me how old Husna is?'

'Er … she's about thirty-seven, I think.'

'Do you know whether she has any underlying medical conditions, or if she's on any medication?'

'No! I haven't got a clue! Where's this fucking ambulance?' he shouted, shooting another glance out into the night, searching for any sign of help.

'Me asking you any these questions isn't delaying the ambulance – it's already been requested and is on its way. I'm just trying to get as much information for them as possible before they get to you.' There was a brief pause, then Lisa asked him, 'Have you got any injuries?'

'What? Er, yes, I've got a cut on my leg and my ribs hurt.'

'Is the cut on your leg gushing or spurting blood?'

'It's not gushing, but it's bleeding a lot.'

'Where on your leg is the cut?'

'It's on my left thigh.'

'Can you apply pressure to it to stem the bleeding?'

'I can press my hand on it – is that OK?'

'Yes, press as hard as you can, to try and stop the bleeding. Can you tell me, is there any change in Husna's condition, Raj?'

'Er, no, I don't think so.' He took short, jerky breaths, struggling to fill his lungs. The air in the car felt as if it was getting heavier, harder to take in.

Raj let out a sigh of relief as he saw an ambulance come into view.

'Husna, Husna, there's someone here – you're going to be OK, please be OK.'

Husna was motionless and silent. He'd checked her breathing just a few seconds earlier and was sure he could still feel the faint warmth against his hand. She was slumped forward in her seat, suspended by her seatbelt, the angle of the crashed car and gravity trying their best to pull her forward.

He saw the ambulance pull over. Within seconds the crew were out and heading towards him. A female paramedic pulled Husna's door open. As she did this, Lisa finished off the call with Raj.

'Raj, the ambulance should be with you now. Can you see it?'

'Yes, yes, they're here. Thank you so much.'

'No problem. I'm going to end the call now and leave you with the crew.'

'OK, thank you again.'

Lisa cut the call and Raj turned his attention to the paramedics.

'Raj? I'm Amanda. Can you tell me what happened?'

He explained how they'd been driven off the road by an X5, then how the car had dug into the ground and flipped until it hit the tree against which it now leaned. Amanda was checking Husna as he spoke, and he could hear her partner calling for the fire service.

'Why do you need the fire service?' he asked anxiously.

'We can't get your door open, sweetheart, and we need to get you out and see what injuries you have. You told my colleague on the phone that you'd felt blood on your leg. Can you tell me if it's still bleeding?'

Raj didn't even know they'd tried to open his door. He'd been so focused on Husna and getting help that he'd forgotten about keeping his hand pressed against his leg. He slipped his hand down to his leg. Instantly, he could tell that it had continued to ooze blood while he'd been waiting for help. In the ambulance's bright lights he could see thick, dark red blood on his hand.

'It is still bleeding quite a lot, I think.' His chest heaved as he took in rapid gulps of air.

'OK, Raj, try to stay calm for me. You're doing really well. We'll have you out of here as quickly as we can.'

Raj closed his eyes for a second. His body hurt everywhere, his head was banging, and the lights from the ambulance were too bright. He was snapped back into consciousness as the door on his side of the car was ripped away by the fire service and a voice he recognised as Amanda's partner invaded his thoughts.

'Raj, I'm Dean. We're going to get you out of here soon, buddy, you're doing really well.'

He looked over to his right. 'Where's Husna?'

'She's already on her way to hospital. Try not to worry – let's concentrate on getting you out.'

'But is she OK?' He felt his head swimming.

'My colleagues are looking after Husna. I need you to stay with me.'

Raj turned back towards Dean and tried to focus, but his eyes were blurred and he could hear a ringing in his ears, which was getting louder and louder. His arms started to jerk uncontrollably … and then all went black.

***

In his Portsmouth nightclub, Valmir Shala's mobile phone rang. He picked it up after the first ring.

'It's done, Mr Shala,' said a heavily accented voice. 'There were no witnesses. We were the only two cars on the stretch of road.'

Shala ended the call and placed the phone back on his desk. He swung around in his large chair and, with a smile, asked his bodyguard for a drink.

30

Larry sat in wait across the road from a large detached house in Castleton. He'd driven up there as soon as Inzamam had got them back to Southampton from Brighton. He'd been thinking about what Raj had said about the contact in Brighton, Roman. Larry figured that Inzamam was blinded by the prospect of taking over the drug supply in Brighton and wouldn't pay much attention to Raj, but Larry thought that Raj's assessment of Roman was spot on. He was definitely not to be trusted – a junkie with an unhealthy taste for his own product, as was common.

Having scoped the residence to make sure there was no recording equipment set up, he watched the stone house, unmoving, for well over an hour. It was dark, but the street light about six feet to the left of the gate illuminated the gate and driveway perfectly.

There was no one in. The lights all over the house were off and Larry intended to sit patiently and wait for the owner to return.

While he waited, he fitted the suppressor onto his HK VP9 9mm pistol. He'd been a Glock man for years, but ever since an associate in the same line of work recommended he try the German pistol, he'd been a convert. It was comfortable to grip, accurate, and had a well-weighted trigger. When suppressed and fired, it made a sound like a plastic ruler slapping skin. Another bonus was that it was easy to conceal.

Just as he'd finished attaching the silencer, a blue Porsche pulled into the driveway of the stone house. Larry shot a cautious glance up and down the road, tucked the HK inside his jacket and got out of the car. He darted across the road and tucked himself against the wall that ran in front of the house. He stepped slowly, but casually, across the driveway, shooting a look to his right, checking to see if the home owner had got out of the Porsche. As he looked, the driver's door closed. Larry could clearly see the person he'd been waiting for. He stepped into the drive and spoke to get the man's attention.

'Mr Langra?'

'Yes, can I help you?'

'I hope so. I wondered if you would mind confirming something for me?'

'Oh, what might that be?'

The Asian man shifted his weight from one foot to the other, showing no signs of fear.

'Well, it's a rather delicate matter. Why did you never choose the same girl twice when you visited Arjun Bakshi's brothel of underage girls?'

Langra's eyes flickered, an instant, unmistakable anger that Larry had seen in many a man's eyes over the years. A look that screamed 'how dare you question me?' Larry drew the HK from under his jacket and aimed. There was a noise like a slap, and a perfect red circle appeared directly between Dalir Langra's eyebrows. His knees crumpled and he sank to the ground. Larry returned to his car, took out his phone and opened his notes app. He put a tick in a circle next to Langra's name and threw his phone onto the passenger seat. Then he fired up the engine and headed back towards Southampton.

31

One day earlier

Raj looked around the private hospital room, his eyes wide and awash with pain. His head was groggy and he tried to swing himself out of bed, stopping as soon as he realised he was hooked up to a drip via a cannula in his left hand.

'Nurse! Nurse!'

No one came. He saw a button by his bed and pushed it. In the corridor, a light came on above the window to his room. Raj pulled the sheet back to see that his left leg had been neatly bandaged from his hip down to just above his knee. His neck hurt. He winced as he turned towards the door, hoping to see someone. He pressed the buzzer again, taking in a huge lungful of sterile-tasting air.

A nurse in a light blue uniform opened the door. 'Raj, you're awake, good. I'm Maya. How are you feeling?'

'How long have I been here?'

'A few hours. Now, how are you feeling?'

'A few hours? Oh fuck, really? How's Husna? Have you called Mr Khan?'

'I think one of my colleagues has called Mr Khan. Husna is stable.'

'Stable? What does that mean?'

'It means we're treating her – she was quite badly injured. It would be good for you to try and stay calm, Raj.'

'Has Inzamam arrived yet?'

'Sorry, who?'

'Inzamam – Mr Khan. Is he here yet?' His speech was getting faster and he could feel his pulse throbbing in the side of his head.

'I don't know. Why don't we concentrate on how you're feeling for a minute, Raj? It would be really useful if you could let me know how you feel and let me have a look at your dressings.'

'Never mind how I'm feeling. You don't understand. I need to get out of here before Khan gets here.'

'That's not possible, Raj. Your injuries are going to need time to heal and Mr Johnson, your consultant, hasn't seen you yet.'

'You're not listening to me! I need to get out of here.' He looked at Maya with pleading eyes. Then, over her shoulder, he saw something that made his blood run cold.

Standing in the corridor, looking at Raj through the window of his private room, was Inzamam Khan. He was motionless, a bemused smile on his face. His head was tilted to one side and he was looking straight at Raj. As they made eye contact, Inzamam winked and held a finger to his lips. Then he pressed his hands together, as if he were about to pray, then put them against his cheek, under his tilted head, and closed his eyes for a second. Raj watched, unable to take his eyes off his boss. Khan opened his eyes, waved, smiled, then turned and walked away, disappearing from view.

Raj's mind flew into overdrive. A million scattered thoughts fought for space in his head, each one shouting louder than the next, so loud that he could see Maya's mouth moving but couldn't hear what she was saying.

I need to get out of here.

What the fuck is he going to do to me? He's going to fucking kill me for sure.

I'm fucked, absolutely fucked. It's over – my life is over.

He's never going to let me out of here alive. What the fuck am I going to do?

Think, Raj, think!

He tried to calm himself by taking deep breaths. It didn't work. He couldn't hear his own breathing over his panicked thoughts. He closed his eyes and pressed his hands to the sides of his head, feeling the cannula tug as he moved.

Breathe, Raj, breathe.

He filled his lungs twice, keeping his hands pressed hard against his head. Three breaths, then four. With each breath, the volume of the commentary inside his head turned down a notch and he felt himself coming back into focus. He looked Maya square in the eye. 'Maya, is it?'

'Yes.'

'Maya, I really need to get out of here. I'm sure you know that some of the people who use this hospital would rather not end up in a normal hospital. Yes?'

'Er, I guess so.'

'Believe me, they don't. When they come in here with their gunshot or stab wounds, do they ever have the police following them in?'

'No, they don't.'

He sensed he was getting somewhere, so he carried on. 'That's because if they did, they would be leaving here in handcuffs and they know it. Now, I'm not saying I'm a good man, Maya – in fact, I've done some things I'm really not proud of. But if I stay in this bed, I'm going to be killed – right here.'

The look on Maya's face reassured Raj that she understood. He smiled at her and held out his hand. 'Look, I know this puts you in a difficult position and I wouldn't ask if there was any other way, but I need you to help me get up and get out of here. Please. Can you do that?' He looked at her, unflinching, and she held his gaze, clearly considering his request. She reached out and took his hand.

'OK, but we'll need to be quick. I can't risk getting caught – I really need this job.'

'Thank you so much. I don't want you to get into any trouble. If I get caught I won't let anyone know you've helped me, I promise. I just need help getting out of the hospital.'

She smiled warmly at him and removed his drip, then started to help him out of bed. His leg was agony whenever he tried to move it. He winced with pain.

'You're not going to be able to walk out of here. I'll get you a wheelchair,' said Maya.

Raj thought about it for a moment. What if Khan saw him leaving the hospital in a wheelchair? He'd never be able to get away. He'd be dead for sure. But what choice did he have? He couldn't walk, and he absolutely needed to get out of there. Raj nodded at Maya and sat on the edge of his bed. She helped him get dressed into a set of hospital whites. They were baggy and slipped easily over his dressings.

'Right, wait here. I'll go and get a chair.'

Maya hurried out of the room, leaving Raj perched on the edge of his bed, feeling vulnerable. His eyes darted between the window and the door. He hoped Khan wouldn't return. His thoughts turned briefly to where he would go, but he decided instead to concentrate on getting out first. He'd worry about where he might go afterwards. Maya came back pushing a wheelchair, her cheeks red as she hurried through the door.

'We need to get you out of here quickly. There's no one out on the ward at the moment, but my colleagues will be back soon and then we'll never get you out. They all know you should be on bed rest and most of them have seen you since you came in.'

Raj managed to transfer himself from the bed to the chair. Maya placed a bag of his personal belongings on his lap and they headed for the door.

***

The door swung back against its hinges and Maya pushed Raj cautiously out into the corridor. Her heart was racing. She had always been the kind of person who followed the rules and didn't buck the system. She lived on her own with two cats, Bilbo and Jingles, and had little time for anything that messed with her nice, well-ordered life. At twenty-eight, she'd been qualified for about four years and loved being a nurse. It gave her a sense of purpose that her disastrous love life had never managed to match. She was average height and build, with unremarkable features. Her mousey-brown hair was tied up, out of the way, as it was most of the time. She had no patience for putting on a face of make-up before work and shaved her legs when she could be bothered – a habit that her mother frequently joked would keep her single for longer. Maya was, however, a true people person and cared deeply for the well-being of others. That was why nursing suited her so well.

What the hell are you doing, Maya? You don't even know this man. She had no clue why she'd felt compelled to help Raj. Maybe it was the terror she'd seen in his eyes, his panicked breathing and tangible air of helplessness. Whatever it was, she knew that if she got caught, regardless of Raj promising that he wouldn't say she'd helped him, she would be in deep trouble.

That was also without Mr Khan finding out she'd helped Raj. She was well aware that some of their clients were criminals. She'd seen more stab wounds and gunshot wounds than any of her friends who nursed in general hospitals, and they'd seen enough. Until Raj had pointed it out, she'd never thought about the fact that the police never turned up to interview any of her patients. She just got on with her job of nursing them back to health, or making them comfortable until they died, without questioning things.

Yet here she was, not only cutting short someone's treatment, but also conspiring to getting them out of hospital. She turned the chair right out of Raj's room and pushed him hastily down the hall. It was the longest way to get to the lift, but the nursing station was to the left on the quicker route, so that way was out of the question. She gripped the handles of the wheelchair and pushed much more speedily than she would normally. At the lift, Maya prodded the call button repeatedly, as if doing so would make the lift appear more quickly. A familiar ping marked its arrival and Maya held her breath. She let out a heavy sigh as the door opened to reveal an empty lift. She patted Raj on the shoulder and hurried into the lift, pushing the button for the basement that led to the staff car park. Maya had decided, as she had been getting Raj a set of patient whites, that if she was in for a penny, she was in for a pound. Knowing Raj had no way of getting away from the hospital, even if she got him as far as the door, she had decided to drive him to wherever he needed to go.

The lift descended quickly from the third floor. As number one illuminated on the panel, the lift stopped and the door opened.

Maya held her breath and her stomach flipped. A porter she didn't recognise nodded at her, then said hello to Raj. Raj replied. Maya knew that she couldn't manage even a simple hello without being sick, so she just nodded in response. The porter got out one floor down; luckily, no one got in. Maya pressed frantically at the close doors button and saw Raj looking at her.

'Why are we going to the basement?'

'That's where the car park is. My car is there and I can get you out of here.'

'I can't ask you to do that! You've done enough for me already.'

'OK, so tell me, how else *are* you going to get away from the hospital?' she asked. Raj looked embarrassed and she instantly felt bad for being so blunt. 'I'm sorry, I didn't mean to snap, but I've never done anything like this before and I'm pretty scared right now.'

'Just get me into the car park and I'll work it out,' said Raj.

'No, I've already decided I'm going to put you in the back of my car. There's a throw in the back that can go over you while I drive us out.'

'But what about your shift?'

'I'll phone and say I've been sick, and couldn't find anyone to tell that I needed to go home. It'll be fine. I'm never ill, so they won't question me. There's been a bug going round.'

Raj nodded. 'Only if you're sure?'

'I'm not, so if I were you I wouldn't go on about it too much, or I might change my mind and leave you in the lift.'

She smiled at him and he let out a small chuckle, then winced.

At the basement, Maya pushed Raj out into the concrete car park. She parked the wheelchair at the side of a blue Ford Fiesta and pressed the key. The car unlocked and she yanked the rear door open.

'Can you get yourself in, or do you need help?'

'No, I think I can do it.' He shuffled to the edge of the wheelchair and pushed his right foot onto the floor, swinging into the back of the car. Maya went to the boot and got out a tartan throw.

'Right, lie down across the seat and pull this over you.' She draped the throw over Raj and shut the door.

Jumping in and starting the engine, she cast a glance around the car park. She couldn't see anyone, but she knew there were cameras. She just hoped that her disappearance didn't make her manager want to check the CCTV. She had no idea how she would explain her actions.

'OK, lie still, here we go.'

She dropped the Fiesta into gear and headed for the out-ramp. Her stomach was still churning but she also felt excited; she'd never done anything remotely risky, not even thrown a sickie, and here she was helping a man she'd never met escape from someone he said would kill him. She didn't know where she was driving as she left the hospital, but decided on instinct to head east. She grabbed a half-empty bottle of water out of the door pocket and glugged it, until the plastic crackled in protest, then passed it between the seats.

'Raj, it's OK, you can sit up now. Here, have some water. You must be really thirsty – we need to keep you as relaxed and hydrated as we can. I'm also going to have to get you some pain relief or you'll be in a lot of pain.'

Raj threw the cover off and took the bottle from her. He took a long drink, nearly finishing the bottle. He looked at her in the rear-view mirror. She thought he had kind eyes.

'Where are we?'

'We're heading out of Bournemouth but, if I'm honest, I have no idea where I'm going.'

'I'm not sure who I can trust at the moment. I need to make some calls.'

'What direction would you like me to go?'

'Er, can you head towards the M3? Once we get on there I'll work out how far we need to go to be safe. Then you can drop me off and be rid of me.'

His last sentence deflated her a little, although she didn't know why.

'It's fine. I don't have anywhere I need to be – just let me know where to take you.' As the words escaped from her mouth, she bit her bottom lip, as if trying to stop any more words making their way out without permission. They drove on in silence for a while until they joined the M3.

'We're on the M3. Where would you like to go?'

'Let's head to Winchester. I know some people I can trust who live on the outskirts of the city, and I think they'll be around. Is that OK?'

'Yes, of course. Do you know where in Winchester? I don't know my way around there very well.'

'I'll direct you when we get closer. I can never remember which junction to get off at until I see it.'

'No problem, why don't you try and relax a little? Your injuries are quite bad and you need to get as much rest as you can or you're going to feel wiped out.'

Raj rolled the throw and tucked it under his head, against the window. He closed his eyes. She turned her attention back to the road, still unsure why she was doing what she was, but getting a buzz from the spontaneity of her actions.

As she approached the first Winchester junction she felt a pang of guilt for disturbing Raj, who was snoring softly.

'Raj, Raj, we've nearly got to the first Winchester turning. Is this the one?'

He sat up and rubbed his eyes. 'Yes, this is the one. Get off here and head towards Twyford. I'm just going to make a quick call and get somebody to meet us.'

She did as he asked and left the motorway. Raj made a hurried call to someone called Tom. He arranged to meet at a pub called the Phoenix in Twyford, and hung up. Suddenly she felt a cool breeze waft through the car as Raj opened his window. He launched his mobile phone out into the trees they were driving past. She made eye contact with him as he closed the window.

'My phone can be traced, and I don't want anyone knowing where we've headed. Tom will meet us at the pub and he'll have another phone for me. When we get there, just drop me off and leave me there. You've done enough and I really appreciate it. I can't thank you enough, and I don't want you getting caught up in what I've got going on.'

'It's nothing,' she heard herself saying. 'I don't mind. Where are you going to go when you've got your new phone?'

'I'm not sure yet. I'm going to see if Tom can get me to my place so I can pick up some bits, then I'll need to get out of Southampton before Khan gets back.'

'I can take you – honestly, it's fine. I've got nothing else planned and I haven't done anything this exciting – well, ever.' She smiled, embarrassed. Raj smiled back. She could see him working through his options, silently weighing up what he was going to do next. She still couldn't quite believe that she was mixed up in this — but after skipping out of work and smuggling Raj out of the hospital — she was already involved, so why not see it through? Whatever *it* was.

They pulled into the car park of the Phoenix Inn in Twyford, an olde-worlde pub that sat on the main road through the pretty Hampshire village. The car park was deserted but for a dark-blue Ford Mondeo.

'That's Tom – pull up alongside him, would you? I'm not sure me getting out is the best plan.'

She did as requested and parked beside the blue car, Raj closest to the driver. Raj pushed the window switch and Tom, a smartly dressed guy with cropped dark hair, who was younger than Maya had expected, put his window down too.

'You OK, mate?' Tom spoke first.

'No, I'm pretty fucked if I'm honest.'

'Anything I can help with?'

'You're helping plenty, mate, if you've got me a clean phone?'

Tom extended his arm out of his window and handed Raj a small box.

'As requested – clean as you like. In fact, brand new, never been registered. The SIM is activated for a pay-as-you-go and topped up. It should last you a while.'

'You're a star. Not a word to anyone, not even our mates, OK? I need to disappear for a bit. I'm not sure how long for.'

'Jesus, you must really be in the shit.'

'Honestly, you have no idea.'

'You going to introduce me to your friend?' Tom grinned.

'No, now fuck off and remember you haven't seen me.' Raj laughed and wound his window up, flicking Tom the finger as he did. Tom grinned some more and started his car.

'Right, before we go anywhere, I need to know if you're really OK with taking me any further. You don't know me, you don't owe me anything, and I'm involved in some really dangerous stuff and don't want you to get hurt. If you say you're out, that's fine. I've got people I can call to come and get me.'

She thought for a moment, but she was sure that she wanted to carry on and take him where he was going next. 'No, really, I'm fine. So where to?'

'OK. Thank you again. You have no idea how much you're saving me right now. We need to go somewhere I can get some normal clothes – I can't spend the rest of the day in these.' He pulled at his top. 'I know just the place.'

She started the car and spun it around to face the road.

32

Inzamam took Husna's hand as he heard the door to her room open. He turned to look at the doctor who had entered.

'Mr Khan, how are you doing? You must be tired. Why don't you try and get some sleep? I think it may be a while before your wife regains consciousness.'

'Thank you, doctor, but I'm fine. I wouldn't want her to wake up and me not be here.'

'I understand. Stay as long as you like.' The doctor checked Husna's charts then pulled her eyelids up and shone a light into her eyes. This got no reaction, just like the previous times they'd done it.

'I'll check in again in a while. Can we get you anything, Mr Khan? A cup of tea, maybe?'

'That's very kind, thank you.'

'No problem. I'll ask someone to get you one.'

And then he was gone. As the door closed, Inzamam dropped Husna's hand, as if it was a broken toy, onto the bed beside her unmoving body. He took his phone out of his pocket and dialled Raj's number. Straight to voicemail – again.

His brain had been spinning ever since he'd got the call to say that Husna had been involved in a car accident. The caller had told him, 'Both the occupants of the car are on the way to hospital.'

'Both?' he'd asked.

'Yes, Mr Khan – your wife and a Mr Raj Gadhi. He called us from the car. They're on their way to hospital now.'

Khan had thanked the caller without reacting but, once he'd ended the call, his imagination had gone to work, spitting out one theory after another. Why would his faithful lieutenant be with his wife? And why had they been heading into the New Forest together, at night, when the accident happened, when Husna had meant to be away on business?

As he'd packed a bag for Husna, he had decided to see Raj as soon as he'd found out how Husna was. He also decided not to tell his girls, Kamila and Muna, straight away. Instead he called his mother, let her know about Husna and asked her to go over to the house and check on his daughters to make sure they didn't suspect anything was wrong. She had sounded shocked and worried, but agreed to his request.

Once at the hospital, he'd immediately gone into concerned husband and boss mode, wanting to know everything the medics could tell him about Husna and Raj and their respective conditions. One of the benefits of buying the kind of service Khan, and others like him, bought from the hospital, was that the senior clinicians were much more honest about the extent of injuries and chances of survival than their general hospital colleagues. Khan paid well to make sure that reports weren't filed in the normal way and police weren't informed as soon as they might be in a normal hospital setting. When Ray had first told him about this service and where to find it, he'd been amazed by what you could find, once you accessed the dark-web.

During his chat with the medics he'd also managed to find out that Husna had been unconscious at the scene and Raj had stayed pretty much conscious all along, only passing out briefly.

He hadn't been prepared for seeing Husna rigged up to all manner of medical equipment, and still unconscious. He found himself staring at her from the doorway, unable to look away, but unable to go in. Once he'd satisfied himself that she wasn't going to suddenly come round, he'd gone to Raj's room. He had decided there was a strong possibility that Husna and Raj had been having some kind of affair, as he couldn't think of a business-related reason why they would be together – or why they would be in the New Forest. The penalty for such a betrayal was clear to Inzamam. He would make Husna suffer – once he'd got a confession out of her. The only things he hadn't decided were how swiftly he'd deal with Raj, or how long he'd make Husna suffer, but suffer she would.

Bubbling with controlled rage, he made his way to Raj's room. When he reached the window to Raj's private room, he could see a nurse tending to him. Inzamam stood for a moment, watching intently, until he caught Raj's eye. A look of fear crossed Raj's face instantly. Then, without giving it much thought, Khan had motioned to Raj to be quiet and to rest. Once he was satisfied he'd intimidated his young apprentice enough, he turned and walked slowly back to Husna's bedside. There would be plenty of time to deal with Raj, he wasn't going anywhere.

The monitors Husna was hooked up to beeped and numbers flashed across their screens as Inzamam sat by her side. He looked at her lying there, quiet and helpless, and felt complete disdain for her. How could she betray him in such a way? She was the woman he had shared everything with, the woman who had mothered his children. He knew he hadn't been a saint, but he expected more from Husna. She'd always been the morally superior of them, stayed away from all his business dealings, putting the safety of their girls first. On top of this, here she was, lying in a hospital bed, unable to explain why she had been heading into the forest with Raj. The more he thought about it, the more angry he became – and the more he wanted to make someone pay.

He stood up from the bedside chair just as a nurse came in clicking a pen open. He pushed past her and stalked down the corridor to Raj's room. Nurse or no nurse, he was going in this time, and he was going to find out what had been going on between them, even if he had to beat it out of Raj.

As he got near Raj's room he could hear raised voices. Three nurses stood in the corridor, he parted them with the backs of his hands and walked between them.

'He was here the last time I walked the ward,' he heard one nurse say. He got to the window he'd watched Raj from earlier. But this time, when he looked through the window, instead of seeing Raj, all he saw were puzzled medical staff and an empty bed. He burst in through the door.

'Mr Khan?' said a surprised doctor.

'Where is he?' demanded Inzamam.

'Er, we're not sure.'

'He's in no state to be out, is he?' Khan added quickly, remembering his role as concerned boss.

'No, he was pretty badly injured and shouldn't be up and about. If I'm honest, I'm surprised he managed to get out of bed,' replied the same doctor who had come in to check on Husna.

'What makes you say that?'

'He had a drip in, and his leg was badly injured. I'm not sure he could have walked out of here without anyone noticing.'

'So, he had help. Is that what you're saying?'

'Yes, I suppose I am.' The doctor turned to the nurse in charge. 'Where are all your staff, Mary?'

'They're all on the ward, with patients … except…'

'Except what?'

'Except Maya. She called a little while ago to say she'd been sick and had needed to go home.'

'How long ago was that?' asked Khan.

'Within the last hour.'

'And how long is it since anyone saw Raj or your nurse?' He took over.

'I don't know, but Maya was the nurse who was supporting Raj earlier, so it's quite possible that she was with him most recently.'

'Is there any way of knowing when Maya left the hospital?'

'Yes – security will be able to track her fob through the door system,' said a support worker, who hadn't spoken so far.

'That's great, thank you. Can you do that? I'm really worried about Raj and want to make sure he doesn't make his injuries any worse,' Inzamam lied.

'Of course, Mr Khan, we'll do it straight away,' replied the doctor.

The hospital ward turned into a frenzied hive of activity. Inzamam watched as people hurried around contacting security and checking every room on the ward, including cleaning cupboards and toilets. He heard staff say that they'd checked the staff changing rooms and break room and had even sent someone down to the canteen to see if either Maya or Raj had gone down there for something to eat. All their checks produced nothing until a member of the security team came up to the nursing station, where Inzamam had decided he was going to stand, despite the nursing staff trying to get him to go back to Husna, as he had a commanding view from there and could hear everything that was being said.

'Mary, I've checked the door system and the CCTV. It shows that Maya went down to the parking garage – and she was pushing someone in a wheelchair.'

'Thank you, Bill.' Mary smiled at the security guard, who turned to leave.

Heath Gunn

'Excuse me, Bill, but did you see where they went when they got to the garage?'

Khan asked, not wanting to let the security guard leave. Bill looked at Mary.

'It's OK, Bill. Mr Khan is the patient's employer; he's quite concerned about him.'

'Oh, OK. Yes, they got in her car and drove out of the garage and turned left, but I don't know where they went after that. Our cameras only go to the corners of the hospital, and I can't see past the end of the road,' Bill said helpfully.

'Thank you, Bill, that's great,' said Mary, clearly closing the conversation down. Inzamam figured she was doing that to stop him questioning Bill further. 'Mr Khan, please leave it with us. We'll get hold of Maya and find out what's happening and we will ensure that she brings Mr Gadhi back to the hospital.'

'Yes, of course, thank you. It's such a worry. Raj doesn't have much in the way of family,' said Khan.

'I'll let you know the minute we get hold of them.' Mary turned away from Khan, and he knew the conversation was over. He left the nursing station and headed away, as if going back to Husna's bedside, but instead, when he reached a turn in the corridor he ducked into a stairwell. He made his way down a level then asked a passing medic where he could find the security office. The medic helpfully directed Khan towards the lower floors of the hospital, and Khan set off in search of Bill.

It didn't take him long to locate the helpful security guard, and even less time to bribe Bill to let him look at the CCTV footage. As Bill proudly guided Inzamam through the recording, he pointed out when the nurse they'd called Maya entered the garage, pushing Raj. He followed them with his finger across the screen, as if Inzamam couldn't see for himself. Khan smiled politely and watched as the pair made their way to a small car.

'Bill, does your system have zoom capability?'

'It does indeed – let me show you.'

Bill zoomed the image in on the pair and held it steady until they got into the car and moved off. Then Khan asked him to pause it while he took a photo of the screen, which showed a Ford Fiesta and a clear registration number. Bill switched the view to an outside camera and fast-forwarded to where the Fiesta drove past and went out of sight.

Inzamam passed Bill five £20 notes and patted him gratefully on the back. 'You're a legend, Bill – thank you.'

'No problem, Mr Khan. You didn't see anything here.' He winked as he slipped the folded cash into his breast pocket.

'See what?' Khan grinned and left the security office.

Inzamam bypassed the lift, which would have taken him back to his unconscious wife's bedside. Instead he headed straight for the car park and his Range Rover. As he jumped in and fired the engine into life, Inzamam knew what call he needed to make. As soon as his phone was paired, he commanded it to call Lawrence.

He answered within a couple of rings, and Inzamam launched into a rant.

'Lawrence, that little shit Raj has been fucking my wife! My fucking wife! Can you believe it? The fucking gall of him. I give him everything – a career, an income, watch his fucking back and offer him a cut of the business in Southampton – and he repays me by screwing Husna. The disrespectful little fucker!'

There was a pause before Lawrence answered. 'No, I'm not sure I do believe it, Inzamam. Are you sure?'

'Am I sure? They've been in a car crash in the New Forest in Husna's Merc. Both hospitalised and now Raj fucking Gadhi has done a runner, aided by a nurse. So, am I one hundred per cent sure? No, but the evidence looks pretty fucking damning, wouldn't you say?'

Again, he heard Lawrence take a deep breath before replying. That annoyed the hell out of Inzamam.

'It certainly sounds incriminating, but if you don't know for definite, shouldn't you find out first?'

'Why the hell do you think I'm calling you?'

'OK, what would you like me to do?'

'I'd like you to find out what the fuck they've been up to. The pair of treacherous bastards. Then I'll decide what to do with him. She's still unconscious, so at the moment I can't do anything with her.'

'Husna's unconscious? And where are you? You sound like you're driving, which probably isn't the best idea.'

'Yes, she's been out of it since they brought her in. Lucky they called me, or I wouldn't have known anything.'

'And where are you heading?'

'I'm going home to see my girls. I need to work out how to tell them that their mother has been in a car crash while out in her car with another man. Any suggestions?' Rage boiled inside him –

at their betrayal, the lies, the deceit. He hung up, not wanting to hear whatever Lawrence was about to suggest.

He floored the Range Rover and sped along the dual carriageway out of Bournemouth towards Southampton, ignoring the speed camera signs. His mind was spinning with thoughts of Husna and Raj together heading into the New Forest, laughing and chatting, the way *he* used to do with her.

He threw the 4×4 onto the motorway and headed for home, with no idea what he was going to say to his girls.

33

What the hell have you been up to, Raj? You dumb fucker, Larry thought as he made a couple of rounds of toast and marmalade, golden brown, with a scraping of butter.

As he chomped his way through his toast, unconcerned by Inzamam hanging up on him, he called Raj's number. Predictably, it went straight to voicemail. *Good lad,* he thought, pleased that at least some of what he'd taught Raj had stuck.

He had taken Raj under his wing over the last year or so, seeing a potential in the youngster that Inzamam seemed to ignore. Larry saw a young, eager mind that would soak up learning and new experiences as fast as anyone could throw them at him. He didn't need to be shown or told anything more than once, and he grasped the subtleties of intimidation and manipulation more quickly than anyone Larry had come across.

So, you've ditched your phone and talked a nurse into helping you get out of hospital and away from Khan. Smart boy. But it's not going to get you far if you can't disappear properly, so what are you going to do next? You're going to need money, clothes, food, somewhere to go and a way of getting there, although you may have got the transport bit sorted with your nurse helper. You're going to need a phone too. But who will you call?

Larry finished his toast, grabbed his phone, wallet and keys and headed for the door. He had a hunch about where Raj might have gone – at the very least for a phone, if not for more help in getting away, which he was bright enough to know he had to do.

After half an hour and making a few phone calls, Larry's hunch had been confirmed. A guy called Tom was one of Raj's oldest friends. His official occupation was a mobile phone salesman, but Larry remembered Raj telling him that Tom was one of those 'handy to know' guys, who could get their hands on pretty-much anything. Larry knew that Tom had helped Raj source some high-end tech gear for the cutting lab, at prices that Inzamam had talked about for ages, as they were so cheap. He was pretty sure it was Tom that Raj would have gone to for help.

A little later Larry parked behind a dark-blue Ford Mondeo. He waited for a couple of minutes and a smartly dressed young guy in a blue suit and open-collared white shirt came out of a quaint cottage. Larry lowered the window as the man approached.

'Tom, thanks for agreeing to meet me.'

'That's alright, I know who you are. Didn't think it was very clever to say no, if I'm honest.'

'Fair enough. Well, thank you, anyway. Can you tell me when you saw Raj and what he wanted? He's in a lot of trouble and I want to help him.'

'Really?'

'Yes, really. Look, I can understand that you probably don't believe me, especially if you know who I am. But I do want to help him and if I don't get to him before his employer does, he's dead. You know it, and I know it.'

He sat while Tom thought through what he'd said. Then, unexpectedly, Tom turned to his left and looked for a moment as if he was going to walk away. Instead he walked around the back of Larry's car to the passenger door. Larry unlocked the doors and Tom got in.

'I'm coming with you. It's the only way I'll know you're not going to kill him.'

'If I did, what makes you so sure I won't kill you too?'

'I dunno, but I'm fucked if I'm going to let you kill my mate without a fight, so you're stuck with me for now. Besides, you don't know where he's gone, but I do, and I'm not going to tell you unless you take me with you.'

Larry smiled, impressed that Raj could inspire such unconditional loyalty from a friend – something he knew Khan couldn't do.

'OK, let's do it. You can come along for the ride. But just to be clear, if you get in my way, I won't hesitate to take you out.'

'Understood.' The young man nodded at him and reached for his seatbelt. Larry started the car.

'So, where to?'

'I don't know yet, but I've got a couple of ideas. Let me do a bit of googling and I'll let you know, but it'll be Southampton way.'

Larry smiled again. 'OK. I'll start driving. You let me know where we're headed, but if you fuck me about they'll find you dead at the side of the road.'

'Understood.'

34

Raj woke with a start as Maya switched off the car engine at the end of the road where he'd directed her to go. Exhaustion brought on by the day's events had overtaken him and forced him into an uncomfortable slumber.

'We're here, wherever here is,' said Maya. Raj rubbed his eyes and winced, as the pain came flooding back.

'Great, this is the road where my cousin lives, but we've got to be really careful. Some of Khan's crew know where this is, and if they think quickly enough about all the places I might go, they'll head here. Hopefully this is far enough down anyone's list for them not to be here yet.'

'What if it's not?'

'I'll know when you drive down the road whether anyone is here. There are some regulars that should be around, and if there's any chance of any beef, they'll have moved somewhere they can get a decent view.'

'Ah, I see. I think.'

'Don't worry – just drive a bit slower than you would normally, but not at a crawl, or you'll attract the wrong kind of attention.'

'So, slow but not too slow.'

'I know it sounds weird, but trust me, too slow and you'll have kids coming out of dark corners trying to sell you drugs.'

Raj sat back and Maya set off down the long road, flanked by terraced houses. As Maya kept the Fiesta at a nice steady pace, Raj looked to see if the people he expected to see were out on the rundown street. They were youths he'd either known through his cousin, or their own network of dealers. If all was quiet they would be hanging out in their usual spots, if not, they'd have disappeared.

As they got towards the bottom of the road, a gang of kids who looked to be in their early teens, wearing hoodies and baseball caps, had gathered not far from a shop on the street corner, with crates of fresh fruit outside. Raj had seen enough and ducked down.

'At the end of the road, can you go right and first right again into an alleyway?' Maya looked at him in the rear-view mirror, biting her bottom lip.

'It's OK – my cousin's not part of all this, he's just someone who's safe. I can go to him to get clothes and stuff. We'll be out of here before you know it. Unless of course you want to drop me off, which I would totally understand.'

'No, I'll sit in the car and wait, if that's OK?'

'Yeah, sure. Can you park here behind these houses?' It was quiet, which Raj liked. He needed to be in and out as quickly as he could. If he hung around too long, he knew that Khan or one of their crew would track him down.

Raj opened the rear door and shuffled to the edge of the seat.

'Are you going to be OK?' asked Maya.

'I think so. Are you?'

'I think so,' she said with a smile.

He pushed up onto his feet and took a moment to steady himself. Pain shot through his left leg and for a second he thought it was going to buckle underneath him. It was only a few steps to the gate at the back of his auntie's house, and with determined effort he made it. He was relieved to find that it wasn't locked. He flicked the latch and, with a glance back at Maya, he went into the garden.

He could see his auntie, Sarbjit, through the kitchen window, cooking, which was the norm. He couldn't remember a time when she wasn't cooking something amazing – and he loved her food. His auntie and uncle, his dad's brother, had brought him up for most of his early childhood; his dad had been working in Dubai and his mum had accompanied him out there. They had left Raj with Sarbjit and Tushar for what was to be six months, and ended up being seven years. He had fond memories of his time with them: the house had always been full of laughter, love and great food.

Sarbjit turned as he got near the door, made eye contact and smiled at him, waving him towards the door. He caught a waft of warm spices drifting out from the kitchen, and he glanced upwards towards his cousin's bedroom window.

'Rajiv!' his aunt greeted him in shrill, excitable tones. She'd always refused to shorten his name, saying that its meaning – which was 'successful' or 'achiever' – was lost if you shortened it.

'Auntie Sarb, how are you?' he said as he limped through the door.

'Rajiv, what has happened to you? Why do you look like you've been beaten up?'

Raj took a moment to gather himself and answer Sarbjit. He could feel pain flowing in waves all over his body. 'I was in a car accident, but it's not as serious as it looks. Don't worry, Auntie. Is Jai in?'

'Hmm, nothing serious, really? I haven't seen a limp like that since you and Jai fell off your BMXs, jumping those home-made ramps.' She shook her head. 'He's upstairs, where he always is. Are you hungry?'

'Thanks, and yes, starving, but…' He paused.

'What is it?' she asked.

'It's just, well, I got a lift here and I have someone waiting in the car.'

'By someone, do you mean a girl?' She smiled.

'Um, yes. Her name's Maya, but she's really shy. Please don't go out to speak to her when I go upstairs to see Jai, Auntie.'

'Oh, OK, you're such a killjoy.'

Raj laughed and headed slowly for the stairs. He stood at the foot of the stairs, looking up, and decided to call his cousin down. Jai appeared at the top of the stairs, with a massive grin on his face at the sight of Raj.

'Come on up, mate.'

'I can't, I've smashed my leg up,' Raj said, shooting a look in the direction of the kitchen. Jai nodded and hurried down to his cousin.

'What's going on, mate?' he asked quietly, leading Raj through to the lounge. Raj followed and was relieved to sit down on the sofa, taking the weight off his leg. Jai knew exactly what Raj did for a living and who he worked for, but Raj knew that Jai had tried to keep himself away from the world that Raj lived in. They'd chatted many times about Raj's intention to work for Khan long enough to have the money to set himself up in a legitimate business. Jai was the only person Raj could trust with that kind of plan.

'It must be pretty bad for you to turn up here in the middle of the day, limping like that. You know Mum's going to ask loads of questions when you've gone, don't you?'

'Yeah, I know. I'm sorry for just turning up, but I really need your help. I'm in deep shit, cuz.'

'Come on, then. Spill.'

'So, I was in a car crash last night. I was run off the road in the New Forest – the car I was in flipped and hit a tree. I spent last night in hospital—'

'And why aren't you still there?'

'Hang on, I'm getting to it. The car I was in was Husna Khan's, and we were on our way to a hotel—'

'Fucking hell, Raj! Are you insane? You're banging Khan's wife?'

'Nicely put, Cuz. Subtle. But in a nutshell, yes. She's still in hospital, but Khan knows. He came to the hospital and looked at me, didn't say a word, just stared at me. I've really fucked up.'

'So how did you get out of hospital and over here?'

'A nurse called Maya got me out of the hospital and drove me here.'

'What? You convinced a nurse to get you out of hospital the day after a car crash, then drive you over here? Fuck off, you're not that persuasive? How much are you paying her? Where is she now?'

'Fuck you. I'm not paying her anything, in fact she offered and when I tried to give her an out, she said no. She's outside in the car.'

Jai sat in silence for a moment, taking in what Raj had told him, shaking his head slowly.

'So what do you need?'

Raj smiled at his cousin. The bond between them had always been strong and he knew he could count on him.

'I need money, clothes and some clippers.'

Heath Gunn

'Clippers? You going to cut your hair? Fuck, you really do need to disappear. Rajiv Gadhi, shaving off his precious locks. This I've got to see.'

'Not *me* cutting my hair, you,' Raj replied.

'Ha ha, even better. Come on then, man, let's do this. What about your nurse friend?'

'What do you mean?'

'I mean, how long are you going to leave her out in the car, alone?'

'I'm not sure she will be alone. I told Auntie she was out there, then asked her not to go out.'

Jai laughed. Raj waited while he popped through to the kitchen, only to report back, grinning, that, as Raj had expected, the back door was open and Sarbjit was not in the kitchen.

'That should buy you half an hour. Right, let's get that mop cut off. I'm going to enjoy this.'

They moved through to the dining room and Raj sat on a dining chair while Jai gave him a buzz-cut, as if he was off to join the army. While Raj brushed the loose hair from his body, Jai ran upstairs and returned with £250 in cash, a change of clothes and a rucksack.

'That's all the cash I've got indoors. Is it going to be enough?'

'Thanks, cuz, it should do me for a while. What's in the bag?'

'More clothes and some deodorant and shit.'

'You're a star. Thanks, Jai. I really appreciate it.'

'No worries – you'd do the same for me.'

Their conversation stopped abruptly as Sarbjit came through from the kitchen.

'She's a lovely girl, Rajiv, and a nurse too. That's lucky.' She gave him a knowing look and left a plate of food on the dining table in front of him. Raj didn't reply, but grabbed the fork from by the plate and tucked in as if he hadn't eaten for a week. Once he'd cleared the plate, he hugged Jai, kissed Auntie Sarbjit and headed back out to Maya.

As he clambered into the front of the car, beside Maya, she did a double-take at his freshly shaved head, but didn't comment. He pondered asking her what his auntie had said to her when she had come out to the car, but decided to wait and see if Maya brought it up. He didn't have to wait long. Before they had driven a mile, Maya fixed him with a glare – the kind you couldn't escape even if you looked away.

'You could have warned me that your auntie was going to come out with food, Raj.'

'Sorry. I asked her not to, but she's quite nosy.'

'She was lovely, but she had a lot of questions and I didn't know what I should or shouldn't say.'

'Why, what did she ask?'

'She wanted to know if I'd known you for long, and how we'd met.'

Raj took a deep breath before he asked his next question. 'And what did you say?'

'I said I'd known you for about three months and we'd met on a night out.'

He let out a massive sigh of relief. 'Maya, I could kiss you. Seriously, that's fucking genius. You're a lifesaver. I'm not sure where I'd be right now if it wasn't for you.'

'Well, according to your auntie, it's about time you found yourself a nice girl like me and settled down a bit instead of running around town like a Lothario. I don't even know what a Lothario is.' She giggled, and for the first time he saw her – really saw her. He felt himself staring. She turned back towards the road, a playful smile painted across her face.

Raj looked straight ahead while he gathered his thoughts and then, with a strange pang of guilt, for the first time in a while his thoughts turned to Husna. He wondered if she'd regained consciousness yet, if she was even alive… Then, seamlessly, his thoughts moved to Khan. The thought of Khan hunting him down and what he would do to him if he caught him refocused Raj's mind on the task in hand.

'We need to get back on the motorway and head east – is that OK?'

'Sure. Where are we going?'

He took a while before he answered, unsure how far to pull her into the dangerous world he lived and worked in. The break in conversation seemed to drag the air out of the car. He could tell that Maya was finding the silence uncomfortable, but she was also clearly unwilling to break it, instead concentrating on driving. He stayed silent for the next fifteen minutes, then as they passed the turning for Fareham, Raj spoke.

'We need to get off soon.'

He bit his lip, tongue-tied for the first time in a long while. He'd come up with a plan, but had no idea how it was going to play out – and he'd realised that he liked Maya and didn't want to see her caught up in something she wasn't prepared for.

'What is it? What's wrong? I asked you where we're going and you've gone all weird.'

'Sorry, I didn't mean to be weird. It's just ... difficult, that's all.'

'What is? Telling me where we're going? I don't understand.'

'No – that's the problem, you don't understand and I'm not sure you're going to.' Her soft features hardened as the sentence came out of his mouth.

'Why? Because I'm a poor, innocent nurse? I couldn't possibly understand what illegal activity you're involved in that means you had to escape from the hospital? Look, Raj, the way I see it, you haven't got a whole load of options and there are a limited number of people you can turn to for help without getting caught. If that wasn't the case, let's face it, you'd have ditched me as soon as I got you out of hospital. So why don't you stop with the mysterious gangster shit and tell me where the fuck we're going and what you're planning on doing when we get there? Either that or I stop the car here and you can get out.'

35

Inzamam Khan stood on his driveway looking at his house, frozen, unable to go in. As impressive as his Chilworth home was, today it filled him with dread. Inside were his two girls and his mother, Maneet, who would want to know where he had been and what had happened. If his mother had been true to her word, his daughters didn't yet know that their mother had been in a car crash and was fighting for her life in hospital. If he was going to be true to his word, he would need to update his mother about what had happened and why he wasn't with Husna when she crashed.

He took a deep breath and put his key in the door. 'Dad!' Muna shouted.

'Inzamam, we're through here,' his mother said, just loud enough for him to hear. She had never been one for raising her voice – something he had taken advantage of as a child. He walked through to the kitchen, where the air was scented with the sweet smell of baking.

His younger daughter, Muna, was on her feet straight away. She was the image of Husna, kind and sensitive. She gave him a huge hug. Kamila turned and said hi before turning her attention back to her phone. She was much more like Inzamam in her attitude; while Inzamam knew she loved him, Kamila wasn't one for overt shows of affection. Like most sixteen-year-olds, she was more interested in her phone and her friends than anything Inzamam or Husna had to say.

He gave Muna a kiss on the top of her head then sat at the head of the table, the girls on either side of him.

'Kamila, can you put your phone down? Muna, take a seat. We need to talk.'

Both girls did as requested, looking serious.

'What is it, Dad?' asked Muna. He reached out and held their hands as he started to speak.

'It's your mum. She's been in a car accident and she's in hospital.'

'What? What do you mean, an accident?' asked Kamila.

'It's difficult to explain as I wasn't there, but what I know is that her car went off the road and hit a tree. She was taken to hospital and she's still there.'

'Is she OK?'

'She's been unconscious since the ambulance got to her and she was still unconscious when I left the hospital to come home. But they're taking really good care of her.'

Muna let go of his hand and stood up, her eyes brimming with tears. 'We've got to go and see her, Dad. Please, can we go and see her?'

'We will, but not just yet. The doctor said I should come home and get some rest, as they don't expect her to come round anytime soon. I'm so sorry, girls. I know this is a shock, but like I said, your mum's getting the very best care. We can go and see her later.'

'Where was she when she crashed?' asked Kamila.

'In the New Forest.' He decided it was pointless trying to cover it up.

'What was she doing there?'

'I don't know, Kamila. She crashed late last night. I didn't want to worry you both until I knew what had happened, so I asked Nana to come over and be with you so that I could go to the hospital, to see your mum and talk to the doctors.' Inzamam looked from one to the other, unsure whether it was best to stay quiet and let the news sink in, or to carry on trying to reassure and comfort them. He opted for the former. Muna got up and came to him, leaning against him, her head resting on top of his. Kamila stayed seated and for once didn't retreat behind the safety of her phone screen. Instead, she held Inzamam's hand as if she was scared to let him go.

He looked at his mother, who sat at the other end of the table. She smiled and nodded reassuringly at him, then walked over and filled the kettle.

Khan sat for a while with his girls. They didn't move, they didn't speak, they just held on to him, each in their own way. His mother brought over a cup of black tea and returned to the other end of the table. As his tea cooled, he decided a distraction was probably needed. He wanted to speak to his mother without the girls being in earshot.

'Why don't you go and put something on TV? There must be something you've got recorded, ready to watch. One of your reality TV shows? We'll go and see your mum later.'

Neither of them protested. He stood and kissed them both on the forehead, smoothing their hair away from their faces. He waited until he heard the TV go on in the lounge, then took a seat next to his mother.

'They are good girls, Inzamam. You and Husna should be very proud.'

'They really are, and we are. Thank you for coming over and being with them while I went to hospital—'

'Inzamam Khan, you have always known that your father and I are here for you all, if and when you need us. At times like these, who else do you call on but family? Now, tell me, what happened to our darling Husna?'

'I'm not sure. I don't know why she was in the New Forest. I don't know why her car left the road. And I don't know how long she's going to be unconscious.' He glanced over his shoulder to check the girls weren't in earshot.

'Listen to me carefully, son. Do not lose yourself in ever-decreasing circles of doubt. When your father was at the height of his career and playing his part in the fight for Islam, he faced many situations that would have struck fear and doubt into his mind – if he had been a weaker man. But he was able to look at where he found himself and the actions of others, then assess how best to deal with the situation he was presented with. He made sure that anyone who stood in his way was left in no doubt who he was and what he stood for. You need to tackle this with the same mindset. Think about this as if it were a business-related problem. How would you go about understanding what had happened? And what would you do, once you did?' His mother clasped her hands over one of his as she spoke, and she never broke eye contact.

Khan sat for a moment, feeling his thoughts arranging themselves into a logical order, removing the emotion and clearing the way for rationality.

'You're brilliant, thank you. Could you stay with the girls for a little while longer? There are things I need to do.'

'Of course – take as long as you need. I get to spend time with my beautiful granddaughters and avoid listening to your father go on about the cricket.'

He kissed her on the forehead, then popped his head around the lounge doorway.

'Girls, are you OK while I pop out quickly? There's something I need to do and then I'll be back.' They looked away from the reality TV show they were watching and nodded, then turned back to the TV show.

He grabbed his keys and headed for the door. As he turned out of his driveway, he commanded his car to call Lawrence. The phone only rang twice before it was answered.

'Inzamam, how are you doing?'

'I've had better days. Listen, now I've calmed down a bit, there are some details that might help with finding Raj. I managed to get a look at the hospital's CCTV. When the nurse took Raj out of his room in a wheelchair, they headed down to the parking garage and out of the hospital in her car.'

'Raj is a smart guy, and if he's not hanging around there'll be a good reason. What can you tell me about the nurse that took him out of the hospital?'

'I'll send you a message with her details on – it sounds like we're both driving.'

'Good idea. Look, Inzamam, I'm sure Husna is going to be OK. Just quickly before

you go, do you know any more about what happened?'

'Thanks, Lawrence. Husna's car left the road and hit a tree is all I know for sure. Anything beyond that, I'm just guessing.'

'Let me know how she is later. I'll get on with finding Raj.'

'Thank you, Lawrence, that's a weight off my mind. Bye.' He ended the call and planted his foot on the accelerator, making the Range Rover lurch forward like a pouncing lion.

Half an hour later, Inzamam was parking in the visitor car park of the private hospital in Bournemouth. He made his way through the identical-looking corridors, following the signs to the ward Husna was on. His pace – and his heart rate – quickened as he got closer to his wife's room. At the nursing station he saw the familiar face of Husna's doctor. He smiled and checked his watch.

'I don't think you've been gone long enough to have rested, Mr Khan.'

'I know, I know. I found it difficult to stay away. I've been home to let our girls know about their mother, then I had to come back.'

'Of course. I understand it's difficult, but there is unlikely to be any change for a while.' The doctor guided Inzamam towards Husna's private room. It was difficult to see his wife with machines monitoring her every function, breathing for her, monotone beeps sounding out her pulse. 'Mr Khan, let me explain. Your wife was very badly injured in the crash and we've had to put her onto a ventilator. She suffered significant brain trauma and needs support to breathe. This may be a temporary measure, but you need to know that her injures are very serious and it may be quite a while before she regains consciousness.'

'So you don't know how long she's going to be like this?'

'I'm sorry. At this time it's impossible to say, but I can assure you, your wife is getting the very best care.'

Khan looked at Husna, lying helplessly on the bed, tubes sticking out of her mouth and hands, wires joining her to her techno lifeguards. She looked smaller.

'I understand, doctor, thank you.'

The doctor smiled and walked towards the door. 'Try and get some rest, Mr Khan.'

'I will. Thank you again.' Inzamam perched on the side of Husna's bed and took her hand in his. As his thumb caressed the back of her hand, thoughts of her and Raj together began to sprint through his mind, as they had done since he'd seen Raj in the room down the hall. He couldn't shift the thoughts and images.

He was confident that Lawrence would find Raj and, when he did, Khan knew he'd be able to find out why Husna and Raj had been together in the New Forest, in Husna's car. For the act of betrayal he was convinced Raj had committed, Raj would have to suffer. As his father had told him many years earlier: 'Betrayal must be punished with suffering. It shows those who may consider doing the same in the future what the consequences of their actions will be. If, with this knowledge they choose to betray you anyway, then they have brought their fate on themselves.' Even though he had been a relatively young boy when this lesson had been passed down to him, it had become engrained in him and guided his actions on many occasions.

But this was different. This was his wife. How could he make her suffer for her betrayal? She was already fighting for her life, dependent on a machine for her every breath. Then he thought about what his mother had said about how his father had dealt with betrayal: 'He made sure that anyone who stood in his way was left in no doubt who he was and what he stood for.' And suddenly he knew what he must do. It came to him like a wave of enlightenment.

Inzamam leaned over Husna and planted a tender kiss on her forehead, cupping her face in his hands. He brushed her hair away from her face. Khan then walked around her bed to the ventilator. He took hold of the coupling that joined the tube coming out of the humidifier to the tube going into Husna's mouth. He glanced through the window.

There was no one in sight.

Looking at his incapacitated, vulnerable wife, Inzamam Khan eased the two tubes apart, carefully laying the half leading to Husna in the same position it had been in before he touched it. He let the other half hang, no longer serving its purpose. He thought for moment about the hospital staff finding it, but was pretty sure that even if they suspected he was responsible, given the underground nature of his medical arrangements with them, they wouldn't say anything.

He kissed her once more on the forehead and a tear rolled down his face. He wiped it away and left Husna to take her last breath.

36

Tom had decided to try and buy Raj some time to get away when he got into Larry's car. He knew this was a dangerous strategy, but figured he could lead him to a couple of red-herring destinations, before taking him where he was pretty sure Raj would have gone.

They'd sat in relative silence since Larry had started driving towards Southampton.

'So, are you going to give me a clue where we're heading first?' Said Larry as he drove down the M3.

'Yeah, I think we should try his place first, he'll need clothes and money I would imagine. If he's not there, there are other places quite close-by he might have gone.'

'You really think he's going to go home?'

'I think he's smart enough to figure out that Khan will think it's the last place he'll go and won't be looking there.'

'Hm, fair point. OK, let's head to Raj's place then.'

They drew a blank at Raj's home and at the next two addresses Tom guided Larry to. Tom could sense the frustration building in Larry and much as he wanted to help Raj, he also didn't want to end up dead.

'Well, that was another pointless trip, any other bright ideas?' Asked Larry. His fingers drumming on the steering wheel.

'Just one. Raj has family over the other side of town, a cousin called Jai. I've met him a few times. Raj was more-or-less brought up by Jai's parents while his folks were over in Dubai.'

'You're right, he's talked about them before. Good thinking Tom. Do you know where Jai lives?'

'Yeah, roughly. It's been a while since I've picked Raj up from there, but I think I remember the way.'

'Good-lad, right, let's go.' Larry seemed to perk up at the suggestion of going to find Jai's house and Tom figured that if Raj had been there, he'd be long gone by now.

Larry drove quickly across town, following Tom's directions. Tom had decided against taking Larry the long route there, figuring Larry would twig what he was doing and get pissed off.

'It's just down here on the right I think.' Said Tom. 'Hang on, that's Jai, I think.'

'Where?'

'There, that guy walking down past that red Golf.'

'I see him. OK, I'm going to drive past him and then you get out first and speak to him. I don't want to freak him out. I'm not up for chasing anyone down the street.'

'OK.'

'Oh and Tom, don't do anything dumb like telling him to do a runner.'

'I won't. I pointed him out, remember?'

'OK, well, just play it cool.'

'I will.'

Larry did as he said and pulled up about fifty feet ahead of Jai. Tom got out and called to him.

'Jai! That is you isn't it? It's Tom, I'm a mate of Raj's, re-member we met at that New Years party.' Jai stopped walking and studied Tom from about twenty feet away.

'Yeah, I'm Jai. What do you want man?'

'I need to find Raj. Has he been to see you today?'

'Nah-mate, I ain't seen him for ages.'

Larry got out of the car and leaned his arms on the roof.

'Hi Jai, I'm Larry, I work with Raj. Look I know you're prob-ably trying to protect him, but we're here to help him. You know he was in a car crash last night and he's skipped hospital. We need to make sure he's OK, he shouldn't really be up and about yet.'

'Like I said, I ain't seen him.'

'OK, if you say so. Look, take Tom's number and if you hear from him can you give us a call. We're worried about him and want to make sure he gets the right medical attention.'

'You can give me your number but I ain't seen him and I'm not expecting to.'

'OK, thanks Jai. Tom give Jai your number would you?'

'Yeah sure.' Tom walked slowly over towards Jai and gave him a business card for work that had his mobile number on it. As he passed him the card, Jai spoke softly.

'You know I ain't gonna call, don't you bruv?'

'Yeah I know. Make sure you don't.' Said Tom as he released the card. He turned and walked back to the car, got in, and Larry drove away slowly.

'You know he's lying don't you?' Larry said.

'Yeah I'm pretty sure he is, but Raj must have been and gone.'

'Yeah guess we got here too late.'

'Guess we did.' Tom shrugged.

'I think we'll knock it on the head for today. I'll drop you off.' He looked at Tom, smiled and pointed the Audi towards the motorway.

37

Vihaan Patel listened as Sadiya chatted to a friend on the phone. He was trying to find an electrician who wouldn't charge him the earth to put security lights and cameras on Bakshi's house. Inzamam had sent him a very brief message telling him to get it sorted. Vihaan had already seen four electricians and all had quoted figures he knew Khan wouldn't pay. His face hurt like hell and the bruising was coming out: he looked like someone had been playing with Snapchat effects on his face, such was the swelling. He was not in the mood for sorting out sparks.

'She did? It doesn't surprise me – you know she doesn't care who knows,' he overheard Sadiya say. He sighed, loudly enough for her to hear, and she shot him a disdainful look. They'd hardly spoken since he got beaten up. Sadiya, while concerned and worried about him being injured, had offered little sympathy after her encounter with Larry in their own home. She had been very clear with Vihaan that she was not prepared to tolerate his business associates landing on their doorstep. He'd tried in vain to assure her that it was a one-off and wouldn't happen again, but even as he was saying the words, he knew she didn't believe him. He didn't blame her. He didn't even believe himself.

His phone saved him from further irritation, vibrating on the arm of his chair. The display showed a FaceTime request from Arjun. He made his way as quickly as he could into his garden and answered. Arjun's face popped up on his phone screen, with a bright-blue sky as his backdrop. He waved with both hands.

'Vihaan, my good man, how are you today?'

'Arjun.'

'The very same. I did say we'd keep in touch. How are you?'

'I'm OK, thanks. It's good to hear from you. How are you?'

'I'm enjoying my new-found freedom. I should probably thank Inzamam Khan – it is the most fantastic place. Maybe a thank you is a bit much, though.' He laughed.

'Oh, I don't know, Arjun. He'd probably get a kick out of a postcard from you.' As Vihaan looked at his friend on the screen, he noticed something unusual. 'Arjun, where are you sitting?'

Bakshi's expression slipped for a moment. 'Ah yes, I'm not sure we discussed this in our last call,' he said, placing his hands out of camera shot then manoeuvring backwards, revealing a wheelchair.

'What the hell?'

'I know. Lawrence hit me at the airport – warning me to board the plane. He seems to have damaged a nerve in my spine. As a result, walking is a bit of a challenge.'

'Arjun, that's horrendous! Are you OK? I mean, clearly not. But, how? I mean, where did you get the chair?'

'It wasn't easy, but it appears my new friends out here are rather well connected and can get pretty much anything – given sufficient funds. It does make getting around a bit tough at times, as Brazil is not the most accessible place in the world. But it's amazing how it changes one's perspective. As with all things in life, there are positives to be drawn from the experience. Anyway, enough of that – back to business. I need you to do something.'

'Yes, of course. Anything.'

'How well do you know Mr Khan's other business associates?'

'I know some of them. Why?'

'I'd like to know more about his main operation and wondered if you could put me in touch with his key competitor. I'm guessing at some point he's ranted to you about his competition. After all, an empire like Inzamam's isn't built overnight, nor is it built without upsetting other people. I just want to know who they are so I can contact them and have a chat about a mutually beneficial arrangement we may be able to come to. So, could you find out who I should be speaking to and how to contact them? Or do I need to source my information elsewhere?'

'I'm not sure that's a good idea, Arjun.'

'I understand your hesitation but, as I said in my last call, Mr Khan has to atone for his actions. As I also said, I will ensure it won't impact on you and your lovely wife.'

'Huh, I wouldn't worry about that right now.'

'Oh? Things not good in the Patel household?'

'You could say that. Ever since Larry turned up here and scared the shit out of Sadiya, she's hardly said a word to me.'

'But she's still there with you?'

'Yes.'

'Then all is not lost. It just means you have work to do. You need to win back her trust and let her know she can rely on you, and that your business activities won't put her at risk. Who can blame Sadiya? She didn't invite Larry to your door. No, you have work to do. If you lose Sadiya, you place her at greater risk, for she knows enough to put her in danger. I would suggest you concentrate your romantic efforts on your wife and leave young Tracey alone for a while.' Arjun grinned as he finished his sentence, tapping the side of his nose with his finger. Vihaan took a breath as if to reply, then closed his mouth.

Arjun continued. 'You must concentrate – now is not the time for frivolous distraction. There is everything at stake, your entire existence could be changed by the decisions you make over the coming days. Are you still alright for money?'

'Yes – thank you for the money you put in my account. It was really generous.'

'Nonsense, you've more than earned it. If my assessment of your loyalty is correct, you will earn much more over the coming months – and indeed years. Now I must go – things to do, places to go, and this chair does not make that a quick process. Take care, Vihaan, and take Sadiya out somewhere nice. You have the money.' Bakshi reached forward as if to end the call, but Vihaan stopped him.

'Arjun! Wait. What do you mean, my entire existence could be changed by my decisions?'

'As I said, there must be atonement, and I am not in the UK to ensure it is administered appropriately. You are my eyes and ears over there. If you want to keep Larry from returning to Rotherham, you will have to take some very tough decisions to protect our future livelihood. Don't worry about it now – all will become clear in good time.'

This time Vihaan didn't interrupt as Arjun ended the call. Vihaan stood for a moment in his garden, looking at the blank screen of his phone, scratching his head. He went back indoors as Sadiya was finishing her phone call. Reaching out, he ran a hand through her hair. She turned and gave him a quizzical look.

'It's been a crap couple of days. How do you fancy going out somewhere nice to eat tonight?'

She looked surprised, but didn't say no, as he'd expected. 'That would be nice. Where were you thinking?'

'Anywhere you like as long as they've got something on the menu I don't have to chew too much. Why don't we get dressed up and go somewhere posh? We haven't been anywhere really nice for ages.'

'What's got into you all of a sudden?'

'I've been a bit of a dick and think I should be treating my amazing wife a bit better. Is that so bad?'

'No. I'm not complaining, just surprised.'

'Good – I like surprising you. I've got to go out but I won't be long. Shall we go out about eight?'

'Yeah, sounds great.'

Vihaan smiled as best he could and kissed Sadiya's hand. *Arjun was right*, he thought. *Maybe everything wasn't lost.*

38

Raj leaned against the side of Maya's Fiesta and stretched. He felt like he'd been hit by a train, with pain ebbing and flowing through his body in waves. He straightened up, turned and knocked on the car window.

'Are you sure you're going to be OK?' Maya asked him.

'Yes, I'll be fine. Remember what I said – I'll phone you as soon as I come out. Make sure you park a couple of roads over. I don't want anyone to connect you with me – at least until you come back and get me. There are some people here you really don't want to be associated with.'

'OK, if you're sure. Be careful. I won't be far away. If you need me, call.'

'Thanks, will do.'

With that he took a step towards an imposing set of double doors. Raj took a deep breath, which hurt like hell, then banged the side of his fist on the door. It took a couple of minutes before anything happened. He stood there uncomfortably, wincing every time he put his body weight on his left leg.

An intercom to the left of the doors crackled into life.

'Hello, how can we help you?' came a heavily accented question.

Raj looked up at a camera bolted on the wall above the door, out of reach. 'I'd like to see Mr Shala.'

'Mr Shala doesn't take visitors, sorry. Good day.'

'Tell him it's Raj Gadhi. I work for Inzamam Khan.'

There was a long silence. Raj waited. Then he heard what sounded like a bolt slide back. Slowly, the door opened, A huge figure stood in the doorway. Raj was well over six feet tall, but whoever was opening the door made him feel small. Once the door was fully open, Raj did his best not to look intimidated by the suited giant in front of him, although it was difficult. When the giant spoke, Raj realised he was the one who had answered the intercom. His accent was a heavy Albanian, which made him sound as intimidating as he looked.

'Mr Gadhi? Come in, please. Mr Shala would like to meet you.'

The giant stood to one side, gesturing for Raj to come inside. Raj walked in the direction the giant was indicating and stopped while he closed the door behind him. As the door shut, the hall-way he was standing in went temporarily dark, then a sensor- operated light flicked on, bathing the walls in a soft wash of purple.

The giant walked around him. 'This way, please,' he said, walking down a corridor. Raj followed as quickly as he could. The big man glanced back over his shoulder and Raj saw that he had registered that he wasn't keeping up.

'Would you like to take the lift? Perhaps it would be easier?'

'Er, yes, that would be good.'

'Very well, just around this corner.' Again he gestured, this time to the right, then led the way. Raj was relieved to see that there was a lift door very close by. By the time he'd hobbled to it, the giant had summoned the lift and the doors were open.

They stepped inside the relatively small lift. The big man almost filled the space. Raj leaned back against the wall as casually as he could manage. The giant smiled. Raj was sure he knew how intimidating he was, and probably quite enjoyed it.

As they exited the lift, his guide pointed to a door.

'Mr Shala's office. I'll open the door for you. I hope your injuries heal soon.'

'Thank you. Me too.'

The giant held the office door open for him and Raj hobbled through. As soon as he was inside, the door closed behind him. Like a Bond villain, Valmir Shala, a man Raj had often heard Inzamam talk about, spun his chair around to face Raj. Beaming, he stood to greet Raj.

'Mr Gadhi! Please take a seat.'

Fuck me, is everyone around here a giant? Raj thought as his host reached over his desk to shake his hand, his huge paw enveloping Raj's hand.

'Would you like a drink? Vodka?'

'Er, sure, thanks.'

'Excellent. I have some of the best vodka available in the country – you will like it, I'm sure.' He waved a hand and a normal-sized suited man appeared from the shadows at the other side of the enormous office.

'Two vodkas please, Erag. Make them large ones.' He smiled at Raj again and Raj prepared what he was going to say. 'Now, while we wait for the drinks, what can I do for the right-hand of, Inzamam Khan'?'

Raj gulped. Shala knew who he was and what he did. *That should make life easier – or make this a very short conversation,* thought Raj. 'I'll get straight to it, Mr Shala, as I know you're a very busy man.' The Albanian nodded at him and steepled his fingers under his square jaw. 'Last night I was in a car accident, hence the limp and my cuts and bruises…'

'That's terrible. Why are you not in hospital, or home?' Shala interrupted.

'Because, how can I put it? I wasn't alone when I had the crash.'

'Oh?'

'No. I was with Inzamam Khan's wife.'

Shala burst into a roar of laughter. It was so loud, it silenced Raj.

'I apologise. Please, carry on,' Shala said, regaining his composure, although he wore an amused smile.

'To make matters worse, Inzamam knows. He came to the hospital to see his wife and looked in through my hospital room window.'

'That explains why you are not in hospital, but it does not explain why you have come to see me.'

'I'm getting to it. Once he'd seen me through that window, I knew I needed to get out of there and get away quickly. I've seen how he deals with people who betray him – and let's just say, it isn't pretty.' Raj paused as Erag brought over two glasses and placed them on the desk in front of them.

'Come, drink, Mr Gadhi. It sounds like you need it.'

Raj knocked the vodka back in one. He was surprised by how good it tasted – smooth, too.

'Thank you. So, as I was saying, I don't want to end up dead, so I thought I'd come and see you and ask if, in exchange for some useful information, you could help me get away from here permanently. I'm pretty sure that, like Khan, you have some well-tested routes out of the country that won't leave me exposed to getting caught by Khan.'

'I see. They were right about you, Mr Gadhi – you are a very smart young man. My people have told me much about you. They say you are largely responsible for the success of Mr Khan's empire.'

Raj felt conflicted. He was flattered that Shala knew so much about him and that the Albanians thought so highly of him. But he was also uncomfortable about the amount Shala seemed to know about him. He decided to try to play it cool. 'That's very nice of you to say so, Mr Shala…'

'Valmir – please call me Valmir.'

'OK, Valmir. It's nice to hear that your people think so highly of me, but really I'm only a small cog in a very big machine.'

'Nonsense – you are being modest. I like that. A lesser man would sit and take the glory, but not you. I like it. I heard that scorpion is your doing. I also heard that the chemical engineering that goes into it is also done by you. Am I right?'

'Er, yes, I suppose that's true. But really, I only do as I'm asked.'

'So, you have come to Mr Khan's direct competitor to share information in exchange for freedom. But, as you have heard, I already have information. I know that soon scorpion will be flooding the streets of Brighton, under the watchful eye of Mr Khan.'

Raj struggled not to let his jaw hit the floor. Shala knew everything – and it was up- to-the-minute information. Raj was thinking how impressed he was when Egra placed another vodka in front of him.

'No, really, I'm fine.'

'Drink,' Shala commanded. Raj took the glass, and again downed the shot in one. It really was good.

'Now, Raj – may I call you, Raj?'

'Yes, sure.'

'Good. Raj, listen to me very carefully. I have a much better idea. You are too valuable and talented to run, your tail between your legs, because you made the mistake of sleeping with Mr

Khan's wife. I'm sure she was a consenting adult and I am sure she had good reasons for being with you.'

As Raj listened to Shala, he felt a pang of guilt for leaving Husna in hospital and not even checking to see if she was OK.

'You will come and work for me. I will provide you with state-of-the-art equipment. You will have whatever assistance you need to make your exceptional product. Then we shall take over control of the south coast and head into London. Your skills and knowledge will make you a very rich man. Why would you squander that by running away and seeking refuge? What would you do, hide forever? No! Use what you have – do not trade trivial information, think bigger! You could make a lot of money.

Currently you supply most of the product across one of the largest areas in the country. I can give you a purpose-built lab for making your product and you will direct a team. Erag, more vodka!' He clapped his enormous hands together as he ended his speech.

Raj sat, stunned that he'd just been offered a job by Valmir Shala, one of the biggest drug lords in Europe – and Khan's nemesis.

'That sounds very generous, Mr Sha— Valmir. Can I ask what you mean by directing a team?'

'You will have a team of people that you will train to make your product. Your scorpion is far superior to ours: it makes sense that my production engineers report to you and you train them. You would not need to mix the product – once you have shown them how to do it, you will oversee the purity. I believe with your expertise and my distribution networks, we can take over the whole of the south – and that is just the start. Your cut would be more than you would have ever earned working for Mr Khan.'

'My cut?'

'Of course – you would take a cut of the profits. How else would I ensure your loyalty and that you didn't sleep with my wife!' He roared with laughter again and knocked back his vodka, slamming the glass down onto the desk. 'It is a big decision – do not answer me now. Think overnight. Allow my driver to take you and the young lady who dropped you off to a hotel, where you will stay as my guest. No one will know you are there, and you can rest which – if I may say? – you look like you need.'

Raj was shocked that Shala knew Maya had dropped him off; he really was very well informed. Before Raj could respond, Shala had risen from his chair and pressed a button on his desk. Behind Raj, the office door opened. Raj turned and saw the giant walk through the door.

'Saban, once Raj has contacted his lady friend and she returns, could you ensure her car is parked safely and take them both to the hotel? I will make sure they have a room ready when you get there, Raj. It is the best hotel in Portsmouth and I am very good friends with the owners. They are very discreet, and no one will know you are there. And do not worry about the cost – you are my guest. Saban, can you make sure you arrange a time to pick Raj up tomorrow? We have more business to attend to.'

'Yes, Mr Shala, of course.' The giant had the deepest voice Raj had ever heard.

Raj stood up. His head was swimming from a mixture of what had just happened and the vodka. He took a deep breath, as discreetly as he could.

'Valmir, that really isn't—'

Shala held up a hand. 'You have better place to go? Go. Enjoy the hotel, have a restful evening. Saban will also make sure you have pain relief to take with you. We have some excellent painkillers, very strong. Do not worry, you will be safe and can rest easy.'

Raj had to admit it; he didn't have a better plan, and the thought of a hot meal and a comfortable bed was very appealing. 'OK, thank you, Valmir. You're very kind and I really appreciate it.'

'Do not think of it as kindness – think of it more as the first part of our new business relationship.' He patted Raj on the back. Raj's face contorted as pain shot through his body.

'My apologies, I didn't think. That must have hurt.'

Raj hobbled towards Saban, who was standing, holding the office door open. Beyond him, Raj could see the lift door was already open. 'Thank you again, Valmir. See you tomorrow.'

When they got out on the ground floor, Raj messaged Maya.

Hi, could you come and get me pls? Slight change of plan, will explain when here X

He deleted the kiss at the end of the message, then retyped it and pressed send, trying not to overthink it. Within seconds, a reply popped onto his screen.

OK on way X

'She's on her way,' he said to Saban, who was waiting silently.

'I will get you some painkillers. They are very good and you need them, I think.' He returned with an unopened bottle of water and a strip of tablets. He handed them to Raj, telling him there were enough to get him through the night and help him sleep.

Raj thanked him and immediately took two of the tablets, with a swig of water.

They walked to the main doors and stepped outside the club, just as Maya pulled up in her Fiesta. Saban stepped forward and gestured for Maya to roll her window down.

She did as directed, lowering the window a couple of inches. Raj could see she was a little unsure of the huge man.

'Please go down the road fifty yards. There is a turning on the right, which goes into our car park. Drive in there and park in any space. I will meet you there.'

Maya nodded and looked at Raj, who walked around to the passenger side of the car. By the time he'd got into the car, Saban had walked down the road towards the car park.

'What's going on? What do you mean, change of plan? And why am I following a giant into a car park?'

'It's OK. They're going to take us to a hotel. He offered me a job.'

'He did what?'

'He offered – well, actually, he pitched a job to me. He wants me to come and work for him. I'll tell you all about it when we get to the hotel. Apparently the owners are friends of Valmir's…'

'Who's Valmir?'

'Valmir Shala, the owner of the club. They're friends of his and we're going to stay the night as his guests. That's if you want to? I'll understand if you don't.'

He watched her. She was clearly trying to process what he'd told her and decide whether she wanted to run away.

'No, a free night in a hotel sounds great. Don't get any ideas, though.' She laughed, a nervous-sounding laugh.

They pulled into the underground car park, where Saban stood beside a black Mercedes. He pointed towards a line of empty spaces and Maya parked in the middle of the row. They got out of the car and walked over towards Saban as he opened the rear door of the Merc and gestured for them to get in. They did, then looked at each other as he closed the door on them.

'This is very nice,' said Maya. 'You don't see anything like this where I come from.'

'It is really nice, isn't it? Hopefully the hotel is just as nice,' said Raj.

They didn't have to wait long to find out. Within minutes, they had pulled up outside a large, brightly coloured hotel not far from the seafront. It was floodlit and looked homely and inviting.

Saban got out first and opened the door for them again. 'They are expecting you. I will come for you at ten o'clock tomorrow. If you need anything while you are here, just ask. The owners are very good friends of Mr Shala and will make sure you are well looked after. Good night, Mr Gadhi, Miss.' He nodded politely and closed the door, leaving them looking at the hotel.

'OK, in we go then,' said Raj.

'I could murder a glass of wine,' said Maya.

'I've had three vodkas already, but wine sounds good. Let's get checked in and then eat. I'll tell you all about my meeting while we get some food.'

They entered the hotel and were greeted by a woman in her mid-forties with bobbed brown hair and a friendly face.

'You must be Mr Shala's guests. I'm Abbey. We've got a suite with a sea view for you, right by the lift. Mr Shala said you had hurt your leg and he didn't want you to have to walk far to a room.'

'That sounds great, thank you,' said Raj. 'Is it possible to get something to eat?'

'Yes, of course. Why don't you go and get settled in and then come down to the bar when you're ready? We'll get you something nice to eat and maybe a glass of something to go with it.'

'Lovely, thank you,' said Maya.

'The lift is on your right and your suite is on the third floor – number twenty-five. If you need anything, just call zero from your room. Reception is open twenty-four hours.'

She passed Maya a key-card and pointed towards the lift.

'Are you OK?' Maya asked as they got out of the lift and walked slowly to their room.

'Yes, I'll be fine. I just need some food and some sleep, I think.'

Maya gasped as they walked into the suite. Raj took a sharp intake of breath for a different reason – a searing pain pulsed down his left leg. He buckled towards the bed. Maya lunged towards him and helped lower him onto the thick mattress. Lifting his legs carefully onto the bed and easing his shoes off, Maya checked he was comfortable, before reaching into her bag and removing some fresh dressings and antiseptic wipes.

'Where did you get those from?' he asked.

'When you went into the club, I figured you weren't only going to be five minutes, so I drove to a pharmacist and bought some dressings. I might have helped you escape from hospital, but I'm still a nurse. And I can't leave you in dirty dressings. I bought enough for a couple of days.'

'You are an absolute star. I can't believe you did that, but I'm so glad you did. Thank you.'

'Yeah, OK. Shut up and undo your jeans.' Maya carefully cleaned and redressed Raj's injuries with the same level of care as she had when Raj was in hospital, making sure he was comfortable the whole time.

Once she was done, he got dressed and they went down to eat. His leg felt much better and the painkillers Saban had given him had kicked in.

They were the only ones in the bar. They sat at a table in a far corner, out of direct sight of the door. Raj's paranoia about being seen made the table selection easy.

After a good meal and making a start on a second bottle of wine, Raj explained in detail the pitch he'd had from Shala. Maya listened to him without interrupting. Raj could see her trying to comprehend what he was telling her.

They talked for hours – about his life, her life, how he'd got involved with Khan, and his original plan to stash enough money away to go legit'. How she had enjoyed a fun, if sheltered upbringing on the south coast, just outside Bournemouth. Then decided she wanted to help people and qualified to be a nurse. As they spoke, the wine flowed and Raj temporarily forgot his pain and the situation he'd found himself in.

***

Maya sat listening to Raj explain how he'd got mixed up in the world he lived in. He was clearly a smart guy and nothing like the usual type she found herself going for. Besides the fact that he was apparently running for his life from a homicidal, drug dealer and had experienced things she'd only read about, he really seemed like a decent guy. He hadn't encouraged her to stay involved beyond helping him escape from hospital. His family seemed lovely and he seemed genuinely sad, whenever he mentioned Husna.

Maya had no idea how he was managing to stay awake with the combination of painkillers and wine and if she'd been advising him as a patient, she'd have been telling him to rest. But that didn't seem to feature very high on his list of things to do.

As Raj excused himself and went off to the loo, Maya looked around the hotel bar they were sat in.

What are you up to Maya? You don't know this guy, as nice as he seems. He's a drug dealer and most of them end up dead, or in prison. She thought. But the more she pondered whether she wanted to run away and leave Raj to it, the more she realised she'd never felt excited in this way before. Being with Raj was dangerous, really dangerous and that made her feel alive and needed.

39

Inzamam Khan drove home from the hospital in a daze. After tampering with Husna's ventilator, he sat in his car in the hospital car park for what felt like an age going over and over what he'd done. Eventually he left the hospital and started to drive home. About twenty minutes into his journey the hospital called, asking him to return. When he'd got there, Husna's doctor had taken him into a side room and broken the news of Husna's death. Inzamam had been unable to speak. He had just stared at the doctor, tears welling in his eyes. But no words came.

After being comforted for a while and having a final visit to see Husna, he left.

He felt numb. He could hear that people who passed him in the corridor were speaking, but he didn't hear anything they said; they were just faceless forms, passing him as he walked.

Despite knowing that he was responsible for Husna's death, hearing the doctor say out loud that she was dead hit him harder than he had expected. What had he done?

Khan got back into his Range Rover and drove, on autopilot, the whole way home.

When he arrived home he sat on the driveway for a while, unable to turn off the car engine and face his next task. His girls were innocent – they had committed no act of betrayal, yet he was about to tell them that their mother was gone forever.

Khan went in. His mother stood in the kitchen doorway. He looked at her, searching for the words, grappling with his guilt at robbing his daughters of their mother.

She walked towards him and took his face in her hands. 'She's gone, isn't she, Inzamam?'

'Yes, yes she is.'

'Was it a good passing?'

'It was quick and painless, they said.'

'Then that's the best you could have hoped for. Take a deep breath and go and speak to your girls. They are going to need you more than ever now. You will need to be strong for them, Inzamam.'

He nodded, took her hands in his and kissed them.

He walked into the lounge and saw his beautiful girls, where he had left them, sitting innocently in front of the TV.

He sat between them and quietly destroyed their world.

40

Gonzo was slumped on the sofa in front of the TV, his arms folded. The TV was showing an Australian airport border control show on loop, but he wasn't really watching. He was giving himself a talking-to for being bothered that Emina hadn't replied to a message he'd sent half an hour earlier. He told himself she could be on the phone to a friend, or with her family. He had been checking for a reply every few minutes, even though his phone had remained silent.

Then his phone flashed and a number he didn't recognise appeared on the screen, accompanied by the *A Team* theme music –

one of Gonzo's favourite shows growing up. He grabbed it, hoping it might be Emina calling from a different phone.

'Hello?'

'Gonzo, it's Raj.'

'Oh, hi mate, sup?'

'You could sound a bit more pleased to hear from me.'

'Sorry. It's like a fuckin' ghost town here, I've never known it so quiet.'

'Listen, we need to talk. Are you at Khan's?'

'Course I'm here – where else would I be? You and the boss told me not to go anywhere, so I'm stuck here watchin' TV. Where are you?'

'It doesn't matter where I am. You need to get out of there, now, and I need you to come and meet me. Make sure you've got a decent amount of cash on you and a bag of clothes.'

'What the fuck, Raj?'

'Just do it. I haven't got time to fucking argue with you. Call me on this number as soon as you're far enough away – and don't tell anyone I called. Do you understand? No one.'

'Yeah, OK. You'd better tell me what the fuck is goin' on though.'

'I will, but get out of there and do it quick. Speak to you soon.'

With that, Raj was gone. Gonzo stood in the middle of the room at Khan's, scratching his head and looking around him in dismay. He stuffed some clothes into a bag and briefly thought about calling Emina, then thought better of it. It could wait. He could always call her later when Raj had told him what was going on.

He had a weird feeling in the pit of his stomach – a feeling that didn't get any better when his phone rang again. This time the initials EH popped onto his phone screen.

Hasani? What the fuck does he want? Gonzo wondered. 'Hi, Mr Hasani.'

'Mike, how many times? Call me Erion.'

'Ha ha, maybe a few more times, Mr … I mean, Erion.'

'That's better. How are you today?'

'I'm good. thanks. You?' This felt weird – first the call from Raj, then Hasani straight afterwards.

'Excellent. I'm very well. Tell me, are you local? Somewhere my driver can pick you up?'

Gonzo thought quickly. 'I'm just on my way out, but I'm only goin' to be about half an hour. How about I make my way up to you when I'm done? Are you at the club?'

'You are a busy man – that is fine. I have something very important to discuss with you, get here as soon as you are free.'

'Sure. I'll come straight over as soon as I'm done in town.' He tried to sound nonchalant. He ended the call abruptly, glad to be out of the conversation, he hoped, without digging any holes for himself.

Gonzo zipped his bag closed, but not before he stuffed a wad of cash into it, which he had left over from the last payment he'd had from Khan. He peeled off a few notes, folding them neatly into his scruffy wallet, swigged the last of his cuppa and headed for the door. Just as he reached for the handle, Khan burst through the door, throwing it back against the wall. Gonzo jumped backwards.

He saw Khan look down at the bag that was hanging from Gonzo's hand. 'Going somewhere?'

'No – I mean, yeah. I'm goin' over to stay with a girl I've met, if that's OK?'

'A girl? You? Are you taking the fucking piss?'

'No, boss. She lives over the other side of town and asked me if I wanted to go over and stay for a couple of nights. I told her I was sleepin' on the sofa here and I guess she felt sorry for me.'

'Well, if she feels sorry for you, that explains it. It's not like you're going to get a woman any other way with that face, is it?' Khan sneered.

Gonzo felt his insides twist into a tight knot and his face flush. 'Guess not, boss.

You OK?'

'Course I'm OK. What are you? My fucking therapist?'

'No, just askin'. I thought you were goin' to take the door off its hinges when you came in.'

'Shut up and do something useful, like getting me a coffee,' Khan snapped, clearly ignoring Gonzo's comment. Then he turned his back on Gonzo and stalked off towards his office.

For a second, Gonzo thought about legging it out of the door, then he thought better of it. If what Raj had said was true and he was in danger, he decided he needed to act as normally as possible. He walked over to the counter, where an empty coffee pot and a kettle stood side by side.

'There's no fresh coffee, boss. Do you want me to make a pot, or instant?' he shouted through to Khan.

'Make a pot. I'll wait, I suppose.'

Gonzo glanced nervously over his shoulder. Khan was rooting through his office, clearly looking for something. He looked as though he was in a rush, almost hectic, as he opened one drawer after another, rummaging through the contents then slamming them shut.

A few minutes later, Gonzo took a steaming coffee through to Khan. As he stepped into the office, he saw there were files strewn across the floor. Beads of sweat popped from Khan's forehead. Gonzo had never seen him look like this. He felt like he should say something.

'Lost somethin', boss?'

'No, I felt like doing some spring cleaning. Course I've fucking lost something. Well, that fuckwit Raj has. Where the fuck does he put things?'

'What are you lookin' for? Maybe I can help.'

'Never mind, I need to go.'

Khan grabbed the coffee cup from Gonzo and raised it to his lips.

'Boss, it's hot!'

The warning was too late. Pain and anger flashed across Khan's face.

'Fuck!' Khan screamed. He threw the cup across the office. It smashed against the wall, leaving a dark brown spatter pattern decorating the smooth surface. Gonzo jumped and instinctively took a step backwards, away from Khan.

Khan stormed past him, through the door and out of the office. Gonzo watched as he went to the sink and drained a glass of water. Then, screaming with rage, he swept his arm across the work-top, sending everything crashing to the floor.

Gonzo stood in silence as Khan marched out of the back door, slamming it shut behind him. He let out a sigh of relief. Khan had clearly been distracted and Gonzo was surprised that he hadn't demanded to look inside his bag.

He decided to give it a couple of minutes for Khan to be well clear of the building – then he would make his escape.

41

Larry's next kill, from Vihaan's list of customers, was carried out with just as much precision as his execution of Damir Langra in Castleton. He sat in a coffee shop in Derby. It was owned by one of Langra's associates, an Indian man called Harish Anand, who owned a chain of coffee shops and nail salons in town.

When Anand walked into the cafe, Larry recognised him instantly. He wore a bright blue and white striped shirt and stone-coloured chinos, a blazer draped over his arm.

Larry stood to greet Harish with a smile and a handshake, then asked him very politely to accompany him. He tucked the tip of a knife into his ribs – hard enough for Anand to understand that his words weren't a request but an instruction.

They walked to a park across the road from the coffee shop, and sat on a bench.

'Who are you? What do you want?' asked Anand, a tremble in his voice.

'It doesn't matter who I am, Harish. What matters is that I know who you are, and how you like to get your kicks … in a certain house in Rotherham.'

Anand's eyes widened as Larry spoke but, before he could respond, Larry added,

'Now is not the time for defensive speeches, Mr Anand. I'm sure you didn't give the young girls you abused the chance to tell you why you shouldn't rape them.' Larry put his arm across Anand's shoulders. Anand started to shake.

'What are you going to do to me?'

'Not half as much as you did to those young girls.' Looking directly into Anand's eyes, Larry slipped the knife smoothly between his ribs. He kept his arm around Anand's shoulders as his lungs filled with blood. Unable to scream for help, Harish Anand slipped quietly into a struggle-free death. Larry placed Anand's blazer against the wound, sheathed his blade and walked calmly out of the park.

Getting back to his car, he saw that he'd missed a call from Khan. He thought for a second. Did he want to return the call, or not? He decided he would. Khan's phone rang three, four, five times, then he answered.

'Lawrence, hi, thanks for calling back. Have you managed to track Raj down yet?'

'No not yet, but I've put some feelers out. It shouldn't be long. How's Husna?'

There was a long, heavy pause – the kind of gap in a conversation that drags the air out of it.

'She … she's dead.'

'Oh, Inzamam, I'm so sorry.'

'Thank you. She died in hospital last night. Her injuries were just too bad and the doctors said she was unlikely to regain consciousness. Just after I left the hospital to go home, they called me back. She died alone, within minutes of me leaving her.'

There was another long pause. Larry tried to work out what to say. He'd killed a lot of people, but rarely had to support anyone with their own grief or loss. It was an alien feeling, and not one he was well equipped to deal with.

'I am so sorry. If there's anything I can do, let me know.'

'I think the help you're giving me tracking down Raj will be plenty. It will save me from worrying about it – I know if anyone can find him, you can.'

He didn't respond, figuring Inzamam must be in a bad place. For all his faults, and he had many, Larry knew that Inzamam loved Husna, even if he had a strange way of showing it.

He ended the call and turned his thoughts to Raj.

Raj, you dumb fuck, where are you? Larry was very aware of what Inzamam was capable of – and what he would do to Raj when he found him. He also knew that Raj was savvy enough to know this too.

Larry knew he had a very short window of time, once he'd located Raj, to find out what he was up to, why he'd been with Husna, and how he could help him to not end up dead at the hands of Khan.

He accelerated hard down the motorway. It took him just over two hours to get from Derby back to Southampton. Once he was back in the city, he headed towards the docks. Halfway along a dual carriageway that ran parallel to the water, he took a right, doubling back into the forecourt of a petrol station.

Larry fuelled his car. He swaggered into the shop and clocked the two customers ahead of him. Out of habit he mentally checked the position of the security cameras and noted the angle they were panned to cover. Making his way around the edge of the shop, he caught the eye of a well-built black woman behind the counter. She wore a uniform shirt and coloured beads in her long, braided hair. She smiled when she saw Larry making his way around the shop, looking directly at her the whole time.

He got to the staff door and heard an electronic lock click open. He slipped through the door and waited for the woman to finish taking payment from the last of her customers, which she did with a warm smile and loud laugh at some exchange they'd had. Larry grinned and waited for her.

As soon as the shop was empty, she turned to face him.

'Larry!' she shrieked. 'Are you a sight for sore eyes. You haven't been around here forever. I was starting to think you were ignoring me. Come here and give me a hug.' As she walked to-wards Larry, her arms thrown out wide, he felt an irresistible pull towards her. He wrapped his arms around her and felt her press against him.

'Ignore you? Never!' he said, as he released her.

'I should think so – your skinny ass ain't gonna find a woman as fine as me nowhere,' she said in a fake American accent.

'That's the truth, Elsie. I can't argue with that.'

'So, what brings you here? And don't tell me your car needed petrol.'

'Ha ha, no – well, yes. I need your help finding someone.'

'Oh? And why do *you* want to find them?'

'It's complicated…'

'Huh, always is. So who is the poor soul?'

'Raj Gadhi. He's a young—'

'I know who he is,' she snapped. 'I know exactly who he is, and who he works for. Which begs the question, why don't you know where he is?'

'That's what I like about you, Elsie – you know just enough about everyone.'

'I know more about some people,' she said, flashing him a smile and a wink he'd seen before.

'I haven't got time for that today. I need to find Raj quickly and I figured you might be able to help me. But Elsie, I need you to do it on the quiet. I can't have anyone knowing I'm looking for him. If anyone finds out, he could be in real danger.'

'You can trust me, you know that.'

'I know. I didn't mean to teach Granny to suck eggs.'

'Hey! Who are you calling Granny?' She laughed. Larry gave her a softer, slightly longer embrace.

'I suppose I'd better pay you for the petrol and let you get back to work.'

'You can distract me for free any time, you know that. But yep, you gotta pay for your petrol like everyone else.'

Larry walked around to the customer side of the counter, paid for his fuel and left, promising Elsie – and himself – that he would be back to see her again soon, and not for fuel.

42

Raj got off the phone to Gonzo and glanced across the hotel room at Maya, who was starting to prepare a new set of dressings. She'd asked reception for a large bowl the night before and walked past him with it in her hands.

'Warm water to clean you up,' she said, without looking at him. She was wearing one of his T-shirts, which skimmed the top of her thighs. He watched her walk into the bathroom. He had woken up to find Maya sat in a chair, looking out of the window. She said she'd been awake for a while, but figured he needed the rest.

He popped a handful of the painkillers he'd got from Saban, the giant. Shuffling to the end of the bed, he was instantly aware how much of his body hurt.

Maya came out of the bathroom with the bowl, half full of water, and a flannel.

'Let's get you cleaned up and get those dressings redone.'

'Yes, nurse,' he said, lying back down on the bed.

Maya worked quickly, cleaning and re-dressing his injuries. He watched her as she worked, her hands moving methodically but gently.

'Maya, I really appreciate you taking care of me. I wouldn't have a clue where to start, but you don't need to do this you know. I feel bad about getting you involved in all this. You were quite happily going about your business when I asked you to break me out of hospital.'

'Don't be silly, like I said last night, I don't do anything I don't want to do and although I may not be part of the world you live in, you need help at the moment and I *am* a nurse. What kind of nurse would I be if I let a man who should be hospital fend for himself? And anyway, it's not often I do something this spontaneous, in fact, I never do anything this spontaneous and I'm sort of enjoying it.'

'OK, well thanks again. When I go to the club to see Shala today, I'd like you to get in your car and drive somewhere out of the way until I'm done. I don't think you should stay here. We don't know if the people who work here also work for Shala.'

'Do you think they might?'

'I think there's a good chance that lots of people either work for him or are very loyal to him. Until I've spoken to him, I don't want you being left exposed.'

'I'm exposed enough,' she said with a smile, flicking up the bottom of the T-shirt.

'Smart arse. Can you help me get dressed? Saban will be here soon.'

'Yeah, sure. Have you decided what you're going to do?'

'Yes, I think so.'

She helped him to dress then went into the bathroom, coming out of the shower just as he was ready to go.

'You will stay safe, won't you, Raj?'

'I'll try,' he replied, as he hobbled to the door

***

Saban was outside the hotel by the time Raj managed to make his way down. It was a struggle to walk, but the painkillers were doing their job.

The large Albanian got out of the car and opened the back door for Raj. 'Good morning, Mr Gadhi. How did you sleep?'

'Morning, Saban. Good, thank you – it's a nice hotel.'

They drove to the club and once more Saban took Raj up in the lift to save him walking too far. The club had the same dark, menacing air that it had the night before, without the benefit of daylight to brighten the corridors and bars.

Saban showed Raj to a seat at a large meeting table on the far side of Shala's office and gave him a cup of tea. The drug lord was nowhere to be seen. Raj looked nervously around the huge space.

'Mr Shala will be with you soon. Please make yourself comfortable,' said Saban, smiling at Raj and leaving the room.

A quiet classical music track played through unseen speakers, with violins that sounded as though they were seeping from the walls. Raj sat and sipped his tea. After about ten minutes a door Raj hadn't spotted, as it was blended into the wall, opened. Shala stepped into the room.

'Raj. Good to see you. I trust you slept well. How was the hotel?'

'Lovely, thank you.'

'Good, and how are you feeling this morning? Your injuries, they must be painful, yes?'

'Yes, they are a bit, but I'm fine. Saban gave me some painkillers on the way out yesterday, which have worked really well.'

'Excellent. Saban was a doctor in our homeland – he is very good at repairing the body.'

Raj was shocked that the giant used to be a doctor; that was the last profession he would have guessed.

'That would explain why the pills are so good,' he said with a smile.

'Indeed! So, down to business. You and your pretty nurse have had a pleasant night in the hotel. I am sure you will have thought about our conversation, perhaps even discussed it with the young lady, yes?'

'Yes.'

'And? What decision did you arrive at? Please understand, this is not a weighted question. I just want to understand what you are thinking.'

Raj pulled himself up in his chair, making sure he was at his full height, although that still left him short of Valmir Shala.

'I've considered your offer very carefully. It's a very good offer…'

'But?'

'But I would like to know a bit more about your intentions and the detail behind your offer.'

'Meaning?'

'For example, you said that I would have a cut of the takings. What kind of cut are we talking about? Given that my product, as you said, is superior to the product your street team are currently distributing.'

'Ah, you are as astute as I understood you to be. Of course you want to know the finer details of our agreement. I admire you for being direct. Too often people dance around what they actually mean to say, but you come straight to the point.' Shala took a breath. 'Let us look at the costs for distributing the product. There are import costs, cutting compounds and lab costs. Then storage and distribution must be paid for. The street teams must be paid and managed, to ensure they stay loyal and deliver the volumes we need to ensure the venture is viable. When you take out all these variables, you are then left with profit – from that comes our cut. What I propose is you have five per cent of gross, which roughly equates to the cut I take for myself.'

'What kind of volumes are you currently moving, if you don't mind me asking?'

'Of course I don't mind. How else are you supposed to know whether it is worth the investment of your time and considerable talent? We currently distribute £80,000 —'

'A month?' Raj interrupted.

'A week. That is only of the equivalent to your scorpion. The other products you would be involved in make us around £200,000 a week across all our networks.'

Raj took a moment to absorb the figures. Five per cent of this would mean at least £10,000 a week. He also knew that Khan moved more drugs than Shala, and Khan had never paid him anywhere near what Shala was offering.

'This surprises you, yes?' Shala asked.

'Er, no, of course not. I knew that you moved a significant amount of product. To be clear, you said I would get five per cent of gross?'

'That is correct. More than from Mr Khan, I'm sure.'

'Yes, that would be a bit of a pay increase. So tell me, if you would, why me?'

'That's always a good question to ask. In fact, it's one of my favourites. The reason is simple. You are better at what you do than the people who currently work for me, and you find yourself in a position where you cannot go back to your previous employer. To me, that looks like a gift horse I should not look in the mouth.'

Raj sat in silence for a couple of minutes. Shala sat opposite him, sipping on a large mug of tea, seemingly in no hurry for an answer.

'OK, so we're talking about roughly £10,000 a week, based on current volumes, but five per cent of gross for all products, and my own team?'

'That is correct. And do not forget - your own lab.'

'And I have your assurance that, if I stay around here, I'll be safe from Khan?'

'You have my security team at your disposal. Once you accept my offer, you immediately become one of the senior members of my organisation, and my personal security team would take direct instructions from you, as they do me. You would have your own car and driver, and Saban would help you find a suitable accommodation where you would be safe when you are not working.'

Raj was stunned. It sounded almost too good to be true, and he didn't want to push his luck and keep firing questions.

'OK, I'm in.' Raj was shocked by how quickly and confidently he had agreed.

'Excellent!'

Shala pulled two shot glasses from a drawer and poured a clear liquid, which Raj assumed was vodka, into them and they each downed their shots.

'Before you start work, you must recover. Saban will take you back to the hotel. Unless there is anything else you would like to discuss?'

'No, I think that's all. Oh – there is just one more question.' He looked at Shala, expecting him to look tired of his questions, which is what Khan would have done by now. Instead he saw him looking inquisitive, waiting for the question.

'Of course. Now is the time for questions.'

'How and when will I be paid? It's not like you can set up a bank transfer.' Shala's laugh boomed around the office.

'Indeed! I'm very glad you asked.'

Shala reached into the drawer he had pulled the shot glasses from. First he pulled out the bottle, which he placed on the table, once he had refilled their glasses. Then he pulled out a clingfilm-wrapped stack of £20 notes, about four inches thick. He placed it on the table then took out a second, identical stack, which he placed next to the first. Dropping one of his huge paws on the piles of money, he pushed them towards Raj.

'That should cover your first four weeks – and be enough to rent somewhere pleasant to stay, yes?'

'That's £40,000?'

'Very impressive. Yes, it is roughly £40,000. We pack used twenties in bundles of £20,000. It makes counting easier – I am sure you understand. Please take it. There will be plenty to follow. To answer your question, I believe money is a personal matter and I will always give you yours in person.'

Raj paused before reaching forward to claim the money, knowing full well that as soon as he accepted Shala's golden shilling, he was committed.

'Hesitation, while you consider the implications,' said Shala. 'Many people would have taken the money before I finished moving it. I think I am going to like working with you, Raj.'

43

Where the fuck is that treacherous little bastard? Khan raged internally.

He'd been into the office to find the detailed files on contacts, pushers and cutting-compound suppliers that he knew Raj kept on his laptop, but he hadn't been able to unlock the password. He launched it across the office. He'd also been unable to find the backup paper copy Raj had shown him. This had really pissed him off. *How could I be so fucking stupid?*

The image of Husna lying helpless and unconscious in her hospital bed played over and over in his mind's eye, taunting him as he drove. The blast of a car horn snapped him out of his thoughts, and he realised he'd drifted over the white line into the path of an oncoming truck. Then, inspired by his near miss, a thought hit him. What if Husna had been forced off the road? What if she hadn't simply lost control of the car? That would mean someone had been following her. Someone knew that Raj was with her, and someone could have been trying to get to him – perhaps to punish him for some wrong or other. He dialled Lawrence, who answered almost immediately.

'Inzamam. You OK?'

'Lawrence, who hates me enough to want to kill Husna to get to me?' There was a silence.

'Oh, come on, don't be coy. We've known each other long enough that you can be straight with me. I was just thinking, what if someone ran Husna off the road to get at me? It's possible, isn't it?'

'I'm not saying it's not possible. The trouble is, that's not a short list.'

This time it was Khan's turn to pause, as he mulled over the truth in his friend's statement. There were a lot of people who hated him enough to kill Husna. He hadn't exactly been on a friend-winning frenzy lately.

'Well, humour me. Who would be at the top of the list, if you were going to rank them?'

'I guess top of the list would be the Albanians – they probably know by now that you killed their men, and you are their biggest competitor.'

'Yes, I agree, I had them top of the list. Who else?'

'Anyone who sympathises with Arjun Bakshi. I'm sure Vihaan has told someone what happened by now.'

'Hmm, yeah, I guess.' He left a deliberate gap for Lawrence to fill.

'Then there's nut-job jealous boyfriends of some of the women you've been with recently. Smaller up-and-coming rival drug gangs, like the crew from Bournemouth, trying to make a name for themselves. Have you had any trouble at your mosque Anyone taking exception to how you conduct yourself? Then I'd add them to the people you've beaten up, humiliated or threatened. Like I say, it gives you quite a list.'

'Alright, take it easy. That was just off the top of your head? I'd need to draft in professional help compiling the list, if you actually gave it some thought.' Khan wasn't particularly happy that Lawrence had reeled off the names of so many people, but he wasn't surprised. 'So, do you think Husna was run off the road?'

'It's possible. In fact, I'd say it's likely. I would, if I wanted to send you a message without fronting up to you.'

Just hearing Lawrence say this was enough for Khan to be convinced he was right. Lawrence was the most thorough, ruthless person he knew. If he'd do it, then others definitely would.

'OK, so my money's on the Albanians. What do you think?'

'I think it's a big list, Inzy, but that wouldn't be a bad place to start. Why? What have you got in mind? Don't do anything rash – it won't end well.'

'Won't end well? Lawrence, my wife is fucking dead, how much worse could it end?' he yelled down the line. 'It was the fucking Albanians, I know it was them!'

'I know you're upset, but these things are always done best after a bit of thought, so promise me you won't do anything hasty.'

Khan's blood was boiling: he wanted revenge and he wanted it now. But he also knew that his friend was just trying to protect him.

'OK, OK, I'll wait. But they're going to fucking pay for this. Every one of them. You mark my words.'

'I get it. I'll be with you later. Just tell me you won't do anything until we've spoken and at least formed a plan.'

Inzamam didn't answer, he ended the call then glanced around to get his bearings, as he'd been driving on autopilot throughout the conversation. He was shocked to realise that he was in Bournemouth, just around the corner from the hospital. His eyes burned and he wiped them, hot tears smearing the back of his hand as another surprise wave of grief swept over him. He turned his car around at the first opportunity and headed for the seafront. There was something calming about being by the sea, and he figured that sitting for a while, listening to the waves, would help him clear his head. He was ready to figure out how he was going to make the people who had put Husna in hospital pay.

44

Gonzo rapped heavily on the door of Jete Nate. He waited a little while and banged once more, then heard the doors being unlocked. Dardan Rama answered the door, imposing as ever with his shaved head and tattooed neck.

'Mr Hasani is expecting you.'

They took the familiar route through the club to Hasani's office, but instead of opening the office door, as he had previously, Rama looked at Gonzo and nodded towards the door. Gonzo stopped for a moment outside the office door and watched Dardan walk away down the corridor. He hesitated. Did he knock? Or just walk in? He decided to knock, but he got no response. After a few more seconds of standing in the corridor, he pushed open the door. Hasani perched on the edge of his desk, drink in hand, clearly waiting for him.

'Mike! Good day. Come, have a drink.'

Hasani reached behind him and produced a glass with a shot in it. Gonzo stepped forward, looking as confident as he could, and took the glass, knocking the vodka back in one swift movement.

'You are getting accustomed to fine vodka. This is an expensive habit and one that will mean you need plenty of money.'

'It is good, and yeah I intend to earn plenty of money workin' with you.'

'Yes, our arrangement. It seems events have taken a mysterious twist since we spoke.'

Gonzo instantly felt nervous. 'A twist? What do you mean?'

'It seems that your colleague, Raj Gadhi, has approached my employer, Mr Shala, and wants to work for us, instead of Mr Khan.'

Raj wants to work for the Albanians? What the fuck?

'I'm sorry, I'm not sure what you mean…'

'Ha – it is a shock, yes? Let me explain. Your friend was in an accident—'

'Yes, yes I know that.'

'And it seems he was with Mr Khan's wife when the accident happened.'

'What?' Gonzo couldn't believe what he was hearing. He knew Raj had balls, but Khan's wife? That was suicide. 'So you're tellin' me, Khan's wife and Raj were in a crash and now Raj wants to work for your boss?'

341

'That is short version, yes.'

Gonzo heard the irritation in Hasani's voice. 'Sorry, Mr Hasani, I didn't mean to interrupt. It's just … well, I've known Raj for a long time and he's always been loyal to Khan. So the thought of him with Khan's wife's a bit of a head-fuck.'

'Don't worry, Mike, I'm sure it's a surprise. But one of the things I've learned in life is that loyalty is flexible. Allegiances often shift when someone is in trouble. From what I know of Mr Khan, I cannot imagine he will take too kindly to finding out this information.'

Gonzo didn't butt in this time. Neither did he think that telling Hasani that Raj had called him would be a good idea. *That explains why Khan was in such a foul mood earlier*. Thought Gonzo.

'So, how does this affect our arrangement?'

'It will have a positive impact. Allow me to explain. Mr Shala and I had a long conversation earlier and we know you and Raj already work well together. So having you both working with us would mean we can take over both Portsmouth and Southampton, absorbing Mr Khan's street teams. It also means a change in your working relationship. Instead of working directly with me, you will become part of Mr Gadhi's senior distribution team. Your income will not be affected by this but, if we are correct, we think that Mr Gadhi has more experience in cutting and coordination of supply. Would this be correct?'

Gonzo felt a wave of relief wash over him. He had been worried, after speaking to Raj a few days ago, about how he was going to blag his way through running the whole of Southampton.

This meant he and Raj could pick up where they had left off, only with the Albanians instead of Khan.

'I mean, I could have done it, but yeah, Raj has been doin' it longer than me.'

'So this is good for both of us, yes?'

'Er … yes, I suppose it is.'

'Of course it is. You and Raj will earn a good income, doing what you were doing already.'

As Hasani refilled their shot glasses Gonzo saw something over Hasani's shoulder that made his blood run cold. On the CCTV monitor from the club's front door was Inzamam Khan. He was looking directly into the camera. Gonzo was unable to move or speak. He just stared at the screen.

Hasani saw the look on Gonzo's face change and must have felt the fear oozing from him. He followed Gonzo's eye-line and turned to see Khan staring up at the camera. Unlike Gonzo, Hasani wasn't fazed.

'Ah, Mr Khan has come to pay us a visit.' They watched Khan bang on the door, three, four, five times, never moving his eyes from the CCTV camera above the doorframe. He waited five-seconds then beat his fist on the door again, three, four, five times.

***

After the fifth strike, Khan heard the doors being unlocked from the inside and shifted his attention away from the camera. One of the doors began to open, revealing a huge suited man. Khan reached into his jacket pulled out a suppressed handgun, and pumped two bullets into the forehead of the man. The bald guy stumbled backwards then folded to the floor, lifeless.

Khan turned to face the camera once more and put a well-aimed bullet into the centre of the lens, then stepped inside the club. He could feel adrenaline coursing through him: his grip tightened on the pistol and his heart thumped in his chest. As he closed the door, he took care to lock it and mentally registered that he had twelve bullets left in the clip and a spare clip in his pocket, giving him twenty-seven to get the job done.

Right, time for you fuckers to pay.

Holding the gun upright in front of his chest, he stalked along the corridor, staying close to the shadowy wall. He heard footsteps hurrying towards him. Two suited men came running around the corner ahead of him. Khan stepped from the shadows and aimed for their centre of mass, putting two bullets into the guy in front and three into the second one. They collapsed, one on top of the other.

He felt no remorse as the would-be defenders of the club fell before him. Fuelled by his anger over the betrayal by Raj and Husna, the building sense of guilt he felt over ending Husna's life, and convinced that the Albanians were wholly responsible for putting her in the hospital, Khan's path to retribution was set. He looked through to the dimly lit bar, but couldn't see anyone else around, so he made his way through towards the back of the club. Here, he found a door marked 'No entry – staff only'. He pushed the door open slowly with his foot, leading with the suppressor. There was a stairway ahead of him that wound up to the left.

Khan

By the time he got up the four flights to the next door, he'd taken out another two Albanians. He had stayed low as he made his way around the turns in the stairs, remembering what Lawrence had once told him: 'People don't expect you to come upstairs, crouching.' He'd killed one with a single shot to the head and double-tapped the other in the chest.

So far, so good. Now, where the fuck is Hasani?

He paused before making his way through the next door, positive that all Hasani's crew knew he was there by now; the second guy on the stairs had got a shot off, which had rung out in the stairway. He didn't know how many men the Albanian boss had in the club and he didn't care.

He took a deep breath and kicked the door open, pushing the gun out in front of him and crouching, as he stepped into the corridor. He swept to the left: no one there. Then, still moving low, he spun around to his right. A door banged open in front of him and someone stepped out into the corridor, their back to Khan. He shot them without hesitation. A young woman, holding a tray of glasses, fell forward against the open door, dead, glasses smashing as they tumbled from the tray.

'Shit!' he hissed through gritted teeth.

He shook his head to clear it, took another deep breath and stepped carefully around the dead woman and the broken glass. He saw a sign on a door to his left: 'Mr Hasani'.

Khan slid his trigger finger back and dropped the extended clip from the gun. He knew he had one bullet in the chamber and only two left in the clip, and decided he would rather go into Hasani's office with a full clip.

Once he'd reloaded, Khan stood facing the door. Beads of sweat popped out on his forehead and his heart thumped harder than he'd ever felt it.

He took a deep breath, grabbed the door handle and pushed open the door, entering as if he was walking into his own office, full of confidence and bravado.

It took him a second to take in what he saw on the other side of the door. Hasani, he had expected, but opposite the Albanian was a wide-eyed Gonzo.

Out of the corner of his eye, Khan saw movement. He turned and shot a silenced bullet into one of Hasani's men. At the same time as he was checking that the guy had gone down, he saw Hasani raise a gun. It looked like a Desert Eagle 50.

Khan threw himself into a forward roll towards the guy he'd just shot and fired three rounds into him at close range, then scrambled up and ducked behind a cupboard. He heard the big gun go off. The back of a nearby chair exploded, scattering around him.

'Fuck me, that's loud,' Khan said, glancing around him. There was no way back now. Another shot boomed from Hasani's gun, taking a chunk out of a table near Khan's head. He stood up and fired three shots at Hasani. As he did, he managed to get his bearings and saw Gonzo duck down behind Hasani's desk. Khan folded himself back against the wall, the corner of which gave him enough cover.

'Gonzo, you treacherous bastard!' he yelled.

Khan

Gonzo didn't answer, but Hasani did. 'Mr Khan, you have killed some of my best men. What do you want? I'm sure you are not here for young Mike.'

'Mike?' Khan whispered to himself. 'I want to know why you had my wife run off the road, and I want the fucking scumbag who did it, so I can make him pay.'

'What makes you think I targeted your wife, Mr Khan? She is of no interest to me.'

'You're a lying bastard! I know it was one of your fucking gofers. You killed my wife!'

'I understand your frustration, Mr Khan, but perhaps the source of your anger lies closer to home? Mr Gadhi, for example. I believe he and your wife were – how shall I say it? Very close?'

Khan couldn't listen to any more. He stepped out and fired another three shots. Hasani's cannon boomed in response. A bullet tore through Khan's left shoulder and threw him backwards into the corner of the room.

Red-hot pain seared through his shoulder and down his arm, and he heard a noise that sounded like Hasani dropping his gun.

A croakier version of Hasani's voice spoke to Khan. 'You have come here with accusations and anger, but no foundation, Mr Khan. You have only yourself to blame for your wife's death – for her affair with Raj and for Raj and Mike leaving you to work for us. You are careless, and allow your emotions to control you. This will be your undoing.'

Bang! The big gun went off again, this time missing Khan by quite a way and putting a hole in the back wall.

Khan held his shoulder, blood oozing onto his hand. He knew, if he stayed where he was, he was dead for sure.

Raj and Gonzo – working for the Albanians? What the fuck is going on? He felt a tingly feeling in his left hand. He braced his back against the wall and pushed up onto his feet. He stepped from the cover of the corner and fired towards Hasani. As he did, he saw the big Albanian on the floor, slumped against his desk. The cannon was hanging loosely in his hand. Hasani's eyes were wide as he looked at Khan, trying to lift his gun. His body was covered in blood. Khan had clearly hit him a few times.

Khan screamed at the top of his lungs and fired four times into Hasani's chest, the slap of the silenced rounds quieter – but no less deadly – than the boom of the Eagle.

His anger and sense of betrayal drove Khan forward, making him forget the pain in his shoulder. Hasani's body jerked with every shot, the Desert Eagle flying from his hand. Then Gonzo leapt up from behind the desk, grabbing the big gun as he moved.

Khan still had his gun trained on Hasani as Gonzo fired the Desert Eagle. The sound was ear-splitting and the impact knocked Khan off his feet. His body crashed to the floor.

He could feel blood pumping from his stomach and his back. Instinctively he clutched his hands over the hole in his abdomen. With every beat of his heart, more of Inzamam Khan's life ebbed away onto the floor of Erion Hasani's office. His eyes began to feel too heavy to hold open. He saw Gonzo standing above him, the huge gun in his hands and tears streaming down his face.

'I'm sorry, boss,' were the last words Inzamam Khan heard.

45

Gonzo crouched behind Erion Hasani's desk. Seeing Khan come into the club on the CCTV then hearing shots being fired as he made his way through the building had freaked Gonzo out enough. But when Khan had walked into the office as if he owned the place, Gonzo had been paralysed with fear. Then, as the gun-fire between Khan and Hasani raged, he'd dived for cover behind the desk.

And there he was, hearing them shouting across the office at each other: Hasani taunting Khan. Khan spitting accusations, venom in his voice.

Gonzo looked around the corner of the desk just as Hasani crumpled to the floor. His gun had come out of his hand. Gonzo saw that Khan had been hit too. Then Khan stepped towards Hasani and pumped bullets into him, a look of rage and hatred painted across his face. Gonzo knew he'd be next – unless he did something first.

He scuttled across the floor, behind the desk, staying low, and grabbed the gun Hasani had dropped. He leapt up, pointed it at Khan and, without pausing to think, pulled the trigger.

The massive gun recoiled, forcing him back half a step. Gonzo watched in shock as Khan flew backwards. He'd never seen anything so brutal.

He walked over to see if Khan was actually dead, or just wounded. As he got closer, it was obvious to Gonzo that, although he was still clinging to life, Khan wasn't going to last for long.

A wave of guilt swept over him as he stood over Inzamam Khan – a man he'd feared for as long as he'd known him. A man who had seemed indestructible.

He felt tears burn in his eyes as Khan looked at him, clutching his stomach.

'I'm sorry, boss.'

Gonzo watched, as without the strength to reply and with blood pooling around his body, Khan breathed his last.

Instantly, panic started to set in. Gonzo began to realise that he was the last man standing in a club that was full of corpses, including Hasani and Khan. On top of this, he was holding the gun that had killed Khan.

His tears stopped and a nervous knot began to form in his stomach.

Khan

W*hat the fuck am I going to do? How do I get out of this?* He thought through his options quickly. He could run, but the CCTV showed him coming in and Hasani's phone would show a call to him earlier. He could take it and destroy it, but then what? There were all the dead bodies, the guns, the two dead drug dealers. He began to breathe faster and faster, rubbing his hands over his head, fear welling inside him.

C*ome on, think, Mike, think.*

He grabbed his phone, searched for a number and pressed call. 'Raj, it's Gonzo.'

'Hello mate, you alright? You sound awful.'

'Raj, listen, I need help. I've really fucked up and I don't know what to do.' His speech was fast and pressured.

'What do you mean, you've fucked up? Calm down. Tell me what's happened.'

'It was fuckin' mental – there were bullets flyin' everywhere. I don't know what to do. I need help. I'm fucked.'

'Bullets? Gonzo, what the fuck has happened? Calm down and tell me everything.' Gonzo took a couple of deep breaths and walked to the other side of the office, facing away from the bodies of Khan and Hasani.

'Khan came to Hasani's club. He had a gun and he went fuckin' mental. He was shootin' everybody, startin' with Hasani's doorman and workin' his way through the club.'

'What? Are you fucking kidding me?'

'No, he made it all the way through the club to Hasani's office. As soon as he walked in, he started shootin'. He killed Hasani,

Raj, fuckin' killed him, right there in front of me. I was shittin' myself. I grabbed Hasani's gun and I-I-I killed Khan.'

'You did what?'

'I killed Khan. I was sure he was gonna to kill me next, after he'd shot Hasani, and he was already bleedin'. So I grabbed Hasani's gun and I shot him. And he's dead. They're all dead, and I don't know what to do. What the fuck do I do, Raj? Please help me.'

'OK, just calm down for a minute and let me think.' The line went quiet for what felt like an eternity, then Raj spoke. 'Right, this is what you need to do. Clean the gun off and anything else you've touched since you've been there. Door handles, glasses, surfaces, anything. Do you understand?'

'Yes, I think so. I need to clean everythin' down.'

'Yes, that's the first thing. Next, I'm going to call Larry. He'll know what to do to clean this up. Then I'll call you back. Don't hang about – do what I've told you to do and keep the doors locked. Don't answer it to anyone. Do you understand?'

'Yes. Clean everythin', keep the doors locked, wait for you to call back. Got it. Thanks, Raj. I didn't know who else to call.'

'It's OK, you've done the right thing. We'll get it sorted out.'

Gonzo stuffed his phone back in his pocket and realised he was still holding the Desert Eagle. He dropped it, and it landed on the floor with a dull thud.

He slumped into a chair, his head in his hands, wondering how he'd got himself into this mess. He shook his head hard and stood up.

'Come on, Mike, sort it out. You've got to get this shit cleaned up.' He rummaged through the cupboards in the office and found a cloth and a spray bottle of cleaning stuff and set about wiping the gun down, like he'd seen people do in the movies. Next, he wiped down the desk, chairs and handles – everything he could think of that he might have touched since entering the office.

He went out to the corridor and saw the dead girl lying on the floor, broken glass all around her. He tried to ignore her as he carried on wiping door handles, clearing away all trace of his presence, but his gaze kept getting drawn back to her, like a moth to bright light. He felt an empty sadness looking at her, knowing that she'd had nothing to do with the madness that had happened here. But there she lay, as dead as Khan and Hasani.

His phone rang and snatched him out of his guilty sorrow. 'Raj?'

'No, it's Larry. Come to the door of the club and let me in.'

The line went dead. Gonzo made his way hastily towards the front door, wiping the surfaces with his cloth and stepping over the corpses he passed on the way.

He got to the door and saw Dardan Rama on the floor, two bullet holes in his forehead. Another wave of sadness, he'd liked Dardan. Gonzo closed his eyes and shook his head then let Larry in, locking the doors behind him. Larry looked down at the dead man, snapping on a pair of surgical gloves and passing Gonzo a pair to put on.

'Fucking hell, Gonzo, this is a mess, isn't it?'

'Thanks for comin'. It gets worse,' Gonzo replied, pulling on the thin blue gloves.

'Yeah, I heard. You've killed the boss, by all accounts.'

'Yeah, he's in the office upstairs.'

'How many dead?'

'I'm not sure. I was in the office with Hasani. I don't know how many Khan killed on his way through.'

'How many have you passed on the way down to let me in?'

'Erm … there's Rama,' he said, pointing at him. 'Then there's two more in the corridor, around the corner. Two on the stairs. A girl in the upstairs corridor and then there's Hasani and Khan.'

'So, eight dead that you know of?'

'Yeah, I think so.'

'And what about guns?'

'What do you mean?'

'How many of them have guns?'

'All of them, I guess, except the girl – she was a waitress.'

'Poor bugger. That's not good; she'll be missed. OK, the Albanians aren't our problem – they could have been killed by anyone. Khan and the girl, they're a different story. We need to get them both out of here and try to cover up the fact that Khan was here, otherwise there'll be repercussions for all of us.'

'What do you want me to do?'

'First things first. Take me to Khan.'

Gonzo led the way to the office. Larry shook his head as they passed the girl in the corridor.

'Do you know her name?' Larry asked.

'Becky, I think. Why?'

'I just think it's sad, dying in a place where no one knows who you are.'

'I don't know her. I heard one of the blokes here call her Becky.'

'Well, we'll sort Becky out in a minute.'

Gonzo held the door open for Larry to go into Hasani's office first. He was surprised that Larry didn't comment on the blood-spattered scene. He just looked around, as if he was viewing a house, then put his bag down in a clear space on the floor.

'Where's the gun you shot him with?'

'Er … it's over there,' he said, pointing to the desk.

'Fucking hell, you don't mess about, do you? That's a Desert Eagle. No wonder he's fucking dead – I'm surprised you didn't cut him in two. Right, give it here. Whose gun is this? I know it's not yours.'

'It's Hasani's.'

Gonzo watched Larry pick up the gun, using a piece of cloth. He wiped the grip then put the Eagle back into Hasani's hand, wrapped his fingers around it, then laid his arm gently on the floor.

Next he walked over to Khan.

'He was always going to end like this, you know,' Larry said to Gonzo.

'What makes you say that?'

'He liked guns too much and couldn't control his temper. That's a dangerous combination in a man with as much power as he had. It was always going to end badly.'

Larry worked his way around the room. It was obvious this wasn't the first time he'd cleaned up a scene like this. He walked over to the bank of monitors and opened the cupboard underneath them. Gonzo watched as Larry found the CCTV hub.

'What are gonna do with that?'

'I'm going to delete the last couple of hours so there's no record of Khan or you being here. It's not perfect as it'll leave a footprint, but it's the best we can do in the time we've got and luckily they haven't password protected their admin. Guessing they never thought it would be needed for something like this.'

'Do me a favour – there's a rolled-up body bag over there in my bag. Grab it, would you?'

'Yeah, sure.'

Gonzo opened the bag and saw three body bags, a roll of gaffer tape, two handguns and some other stuff he didn't have time to check out. He walked over to Larry and handed him the bag.

'He's not going to fit into it rolled up, is he? Put it on that clear bit of floor there.' Larry pointed to a bit of floor that had no blood on it.

Gonzo did as instructed and rolled the bag out, unzipping it ready for Khan.

'OK, give me a hand lifting him in. Be careful, he'll feel heavier than you expect. It's not like lifting a table – he'll bend in the middle.'

Larry was clearly relaxed about what he was doing, but Gonzo was still freaked out. They lifted Khan onto the body bag and Larry zipped it shut.

'OK, that's him sorted for the moment. Let's get someone in here to account for this blood.'

'I don't understand.'

'It's a hell of mess and normally I'd clean the place down and get rid of the body and the blood. But the gun you shot him with will have sent bits of him all over the place and I don't think we've got long enough to clear the place completely. I know you guys all think the police are stupid, but they're not. They'll find any trace of blood, DNA, or fibres they can and match them against the victims laying in front of them and when they don't match, they start digging. Now, there's an off-chance, if we're really lucky that the bloke we choose to lay here has the same blood type as Khan. But if not, the police forensic guys will find out and then they'll want to know whose it is.'

'How do you know all this stuff?'

'It's my job to know. Come-on we've got work to do.'

Gonzo followed Larry out to the stairway, where the cleaner chose one of the two dead men on the stairs, who only had a small amount of blood around him. Between them, they carried the corpse into Hasani's office. They set him down then Larry walked over to Hasani's corpse and retrieved the Eagle.

'Sit him up for me, will you, Gonzo? And hold him upright.'

Gonzo did as requested, holding the dead man's shoulder. Then Gonzo watched as Larry stood and took aim at the body.

'What are you doing?' asked Gonzo.

'Er, shooting him with the right gun. He died from bullets shot by Khan's gun, but we need him to have been shot by Hasani, otherwise the police will want to know who Hasani shot at. Don't worry, I won't hit you.'

He pulled the trigger and shot the corpse in his existing bullet hole. The body jerked violently, out of Gonzo's grip, and slumped to the floor.

Larry placed the gun back in Hasani's hand and rearranged the body, mimicking Khan's final pose.

'That should do it. It will take them a while to figure out that he was already dead when that bullet went in. Right, grab another body bag.'

Gonzo did as requested and followed Larry again, this time out to Becky. Gonzo noticed that Larry took much more care when lifting Becky. He sat her up and brushed the pieces of broken glass off her, taking shards out of her hair and straightening her shirt. She had bullet holes in her back. What blood there was had pooled on her shirt, with only a tiny bit on the floor. When they laid her in the body bag, face-up, she looked as if she was sleeping.

'What will we do with her?' Gonzo asked as Larry slowly zipped the bag shut.

'I don't know yet. She's clearly been shot, so she can't just turn up somewhere, like she could if she'd been poisoned or strangled. The police will go full-on murder hunt, and we don't want that – not with a club full of dead Albanians. And, like I said, she'll be missed. They won't.'

Gonzo looked at Becky's face until it was swallowed by the closing bag, wondering what kind of life she might have had, had it not been for Khan.

'Gonzo!'

'Yeah?'

'At last. It only took three times for you to answer me. Are you OK? Look, I know it's tough to take in the first time, but we've not got long to deal with this before someone turns up. Places like this never stay quiet for long and I think we've already been lucky. So let's not push it, eh?'

'Yeah, sorry. I'm OK. It's just that, when you said she'll be missed, it got me thinkin' about what a waste it is.'

'Try not to beat yourself up. You didn't kill her, did you?'

'No. Khan killed her on his way through the club, I'm guessin'.'

'Exactly. Sad as it is, and it is sad, it's not your fault. Now, can you go and get a brush to clear up this glass while I go and get something out of my bag to get rid of that spot of blood on the floor.'

Gonzo went through the door that Becky had come out of. It opened out to a bar he hadn't seen before. On a shelf, low down, was a dustpan and brush. He grabbed them and took them back to sweep up the fragments of glass, as instructed.

Larry was clearing the blood spot, and directed Gonzo to sweep the glass into the dustpan. 'Make sure you get it all – we don't want to leave any sign that Becky fell here.'

'Will do.'

Gonzo stood back as Larry checked the area. Once he was happy it was clear, he turned to Gonzo. 'Right, just the blood to clear up from where our Khan replacement was laying and then we need to know where the back door to this place is. We need to get Becky and Khan out of here, pronto.'

'I think I'd have been fucked if you hadn't come and sorted this out.'

'Don't sweat it. It's what I do.'

Once Larry had cleared the patch of blood from the stairs, the pair of them picked Becky up. Gonzo led the way to the lift.

It wasn't difficult to find the back door, and Gonzo was thankful that Becky wasn't very heavy. They stopped just inside the back door. Larry told Gonzo to wait until he brought his car around. He disappeared out through the door and left Gonzo with the bagged-up body.

He wasn't gone long, which was fine by Gonzo – the thought of getting caught with a dead body filled him with dread. He hadn't thought about anyone coming into the club until Larry had mentioned it, and now that was all he could think about.

When the door opened, he could see that Larry had backed up an unfamiliar silver Mercedes, but he decided not to ask Larry any questions about it, figuring it was probably better he didn't know too much. Larry was a scary guy.

The boot was already open and Gonzo didn't need instructions for what came next. After Larry had taken a quick look around, they moved the body bag as quickly as they could into the back of the vehicle and Larry closed the boot.

'Back upstairs, then Mr Khan can join Becky,' Larry said brightly. Gonzo struggled to reconcile his tone with what they were doing. They went up in the lift and when they got to the office, Gonzo saw someone at the front doors on the CCTV monitor.

'Larry, look!' He pointed at the monitor.

'Shit! Let's get a move on. Do you know who that is?'

Gonzo looked more closely at the image. 'I think he works behind the bar downstairs, but I'm not sure.'

'We need to move, now!' Larry pulled a gun from inside his jacket, checked it and put it back. They heaved the body bag containing Khan off the floor, checking the monitor one final time on their way out of the office. They saw the barman, buzzing to be let in and looking up at one of the CCTV cameras, frustrated. As quickly as they could, they headed for the lift.

When the lift door opened on the ground floor, Larry shoved Khan's body bag in front of the lift door to stop it closing, then held a finger to his lips. Drawing his gun again, he crept along the corridor towards the front door. A few seconds later he was back.

'OK, come on. He's still out front.'

They staggered to the back door with Khan and Larry opened it, very slowly. Gonzo held his breath as the cleaner looked out into the street, then he heard a voice he didn't recognise.

'Hello, mate – do you know why no one is answering the front door?'

There was no answer that Gonzo could hear, but what followed was a strange-sounding thud. Larry appeared at the door, dragging the limp body of the barman.

'Fuck! Is he alive?'

'Yes, he's alive.' Gonzo helped Larry drag the man inside. Once inside, Larry turned, closed the door, took out his gun and put a single bullet between the barman's eyebrows.

'Now he's not. Come on, we've got to get out of here.'

Gonzo stood, mouth open. 'What the fuck was that for, Larry? He hadn't done anything.'

'He'd seen me – that's enough of a reason for me to add him to the body count. That is, unless you want him to describe me to a police artist when they come to investigate the club full of fucking dead Albanians. Now, do as you're told and pick up the end of this bag.'

Gonzo got the distinct feeling that if he didn't do as he was told, he'd be joining the barman. So he lifted the end of the bag and, between them, they threw Khan into the boot of the car, with Becky.

46

Raj's phone rang. It was a call he'd been waiting for. 'Larry, how's it going?'

'Pretty much as you said – fucked.'

'So Khan is dead?'

'Oh yeah, he's dead alright. Gonzo did a proper job – blew a hole straight through the middle of him, with a Desert Eagle, no less.'

'Fuck. What about Gonzo? Is he OK?'

'Yeah, he's fine, he's with me now. We've got Khan and an innocent loaded in the back of my car.'

'Well, at least that's something. How many others are dead? In fact, let's not chat about it on the phone. Can you meet me at Khan's?'

'Yes, of course – it's probably the best place to be right now. We'll be there in ten minutes. How long until you get there?'

'I think we can be there in about forty, forty-five minutes.'

'OK, see you soon.'

Raj pocketed his phone and turned to Maya, who'd been listening to Raj's side of the conversation.

'It sounds bad.'

'It is, really bad. Khan's dead, Gonzo shot him, and I get the feeling there are a lot more dead than Larry managed to tell me about on the phone.'

'If we need to be at Khan's in forty-five minutes, we'd better get going.'

'*I* need to get to Khan's and meet Larry and Gonzo. *You* don't need to get any deeper into this.'

'Are you kidding? You need to get to Southampton in three-quarters of an hour and I'm guessing your new driver wouldn't be great at keeping secrets – like, say, you going to Khan's?'

'Ha ha, no, I guess not. OK, let's go, driver.'

'Oi! Steady, or you might end up walking, and you're not up to that yet.'

They made good time to Khan's. As soon as they got through the door, Raj clocked the look that Gonzo and Larry gave Maya.

'It's OK – she's with me. I'll explain later, but right now we've got more important things to discuss.'

Raj saw Maya point at the kettle and knew that she was distancing herself from their conversation.

Raj, Gonzo and Larry went through into Khan's office, which had paper strewn all over the floor. They sat around a small coffee table. Raj went first.

'Thanks for clearing this up, Larry. Can you tell me what the state of play is at the club?'

'Yeah, sure. In summary, the Albanian club currently has five Albanian gangsters, one Albanian drug dealer and one innocent lying dead throughout the club. All of them have been shot and most of them have been shot by our beloved Mr Khan. In addition, he and another innocent are body-bagged in the boot of my car. Khan was shot by Gonzo and the innocent was another victim of Khan's.'

'You said there was another innocent at the club?'

'Yeah – a slight issue with a member of bar staff who witnessed Gonzo and me moving Khan.'

'Fucking hell, that's a lot of dead bodies.'

'It is, and someone is going to raise the alarm soon, if they haven't already. Then the police are going to be crawling all over the place. On the face of it, it'll look like a bust-up between the Albanians, where they've all ended up shooting each other. But when they get them back to the coroner's and do the autopsies, they'll start to realise it's not as clear-cut as they might have first thought.'

'OK, so what do we do?'

'We need to get rid of Becky and Khan.'

'Becky?'

'The innocent. She was a waitress at the club. I could have left her, but her being there didn't work with the drug gang bust-up narrative. As I said to Gonzo, nobody will worry if the gangsters don't go home. But when Becky doesn't turn up, someone will raise the alarm.'

'Meaning?'

'Meaning, she needs to disappear permanently. With nothing left to link her to the shootings at the club – or to us. Don't worry about her. I've got a friend at the local crematorium who can take care of her.'

Raj and Gonzo looked silently at each other.

'Our bigger problem is getting rid of Khan,' Raj said eventually.

'Yes, we need to get rid of him in a way that doesn't lead back to here,' said Larry.

Raj thought for a moment, and an idea started to form. 'What if we left the police a gift?'

'Go on, you have my attention.' Larry said.

Raj explained his idea in detail, and Gonzo and Larry listened. They spent the next half an hour chatting through the plan to iron out the wrinkles and make sure they did everything they could to avoid being caught. Together, they decided it needed to be done by the end of the day.

Raj told Gonzo where Khan kept the spare key to his Range Rover, and asked him to go and get the car, which they assumed must be near the Albanians' club.

'Gonzo, straight there and back, no fucking about or joyriding – we haven't got time.'

'No problem. I'll go there and back, no detours.'

While Raj was letting Gonzo know what he wanted him to do from the office doorway, he overheard Larry arranging to drop off Becky's body to the crematorium.

'Oh, and Gonzo, make sure you tuck the car away behind the restaurant when you get back. We don't want anyone else seeing you in it, and it needs to be easy to load up.'

'Got it.' Gonzo pulled on a baseball cap and headed off, on foot, to collect the car.

'Could I have a quick word?' Larry asked Raj once Gonzo had left.

'Yeah, sure, what is it?'

'Let's go back into Inzy's office and have a seat.'

'This sounds serious, what's up?'

'Look, there's something I need to tell you and I didn't want to do it with Gonzo around.'

'OK, is there something to do with Gonzo I don't know yet?'

'No, it's nothing to do with Gonzo, just hear me out for a second. I'm not really sure how to say this so I'm just going to come out and say it. I know that you and Husna were having an affair. Inzamam told me. Not that you needed to be a genius to figure it out, once we knew you were both involved in the crash in the forest. I'm not here to Judge you and I'm sure you both had your reasons for being together. But there's something you need to know. Husna's dead. She died from her injuries in hospital yesterday. I'm really sorry, Raj.'

Raj was stunned. 'She's dead?'

'Yes mate, I'm afraid so.'

'I can't believe it. What kind of scum-bag am I? I left her in the hospital to die and I ran away.'

'You can't blame yourself. If you hadn't got out of there In-zamam would have killed you for sure, we both know that.'

'And now he's dead too. What about their poor kids?'

'As harsh as this might sounds. I'm pretty sure that's not your problem and right now we've got bigger problems, like the dead man in the boot of my car.'

'Yeah, of course. I just —'

'I get that it's a shock, do you need a minute?'

'No, I'll be fine, thanks. Like you said, we've got bigger things to deal with at the moment.' His head was swimming with the realisation that Husna was dead, he sat for a couple minutes in silence, his head resting in his hands, unable to look at Larry, but not wanting to cry.

'How about we go and get a cuppa?'

'Yeah, good idea, and Larry, thanks for letting me know and for not judging me about seeing Husna.'

'Like I said, it's not my place to judge you and I'm sure she had her reasons for being with you too. From what I know of her, she didn't do anything she didn't want to do.'

'Yeah, you're not wrong there.' Raj attempted a smile. They left the office and took a mug of tea each from Maya. They drank their tea in relative silence.

Larry got up. 'Raj, can you give me a hand getting Khan's body in from the car?'

'He shouldn't really be lifting anything, with his injuries,' Maya interjected before

Raj could answer. 'But I'll help.'

'Are you sure?' Asked Raj.

'Yes, it's fine. I overheard most of what you said earlier on the phone. You don't need to protect me, Raj. I'm not a delicate little flower.'

Raj saw Larry smirk, but he said nothing.

'OK, come on then, let's get this done.' Larry headed for the door.

Raj limped over to his workbench and cleared a space for them to lay Khan out. He turned to see Larry and Maya bringing a body bag through the door. He couldn't help thinking about how Khan's girls were going to feel having lost both parents within a couple of days. He shook the thoughts off. 'How about over here?' said Raj, pointing at the bench.

'Yeah, that'll do,' said Larry.

Raj gave them a hand lifting Khan onto the bench. Larry bowed out, saying he had to get Becky to the crematorium as his mate had an early finish and there was no one else around for the next hour. Just before he left, he asked Raj to find something to wrap Khan's body in.

'It will be easier to offload the body if it's tightly wrapped, not in the bag.'

'We'll try and find something. See you in a bit.'

After Larry had left, Maya came and sat next to Raj. 'How are you feeling?'

'I'm not sure, if I'm honest. I can't believe he's dead.' He didn't share the news of Husna's death.

'I meant physically, but yes, it must be a shock, knowing he's in that bag.'

He sighed. 'I'm OK. My leg's killing me and my ribs hurt a lot, but I'll be OK. I'm not sure how my next conversation with Shala is going to go.'

'Shit, yeah, he's not going to be happy, is he? Do they all work for him? The dead men?'

'Yep, the whole lot. It's his club too. Although Hasani used to pretend it was his, we all knew it was owned by Shala.'

'Oh, he's really not going to be a happy camper, then.'

'Ha ha – no, you could say that.'

'You'll work it out. I get the impression that you usually do.'

'I'll have to – there's no one else to sort out Gonzo's mess. Well, Khan's mess. It's not fair to hang this on Gonzo. He must have been scared to death when Khan turned up at Hassani's club and started shooting the place up.'

'What can I do to help?' she asked.

'You could help me find something to wrap him in before Larry gets back. We've got some rolls of hessian in the store. We use it for packing sometimes. I think it's in five-metre rolls.'

'That sounds like it might work.'

They rooted around in the storeroom. Sure enough, there were four rolls of hessian, each one about 150 mm wide. They carried the rolls out to the workbench.

'Right, that's ready for when Larry gets back,' said Raj.

'Why are we waiting for Larry to get back? I can wrap him.'

'You? I mean, you can?'

'I'm pretty sure I'm the only nurse among you. Do you have someone with better skills for wrapping a body? The rolls of hessian are basically like big bandages.'

'Then I guess we don't have anyone who is better qualified to wrap a body.' Raj was stunned by how willing Maya was to be involved and – literally – get her hands dirty.

'Let's get cracking, shall we?'

She reached for the zip at the end of the body bag and paused. 'Have you seen many dead bodies?'

'Only a couple, but not really close up.'

'You might want to prepare yourself. It won't be pretty.'

'I'll be fine.'

She pulled the zip down. When it passed the hole in Khan's stomach, Raj had to look away. 'Fuck me, that's a mess!'

'He's definitely dead.'

'What do you want me to do?' he asked, keen not to stand by and let Maya do it all.

'You can help move his limbs as I need to get the hessian around them, if you're comfortable with that?'

'Yeah, that's fine.'

He watched as Maya expertly wrapped a tight hessian binding around each of Khan's limbs, then bound them together. Then Raj helped roll him as she wrapped his torso, packing and covering the holes in his back and stomach with cut-off squares of hessian before she wrapped him. Once she'd finished, Khan looked as if he'd been mummified. There were no scrappy edges, no pieces out of place; he was perfectly encased in the light-brown cloth.

'That's amazing. You're an absolute star.'

'Aw, thanks. It's really not that difficult once you've done it a few times. Like I said, they're just big bandages.'

It wasn't long before Larry and Gonzo returned, both expressing their admiration for Maya's work.

'I think I might have a new sideline for you, Maya. That's the best wrapping job I've ever seen,' said Larry.

'And I'm guessing you've seen a few?' she replied with a smile.

'That, my dear, would be telling.'

Gonzo came over with four cold beers and they sat for a while, preparing themselves for what was to come.

'Did the crematorium go OK?' Raj asked Larry.

'Yes, all straightforward. They'd done with services for the day and once all the families have gone, that's when they cremate the bodies, so slipping another one in is easy.'

'Sounds like you've done that before,' Raj said.

'It's proved to be a useful resource on occasion, let's leave it at that.' Raj didn't press him any further.

47

DI Baxter and DS Taylor arrived at Jete Nate following a call from a distressed member of staff. The young woman reported that she had arrived at work to find multiple dead bodies inside the club. A quick look around confirmed that there were indeed a number of dead males, in various parts of the club, from the front door, throughout the club and upstairs in the offices. One of the casualties, Erion Hasani was known to the police and although never convicted, he was widely thought to be linked to an Albanian drug distribution network.

'Drew, could you sit with Melissa and take a statement please?' Asked Lomas. The waitress looked pale and in shock and he knew that Drew would handle the questions sympathetically.

'Of course. Mellisa, shall we go through here and find somewhere to sit?' Drew motioned towards the main area of the club knowing there were no bodies there. Lomas waited until they were out of earshot, then called through to another of his team.

'Pete, could you go around and take photos of the deceased please? We need to move quickly on this. If its what I think it is, there'll be a follow-up on its way.'

'Yes boss, no worries.'

Lomas stalked through the club, checking out each of the bodies, being careful not to touch anything, or contaminate the scene. His colleagues in the Scene of Crimes unit would need the area as clean as possible and he'd advised those who were first to arrive at the club to proceed with caution as they'd donned their protective suits and over- shoes.

He stood over the body of Dardan Rama which lay just inside the front door. The bullet holes in his forehead strikingly clear.

'Who did this to you then big-fella?' He turned and made his way slowly through the club, stopping at each of the corpses, trying to figure out the chain of events. Lomas took out his phone and called DCI Carlton as he walked.

'Hi Marie, I'm over at Jete Nate. It's quite a mess. Someone's really gone to town. There are seven dead and no survivors that we've found. If they're all connected, it could be a drug related killing.'

'A turf war, that's all we need. Any idea how it played out?'

'My guess is that the shooter, or shooters, made their way through the front door, after shooting out a camera and catching the first of them by surprise. Then I think they worked their way through the club, picking people off until they got to Erion Hasani's office, where they killed him too.'

'Hasani's dead too?'

'Yep, in what I assume is his own office, judging by the size of it. It's even bigger than yours.' He laughed.

'Ha ha very funny. Isn't Hasani one of Shala's crew?'

'Yes, we know they're connected beyond the club, although we've never been able to prove it.'

'Are you planning on going to speak to Shala?'

'Yes, me and Drew will go over there when we've done here.'

'OK, keep me in the loop. Anything else?'

'Only that we need to get on top of this quickly. If it is drug-turf related there could be a revenge attack coming as soon as Shala-and-co find out about it.'

'Good luck with Shala and let me know how you get on.'

'Will do.' He ended the call in the middle Hasani's office. Even with blue over-shoes on he took great care where he placed his feet. The office was a mess. There was a lot of blood. Erion Hasani's corpse was laying next to his desk, a Desert Eagle hand-gun resting on the fingers of his right hand. Lomas shook his head and crouched to take a closer look.

'Whatever this was Mr Hasani, I'm guessing this is not the way you thought it would end.'

Heath Gunn

48

Gonzo and Larry put the wrapped corpse of Inzamam Khan in the boot of his own Range Rover, as Raj stood lookout at the front end of the car.

The light was starting to fade. They'd gone over their plan several times to make sure there were no gaps, nothing they'd left out.

Maya had gone off to book her and Raj into a hotel for the night. She'd then meet them by the docks.

Raj was happy that his plan had come together so far, and thought they should all be able to get away smoothly once they'd dropped Khan's body.

Each of them wore a black balaclava and a plain black or navy top. The Range Rover windows were tinted, the rear ones more so, this meant no one would be able to get a good look inside.

'Are we good?' asked Raj.

'Yep, all loaded up. You ready?' replied Larry.

'As ready as I'm going to be, I guess. Gonzo, how about you?'

'Yeah, I'm OK. Not too happy about being in the boot with him, but it'll be over soon enough.' Gonzo pointed at Khan.

'In you get. Let's do it,' Raj directed.

Gonzo jumped into the boot of the Range Rover and Larry gently pushed the boot closed. Raj looked through the gap at the bottom and saw Gonzo grab the edge of the tailgate, holding it just short of closed with a piece of rope they'd tied on earlier when they'd covered the mechanism to stop it auto-locking. Then Raj and Larry got in the front, Larry driving.

'OK, just like we planned.' Said Raj.

'Don't worry, Raj. It's a good plan. It'll be fine.'

They set off as the evening was starting to draw in, the light fading. They made their way through the middle of town, easing into the flow of traffic. Raj sat in silence, thinking about Khan and Husna. How a couple of days ago everything had been going so well and now everything was as fucked up as it get. He glanced across at Larry who was concentrating on driving. They'd not mentioned Husna since the chat in office and Raj wondered if Larry really wasn't judging him, or if he thought worse of him for being with Husna. He wasn't sure he wanted to know really.

'There's a lot of traffic,' said Raj, wanting a distraction from what was going on inside his head.

'Really, it'll be fine.' Larry smiled and patted his arm.

They stopped at a set of traffic lights and Raj shouted through to the back. 'All OK back there, Gonzo?'

'Yeah, fine. Are we there yet?' He sniggered.

'Fuck off, Gonzo.' Raj laughed but Larry, straight-faced, moved off from the lights.

'You ready, Gonzo?' asked Larry.

'Yes, just let me know when.'

'I've got a decent flow of traffic behind me and to the sides, so it won't be long.' Raj glanced in the wing mirror and could see a white van close behind them. 'He's a bit close, isn't he?'

'He is, and he's going to get a shock in a minute,' said Larry.

Raj felt Larry slow the Range Rover down, pulling the van in even closer. 'Gonzo, now!' shouted Larry.

Raj turned to look as Gonzo released the rope. The tailgate shot up in the air. He heard Gonzo grunt as he pushed Khan's body out of the back of the car and onto the road.

Raj watched as the van that had been too close jammed its brakes on – too late.

Khan's wrapped corpse disappeared under the front of the van. At the same time, Gonzo grabbed the end of the rope and pulled the tailgate shut. Larry hit the accelerator hard, and the Range Rover sped off through the traffic, away from its owner.

It was over so quickly. Once they were a good distance away, Larry dropped to a normal speed.

'You all good, Gonzo?' asked Raj.

'Yeah, man! All good back here. We fuckin' did it!'

'Let's not celebrate too soon, eh?' said Raj.

'Like I said, Raj, it'll all be alright. Let's get rid of this car,' said Larry.

They drove to the meeting point on the docks where Maya was waiting for them, as arranged. Raj smiled as her car came into view.

Raj and Gonzo got out and Larry drove the car into a container, locking it and hiding the car from view.

They all got into Maya's car and headed out of the docks and back the way they'd come. When they got near the scene, the traffic slowed down to a crawl. Rubberneckers were looking over to see what the police were doing.

Raj felt a flutter in his stomach as they crawled past. Only Gonzo looked over to where Khan's body lay.

49

Valmir Shala slammed a hand onto his desk and threw his phone across the room.

'Who the fuck would go into one of my clubs and shoot everyone? Do they not know who I am? Surely no one would be so stupid.'

Saban knew better than to respond to one of Shala's outbursts, especially if it was in relation to one of his clubs, distribution networks, or a betrayal of any kind. He stood silently, waiting for his next instruction.

'The police are crawling all over the Southampton club and want to interview me today. Saban, I need you to start asking around. See if anyone knows what happened at Jete Nate. Also, where is Raj Gadhi? This is his neck of the woods – he must have some contacts we can talk to, find out what went on.'

'I don't know where Mr Gadhi is, Mr Shala. Shall I call him?'

'Yes please.'

'I will start making enquiries among our immediate circle to see if anyone knows anything about the shooting. Perhaps Mr Hasani was having trouble with someone locally?'

'Hmm, perhaps, although he did not mention anything. The last time we spoke, he was sure his new recruit, who is one of Khan's, would give him the edge in Southampton. He was very pleased when I told him we'd brought Raj on board, and we agreed that his man – Mike, I think – would work under Raj, as they have history. Actually, speaking of Raj, don't worry. I will call him.'

'Very well, Mr Shala.' With that Saban left the office, leaving Shala to call Raj.

'Raj, hello, how are you, my friend?'

'I'm good, thanks, Valmir. I heard about the shooting in the club. Were many people hurt?'

'Unfortunately, yes. A handful of my best men, including Erion Hasani. It is a sad day for our business, Raj. It is also the reason for my call. Where are you at the moment?'

'I'm really sorry to hear that. I'm in Southampton, visiting my aunt.'

'Ah, excellent. I need you to start speaking to your local contacts to see what you can find out about the attack on my club.

This cannot go without retribution. Tell me, Raj, do you think your friend Mr Khan could have been behind this?'

'It sounds a bit, er, loud for Khan's taste to me. He's always preferred to do things that can't be linked back to him. But leave it with me. I'll ask around and call you when I hear anything.'

'Very good. This may delay our plans by a few days while everything calms down around me and my operation. Your introduction to your new team may have to wait.'

'I understand, Mr Shala. That will give me a couple of days to find somewhere to live.'

'Excellent. I will wait to hear from you. Goodbye.'

Valmir searched through his contacts and called Saban. 'Saban, do we have location tracking set up on Mr Gadhi yet?'

'Of course, Mr Shala.'

'Good. Can you check it's activated and let me know where he is?'

'Yes, Mr Shala. I will call you back as soon as I've checked.' Shala only had to wait a few minutes.

'Where is our Mr Gadhi?' he asked Saban.

'He is in Southampton, Mr Shala, nowhere that I am familiar with. I zoomed in on the map – it looks like a residential street.'

'Very good, thank you, Saban.'

50

'Thank you for thinking to let me know, Mr Khan. If there's anything I can do, please let me know. Goodbye.'

Vihaan Patel felt numb as he put the phone down from Inzamam's father. He looked around his lounge and the walls seemed somehow out of reach, far away, as if he was isolated in the centre of an island.

Inzamam is dead? Arjun, what have you done?

After taking a couple of minutes to gather his thoughts Vihaan picked his phone back up and dialled the FaceTime number Arjun had called him recently. It only rang a couple of times before Arjun's face popped up on the screen.

'Vihaan, how wonderful to hear from you. I was just on my way out, how are you?'

'I need to tell you something Arjun.'

'That sounds serious, are you OK?'

'I don't know really. I've just got off the phone with Inzamam's father. Inzamam's dead.'

'What?'

'He's dead. Apparently he was shot and his body was dumped in the road, in Southampton. What did you do Arjun?'

'Me? I can assure you this is first I'm hearing about anything happening to Inzamam Khan, let alone his death.'

'But you said, you'd get revenge and don't get me wrong, I'm not surprised after what he did to you. But you did say it and now he's dead.'

'I did say that, you're right. And, if I'm honest I meant it. But I haven't done anything to move that train of thought on since we spoke. I can guarantee you I had nothing to with his death.'

'OK, sorry, but I had to ask.'

'Of course.'

'So, what will you do now?'

'What do you mean?'

'Well with Inzamam dead, I would have thought you might want to come back to the UK?'

'I suppose it does present one with options, doesn't it. But that can wait. He was your friend, or rather you'd down him for a long time. How do you feel about it?'

'I don't really know, a bit numb at the moment. It's his girls I feel for, Malik told me that Husna died in the last couple of days too. She had a car crash and died in hospital.'

'Oh those poor children. How old are they?'

'They're both teenagers, about fourteen and sixteen I think. I can't imagine how they feel, to lose both parents within a week, they must be devastated.'

'Truly awful. Look Vihaan, I really must get on, but if you need anything at all, please don't hesitate to call me, day or night.'

'I will, thanks Arjun. Speak soon.' With that he ended the call.

51

Larry pulled onto a petrol station forecourt, driving around the edge to avoid the CCTV cameras mounted on the pumps. Reversing the Audi into a corner, he got out and walked round to the car boot.

Hidden from view by his boot lid and a row of dense shrubs, he took the HK handgun from inside his jacket. He placed it carefully under a false floor panel in the boot, then took a Karambit from his inside pocket. The knife, shaped like a tiger's claw, was an efficient weapon that had got Larry out of trouble on a couple of occasions. But there was no need for it tonight. Not for what he had planned.

He had a quick look around the forecourt. As he had expected, at this time of night it was empty.

Larry reached inside the boot and took out something else, which he hid behind his back. He closed and locked the car as quietly as he could and moved stealthily towards the shop door. There was only one person inside, and they were busy filling shelves.

The forecourt was still deserted. He opened the door and slipped in without being seen. With well-rehearsed precision, he moved to within inches of the worker. Standing behind them, he slipped a hand around their face, covering their mouth to stem any screams.

The garage worker spun around. Simultaneously, Larry produced a huge bunch of flowers from behind his back. He grinned and gave Elsie a long, passionate kiss that made the events of the past few hours melt away.

'You're lucky I didn't kick your ass all over this garage,' she said, beaming at the assassin.

'Yeah, I know, I was terrified,' he replied.

Elsie locked the shop door and turned out the lights.

52

Gonzo had sat across from Emina for about half an hour without saying a word. His drink sat in front of him, as full as it had been when the waitress placed it on the table. He'd called Emina the minute Maya had dropped him off, and she'd sounded really pleased to hear from him.

'Mike, what is wrong?'

'Nothin'. Just had a bad day.'

'Why was it bad? Do you want to talk about it?'

'I can't. It's not the kind of thing I can talk about.'

She looked worried. Gonzo wasn't used to people worrying about him, and it felt strange. Good, but strange nonetheless.

He looked at Emina, at her eyes searching his face for a sign of what was bothering him. He felt a building compulsion to tell her what had happened at the club, but knew he couldn't.

Another ten minutes passed. Emina reached across the table and took his hand in hers. Her soft, delicate fingers stroked the back of his hand.

'You know you can tell me anything, Mike. I won't judge you, but I can see that you're struggling with whatever is troubling you, and that upsets me. I don't want to see you hurting if I can share your pain.'

Gonzo couldn't hold out any longer. He needed to tell someone, and he trusted Emina. He trusted her to keep his secret and he trusted her when she said she wouldn't judge him. Above all, no one had ever cared this much about him, apart from his gran.

'OK, but you have to promise me you won't freak out and you won't tell another livin' soul. If you do, I'm in deep shit.'

'I promise, but you're really worrying me. What is it, Mike?'

'It's to do with Khan, and Hasani, and the club.'

'Go on.'

'I was round there earlier today, meeting Hasani. While we were talking in his office, Khan turned up at the club. We saw him at the door on the CCTV camera in Erion's office.' He paused and took a swig of his drink, then another. 'Dardan opened the door to him and Khan shot him dead.'

Emina gasped and her eyes widened.

'That wasn't the end of it. Khan made his way through the club, shooting people on his way up to Hasani's office. As soon as Khan walked through the door, Hasani pulled a massive gun and shot at him. Khan shot back and I dived behind the desk to get out of the way.'

'Oh, Mike, you must have been very scared.'

'It was pretty scary. But then Khan hid behind a bit of wall and Hasani was lyin' on the floor by his desk. They'd both been shot and they were just shoutin' shit at each other. You know, windin' each other up. Then Khan came out from behind the wall and pumped loads of bullets into Hasani and killed him. I was convinced he was gonna to kill me next, so I grabbed Hasani's gun and ... and I shot him. I blew him across the room, and he's dead. I killed Khan.'

Emina sat staring at him for a good few seconds, her eyes wide and her hands over her mouth, as if to stifle a scream. Then she leaned across the table towards him, took both his hands and said something Gonzo didn't expect.

'Oh, Mike, that must have been terrible for you. How do you feel?'

He was so overwhelmed by her concern for him that he broke down in tears, sobbing uncontrollably. Everything he'd been through, everything he'd witnessed, all culminated in a massive emotional outpouring.

Emina moved around the table, sat beside him and wrapped her arms around his shaking shoulders. 'You poor thing, that must have been horrible. You are very brave to tell me everything so openly.'

'But I shot him, Emina. He saved my life and I killed him.'

'Like you say, if you had not, maybe it would have been you who died. You did what you had to do, and I'm glad you did. I do not want you to die Mike.'

She leaned towards him and kissed him. He felt her wiping tears from his face.

He'd always tried his best never to cry in front of anyone, but right now, it didn't matter.

53

As the car door closed and Gonzo walked away, Maya turned to Raj with a quizzical look on her face.

'Where to, Mr Gadhi?'

'What do you mean?' he asked.

'What I said – where to? Big, bad Khan is dead. Larry and Gonzo, which I still can't believe you call him, are dropped off. I'm guessing you don't want to go to Portsmouth and see your new Albanian friends. So, where to?'

There was only one place Raj could think of.

About twenty minutes later, they pulled up outside Aunt Sarbjit's house. 'Are you sure it'll be OK?' Maya asked him.

'Course it will. They're my family and you've already had the third degree from Auntie Sarb. It doesn't get more random than that. Besides, she's a great cook – and I don't know about you, but I'm starving.'

They got out of the car and Raj limped up to the back door of his aunt's house, Maya by his side.

The smell of home-cooked food hit him as soon as he opened the door.

'Ah, you're back then,' a voice said. His cousin, Jai, was standing in front of the fridge, the door open and a grin on his face. 'Hey, cuz, how's it going? You look shattered, man.'

'It's been a bit of a day. Jai, this is Maya.'

'Yeah, I know. Mum wouldn't shut up about you when you'd gone. Nice to meet you, Maya.'

'Rajiv!' came his aunt's shrill voice.

'Hi, Auntie Sarb.'

'Have you brought that lovely girl back with you?' she said as she breezed into the kitchen. 'Maya, lovely to see you again.' She walked straight past Raj and gave Maya a hug. Raj smirked as he watched Maya being squeezed.

'I hope you've been keeping him out of trouble.'

'Yeah, I'm trying.' She smiled at Raj.

'Never mind all that – have you got anything we can eat, Auntie Sarb? We're starving, and it's been a long day.'

'Of course I have – you know there's always a good meal waiting here for you, Rajiv. Come, come, sit down, both of you.'

As they sat down, his phone rang. It was Shala. Raj got up from the table and took the call outside. As he left, he heard Sarb say something to Maya about him working long hours.

'Raj, hello, how are you, my friend?' asked a serious-sounding Valmir Shala.

'I'm good, thanks, Valmir. I heard about the shooting in the club. Were many

people hurt?'

'Unfortunately, yes. A handful of my best men, including Erion Hasani. It is a sad day for our business, Raj. It is also the reason for my call. Where are you at the moment?'

'I'm really sorry to hear that. I'm in Southampton, visiting my aunt.'

Shala went on to ask Raj to ask around and find out who might have been responsible for the shootings at his club. Raj listened, making conciliatory noises at appropriate points.

'I understand, Mr Shala. That will give me a couple of days to find somewhere to live,' he said, finishing off the conversation. Raj pocketed his phone and took a moment to compose himself as thoughts of Husna pushed their way into his mind, taking him by surprise. After a couple of minutes he took a deep breath and went back into the house.

'Who is calling you at this late hour? Surely you can't be on the clock,' said his auntie.

'You know me, Auntie, always busy. It was my boss giving me a couple of days off.' He smiled at Maya, who smiled back.

'I should hope so – you have to recover before you can work properly. But at least you have your own nurse,' Sarb said, winking at Maya.

54

Malik Khan put down his coffee cup and looked across the table at his wife. She had been sitting at Inzamam's kitchen table since they'd got the knock at the door late the previous night. The police officer, who was expecting to speak to Husna, had very sympathetically informed them that they believed Inzamam to have died in suspicious circumstances. Malik had accompanied the officer to formally identify their son; an image that would stay with him for the rest of his life. On his return they had both sat in near silence for most of the night, Kamila and Muna asleep up-stairs.

'We should wake them and tell them.' Said Malik.

'Let them sleep, what difference will it make telling them now, or an hour from now? They're still processing their mother dying and now we have to tell them they are orphans. Once we tell them there will be decisions to be made. We will need to decide where to live. They will need time off school and we will have to arrange the funerals and contact our families.' replied Maneet.

'I know there is much to do, but the first thing we need to address is telling Kamila and Muna. They will not thank us for keeping them in the dark, we should wake them and tell them. There is nothing to be gained by spending time sleeping.'

'Malik, our son, their father is dead. He will still be dead when the girls wake naturally, but if you insist we will wake them.' Malik walked around the table and placed his hand on his wife's shoulder. He could feel a subtle tremble moving through her body and although no tears were falling, he knew she was crying. He had never been good with emotions. Maneet had always been the emotionally stronger of the two and he knew that she would be the one telling his granddaughters that they had been orphaned. As Malik stood trying his best to comfort Maneet, the kitchen door swung open.

'Dadda why does Daddi look so sad?' Said Kamila from the doorway.

'Kamila, you're up early, is Muna still asleep?'

'I don't know.'

'OK, let's get you some breakfast, Dadda can go and check.' Said Maneet. Malik went to see if the younger sister was also awake. She was and had had a restless night. Malik and Muna joined Maneet and Kamila in the kitchen and they all sat at the table with a drink, neither of the girls wanted anything to eat.

'Girls, Dadda and I have something we need to speak to you about.' Began Maneet, holding the hands of both girls, as Malik sat at the head of the table.

'What is it Daddi?' Asked Muna. Malik nodded to his wife to carry on, giving her his best reassuring smile.

'Last night, after you were both in bed, a police officer came to the door. He told Dadda and I that something has happened to your Father and I'm afraid that he's dead.' She paused to let her words register with the sisters.

'No, he can't be, he was only here yesterday.' Said Muna, tears instantly filling her eyes and streaming down her face.

'I'm so sorry. It's true, the police don't know what happened to him yet, but Dadda went with the police officer and it was definitely him.' She said in soft tones, smoothing her hand over Muna's hair.

Kamila didn't say anything. She sat silently holding onto her grandmothers other hand, staring into space. She stayed like this for at least ten minutes. Then she said, 'Was it anything to do with mum's death?' Maneet looked at Malik.

'I don't know, I don't think so. The police said they didn't know exactly what had happened to him.' Answered Malik.

'Was he murdered?' Kamlia asked, still staring aimlessly and holding Maneet's hand. Malik paused for a moment and looked at his wife, who was still comforting the crying Muna.

'Yes, we think he was. Why do you ask, Kamila?'

'Because if someone murdered my father, I want to know who it was. I know what you used to do Dadda, training people to fight. I want you to train me and when I find out who killed him, I'm going to make them pay.'

The End

Thank you !

Thank you for taking the time to read Khan, I hope you enjoyed it.

If you could take 5 minutes to drop a review on Amazon, I'd really appreciate it.

Thanks Again.

Heath

Follow me on
Instagram - @heathgunn1
Facebook - Heath Gunn - Author
Twitter - heathgunn

Or join the Gunn Club at
www.heathgunn.com
And I'll keep you up to date with what I'm up to next.

Acknowledgements

There are so many people, who knowingly, or not, contribute towards the writing of my stories. The people below were a great help in bringing my ideas to reality.

A huge thank you to my editor Jane Hammett, who did a fantastic job in helping me to polish Khan into the final version you are holding now.

Thank you also to Tracey Mack for doing a great job of proofreading and picking up my typo's.

Thank you to Amanda Jarvis for fact checking the ambulance section.

Thank you to my sister Lisa Bailey for taking the time to educate me on the what3words app and for talking me through an emergency call.

Books By This Author

Prisoner

DI Lomas Baxter is used to dealing with the criminal underbelly of the south coast and has built his career from hunting down and catching murderers. He is also a dedicated father and husband who strives to keep his family and "the job" separate.

As the arm of victim three is fished from a stream, Baxter knows he has to hunt down and stop a sadistic serial killer. One who is relentlessly abducting, torturing and murdering young women. With the death-toll mounting, DI Baxter and his team race to save the lives of innocent victims, while being taunted by a seemingly untouchable foe.

Can Baxter capture the killer before the threat moves closer to home and his two worlds collide?

If you like gripping, fast paced crime thrillers, and you're a fan of greats like Rankin, McDermid and Patterson, you will love Prisoner, a debut novel by Heath Gunn.

Coming Next !

Coming in 2021 is the long-awaited sequel to Prisoner !

Read the first chapter now...

Prisoner II
(Working Title)

Chapter 1

Monica Silverman heard muffled voices from outside her cell door and the rattle of keys.

'I wish they'd leave me the fuck alone.' She said under her breath.

The hatch slid open and Bob Anderson stuck his cheery face into the gap.

'Monica, it's Bob Anderson, we're going to open the door, please stand at the back of your room.'

She thought Bob was alright, as screws go. He didn't give her any hassle and was always polite enough, but she really just wanted to be left alone and wasn't in the mood for whatever they wanted.

'What's she doing Bob?' Monica heard a voice she recognised as Gill O'Leary - a chubby middle-aged woman, with curly brown hair and thick-rimmed glasses who grated on Monica's last nerve.

She didn't react to Bob's instruction, then she heard him say. 'Nothing, she's just sat on her bed, staring at the floor. I fucking hate it when she doesn't move.'

Monica allowed herself a smile, knowing that her inaction would wind them up. If I sat still enough, for long enough, maybe they'd fuck off. She thought.

'Ask her again.' Said a squeaky woman, a new voice.

'Monica, we need to come in and speak to you, can you please stand against the rear wall of your room?'

For fucks sake, if they're not going to leave me alone, I'm going to have some fun with them.

She stood up, from her bed and walked to the back of the room, without looking in their direction. Then she sat on the floor, cross legged and put her arms on her legs and closed her eyes, like she was ready to meditate. Bob let out a heavy sigh.

'What is it Bob?' Asked the squeaky one.

'She's fucking meditating at the back of the cell.' Said Bob

Monica took his exasperation as a small victory.

'Oh well, it could be a lot worse.' Said Gill - she was right, Monica could make life a lot worse. She opened her eyes just enough to see through her eye-lashes, but to the screws they looked closed.

'Come on then, in we go.' Bob prompted his colleagues, as the handle, to open the door turned slowly.

Bob and the two female officers stepped into Monica's cell in a v formation, the women standing at Bob's shoulders, primed and looking like they were ready to pull him out of the cell.

They took another step forwards, as they did Monica slapped the floor, hard. All three of the screws jumped back, half a step. Bob tried to hide the deep breath he took as he composed himself, but Monica saw him. She saw them all. They absolutely shit themselves. She lifted her head to look at them and couldn't resist a smile.

'That wasn't funny Monica.' Said Bob.

It fucking was. I just about managed to not laugh out loud and stay quiet. She thought.

'We've been sent to bring you to the office, so I need you to get up, slowly, and turn around, so we can put some restraints on you.' Bob told her.

'If she wants to speak to me, why doesn't she come down here?'

'You known that's not how it works, now come on, let's not make this difficult.'

'Why would we make it difficult, Bob? After all, we're all friends here, aren't we?'

Bob was looking for a sign that Monica might be getting up, but she stayed on the floor, unmoving, except for her eyes. She looked from one to the other, figuring out who she could have the most fun with, on the way to governor's office. The squeaky one was new, her ID said she was called Beth and she looked young.

Silverman was a convicted serial killer, who in the judge's words, had abducted, tortured and dismembered a string of women, before being caught. She'd been inside for three months and in that time had assaulted six prison officers, one, they said, was unlikely to ever work again, such was the extent of her injuries. This was along with quite a few of her so-called inmates.

She'd learned a long time ago how to appear removed and cold, it made her almost impossible to read and to date, no-one in prison had come close to giving her anything resembling trouble. She knew she was bigger than most, not an out of shape, big. Monica had been a champion hammer-thrower and strength athlete before she got locked up and this gave her a massive advantage over her peers.

'Come on then Monica, let's get on with it.' Bob said. He glanced over his shoulder quickly and the two officers either side of him, who stood, poised.

Right, time to have some fun, she thought.

Beth and Gill nearly jumped out of their skins when Monica thrust her arms out in front of her, pressed the sides of her feet into the floor and sprang to a standing position. Bob instinctively took a step back, Beth and Gill, moved with him. He didn't take his eyes off her and she just stood there - statuesque, grinning at the three of them. They all looked a bit freaked-out.

'Turn around and face the wall?' Said Bob, clearing his throat and trying his best to sound authoritative.

'Oh, I love it when you're masterful.' She said and laughed. 'Don't you two just love it?'

'That's enough, Monica, now turn around and face the wall please?' Said Bob raising the volume of his voice.

'Oh alright, calm yourself. I was only having a bit of fun.' She decided to play along for a minute and see what happened next. So she turned and faced the wall of her cell and without being prompted, put her hands behind my back. Monica heard them shuffle forwards, all together. Staying in formation in case they needed to restrain her. Bob closed the ratchet handcuffs around her wrists and moved her around to leave the cell. As Bob turned Monica, Beth and Gill moved around to stay at his flank. Staying in formation they started to walk her towards the cell door. About a metre from the opening Monica realised their mistake, but it was too late. They'd fucked up and put her between them and the doorway.

She kicked a foot, hard against the door-frame, throwing herself back into the three of them, bowling them over with the speed she hit them.

Beth was on her knees in front of Monica and she kicked her, with full force, catching her under the jaw, forcing her head back and hearing it smashing against the cold, hard, floor.

One down, two to go. She thought.

Before they could stop her, she rounded on Gill, who was still scrambling to get to her feet. She swept Gill's legs out from under her, easily and stamped-down, on her forearm, as she fell towards the floor; hearing the crack of breaking bone, and the accompanying scream, such a scream. Bob was bigger and slower than both of his team-mates and as Gill screamed, Monica grinned at him, then she threw herself forward towards him, driving her forehead into his face, splitting his nose and smashing his top lip against his teeth. She rocked myself back onto her knees, as he instinctively raised his hands to his bleeding face. He looked defenceless and she was enjoying herself. She dived forwards again and sank her teeth into his forearm, biting down and ripping a chunk of flesh away from his arm. Bob let out a blood-curdling howl.

Monica stood and looked at the three of them, all on the floor, helpless - but she didn't want to kill them, even though she could have done, easily. To her it was just a bit of fun.

Silverman stood for what felt like an age, all the while she just stared at Bob. A full response team came racing through the door. Monica looked at them, her face smeared with Bob's blood, spitting out bits of his arm.

***

Bob watched, holding his arm, as the team took Monica to the floor. She didn't fight back, she just grinned. They dragged her to her feet, Bob didn't move as they marched Monica out of the cell. Next a team of medics came rushing into the cell, accompanied by more prison officers. Beth was stretched out on the floor, where Monica's kick had dropped her. Ignoring his own injuries Bob scrambled to her side, grabbing a wrist and checking for a pulse.

'We need to get Beth out of here and to hospital quickly, along with you and Gill.' Said Charles, one of the Prison medics.

'Can you walk? Gill what about you?' They both nodded. Gill was nursing her arm, in obvious pain. Bob had blood streaming from his face and arm, and was starting to feel drowsy. He swayed back and forth, then felt his legs crumble beneath him. He crashed to the floor, beside Beth, aware of the frenzied activity around him, but unable to focus, unable to speak. Laying, helpless on the floor with blood pumping from the huge, gouge in his arm, Bob's head began to swim The room became a blur of lights and noise, all getting further and further away. He tried to speak, tried to call for help, but nothing came. No sound, no words. His eyes closed slowly, he was too weak to hold them open, then all went black and the sounds around him ebbed away to nothing.

To be released - 2021

Printed in Great Britain
by Amazon

50356582R00246